Also by Teri Anne Stanley

Charming
Texas
Cowboy

TERI ANNE STANLEY

sourcebooks
casablanca

Published by Sourcebooks Casablanca, an imprint of Sourcebooks
P.O. Box 4410, Naperville, Illinois 60567-4410
(630) 961-3900
sourcebooks.com

Printed and bound in Canada.
MBP 10 9 8 7 6 5 4 3 2 1

For Lucy—the barking-est dog we ever did love

Chapter 1

"I THINK YOU HAVE A REAL KNACK WITH THOSE DAIRY GOATS," Jen Greene's mom, Joanie, gushed as she loaded mason jars full of fresh goat's milk into the back of their vintage Suburban.

Jen grinned and turned toward the camera with a wink. "Milking was a lot easier once I figured out which ones were the girls."

Her mother gave a not entirely fake snort. "Do you think we should start a herd at Summer's Ridge?"

"Well, that would really be something, wouldn't it?" Jen asked, drawing a raised eyebrow from Joanie.

"Cut!" Brock called, making his signature—and way overused—move of frustration, grabbing a handful of his hair. It fell back into place as though he'd never touched it. Through clenched teeth, he asked, "Jennifer, what are you doing?"

"What?" Jen pretended not to understand what Brock was talking about. It was a passive-aggressive move, but *come on*— Joanie and Jen lived in a three-bedroom split-level house on a quarter acre in suburban Austin. There *was* no Summer's Ridge. Jen wasn't planning to announce that to their audience, but she loved making little inside jokes about it, even if she was the only one who thought it was funny.

One of the many Nigerian dwarf goats belonging to the farmer they were visiting nudged Jen's backside. She squatted to pet the little guy—er, girl. If she ever got her dream farm, she was totally getting some goats.

"For crying out loud, Jennifer, can you be a little less ladylike?" How was Brock not bald, considering how much he yanked on that hair? "You look more like Johnny Bench than Laura Ingalls Wilder at the moment."

Jen glanced down at her slightly spread thighs, firmly encased in denim, and glared up at their director/manager/lord and master and said, "I'll remember my prairie dress next time."

Brock might or might not have muttered something about a giraffe, but Jen decided not to ask him to repeat his words.

"Come on, Jennifer," Joanie said. "Give him a break."

Jen forced a smile and gave the little goat one last pat before rising to her full five feet, ten inches. Brock was about five four including hair and had a bit of a body image issue. He often tried to pass that on to others. Jen, not being a Baseball Hall of Famer, tried not to catch what he was throwing.

But jeez, he was such a jerkface.

"We need to get to the Summer's Ridge test kitchen before I have to pay the videographer overtime," Brock said. "Joanie, do you want to ride with me?"

Joanie bit her lip in hesitation, but Jen just waved her on.

"I'll see you at the studio," Jen said, refusing to call the rented kitchen with the vintage white cabinets and massive marble countertops "Summer's Ridge."

Normally Joanie and Jen would ride together and brainstorm about their next steps, but things were so scripted now that there wasn't any need, and frankly, Jen needed a few minutes alone to get her head back in the game. No one had promised her this gig was going to be fun every single minute, and it was unprofessional to pout just because Brock had insulted her.

What was wrong with her today? It was true that she'd disliked Brock from "hello," but he usually didn't get to her. Joanie seemed to have drunk whatever Kool-Aid Brock was pouring, which bothered Jen—and not just because there had been a gulf developing in their normally tight mother-daughter relationship. She was really worried that Joanie might be backsliding, but it had been so long and there had been so much therapy since the last time her mother met a *this is the guy who will save me* guy Jen was pretty sure her mom was cured. For a few years there, as in the first fifteen years of Jen's life, there had been a series of losers moving in and out of their home, taking a little more of her mom's sanity and self-esteem in every garbage bag full of personal belongings.

Finally, Joanie had gotten better and had thrown herself into making arts and crafts, eventually starting a blog, and then a couple of years ago, when Jen graduated from college with a degree in digital media, they'd joined forces and started the *Homemade with Joanie and Jennifer* show. Jen loved it because she liked hanging out with her mom, and it gave her a chance to learn new things and to have a little control over her life—something that had been sorely lacking after her father went out for cigarettes the day she was born and never came back.

Until, that was, they'd decided they needed someone to manage all of the little details that came with a runaway YouTube sensation, and that someone had turned out to be Brock.

Jen decided she was probably suffering from PMS. She kind of hoped that was it. A few cramps and a couple of Hershey bars and things would start to look sunnier. The alternative was facing the uncomfortable possibility that she might not want to be the Jennifer half of Joanie and Jennifer anymore.

As she drove, she thought about calling her best friend, Robin, just to vent, but she felt guilty. It seemed like the only time she ever called Robin or any of her other friends was to complain. She never called to ask them about their own lives or their kids or husbands.

It was a teeny bit possible that her hesitancy to check in with friends wasn't so much guilt over how selfish she could be. It might also be a little bit about how bummed out she got when her friends talked about their husbands and kids—because Jen had neither. She'd somehow figured that by the ripe old age of thirty-one, she'd be married and spending her time making Pinterest-inspired snacks and homemade Halloween costumes for her little ones, but instead she was almost painfully single. Even if she had time to date, where would she meet guys? Okay, yeah, online like everyone else in the universe. But as Jennifer the YouTuber, she was supposed to be a proponent of slowing down and living an authentic, wholesome life. Virtual speed dating was *not* part of her brand.

Well, heck. Maybe her next craft project for the show could be homemade personal pleasure devices. Can you say "Ewww?"

Unfortunately, the twenty-minute drive in air-conditioned solitude had done nothing for Jen's peace of mind, and now she had to get in there and be a maker.

She took a deep breath and tried to focus on today's "homemade pleasure"—which had nothing to do with self-gratification beyond the satisfaction of being able to say you'd made something yourself.

Her mother had set things up for the segment, and it was almost Jen's turn.

With her trademark lyrical enthusiasm, Joanie said, "And now Jennifer's going to add lye to the lovely fresh goat's milk, and we'll be on our way to making our own goat milk soap!"

Jen picked up the measuring cup to do her part and said, "Remember, don't ever pour your milk into the lye, or you'll get a caustic volcano."

Fortunately for everyone in the studio, Jen poured the lye into the milk and not the other way around. *Unfortunately*, she poured it into the fresh, warm jar and not the prechilled milk her mother had just taken from the fridge.

Oops. This wasn't going to be good.

She jerked her hand back from the mixture and knocked over the jar of cold milk, which flooded the counter, while the warm milk literally began to scorch from the heat generated by the chemical reaction.

"Oh my God, what's that smell?" Joanie asked as Jen tried not to gag.

At least it wasn't volcanoing, she told herself. It was just stinky. Not sticking to anyone like napalm or anything. Wouldn't that be something? Suddenly the whole situation seemed too ridiculous, and she had to stifle a grin.

"Cut!" called Brock as Joanie hissed, "Don't squinch your face up like that! You'll ruin your makeup!"

"Ugh, it's disgusting!" Jen laughed. "I ruined it, didn't I?"

Brock nodded, scowling, but said, "That's okay. We've got the practice version in the pantry. We can use that."

"Okay, then let's shoot a little explanation—" She looked to the videographer, a new guy Brock had hired, who rolled his eyes before turning his camera back on.

Brock shook his head. "No. We don't have time for that. We can use this and cut before you notice the smell."

"We can't do that!" Jen protested. "People will do it the way I did, and it won't work, and they'll complain, and—"

"We'll deal with that if it happens. You don't really think people try this crap at home, do you?" He laughed and gave Joanie a conspiratorial wink, which Joanie, to her credit, didn't return. Joanie also didn't disagree with him, which was a drag because Joanie and Jen's whole reason for doing *Homemade with Joanie and Jennifer* was to promote authentic do-it-yourself stuff.

Wasn't it?

Suddenly everything—the fake estate, the fake kitchen, the fake smiles, the fake goat's milk soap, all seemed to be crushing Jen from the inside out. And now Brock, who was supposed to be working *with* them, was dismissing her.

"You know what, Brock? You don't have a clue what you're talking about. I *do* think people do this stuff themselves. That's why they watch us. Because we're *authentic people.*"

Brock snorted. "There's nothing *authentic*—whatever that's supposed to mean—about any of this. They don't watch because you're some kind of magical unicorn of living the good life, they watch because you're good at *acting* like a funny klutz, and because Joanie's got perfect tits."

"Excuse me?" Jen asked, because surely she hadn't heard that right.

"You heard me. Joanie's got a great rack. Better than yours, anyway."

Joanie had the good grace to look shocked and put a hand over the opening in her low-cut blouse, but she didn't call Brock out for being a pig.

Jen stared at her. "Mom? Are you going to take this?"

Joanie's forehead creased and she bit her lip. "Maybe we need to take a minute."

Brock threw up his hands. "We don't *have* a minute. Time is money, and if we don't get out of this kitchen in ten minutes, we'll be paying for another half day's rent in addition to overtime for the cameraman."

Jen put her hands on her hips. "I'm not going to demo the finished product if we can't spend a few extra minutes explaining about the milk."

"Then I'll just cut in something else," Brock said.

"Mom, we can't let him do this!" What had happened to their simple little mother-daughter enterprise? And how had Jen completely lost her right to have an opinion in how they did things? Yeah, her mom—just by virtue of being the mom—had always been the spokesperson for the pair of them, but she'd always taken Jen's opinion into account when it was time for decisions. Since Brock had come along, though...

Joanie looked to Brock, who raised his eyebrows expectantly, then turned back to Jen. "We really don't have time right now—"

Something snapped in Jen at that moment. Maybe it was some sort of metaphorical umbilical cord, severed when her mother decided to take Brock's side over Jen's. Maybe she'd been too attached to her mother for too long anyway. "Fine. We don't have time? You'll have a lot more time to do things your way from now on, because I'm done."

She turned and marched away, snatching her bag from the back of a chair and digging for her car keys. "I'm so done with this stupid show. 'You're the funny klutz,' my patootie."

She didn't mind providing a lighter side to their reality show, but she wasn't there to be the comic relief while her mom got to be the pretty, sexy one. Which sounded like jealousy, but damn it, Jen realized, she hadn't had a date in…forever. She'd subjugated her whole self to this stupid show, and she was lonely, exhausted, and miserable.

She had believed in what they were doing. Getting in touch with life, with food and textiles, and back to basics in this plastic, artificial world—all that had been worth a few Saturday nights when she'd been too tired to do anything but fall into bed by nine. But once Brock had come in and started changing everything, it wasn't okay anymore. And then he had the nerve to compare her boobs to her mom's? As she unclipped the microphone from her ridiculous chicken-embroidered chambray shirt, she accidentally popped a few buttons loose. *Screw it.* She tore it the rest of the way open and held the sides out as she turned to face Brock (and her mother, and the damned videographer). "Just so you know, Jerkface, I've got perfectly adequate tits!"

Chapter 2

"TRIXIE, SIT." THE LITTLE DOG OBEYED, WATCHING TANNER expectantly. At about thirty pounds, with long, wavy curls, a pointed nose, and intelligent eyes, she seemed to land somewhere between a sheltie and a labradoodle on the mixed-breed range. She gave him all of her charming, adorable attention, pretending to ignore the five other dogs sitting a few feet away, perfectly well behaved on their assigned spots in the training enclosure. Tanner told her she was a good girl and gave her a tiny bite of hot dog. "Are you ready to try this without a leash?" he asked.

She seemed to nod, so eager to please he couldn't imagine she'd ever not been able to sit long enough for a reward. When she'd first come to the Big Chance Dog Rescue, all she'd wanted to do was chase the other dogs. It had taken a ton of patience and even more hot dog bits, but she was finally following basic instructions. Most of the time. Granted, Tanner wasn't the most experienced dog trainer on the ranch. He wasn't an official trainer at all, but he helped out with the new dogs, working on basics. Trixie had become his special project. She reminded him of himself as a kid, eager to please, and even more easily distracted.

Unfortunately for Trixie, her future also seemed to be taking the same trajectory as Tanner's. He'd been discharged from the army with no hope of a useful future, and Trixie had flunked out of service animal school before she'd even started. So here they were at the Big Chance Dog Rescue, just trying to behave well enough to keep from getting kicked out. At least Trixie was cute and had the potential to be a great pet.

Tanner? He definitely wasn't cute—his bad decisions in the

army had seen to that—and he wasn't likely to become anyone's lapdog, either.

"Ready? I'm going to let you off leash, and you're going to stay right here until I give you the word." Trixie smiled and panted, hanging on Tanner's every word. She leaned her silky head against his leg, eager to be petted.

He complied, unclipped the leash, and before he could even straighten up, the little dog was off. Running toward the other dogs, stirring them into a frenzy.

"Damn it, Trixie, no!" he barked.

She ignored him. Yipping and dancing and twirling around the other dogs like a ballet dancer on meth, urging the other dogs to participate in her madness.

He groaned. It was possible she was never going to get the hang of this obedience thing. He decided he'd take her with him on his run tonight and try to wear her out. She certainly had the energy to keep up with him, but the way she bounced around, she'd probably trip him in the first quarter mile and get them both killed.

"I think you've got your work cut out for you." Adam—ranch owner, dog trainer, army veteran, and Tanner's boss—approached the pen.

"I think I should go back to bookkeeping and leave the dog training to the professionals," Tanner said, leaning back against the fence rail and pulling off his hat to run a hand through his sweaty hair before resettling the hat. *Damn*, but central Texas was hot. His home in Louisiana had been hot, too, but Texas seemed worse somehow. Like the ground collected the heat from one day and saved it up to add to the next day.

"You're doing pretty well with her," Adam said. "Remember how clueless she was when she first came here."

Tanner snorted. He knew the truth. He wasn't any better at being a dog trainer than he was at being a rodeo cowboy—or a soldier.

"I wanted to talk to you about that," Adam said.

Wait, what? Tanner had a moment of panic, afraid Adam had learned the details of Tanner's last patrol and was going to kick him off his ranch. This place—the Big Chance Dog Rescue Ranch—and the other veterans who lived here and ran the place, had saved his miserable life. The "Rescue" in the name wasn't just about homeless dogs. Adam was the owner, and along with the other members of the team, he'd welcomed Tanner and made him part of the family.

Tanner schooled his expression. There were a lot of things he sucked at, but keeping his shit locked down was a skill he'd learned at an early age.

Adam nearly cracked that ironclad emotional control right down the middle when he said, "What do you think about starting some therapeutic riding here?"

It took Tanner a second to put his WTF back in storage before he spoke. "I don't think—"

Adam must have anticipated Tanner's automatic *ix-nay*, because he spoke over his opposition. "Just think about it. It could be a good thing for our veterans to learn—kind of a corollary to working with the dogs. You're the former rodeo star of the team, so I know it's something you can do. You're also the spreadsheet man. Figure out how much room we'd need, how much it would cost to get us started with a couple of horses."

"I don't think—"

"Lizzie and Emma suggested it, and I told them I'd talk to you."

Oh thanks, Adam. Throw your girlfriend and sister into the deal and make me be the one to disappoint them.

Adam slapped Tanner on the shoulder and was gone before Tanner could finish "I don't think" with "there's a chance in hell I'm ever getting back on a horse."

"Hey, y'all, we're almost there!" Jen stopped her little Ford Escape next to a gas pump at the Big America Fuel center and smiled into her camera. "It's me, Jen, ready to start a new adventure! I know it's been a minute since I posted a video, and you'll probably notice that it's just me this time! Mom is carrying on with her own gig, and I'm trying something new, something that I hope is a little more authentic, and hopefully interesting and entertaining, too!"

Was that too enthusiastic? How many verbal exclamation points was too many? And did her own plan for more authenticity imply that her mom wasn't the real deal?

Not a problem. She could edit that out and splice in something else—without worrying about how much she was paying a two-timing director and his sleazebag videographer.

An elderly man in a Big America ball cap shuffled across the parking lot as she got out to pump gas. Her phone buzzed, but she decided to let it go to voicemail. He waved as he passed by, almost as if he knew her.

By the time she finished pumping her gas, the old guy was heading back her way. She didn't need directions, but she did need some local color for her video, and this guy looked perfectly colorful. She'd put her phone camera-side out in the top pocket of her shirt and checked to make sure it was recording. "Excuse me," she said. "Can you tell me how far it is to Big Chance?"

"Are you a cop?" the man asked.

"No…" Why would he ask that?

"Then what's with the body cam?" he asked, pointing at her breast.

"Oh. I'm new here, and I'm recording my trip and all the people I meet along the way."

"Is that so?"

"Is it okay if I record our conversation?"

He seemed to be chewing on something as he considered her. "You going to put me on some TV show, or that Ticking Clock app?"

"TikTok? No, but you might end up on YouTube if you're okay with that."

"Oh, I like that channel," he said. "Not sure I've got much use for them how-to shows about making a man look like a woman, but I sure like how-to-clean-a-fish videos. Not that I get much time to fish, what with how much I work here. Can't seem to get them young ones to show up for work, and I'm always stuck here covering someone's shift."

"Gosh, that's too bad," Jen commiserated. "So is it far to Big Chance?"

"It's straight down this road, about five minutes. You can't miss it, unless you blink." He cackled.

"Thanks so much, Mr…"

"Just call me Wayne."

"Mr. Wayne. Thanks." She started to turn back to her car, but he called after her.

"Hey, why don't you take one of them selfies with me?"

"Okay," Jen said, because why not. "Smile!"

"You send that to me, okay?"

"Um, sure." Wayne rattled off his digits, and she sent the picture before it occurred to her to wonder why he was so anxious to have a picture with a random woman who stopped at his gas station.

Apparently because he'd figured out she *wasn't* some random woman.

He confirmed her fear when he said, "Whoee! Them kids that didn't show up to work are going to kick themselves when they find out I got my picture made with the perfectly-adequate-tits lady!"

"What?" Jen wasn't faking her shock and dismay. It had taken less than twenty-four hours for that butthead videographer to get her naked breasts uploaded to every available website everywhere, but Jen had really believed—well, hoped, anyway—that most of the world wasn't that interested, and by the time she'd made arrangements for her new life to start, no one would care anymore. She tried to pull out some acting and said, "I'm flattered you think I look like her, but my name's Brenda."

"Sure it is," the man said with a wink. "I'll keep your secret, but you have to promise to let me know when that video is going to go on YouTube, okay? You've got my number now."

"Oh. Sure." *Crap.* She hadn't even made it into town and she was busted. Hopefully the rest of the community didn't have as much time to surf the web.

She waved goodbye and wished the Kardashians would do something soon so her bust would stop being news, at least until she had some proof that she could do this on her own.

Here, in Big Chance, Texas, she was going to be mistress of her own domain. No one was going to tell her what to do, or how to do it, or do it for her. She was going to run her own show—literally and figuratively.

She hit Record again. "All righty then! Just a few more miles to go, and then you'll see my new venture—a one-woman homestead!" She flipped the camera back around so her viewers would be able to see the same things she was seeing. "I've used my savings to buy a few acres in the middle of Texas, and I'm going to get a goat and some chickens and start a garden. I know it'll take a few months to really get going, but by the end of summer, I fully intend to be mostly self-sufficient.

"Oh look—here's the town." She slowed down to make sure she got a clear recording of the sign that read "Welcome to Big Chance—the luckiest little town in Texas."

Since she'd studied the Google Maps street view so thoroughly, she felt like she already knew her new town inside and out. "We're coming into Big Chance, Texas, and this is Main Street. Up here on the right is the Shop 'n Save, where I'll be getting groceries until my own garden starts to produce veggies and my chickens start laying eggs. And there's the Dairy Queen. I'll probably have to visit there a few times to be, you know, neighborly. I'll be working all those extra calories off on a daily basis, I'm sure.

"Okay, we're leaving town and are on Wild Wager Road. There's a sign for the VanHook Historical and Recreation Park. We'll definitely have to check that out when we get a minute. Oh, hey! What's that place? Big Chance Dog Ranch? Do they raise herds of dogs? Yikes, I hope it's not a puppy mill."

After a couple more miles of brush-bordered road, she found her turn. "Here's Happy Beef Way," she said. "I wonder how the beef got so happy?" She snorted. "And why did I not realize how dirty that would sound? Oh, no. I'm never going to be able to write my new address without laughing."

She turned right onto her new road, and saw, to the left, her new neighbors. There were a lot of cattle in a ginormous pasture, lazing around in the afternoon sun, munching on grass. "Well, they do look happy. Content, at least. Oh! Here's my place!" She stopped in the middle of the road to make sure she had the camera set perfectly to record her first live view of her new home.

She certainly couldn't see it from the road, given the volume of honeysuckle and something tall and bushy lining the lane. "So I bought this place sight unseen in an estate sale, and I checked it out from satellite images, and it's going to be just great. Let's see, okay?"

She hoped her audience wouldn't be able to detect her trepidation. She was annoyed that she was feeling anxious in the first place. That was not part of her plan. She was confident and in charge!

"Wow, this little lane is narrower and bumpier than it looked on Google Earth." Her laugh sounded nervous, even to herself. "And has a lot more brambly stuff on the edges."

She glanced back to make sure the U-Haul trailer was still attached to the back of her SUV, and when she looked forward again, she slammed on the brakes. "Oh." The lane ended in a clearing. "I guess this is it."

She really couldn't say anything else. So what if her *quaint property perfect for homesteading* was really *rocky, generally useless land between a couple of larger cattle operations*? That was real life, right? Things were not always what you expected them to be. Especially if you were in a hurry to get out of town and start your new life and not willing to take the time to check things out.

A few yards to the right sat an old, rusted motor home. She half expected Cousin Eddie from *National Lampoon's Christmas Vacation* to step out with a sewage tube over his dressing-gown-clad shoulder. Hopefully the motor home didn't have mice. Or anything larger or slitherier.

Beyond the camper was a small overgrown area completely enclosed by a tall fence, which had been labeled *garden* in the online image. On the other side were a couple of outbuildings: a barn that listed precariously to the right and a shed, enclosed by fencing, where she planned to put a goat. The little chicken coop sitting next to the goat shed looked to be the sturdiest of everything. God, what a mess!

She cleared her throat and spoke to the camera. "Not exactly what I expected from the photos, but that's not a problem. This is going to be great!" It really was okay, Jen told herself. To herself and her audience, she said, "I can totally do this."

She almost meant it.

Chapter 3

ONE, TWO, THREE, FOUR, ONE, TWO, THREE, FOUR... IT HAD TAKEN a couple of miles, but Tanner's brain was finally quiet, in sync with the rhythm of his feet striking the ground. The night was warm but no longer stifling, and the sound of crickets and cicadas—or whatever made that buzzing sound—kept his mind on an even keel. His muscles burned, drawing from the excess energy that bounced around in his head, constantly reminding him of his failures, pointing out everything that could still go wrong, the ways he could let down the few people who cared about him.

Well, running *usually* worked to clear his head.

He realized his steps had slowed as his brain sped up. He picked up his pace, hoping to outrun his thoughts before he ran out of road.

"Come on, Trixie, let's step it up."

They were about two miles from home when Trixie stopped in the middle of the road, ears pricked forward, pausing in her panting to sniff the air. Her whole body wiggled when she wagged her tail. It took Tanner a minute to detect anything over the sounds of his own pulse and breathing, but there off to the left, in the bushes that grew next to the road, something rustled.

Trixie darted toward the sound, yanking the leash from Tanner's hand. "Trixie, come back here. You're gonna get eaten by a damned wild boar."

Trixie, of course, ignored him and pawed at the brush. Over the noise of her scrabbling, something cried out. Trixie looked anxiously to Tanner.

It was too dark to go digging around in the brush. There would be scorpions, spiders, and rattlesnakes lying in wait for some fool like Tanner to go stumbling in. Unfortunately the same predators would be just as anxious to take a bite out of whatever animal was crying for help.

"Okay, fine, but if something tries to kill me in there, you've got to promise to go for help."

Wishing he were wearing jeans and cowboy boots—or hell, even combat boots—rather than running shoes and flimsy-assed shorts, and wondering why he hadn't brought his cell phone—he might not have reception out here, but at least he'd have the flashlight function—he took a careful step into the tall grass at the side of the road, peering into the dim tangle of foliage.

Whatever it was, it thrashed and cried harder at Tanner's approach. Trixie, close on Tanner's heels, whimpered and darted back and forth, anxious to see what new and exciting creature would be revealed. She barked in excitement. Which, of course, made the animal cry and thrash harder.

"Damn it, Trixie, knock it off," Tanner said. She didn't knock it off. Tanner yanked a branch aside, cursing again as thorns grabbed onto his skin. He caught a glimpse of flaring nostrils above a mouth that bleated *Waaaaah!* loud enough to cause Tanner to flinch, lose his footing, and land on his ass in the dirt. At least Trixie shut up for a few seconds while she cocked her head and watched him scramble to his feet.

He once again tugged the branch aside and looked at the creature. Where there should have been eyes there was a mop of long, springy coils of hair. It looked like a sheep, but if it was, it wasn't any breed Tanner remembered from his 4-H days. Which were short because his parents got him into junior rodeo as soon as he was old enough, and then he'd paid more attention to horses. And girls.

Whatever it was, it was bucking and thrashing, and Tanner might be inclined to give it a few badass points just for effort.

Trixie shoved her way past Tanner and lifted her face to sniff more closely at the animal.

"Watch out," Tanner said, using his knee to nudge Trixie out of the way. "Mr. Sheep here might not be inclined to make friends, and if he's got horns, we both could be sorry we stopped to help."

Trixie whined.

"I didn't say we aren't gonna help. I just said we might be sorry." Tanner peered into the darkness, trying to see if the animal was injured in any way, or simply stuck. "The good news is he's not likely to eat us."

Tanner reached into the tangle and slid his hand above the animal's head, finding horns. Weird. It sure looked like a sheep but it had horns like a goat. *Ugh.* And it smelled like a goat. Trying not to breathe in too deeply, he grasped a horn and spoke to the terrified creature. "Come on, buddy. Want to come out here away from those stickers?" He was able to tug the beast forward a couple of steps before it stopped to complain.

Vibrating with the need to do something, Trixie let out an encouraging bark. The goat jerked his horn out of Tanner's hand and tore his body free of the brambles, charging Trixie, who refused to back down. Instead, she turned the tables and chased the sheep…goat…four-legged Muppet until he stopped in the middle of the road and panted.

"Whoa there," Tanner soothed.

Then the creature turned, faced Tanner, and pawed the ground. Great. He'd survived an endless tour in a war zone and an explosion that should have killed him along with the rest of his squad, endured months and months of skin grafts, and now he was about to be murdered on the side of a road in Texas by an angry sheep-goat hybrid.

He held his hands out in front of him, ready to grab at the horns as he hopefully stepped out of the way before getting gored.

Tanner had his eyes on the goat but saw the lights from an approaching vehicle in his peripheral vision. Trixie started to bark frantically, running in circles around Tanner and the sheep.

The car was coming closer—fast.

Well, hell.

"Here, Trixie," Tanner called, and lifted the dog in one arm as he dived toward the sheep, moving all three of them out of the middle of the road just in time to avoid being turned into roadkill.

Jen cruised along the dark country road with her windows rolled down and the radio off, scanning to the left and right, listening and looking for Angus. "Oh, please don't be eaten by wolves or coyotes or wild boar. Whatever the heck eats innocent animals out here, please don't be eaten by them," she begged under her breath, though why the stubborn goat would listen to a whispered plea, even if he was within listening distance, was beyond her. Doggone beast hadn't done a thing she wanted him to since she'd brought him to the homestead this morning. And now he was missing. Disappeared.

One of the chorus members in her brain, who looked like her mother and sounded like Jerkface Brock on helium, started in with all of the reasons that moving to the boonies alone to remake herself was a bad idea. "You don't need to do this. Starting a homestead is beyond crazy, even with air-conditioning and access to antibiotics. It's too much work, especially all alone. You could keep this great life you've created here, if you'd just compromise a little."

Well, I compromised myself into a laughingstock of the internet, and apparently the real me seems fake anyway, so there's nowhere to go but up, right?

That was why she was out here in the dark chasing a danged goat instead of home in Austin, curled up on the couch watching Netflix, sharing a big bowl of popcorn with her mom, and hoping Brock would find himself transported to another dimension. One where he couldn't wreck Jen's life.

Nope. Not thinking about him, or blaming the slime bucket for how messed up her own life felt at the moment. "I'm responsible for my own existence, my own reputation, and my own reality. I can start over, make it really real this time, and prove to God, the internet, and most of all myself that I can be a real, functioning homesteader. Who can't keep track of one stupid goat."

She took a breath, then stopped long enough to make sure her camera was aimed at the road and hit Record and went into think-out-loud mode.

"So I'm out here driving around looking for my new goat. I went out to check on him after dinner, and he was gone. It's like he vaporized out of his pen without bothering to open the gate or even crunch down the fence."

The headlights cut a tunnel of light through the darkness, and it occurred to her that anything not in the tunnel could probably see in better than she could see out. Another thought struck her.

"What if he didn't escape? What if someone took him? What if some*thing* took him?

"I don't need to think like that, but it's crazy dark out here. Why aren't there any streetlights? There should be streetlights every-where. Even rural Texas. *Especially* rural Texas. There could be all kinds of terrible things out here." She forced a laugh. "But this is not a problem. I've got this, right?"

Breathe. You're supposed to be you, so it's okay to be a little creeped out, but you also need to remember that you can do this.

"Okay, there aren't any real monsters in Texas. I mean…there might be wild pigs, I think I saw something about that on reality TV, but Bigfoot lives up north." Then she remembered something else she'd learned on "reality" TV. "Texas shares a border with Mexico, and they have something. What's it called…Cthulhu? No, that's a science fiction thing. What's it called? Chupacabra? But it's not real. Except *chupacabra* means goat-sucker in Spanish."

As her anxiety level rose, so did her speed. She was pretty far from her place, and getting more and more freaked out, and she apparently wasn't paying close attention to where she was going because all of a sudden—

"What the—?" She slammed on the brakes as a flash of white darted in front of her—Angus!—but it was chased by something else, right into the ditch on the opposite side of the road.

"What was that?" It had looked like a man—it was tall, with broad shoulders and long human legs—but the top part of it was lumpy, and it had a dog head. There was definitely a canine snout, big white teeth, and eyes that glowed in her headlights. "I think that thing was after Angus!"

Jen threw her car into park and yanked the keys from the ignition. She scrambled to the side of the road, scanning the darkness, deaf to anything but her own rapid breathing before it occurred to her that it might be better to get back in the car and call 911 to report... What? She was about to take a step away from the edge of the road, back toward her car, when she heard something. She froze in terror. A groan, then a cry. *Angus.* The monster was eating Angus. She could hear her sweet little goat bleating, begging for its life. She tiptoed a few steps toward the ditch, peering down into the darkness.

She wondered briefly if after it finished with her goat, it would attack her, so no one would ever know how well she was doing out here on her own, making a legit life for herself, but she shouldn't give a rat's patootie what people thought if she was going to be dead. She had to save her goat!

Another sound, a moan—of anticipation?—came from the monster, followed by another panicked scream from Angus.

Oh, hell no. She might die out here, but her goat was going to survive, and she was going to go down fighting. The thing in the ditch writhed, and she glimpsed white—the fleece of her prize-winning Angora goat. That damned monster was probably trying to swallow Angus whole, like snakes did with mice.

Before she could think any more, she leapt into the ditch, onto the thing's back, and whacked it on the back of the head.

"Oh no you don't, you stupid monster. Don't you hurt my goat. Let him go!" she yelled.

"Jesus!" The monster separated into two parts then. One part broke away—the dog part. Then Jen found herself being dragged through the weeds and flipped onto her back.

Chapter 4

It took less than an instant for Tanner's instincts to kick in and neutralize his attacker, to flip him and pin him under his body and immobilize his hands above his head. Fortunately those same instincts recognized that *he* was a *she*—a terrified *she* who fought and hissed like a scalded cat. His brain kicked in, and he understood that whatever psychosis had led her to attack him, he wasn't helping her by holding her down in a ditch. Good sense, however, suggested he needed to let her go carefully.

"I'm not going to let you suck Angus dry!" she cried, snarling and twisting beneath him.

"What the hell?" he demanded, rising to his knees to take his weight off of her—but not releasing her hands, because he had no idea why she'd attacked him.

She twisted under him. "Let me go!"

"Just hold on a second," Tanner said. "Are you going to attack me again?"

"I will if you—" She paused, squinting at him through the darkness. She took a deep breath and shook her head, so he released her hands and lifted his leg so he wasn't straddling her. He groaned when the movement pulled at uncompromising scar tissue, but fortunately, he didn't fall.

She sat up and scooted out of the ditch onto the edge of the road. She stood, eyeing him warily as she brushed debris from the seat of her shorts. The lights from her car showed him a woman about his age, tall and lean. Twists of red hair sprang from a long braid that hung over one shoulder and brushed the top of one breast. She was pretty, too, in a girl next door meets lumberjack sort of way. Ready for anything, and looking good while she did it.

As he straightened, she edged away. "Don't come any closer!"

Tanner raised his hands and stayed put. "I don't want any trouble," he told her. Except wasn't that what hijackers and kidnappers always said? *Damn.* He did have a way with the ladies.

The woman ignored his words, indicated the shaggy animal calmly chewing leaves like it hadn't just been freaking the fuck out in the bushes, and said, "So…maybe you weren't about to go vampire on my goat?"

He shook his head and grabbed at the only thing in that sentence that made sense. "It's a goat? We wondered."

"We?" She took another step away from him and looked around.

"Yeah, Trixie and I." He looked around for his dog. "Trix? Come here, baby." Trixie trotted up to the woman and sat, smiling expectantly. "This is Trixie."

"Hi, Trixie." She crouched down and extended her hand toward the little dog, who licked her wrist until she received a thorough petting.

He cleared his throat and indicated the goat. "So…Angus?" At her nod, he went on, "Weird-looking goat."

"Yep. He's a full-blooded, registered, award-winning Angora goat. I was actually planning to buy a milk goat, but then I met this guy and, well"—she shrugged—"plans change." She shoved a hand into the animal's fleece and scratched behind his ears.

"No kidding." Tanner eyed the goat, who stared insolently back at him, gnawing a branch.

"I'll spin his fleece this winter and knit sweaters and mittens." She shrugged and laughed. "Or at least a scarf."

"That's…ambitious." He tried to picture her sitting by the fire with a spinning wheel, but he couldn't quite get there.

"I don't think it'll be that tough. I've got some books about shearing and spinning, and I already know how to knit."

Tanner laughed. "I grew up with cattle, but I know you can

pay people to shear your flock. And you can get yarn at Walmart. Presheared, prespun, preknit sweaters, too."

She pursed her lips and narrowed her eyes. "I don't want that fake processed stuff. I want to make it myself."

"Okay." He thought about Emma and Lizzie and how they'd recently been watching some internet thing that had inspired them to start making things from scratch.

"Anyway, I don't have a flock, it's just Angus." She hesitated, then said in a tone that was curiously half-defensive, half-confident, "Besides, if there's anything on my homestead I can't do myself, I don't need it."

Interesting. So, she was a homesteader. Probably living on some dried-up piece of Texas with an Armageddon prepper who'd built his own personal bunker to defend himself against the government, or a hipster growing organic "herbs" to cure what ails you—or at least to make sure you didn't mind the ailment so much.

He should get back on the road and finish his run before the guys came looking for him. Or before her husband or boyfriend came looking for her.

"How do you plan to get old Angus here back home?" Tanner asked, eyeing the woman's vehicle. It was an SUV, but the back end appeared to be filled with junk.

"I'll put him in the back seat. Can you hang on to him for a second so he doesn't get any more ideas about escaping?"

"Sure."

"Thanks!"

She smiled, and Tanner felt something deep inside shift. He didn't want things inside himself shifting; he'd worked damned hard to find space for everything that needed to be kept in. Then their hands brushed while transferring the goat's collar from her to him, and he could have sworn his whole body got a jolt of electricity.

She must have felt something, too, because her eyes widened a fraction as she met his gaze. Maybe something with all that hair on the goat and static electricity, he decided.

The moment ended in a second, and she walked to her car to open the passenger door, bending to find the seat release. "Just a second. I've got a lot of junk back here. I just moved here, and I'm still not completely unpacked," her muffled voice called. Tanner watched as she tossed stuff around the inside of the car. Mostly he watched her. Specifically, her backside. Her shorts rode up a little on the backs of her thighs, just enough for him to see the tiniest hint of butt cheek, and he guessed she probably wasn't wearing regular panties. So a thong. To do homestead chores?

He figured the wife of an Armageddon prepper would be wearing utilitarian white granny panties, so he mentally scowled at the hipster for being a weed-smoking slacker. Tanner would never tell a woman what she could and couldn't do, but he also wouldn't let her take off into the night alone to look for a missing goat.

"Okay," she said, straightening and turning back to Tanner and Angus. "Come on, buddy." She reached for her goat's collar. "We're going to get you home, where you will stay put, right?"

Not his business, though he felt obligated to offer a suggestion, especially since the weed-smoking hipster wouldn't know any more than she did about livestock. "You said your herd is just Angus?"

"Yes," she said, shoving a stray curl from her forehead.

"He might need a friend. The girls in my 4-H group—"

"You were in 4-H?" she asked, eyes lighting up.

And why did that just now make him glad he'd gone? "Yeah. My parents made me go to learn about taking care of livestock before I started doing rodeo." Why had he offered that tidbit? He wasn't exactly proud of his time on the circuit. Especially not that final year.

She tucked that curl back into her hair. "Really? So you're a real live cowboy. That's so cool. I grew up in the suburbs—" She cut herself off, then seemed to reconsider, and said, "And all we had were Girl Scouts and soccer."

Tanner shrugged. "Everything's relative, I guess. Maybe I'd have rather played soccer than shovel manure."

She laughed, and the moonlight sparkled in her eyes. He'd have to see her in the daylight to find out what color they were.

He stepped back, breaking the connection. "So anyway, you and your husband might want to go find another goat or two to keep Angus company, so he's not so inclined to go wandering off. They do better in groups."

"I didn't know that. And I'm not married, but I'll get online and see what I can find," she said, then slapped her hand over her mouth.

He must have looked confused because she said, "I don't think I should have admitted to a total stranger on a dark road that I'm living out here in the boonies by myself."

Tanner smiled, mentally kicking the hipster out of the picture. "I'm Tanner Beauchamp," he said. "I live a couple of miles south at the Big Chance Dog Rescue."

"I pass that place when I drive to town. I'm glad it's a rescue and not a puppy mill," she said. "So you're not a *cow*boy, you're a *dog* boy? Guy? Man."

"I did a little roping and wrangling back in the day, but yeah, I guess I'm a dog boy-guy-man now." He felt his mouth quirk when he repeated her words. "I work with some guys who train rescued dogs to be service animals for other vets."

"Whoa. That's even cooler than 4-H."

Tanner laughed.

"I'm Jennif—Jen," she said.

"Nice to meet you, Jen." And in spite of his attempts to remind himself that he was in no position to get his hormones all fired up over some random woman he met on a dark, abandoned road—nor any other woman anywhere—it *was* nice to meet her. He shook his head. "And I promise I'm not a serial killer, though I'm not sure why you'd believe me. If I were a serial killer, that's also what I'd say."

"Maybe, but you probably wouldn't point out that a serial killer would say that, if you really were a serial killer. Right?"

"Let's hope not," Tanner said.

Jen stood there for a long moment, smiling at Tanner in a way that made him a little light-headed, in a good way. But her eyes traveled over his face, and for the first time in a long time, he was self-conscious about the burn scars that had changed his face, an outward reminder of his damaged, useless soul.

He cleared his throat. "Come on, let's get this goat loaded up."

"We certainly made an impression on our new neighbor," Jen told Angus and the dash cam after saying good night to Tanner. "I don't think it was a good impression, though." She'd nearly killed him, after all. "He was pretty nice, all things considered." Really nice, actually. Even after she'd accused him of planning to do unnatural things to her goat.

Even now, her face burned with embarrassment. It had been pretty dark, so she'd barely seen his face, but her imagination filled in what appeared to be strong features and intense dark eyes.

"It's possible that he thinks I'm a nutcase. I've been too busy working my butt off to be really lonely, but chatting with Tanner reminded me that I like people—in spite of how hard I've been trying to avoid them since *the incident.* I hope I didn't offend him there at the end. We were talking, and then all of a sudden, he was all *Okay, gotta go.* But I suppose I *had* kind of interrupted his run, and then attacked him in a ditch." She cleared her throat, hoping he hadn't picked up on how super aware she was of him.

Even now, her face—and other parts—went hot as she thought about how he'd straddled her and held her down in the weeds. Probably just the heat of the moment, though. It must have been adrenaline that made her notice his strong, hot thighs braced around her own, made her appreciate his scent. She had to be losing it if she thought a sweaty stranger in a ditch smelled good. Context was everything, wasn't it? If he'd turned out to be creepy, her memory of his smell would have been different, she was sure.

She shook her head. How sad that she'd been on her own out here for fewer than two weeks and she was lusting after the first guy she'd met. She tried to hope she'd never see him again, so she wouldn't get a chance to rub herself all over him like a cat in heat.

She forced her mind to get back on topic. "I'm sorry I didn't know you needed friends, Angus. I thought I'd read everything ever written about raising goats." Probably she hadn't actually paid attention to all of it that wasn't about what awesome fleece Angora goats have, which would make amazing sweaters one day.

"But it's not a problem. I'll get on Craigslist tomorrow and see if I can't find some other goats or sheep to keep you company."

She peered through the darkness, but everything looked the same: long, straight roads lined with mile upon mile of fence, broken up here and there by a ton of tangled brush. "On the edge of beautiful Texas Hill Country" the real estate agent's description had said. "On the edge of" really meant "not in," when it came to the lay of the land.

"Whoa! Here we are!"

Angus bleated as she hit the brakes, then swung her car into the lane.

"You hush," she told him.

She pulled her car next to the goat shed and turned on the inside light, so she'd show up better on the last bit of recording for the day.

"Phew! Day ten ended on an exciting note. Angus almost got

eaten by a chupacabra, but I attacked it and saved his life." She made a mental note to add some cheesy animation of a monster. She laughed. "It turned out the monster was really a nice man named Tanner who lives a couple of miles down the road. Check this out—there's a place called the Big Chance Dog Rescue Ranch where a bunch of guys train rescued dogs to be service animals for veterans. OMG, I think my ovaries just exploded." She snickered.

"I'm going to see if I can't find a couple more sheep or goats to keep Angus company so maybe he won't run off, and I definitely have some fence reinforcing to do before I get my garden put in."

She signed off and yawned. "Come on, Angus, let's get you into your shed so I can get to bed. Tomorrow morning's going to come awfully early."

Angus was surprisingly agreeable when she led him out of her car and into the little shed.

After latching the door and double-checking it, she headed toward "home." A couple of moths fluttered around the security light that illuminated her pathetic little camper. One of these days, she'd spiff it up, put her own style on it. After she got that garden in, figured out how to water it, cleaned out the chicken coop, and rigged up some sort of laundry system. Oh. And all of that had to happen after she found a companion for Angus.

She trudged up the steps into the camper and dragged off her clothes, leaving them in a pile inside the front door. This business was exhausting, but the good news was that she didn't have to get back to it for another few hours. Until then, she could sleep.

She washed up, pulled on a sleep shirt, and checked to make sure she didn't have any uninvited guests under the covers before climbing in. She wasn't really freaked out by bugs or snakes, but she sure didn't want to find one in her bed. Aaaand then her mind started to go down the *what to do if you get bitten by a rattlesnake* path. She had a standard first aid kit, but should she have some sort of antivenom stuff available just in case?

What if she got bitten while she was sleeping and didn't wake up? She was out here all alone. No one would even hear her cry for help. She bet Tanner knew what to do for snakebites, but he was tucked up safe and sound at his little dog ranch full of army guys, probably having a beer and telling the story of the crazy lady he'd met on his run tonight.

Suddenly she wasn't quite so sure that heading out on this adventure alone had been such a great idea.

"Oh, for heaven's sake," she said. "You're just fine."

And then she repeated the *You're just fine* part for the better part of an hour, until she finally drifted off to sleep.

Chapter 5

"COME ON, TRIXIE, LET'S TAKE A BREAK." TRIXIE LOOKED LIKE she wanted to argue—*No, human! Let's play foreverrrrr!*—but she trotted after Tanner and his baggie of hot dog bits. She was getting better at following his commands when she was off leash. He was pretty sure the hot dogs were her kryptonite. He eased into one of the rockers on the ranch house porch. Most days were easier: undamaged muscles were usually strong enough to compensate for the damaged ones, and more than a few surgeries made sure his scars weren't so restrictive, but today wasn't one of his better days.

His normal dreams of fire and explosions were always interspersed with screams of people needing his help, or pointing their fingers in blame, but last night he'd awakened sweating and shaking more than once, and his memories of what he'd dreamed were still especially vivid this morning. The woman from last night— Jen—had been there along with the usual suspects. He'd been chasing her, and she'd pushed him away. Then he'd catch up and she'd push him away again.

No need to see Dr. Freud about that one, but Tanner hadn't had any thought of pursuing her. That would just be nuts. He didn't need a subliminal dream to ward him off.

Except she was still hanging out in his brain. He'd never met anyone who just decided they were going to start a farm from scratch. Most people inherited the lifestyle. Or started working as a ranch hand and worked their way up from there.

Tanner had a feeling she was both out of her depth and very likely to get where she wanted to be through sheer determination and wits.

He was sure he'd get the chance to find out. News traveled

fast in a small town, and Chance County had a pretty tightly knit gossip network. Tanner wasn't hooked into the community, but with Lizzie and Emma around, he couldn't help but hear things. All alone here on the porch, he could admit he was intrigued with Jen, and not just because he had a professional interest in her ranching abilities. She was funny, and sexy, and maybe a little fool-hardy, which brought out his protective instincts, he supposed.

He snorted. Who was he kidding? He knew too well he wasn't qualified to protect anyone. Especially some random woman who'd probably never think of him again.

He scrubbed his face with his hands and resettled his hat, propped his boots on the porch railing and pretended to be a man with no worries. Not that anyone was watching. Adam was off with Marcus meeting some potential donors. Seemed like they spent more time begging for money than Tanner spent accounting for it. Jake was in the barn, rearranging leashes or doing one of his other seemingly pointless projects. Jake had suffered a traumatic brain injury a couple of years ago while deployed with Adam and Marcus, and although he'd mostly recovered, he had a few quirks. One of those was an inability to sit still if there was anything he could be doing.

Tanner, on the other hand, had a knack for spending hours contemplating the toes of his boots, or whatever else happened to be in his line of sight. At least until his mind found its way down the path of shame and regrets, but if that happened, he had his "job" which he had been surprised to learn that he actually liked. Turned out that all the bookkeeping junk he was in charge of gave his brain something to do besides obsess over his failures.

"Hey, Tanner. There you are." Lizzie stepped out of the ranch house, followed by Emma and their pit bulls, Loretta and Garth.

Trixie sprang to her feet to try to engage the other dogs in doggy antics. Garth, Loretta's mostly grown pup, wagged and did the front-down, butt-in-the-air thing. They were off, chasing each other around the big oak tree before Tanner had a chance to give the official release word. *Oh well*. She'd remember he was the guy with the baggie of hot dogs pretty soon. Hopefully.

Lizzie said, "I was about to come looking for you. Doc Chance called, said he needs to see Trixie to repeat her blood work."

A frisson of unease skittered along Tanner's spine, reminding him of the way his spidey senses would tingle when faced with a bad situation in combat. Unfortunately, that crap happened to him all the time now when there wasn't a damn thing wrong. It was part of his PTSD—the feeling that another shoe was about to drop, when there wasn't a reason in the world to feel like that. "Why does he need more blood?"

"Something about a lab error," Lizzie said. "He didn't seem too concerned."

"Okay…" It was possible that something got switched. Things had been a bit chaotic when the veterinarian had come out the other day to do wellness checks on all of the dogs at the ranch. It was a pain in the neck to take them all in, so Doc Chance made house calls and said it was community service.

"Anyway, we're heading into town to pick up some groceries, then getting Granddad," Emma said. "We can drop you and Trixie at the vet and meet you at the training center, if you like."

Tanner thought about telling the women he'd go on his own in a couple of hours, but had a feeling he might be tempted to blow it off altogether. And while that would sure give Tanner's anxiety something new to chew on, it wouldn't help Trixie if for some reason there was a problem. "All right," Tanner agreed. "Let me try to catch her."

It took all three humans, the other two dogs, and half of his bag of hot dog bits, but they finally convinced Trixie to let Tanner attach her leash. Tanner belted himself in the back seat of Lizzie's car, between the dogs, and settled back to enjoy the ride.

As soon as they were underway, Emma asked Lizzie, "Did you

hear about this?" She held up her phone so Lizzie, who was driving, could glance at the screen.

Whatever she saw had Lizzie saying, "Omigod, yes. I did see it. That poor woman! I can't even imagine how embarrassed she must be. The internet is practically melting!"

Tanner didn't want to know. Internet drama wasn't real, after all. Real drama was seeing your friends getting blown up and then having to collect body parts in ziplock bags.

On the other hand, there was something to be said for non-real drama. They were making such a fuss that his curiosity was raised a little, which distracted him from his thoughts.

"What a jerk!" Lizzie said. "Whoever this Brock guy is, I hope they kicked him to the curb!"

"Right?" Emma answered. "Here, listen to this. It's from their website." She tapped the phone a few times, then began to read, "We appreciate your support of *Homemade with Joanie and Jennifer* and want to ensure that we always bring you the best lifestyle content on the web. We've been planning some exciting new things for months, but right now Jennifer is taking a sabbatical to refresh her soul while Joanie prepares to stir up some more amazing do-it-yourself fun."

"Jennifer left the show?" Lizzie's shock seemed equivalent to learning that the earth was really orbiting Pluto. "Do you think she's gone for good?"

Emma shrugged. "That's what it seems like. Neither Jennifer nor Joanie has posted on Twitter or Instagram for a few days, and the Facebook fan groups have more conspiracy theories than two political conventions in the same venue."

"Wow, I'm really sad," Lizzie said, though Tanner thought she sounded a little hungrier for gossip than devastated. "I do kind of like her parting shot, though."

Emma nodded in agreement. "Yay for semi-assured body confidence."

Huh? Nothing like getting the back half of a conversation, Tanner thought.

"Too bad the internet's more interested in deciding which of them has fake boobs than which of their shows was faked. Except—do you think Joanie's had work done? I think Jennifer's are probably real."

"Here's to perfectly adequate tits!" crowed Emma, arching her back and thrusting out her chest.

Tanner coughed and tried not to think about his friend's girlfriend's breasts. Or his other friend's girlfriend's breasts. Or anyone's breasts. Or boobs, or hooters, or—

"Oh crap, Tanner, I'm sorry," Emma said, laughing with embarrassment. "Didn't mean for our moment of throwing off the bindings of societal breast-pectations to make you uncomfortable. Although maybe I should, I guess. I mean, we need to stop apologizing for wanting our own natural bodies to be enough instead of some e-version of reality, right?" She looked at Lizzie.

With a shrug, Lizzie glanced in the rearview mirror at Tanner and said, "Right. But we don't blame you for any societal bindings."

Tanner managed to clear his throat and say, "For the rest of my life, I promise to do my best to remove societal bindings anytime I see them."

At Lizzie's raised eyebrows and long blink, he mentally reviewed his words.

"I mean, I promise not to like breast implants." He shook his head. That wasn't right, either. "Not that there's anything wrong with that. Them. I mean, if any woman—"

Emma laughed. "I know what you mean. And we let the whole boob thing distract us from the real story anyway."

"Which is what, exactly?" Tanner asked.

"The online YouTube channel *Homemade with Joanie and Jennifer*. Joanie and Jennifer have apparently broken up." Lizzie made a sympathetic frown, as though she expected Tanner to feel as devastated as she apparently did.

"Okay…?"

Emma rolled her eyes and said, "It's like the YouTube version of Martha Stewart crossed with that couple from Waco with the shiplap."

"Shiplap?"

"Never mind that. Joanie and Jennifer are a mother-daughter team who make videos of do-it-yourself projects and put them online. They make all kinds of down-to-earth things like baskets and maple syrup and quilts."

"How…interesting."

Lizzie snorted. "Yeah, so there are probably a million other videos *you'd* rather watch, but they're cute and funny and *real*, instead of all 'Look at me take this roadkill and turn it into a perfect cutting board the first time I try it!'"

"They turn roadkill into—"

Emma gave Lizzie a pretend shove and said, "That might be a little exaggeration. But they do lots of cool stuff, and they do it in a fun and realistic way. Or at least they did. Apparently Jennifer, the daughter… She's a little fussy about things, and their producer guy tried to get her to try something his way, and she went off on him after he accused her of being a big faker. Then he said something about Joanie's—she's the mom—perfect boobs, and Jennifer said her own boobs were 'perfectly adequate,' and now the internet's melting over who has better ta-tas."

"I see," Tanner said, though he was still trying not to see any boobs that might be in his general vicinity. He glanced through the window. "Oh wow, we're here already!" Thank God for small favors.

Chapter 6

"GIRLS, YOU'RE KILLING ME," JEN MOANED, TURNING UP THE radio and leaning her head out of the window to gulp some lung-scorching Texas air, which was better than the smell of the inside of her SUV.

Unfortunately, the dulcet tones of the Backstreet Boys at full blast weren't enough to drown out the complaints of the two tiny sheep bleating behind her.

They were cute, but in desperate need of a bath. Jen hoped like heck that Angus appreciated what she had gone through to get them. After hours spent surfing every goat and sheep group's website within a hundred miles, she'd finally found someone on Craigslist who was looking to rehome a couple of babydoll sheep. That sent Jen on a journey of many gravel roads, finally landing her at the home of one very overwhelmed Phyllis Gianetti.

It turned out that in the past six months, Phyllis's husband of thirty years had left her for a younger woman, and then her mother died of breast cancer, leaving her responsible for her grand-mother. And *then* her daughter's boyfriend had been deployed, so the daughter and her three girls had moved in with Phyllis and Granny. Needless to say, Phyllis barely had the time or energy to care for herself, much less hobby livestock.

So now Jen was the owner of not only a pair of babydoll sheep (currently residing in the back seat), but also two Angora rabbits (currently residing in the front passenger seat) and a box turtle named Mr. Bigfoot (in a five-gallon bucket next to the sheep). She'd escaped without the one-eared barn cat.

The good news was that all the animals seemed to be healthy, if a little unkempt.

Jen sure hoped that someone at the Feed and Seed in Big Chance would do curbside delivery, because her shopping list had grown from "some more fence stuff" to "all the things" in the past two hours.

"Turn left in five hundred feet," Google Maps told her. Jen slowed and peered ahead for the store, but as she got closer, she didn't see any signs.

"Your destination is on the left."

Still no signs.

"You have arrived at your destination."

Jen stopped in the middle of Main Street and looked to her left, at a place called the Big Chance Training Center. Personal fitness training? Job training? She couldn't tell from the outside, but it definitely didn't look like it sold farm supplies. She looked as far as she could see up the street. Then she looked back the way she'd come. She looked on the right side of the street in case the app was confused.

No Feed and Seed. Nothing even close.

There were a law office, a grocery store, a veterinarian's office, a dog groomer, a barber, and a beauty shop. A little farther down, there was a Dairy Queen.

A car behind her honked, and Jen waved to acknowledge the nudge. She turned left on the side street next to the training center and pulled to the curb under a huge old oak. She got out and resettled the ball cap she wore to keep pigtail-escaping curls out of her eyes. Maybe she should just cut the whole mess off, she thought for the ninetieth time.

While she was pondering her options, and hoping a farm store—or even a pet shop—would miraculously appear before her eyes, another SUV pulled into a spot in the lot of the training center.

Two women and two dogs got out. One of them leaned back in to say something to an elderly man who ignored her. They looked at Jen curiously.

Oh, no.

What if they recognized her?

Stop being so full of yourself, Jen told herself. Even if they had seen the show, they wouldn't know her. She had on a hat and sunglasses, and her hair was in freaking pigtails instead of tamed by a sh-ton of styling product. She was also wearing jeans and a Bart Simpson T-shirt with sneakers instead of her signature quirky overalls and Doc Martens.

The women didn't look like ax murderers, so Jen decided to ask if they knew where she could get supplies.

"Hi there," she called out, crossing the street.

"Hi," the women answered.

"I wonder if you can help me. I'm looking for the Feed and Seed? Google says it should be right here."

"Oh no." The shorter, dark-haired woman winced. "I still haven't gotten that changed."

"So maybe it moved to a new location?" She could hope, right?

"No, I'm sorry," the woman said. "You're in the right place. This used to be the Feed and Seed, but they went out of business and now we use the place for dog training."

"Oh, a *dog* training center?" Then a light bulb went on. "Are you part of the dog rescue place?"

"We sure are," the taller, lighter-haired woman said, looking like she was about to launch into a sales pitch. "The Big Chance Dog Rescue Ranch is where most of us live and where the dogs and veterans stay, but we do a lot of training here in town and have classes for local pet owners as well. We rescue a lot of dogs, but very few make it as service animals. The rest we adopt out with free lifetime obedience classes. Do you happen to need a rescued dog?"

Jen laughed and cocked her thumb over her shoulder. "Not right now. I've just, um, *adopted* a handful of rabbits and a couple of miniature sheep. Oh, and a turtle. I was hoping to pick up some supplies from the Feed and Seed."

"Uh-oh. What do you need?" the dark-haired woman asked.

"A little bit of everything," Jen said. "Where's the nearest next-best place to pick up feed?"

"You'll probably want to head into Llano, there's a Tractor Supply there."

"Okay, thanks." Jen looked at her watch. There was no way she could keep these poor critters cooped up in her car long enough to drive all the way to Llano and back today. She'd have to improvise. She could probably keep the turtle in the bathtub and put the bunnies in the henhouse. She'd figure out some way to keep the sheep separated from Angus until she was sure they'd be friends. Somehow. Maybe.

The blond woman was peering at Jen as though trying to place her. Jen pulled her ball hat down a little more snugly. "Are you from Big Chance? I don't think I know you."

"I'm Jennif—Jen. I've got a place out on Happy Beef Way."

"Oh, is that the place with the perfect fences and sparkly cows?" the blond asked.

Jen laughed. Those cattle did seem awfully tidy. "Not exactly. I'm next door at the place with the overgrown everything and escaping goat."

"Oh." The blond recovered quickly and said, "Anyway, that's not too far from us. I'm surprised we haven't met before now." She looked at her dark-haired friend as if for confirmation that Jen was indeed a stranger. Apparently, Tanner the goat rescuer hadn't mentioned her.

"Well, I don't get into town much," Jen said in an attempt to forestall too much questioning. "I'm usually pretty self-sustaining." At least that was the goal.

"When did you move in?"

So much for deflection. But the women were so open and friendly that Jen found herself answering, "I've only been here for a couple of weeks."

The dark-haired woman stuck out her hand. "Well, it's nice to meet you, Jen. I'm Emma Collins, and this is my almost sister-in-law, Lizzie VanHook."

"Stop that, you'll jinx things," Lizzie hissed, taking her turn at shaking Jen's hand. "Unless you know something you're not telling me?"

"No, he knows I can't keep my mouth shut, but I know he's going to pop the question any minute," Emma said, then told Jen, "Lizzie and my brother, Adam, are very likely getting married in the near future."

"I bet you and Marcus get there first," Lizzie said. "But that doesn't help you right now, does it?"

"Well, I sure wish you all the best," Jen said, trying to sort through the conversation and noticing that no one named Tanner had been part of the boyfriend conversation. Which didn't mean he was single, but...

"We have to have you out to the ranch for a cookout," Lizzie said.

"Oh...that's nice of you." She should totally decline, but suddenly Jen realized how much she missed human contact. Although if she started hanging around with the locals, someone was bound to recognize her before she was ready to go public with her success, if she ever managed to get to a place she could call "success." Well, she could always say no later, right?

"Give me your number," Lizzie said, pulling out her phone. "I'll text you and we can talk about some dates."

"I–I don't want to impose."

"Nonsense. We're going to have a new group of veterans arriving in a few days, and you'll be a welcome addition to the party."

"Well, I..."

"Give her your damned phone number," growled a voice from behind Emma.

Everyone turned to look at the elderly man in the car.

"And this is Granddad," Emma said. "Granddad, this is Jen."

He ignored the introduction and launched right into "You've got to eat, right?"

"I suppose…"

"Right. And God knows those boys out there at the ranch need practice talking to girls."

"Aren't we girls, Granddad?" Emma asked.

"You don't count. You're already hooked up, and those two other ones aren't afraid of you anymore. It's time to bring in some new meat."

"Granddad!" Emma admonished, then looked at Jen and said, "I'm so sorry. Sometimes he's not…polite."

"Aw, screw your polite crap," Granddad said. "Desperate times and all that. You there…new girl. You got a fella?"

"Well, no, I don't, but I'm really b—"

"You get your hide out to the ranch and see if one of them rejects don't suit you."

"Granddad!" Emma was bright red. "Jake and Tanner aren't rejects!"

"But you know exactly who I'm talking about, don't you? That Jake's a loser if he thinks one bonk on the noggin is enough to take him off the market, and the other kid assumes no one wants to get nekkid with him because of them scars. His scars are all in his head, if you ask me. Make him scared of the damned daylight."

Emma rolled her eyes and muttered, "Why we're thankful for your lucid days is beyond me." A little louder, she said, "Tanner's not afraid of the daylight, Granddad."

"Then what's he doing back there hiding behind the shop?"

Everyone looked where Granddad was pointing, to a shady spot behind the training center. Sure enough, Jen's late-night goat hero and his trusty sidekick Trixie were standing there in the shadows. He reached down to adjust Trixie's collar and then approached the group.

Whoa. Tanner had seemed well built last night when he'd been in running clothes and trying to keep her from strangling him in a ditch. In the full light of day and wearing a snug T-shirt, well-worn jeans, and cowboy boots, he was just this side of perfect, as far as Jen was concerned. He was a long, tall drink of lean muscle and looked like he belonged in an ad for pickup trucks or something. He stopped on the other side of Lizzie's car from where Jen stood with the women, but now she could see him a little better. His cowboy hat threw serious shade, but everything about his face seemed…hard. Strong jaw, firm lips, aquiline nose, and piercing eyes. He didn't seem glad to see her, but Jen was helpless to look away. She held his gaze and smiled.

"Hi," she said, giving a little wave. "Nice to see you."

He didn't respond, barely raised his chin in acknowledgment of her greeting, but stared back at her intently.

Okay, well, that friendly guy she thought she'd met last night seemed to have disappeared by light of day. Maybe Granddad was right after all.

"You know each other?" Emma glanced from Jen to Tanner and back again.

Since Tanner didn't seem inclined to answer, Jen did. "Tanner rescued my goat last night."

"Rescued a goat? Tanner, you didn't tell us about that!" Lizzie put her hands on her hips.

"Uh, yeah," he said. "Apparently there was a chupacabra out looking for goats last night, and Trixie found an escapee just in the nick of time."

Was that a wink in Jen's direction? Okay, so maybe he wasn't so unfriendly. She felt her cheeks heat.

"Well, huh," Lizzie said. "Anyway, how's Trixie? Did you get everything straightened out with Doc Chance?"

Tanner looked at Lizzie, releasing Jen from whatever spell he'd cast on her. "Yep, just a paperwork error."

Emma said, "Good." Then she lifted a finger. "Hey, I have an idea," she said. "Tanner, you've got a pretty light schedule for the next couple of days, don't you?"

"I…guess so," Tanner said, clearly not sure he wanted to commit to whatever Emma had up her sleeve.

"Jen needs some help," she told him. "Turns out she's a rescuer, too."

She was? Well, considering her car full of formerly unwanted animals, she supposed she was.

"Great idea!" Lizzie chimed in, in tune with whatever Emma was about to propose.

Emma went on, "Anyway, Jen's got a bunch of new animals and didn't realize the Feed and Seed wouldn't be here to supply her needs—but surely, we've got stuff we can spare to help her, at least until she can get to Llano. Maybe you can run over there and have a look."

Tanner rubbed the back of his neck and looked at Jen's car, where the sheep had shoved their heads through the open window to complain about their captivity. He shot Jen a sideways glance. "You got sheep?"

"Yes, but you don't have to—"

"Oh, it's no problem," Lizzie answered for Tanner. "You can drop by later, can't you?"

"Uh, sure." He didn't look sure. As a matter of fact, he looked like he wished he'd stayed out of sight.

"Listen, you really don't have to—"

He gave a half smile from beneath the brim of his hat. "I reckon since gettin' more friends for Angus was my idea, I oughta follow through."

Oh God. He remembered her goat's name. Her tummy gave a little tumble. "Okay."

"Okay." He nodded. "I'll run by later."

"Do you know where I live?" she asked.

"I'll find it."

Why did that sound like such a…promise? "'Kay." Aaand now she'd been reduced to being a monosyllabic teenager.

"Stop your cow-eyeing and let's get going," Granddad complained from the back seat of Lizzie's car.

"It was nice to meet you, Jen," Lizzie said as car doors were opened and dogs and people piled inside.

"You too," Jen said. "All of you."

As she waved goodbye to her new friends and opened her car door, she could swear she heard Lizzie say, "I think it's her."

Uh-oh.

Tanner spent the first couple of miles of the ride back to the ranch in a mental traffic circle where he kept ending up in the training center parking lot. This time he didn't lurk in the shadows like some kind of perv. Instead, he stepped forward and said hello to Jen and proved that what Granddad said about him being a chickenshit around women wasn't true. Then he'd tell her he'd see about getting Jake to drop by and help her with her fencing issues. Jake would be a good guy to help Jen.

But the thought of Jake smiling at Jen, accepting a glass of sweet tea from her made his stomach clench. But hell, Tanner wouldn't be getting any sweet tea from Jen, and she did seem to need some help. Jake didn't talk much, but he was a great guy, and good-looking to boot. A much better choice for Jen. Tanner should ask Jake to go over there.

He ruffled Trixie's ears. She laid her head on his knee and grinned up at him. She really was a nice dog, but she needed something to keep her occupied. Something to herd.

Which reminded him of Adam's suggestion about horses. Tanner hadn't given him an answer, and Adam hadn't reminded him, thank God. Maybe he'd forget about it.

Besides, a couple of old quarter horses wouldn't be the right "herd" to keep Trixie's mind busy. Sheep, though. Sheep—and yeah, goats—would be perfect. He wondered if Jen was in the market for a sheepdog, now that she had a three-critter herd. That probably wasn't a good idea.

"Earth to Tanner. Come in, Tanner." Emma had turned to look at him.

"I'm sorry, what?" he asked.

"What's her last name?" Emma asked.

"Umm...?" He knew perfectly well who they were asking about, but he was trying not to think about her constantly and sure as hell didn't want the girls to know about his interest.

"Jen. What's her last name?" Emma repeated.

"I have no idea."

"I'm telling you, it's Greene."

"I don't think so," Emma said.

"It's totally her. Jen...Jennifer?"

"What would she be doing here in Big Chance?"

"She's homesteading," Tanner said without thinking.

"Homesteading? Like *Little House on the Prairie*?" Lizzie asked.

Tanner shrugged. "I guess. She's planning to have her own little self-sustaining farm."

"No kidding. But hey, how do you know all this? Did you really rescue her goat?" Lizzie was so busy questioning Tanner in the rearview mirror that she almost missed a stop sign and had to slam on her brakes to avoid a collision with a FedEx van. "When did you meet her?"

"Ah..." Everyone's attention was on him. Even Granddad appeared to be paying attention. "I met her last night when I was on my run. She was out looking for her goat, and Trixie found it stuck in the bushes alongside the road."

Emma asked, "So is it her? Is it Jennifer from *Homemade with Joanie and Jennifer*?"

"I don't know," Tanner said. "I've never seen this show you're talking about."

"We talked about it all the way here," Lizzie pointed out. "She's the one who's all over the internet for talking about her perfectly adequate boobs."

Tanner groaned. He couldn't have this conversation. Yeah, he'd noticed Jen's body last night, and this afternoon she'd worn that Bart Simpson T-shirt to her advantage.

"Here," Emma said. "Here's the clip." She handed him her phone, queued up to the episode in question.

He took the phone, feeling like he was doing something bad. Should he— Too late. He saw the boob flash. And the determined chin, the firm lips, that looked like a woman who'd fight to the death to keep her goat from the grips of a bloodsucking predator.

"Is it her? Is Jennifer your Jen?"

"I don't—"

"Lemme see that," Granddad said, yanking the phone from Tanner's hand and immediately locking the screen so that Emma had to take the phone back and start over at pulling up the video so her grandfather could watch it. He harrumphed. "Better udders on them Victoria's Secret girls. I don't see anything to write home about there."

"What do you think, Tanner?" Emma repeated.

Granddad was wrong. Dead wrong. Everything about Jen was perfectly adequate. *Wait.* Emma wasn't asking his opinion of Jen's breasts. He cleared his throat. "I don't think so. I mean, wouldn't she have introduced herself if she was that person?" *Or if she wanted you to know who she was?*

Tanner was pretty sure the woman in the video was the exact same woman they'd just left, the woman with the great smile and the unruly curls. He was also pretty sure she wanted to stay under the radar. That was what he'd want. The last thing he wanted was to connect with people who knew him from his old life.

"Well, then you'll have to go over there and find out," Emma said.

So much for his big plan to send Jake in his stead. Jake was a little too straightforward—that brain injury had removed the filter that kept everything he was thinking from leaking out of his mouth. He'd just march up there and tell Jen what Lizzie and Emma wanted to know and give his opinion of her incredible body.

That meant Tanner was the guy who'd be going to help Jen fix her fence, and doing his level best to keep his own opinion of her incredible body to himself.

Chapter 7

"Phew!" Jen wiped her brow and tried to smile for her camera. "It's been a day, huh, girls?"

She turned the camera toward the sheep, who had squished themselves together in a corner of the barn. She'd kept them in a stall she'd emptied of machine parts and broken furniture and God only knew what else because it was shady, but now it was time for them to roam free—in their fenced 5,000-square-foot yard.

"Are you ready to meet your new roommate?"

The sheep bleated as she came toward them, venturing to the front of the stall. Jen hooked a lead to each halter and coaxed them out of their temporary home.

"Come on, let's go see Angus," she said, thinking she needed to reinvent her little selfie stick into some sort of harness so she didn't need three hands. Yeah, that would be attractive. She imagined trying to work, upper body encased in straps and bars, camera propped a foot from her face on some sort of remote-control swivel so she could go from selfie to Jen view with a push of a button.

This do-it-yourself thing was a little more challenging than *Homemade*, where they had a guy with a camera—sometimes two guys with cameras—working to catch her every move and word.

But this way she had control, she reminded herself.

And carrying around a tripod thingy was a lot better than letting your neighborhood cowboy catch you in the 2020s version of an iron maiden.

She wondered if he was actually going to show up. He'd seemed a bit reluctant when Lizzie and Emma had asked—told—him to come help her.

Hopefully he wouldn't come to *help* her, as in telling her what to do, how to do it, and/or doing it all himself and telling her to hold his hammer for him.

She snorted. She might not complain if he wanted her to hold his *screwdriver*, though. Yikes. It was entirely possible Jen wasn't suited for a lonely life in the country. The thoughts that had been running through her head about the one and only young, single guy she'd met in the past month were completely inappropriate.

"But he's so sexy!" she said, then cringed, making a mental note to edit carefully.

The sheep didn't seem in a hurry to leave the barn, but when they saw the goat a few yards away, they began to run around in circles, twisting Jen this way and that. At least they were both going the same direction. "Hey, Angus! Look who I brought to meet you!"

Still (thankfully) secure behind his fence, Angus was bleating and braying up a storm. Hopefully that was friendly chatter. He shoved his nose through the fence to sniff at the new arrivals, who stopped their carousel dance and sniffed back.

"Angus, I'd like you to meet Kim and Khloe. Kim, Khloe, this is Angus."

Nothing terrible happened, so Jen walked the sheep a few yards down the fence to the gate and opened it. At which point Angus trotted—ran toward them.

In half a second, Jen realized she didn't know anything about introducing strange animals—of different species—to each other. Fortunately, Angus stopped a few feet away, peed, and bleated at the girls as they baaahed at him. He lowered his head.

"Oh, no. Should I have gotten his horns trimmed?"

But he only waited while Kim, then Khloe, sniffed at him.

Jen waited a few minutes and, when it seemed there wasn't going to be any carnage, went to get their supper. After they were happily munching their dinner, she took her camera for a walk to show off her hard work.

"The bunnies are looking good," she said. "They're staying in the chicken coop for now, but we'll have to get something else set up soon. My baby chicks are due to arrive in just a couple of days. They can start out living in the kiddie pool I found, but that's not going to hold them long. As for the rabbits, I'm not going to bother them tonight, but tomorrow I'll start giving each rabbit a regular brushing to keep them from getting the bunny equivalent of hair balls. I really wasn't planning on another breed of fiber animal, but if I can figure out this spinning business, I think I'll be able to make some awesome soft yarn over the winter.

"And over here in the old stock tank is Mr. Bigfoot." She walked to the beat-up galvanized swimming pool (at least, that's what she thought it looked like) where Mr. Turtle was to reside. "I'll see about making this look nicer when I have a few minutes, but for now, he's under a tree, and the tank has enough old leaves and weeds growing, he probably thinks he's in the wild. At least, he might if he ever comes out of his shell."

She then turned the camera toward the acre of weeds on the other side of her camper. "Over there is my garden-to-be. I'm going to start working on it tomorrow. I really mean it this time." She laughed at herself. "I know we've got a pretty long growing season, but I'd like to get a lot of stuff started soon so I'm not living on hay and goat pellets next winter."

She yawned and realized the shadows had grown long while she'd been moving in her new family members. "I think it might be time to call it a day. I kind of thought a neighbor of mine might be stopping by, but I guess he got busy. He's an army veteran who works with other vets to train service dogs, which I think is really cool, but he's also a cowboy—and he's the guy who found Angus last night when he escaped. Tanner's going to give me some pointers on shoring up the goat pen so we don't have any more escapes."

She panned the farmyard and the very sad-looking fence containing Angus, Kim, and Khloe.

"Let's hope they're secure for tonight."

She was not disappointed that Tanner hadn't shown up. She didn't want him to come over and boss her around, she reminded herself.

She entered her camper, opened the tiny freezer to grab a frozen meal, then popped it in the microwave. The timer dinged just as she was getting out of the shower.

She settled on the little couch and practically inhaled tonight's processed masterpiece of pasta and some sort of cheese sauce. Five minutes later, she was fast asleep.

"Have a good run," Jake said, as Tanner laced up his running shoes.

"Thanks," Tanner said absently, his mind whirling with everything he'd learned today.

Not only was his Jen—*his Jen, if only!*—the same Jen that had the internet buzzing over a split-second video of her bra-covered breasts, but she was pretty well-known beyond the flashing incident for the YouTube show she had with her mother. The "refreshingly wholesome but not annoying duo" had even won awards for their how-to videos. So *his* Jen might not know much about keeping goats happy, but she could do a sh-ton of other crazy pioneer junk like make candles from tallow. Hell, she could make tallow. She was so darned wholesome, too. He'd bet she went to church regularly and taught preschool in her spare time.

She probably also knew how to keep track of time. He'd meant to head over her way an hour ago, while it was still light, but he'd gotten sidetracked by the internet. By *Jen* on the internet.

He caught a glimpse of his reflection in the window. The scars really weren't so bad anymore, he reminded himself. But sometimes, like today when he was out of sorts, everything looked worse and felt bad. Numb and painful at the same time.

Which was really, his inner therapist pointed out, a superficial manifestation of self-hatred over what had happened in Afghanistan. In his life before Afghanistan. His whole life, actually. At least that's what the VA doc had tried to tell him for all three of the therapy appointments he'd gone to. And no amount of antidepressants and anti-anxiety meds, no length of time spent whining in someone's office was going to take that from him. He was stuck with the knowledge that he was a selfish asshole who ruined lives.

Yeah, he definitely needed a good long run or he was going to wind up drunk tonight, which would be frowned upon.

"Come on, Trixie, let's hit the road." The sun had dipped low enough to touch the horizon, which meant it would be getting dark by the time he got to Jen's place. Not exactly conducive to taking inventory of her fence, but he'd see what he could.

Trixie was getting better as a running partner. She kept up with Tanner's easy pace for two miles before she tried to kill him when something on the other side of the road distracted her. Tanner tried to avoid the leash, but his right foot got tangled and down he went—right knee, right hand, elbow, shoulder, hip—until he lay in the middle of the road, panting and cursing while Trixie barked and tugged at the leash trapped under his body.

He took a quick inventory. This wasn't a busy road, but sometimes women searching for goats didn't pay attention to what was right in front of them. When he'd determined he hadn't sustained any more damage than bruises and probably a little road rash, he found his end of Trixie's leash and carefully got to his feet. He limped to the side of the road and bent to brush gravel from his—fortunately not bloody—knee, and that was when he heard it.

"Baaaah!"

He'd know that bleat anywhere. It was Angus.

"Baa, baa, baa!"

Except that wasn't just Angus. He had company.

Yep, right there, tangled in the bushes along the road, were one big fuzz-ball goat and two tiny cotton balls. He'd only seen their heads sticking out of the window this afternoon, but he assumed they must be Jen's new sheep. They were really freaking short.

He paused, hands on hips. Jen would probably be along any minute, looking for them. In the meantime, he'd get them untangled and ready to travel. Now he really felt bad about taking so long to get on the road.

He looped Trixie's leash around a nearby tree and started untangling livestock. It took him the better part of an hour—every time he got one free and started on the next, the first would get stuck somewhere else. He finally had to use a sharp rock to hack off a length of Trixie's leash—fortunately he'd brought a long training leash for their run—and tied Angus to another tree. When he got the little sheep free, they migrated to Angus and hovered around him. Hopefully they'd stick with their hairy Pied Piper all the way to Jen's homestead. Hopefully Jen's place wasn't too far off.

Once the last sheep was untangled, Tanner untied Angus and then Trixie, who was thrilled to have something to herd— something other than disinterested dogs or stubborn humans. Tanner wiped the sweat from his face with his arm, and they were on their way.

It wasn't hard at all to tell when he'd reached Jen's property. He just followed the immaculately groomed board fence (did these people think they were in Kentucky?) belonging to the blissed-out cows until it ended. Then he followed the honeysuckle-covered barbed wire until a break in the foliage showed hints of a gravel driveway. He might not have ventured into the dark tunnel, assuming that it couldn't lead anywhere he should be, but there was a mailbox there. The mailbox had a wood-burned sign hanging from it, telling anyone who cared that this was "Greenish Acres, a perfectly adequate homestead."

Tanner laughed and said, "Come on, gang. I think we're home." The lane was long and dark, but between Angus and Trixie, they managed to make it to a clearing, where there was enough moonlight to see Jen's car and, beyond that, a rather sorry-looking camper. Across the clearing were a couple of outbuildings. Presumably the goat pen as well.

Everything was dark and quiet, except for a faint light showing through the cracks around the camper's window shades and the song of a few local crickets. Jen must already be tucked up in bed. Tanner didn't want to scare the life out of her when he banged on the camper door, but he wasn't sure how else to wake her. Maybe he should get Angus and his new friends back to their pen, make sure it was secure, and slink off home.

His parade of critters solved the problem for him. Something small and dark darted across the clearing, and Trixie jerked the end of the leash from Tanner's hand as she let out a series of barks worthy of a much larger, meaner dog. The goat and sheep joined in, bleating and baaing so loudly that Tanner wished for hearing protection—and he'd been around some really loud noises in his time. Trixie gave up on the squirrel and came back to the other animals, yapping and making sure they stayed together.

"What the hell is going on out here?" The camper door slammed open to reveal Jen, holding a baseball bat poised to swing.

Tanner's mouth went dry. Not from fear, but from the wave of lust that hit him from the way her body was backlit by the light inside. She wore nothing but an oversize T-shirt, and he could see every curve and dip of her body.

A spotlight came on, and Tanner held up a hand to protect his night-adjusted eyes. "Hi."

"Oh. It's you."

He lowered his hand to see her face, because he couldn't tell if that was a glad-to-see-you statement or if she was going to advance on him with that bat.

Rubbing sleep from her eyes, then running a hand through

pillow-tousled hair, she looked more confused than menacing. "What are you doing? Are you stealing my animals?"

"Yep. I'm practicing with yours so I can be a cattle rustler if the dog-ranch gig doesn't work out."

She groaned and shook her head, stepping out of the camper and tiptoeing closer on bare feet, bringing the scent of flowers and warm woman to him. "Sorry. I was dreaming that my mo— Anyway, I was having a bad dream when the barking started."

As though knowing she was being discussed, Trixie rose on her hind legs and put her front paws on Jen's belly, asking to be petted. Jen complied. "Hi, sweetie. It's good to see you again." And then to Tanner, "Did they really get out again?"

"Yep."

Jen sighed, looked at Angus, then back at Tanner. "This is getting to be a habit," she said. "The neighbors are going to talk."

Tanner looked around at the cows from the ranch next door, just visible on the hill beyond their fence. "I'll ask them to be discreet."

Chapter 8

THE LAST THING JEN EXPECTED TO BE DOING AT TEN THIRTY on a Thursday night was holding a flashlight so Tanner could rebuild the latch on her goat shed. She quirked her mouth. Hadn't she just been thinking she didn't want to be the hammer-holder for some guy?

Okay, she gave herself a break this one time. He knew what he was doing, and she didn't. So she held the flashlight. And if the light wobbled every now and then and illuminated Tanner's backside in those flimsy running shorts? Well, sue her. His body was a study in contrasts. Rippling muscle over long bones, covered in skin that was smooth and gleaming in the moonlight—except where it wasn't. His left arm was covered in an intricate tattoo—some sort of a map, maybe? His left calf was different from the right—it had an almost patchwork appearance. Were those skin grafts? She thought they probably were. He'd been burned, apparently badly, though the scars on his cheek were faint.

"It looks worse than it is."

Jen jumped when Tanner spoke, and realized she'd taken the light off of his work and had it shining right where she was looking.

"I'm sorry. I—"

He put a hand up to avoid being blinded—or to keep her from scrutinizing him. "I'm sorry!" she repeated, moving the light away. She shined the light toward the ground, and then she could still see his dark form, but not specifics.

Tanner said, "Sorry, I should have warned you not to shine a light on me after dark."

"I…" Jen didn't know what to say. She wasn't freaked out, just surprised, but she was reacting badly, and—

"That was supposed to be a joke. You know, like don't feed the gremlins after midnight? They turn into monsters?"

"Gremlins?" She clutched at his words like a lifeline in a pool of awkward.

"Yeah. It was a movie in, like, the eighties. This guy gets his kid a cute little pet at a shop in some back alley, and it comes with a warning not to get it wet or feed it after midnight. *Shockingly*, the kid screws it up."

She laughed. "I'll have to see if I can find it online."

There was a beat of uncomfortable silence. What should she say?

He saved her again by asking, "Can you shine that over here for another minute? I've almost got it."

"Sure." She pointed the light at the door, and Tanner bent back down. Trixie, who had been lying nearby, got up to investigate, blocking the light.

"Move it, dog," he said and gently shoved her aside. "I think one more good whack—" Trixie was not to be dissuaded, however, and shoved her nose back toward the action. There was a thump, and then Tanner cursed.

"Are you okay?" Jen rushed toward him, the light bouncing everywhere as Tanner semi-straightened, holding one hand with the other, while Trixie pranced and yipped. "What happened?"

"Hit my thumb with the hammer. Damn, that hurts."

"Let me see." She held the flashlight up and with her free hand grabbed his wounded one. Blood welled around the edge of his thumbnail and dripped onto her hand. "Come on, I've got a first aid kit inside."

She turned and started to tug him along toward the camper.

"Wait, you've got blood on you." He pulled his hand back and yanked his shirt over his head and handed it to her. "Wipe that off."

She took the soft cotton, damp from his exertion. She caught a whiff of clean sweat and fresh-cut grass. She was tempted to raise the shirt closer to her face—but that would be weird, right? Instead, she wiped the small smear from her palm. He took the shirt back and wrapped it around his thumb.

"Can I borrow your flashlight for a minute?" he asked.

When she handed it to him, he shone it around and surveyed the work she'd done earlier in the day, before she'd realized her new sheep would only be taller than a beagle when they had a full coat of wool. She'd taken the extra chicken wire she'd bought for her coop and secured it to the top of the existing fence to reduce the possibilities that Angus could escape by jumping or climbing over. It was wonky as heck because her fence posts weren't long enough to support the extra weight of the wire, so she'd had to rig up some extra supports made of all the long, straight things she could find, including but not limited to: a broom, a shovel, two table legs, and a ridiculously long grill spatula.

After a moment, he said, "I think we have some stuff around the ranch we could use to reinforce that fence."

She snorted. "Are you saying my avant-garde upcycling project doesn't meet your standards?"

"I, uh…"

She laughed. "That's okay. It looked better in my imagination, and obviously it didn't work."

He shrugged. "Seems like they escaped through the gate, which we can also fix tomorrow. In the meantime, they should be okay in the shed for the night."

She liked the way he'd said *We can fix*. Like he wasn't taking over, and was including her. Hopefully that didn't mean more flashlight holding. "Come inside and let me patch you up."

"Lead the way."

"Welcome to my humble abode," she said, holding the door open and stepping aside to let Tanner in, quickly followed by Trixie who scooted in around his feet. Jen brought up the rear, stopping to shut the door behind her. When she straightened, she bumped against Tanner's broad back, which was warm and firm against her front. Her nose was barely two inches from the back of his neck, and she smelled that enticing scent again.

Without thinking, she put her hands on the sides of his waist and backed up a step as he turned toward her, and there they were, up close and staring at each other in the dim glow from the light over her kitchen sink. His bare chest was broad with a light sprinkling of hair leading down to— She jerked her hands back. "Sorry. Didn't mean to get fresh," she stammered.

He took a breath and seemed about to say something, but then changed his mind and cocked his undamaged thumb over his shoulder toward her tiny kitchen/living area, which took up the front half of the camper. "I love what you've done with the place. That's pretty bold, installing a swimming pool in the living room."

Oh. She'd forgotten about that. "That's the nursery."

"Nursery?"

"For the chickens."

"You have chickens?" He glanced back at the kitchen, then behind her, where the rest of the camper—her bedroom and a minuscule bathroom—was hidden behind a wall. "Are they in bed now?"

She smiled. "No, they're coming by mail next week. I'll pick them up at the post office."

"Wow, you're really diving into this farm thing, aren't you?" He smiled, his smile a little crooked, a little dangerous to her sanity.

She cleared her throat. "I thought I'd start off with a goat and a few chickens, but my livestock plans got deeper faster than I planned what with the turtle and the rabbits…"

He looked around again, lifted the pool from the table, pretending to look underneath. "Rabbits? A turtle?"

She said, "Mr. Bigfoot—that's the turtle—he's outside, and the rabbits are in the henhouse for now. I'll figure out what to do with them before the chickens move in."

He shook his head and said, "Well, since you're going in head-first, you might want to find a pool deeper than this one."

"The turtle's in that one." She sighed. "Just shove that thing off to the side," she told him. "Let me see your thumb."

When he'd turned the pool onto its side and rolled it against the tiny refrigerator, she pointed to the bench seat next to the table, beneath which Trixie lay, head on her paws, watching everything. "Sit."

Tanner glanced up at Jen's face as he unwrapped the bloody T-shirt from his hand, and there were those big brown eyes staring at him again. Just looking curiously, not with fear or disgust, just as she'd been looking at him outside and then when they'd first come in here. He hoped she wouldn't start asking him a lot of awkward questions. He didn't have any problem talking about how much the burns had hurt (a fucking lot) or if he still had pain (sometimes, as nerves were still growing back into tight skin). He was willing to tell her how many skin grafts he'd had and how many hours of surgery he'd had to endure, and how glad he was for donor skin. How grateful he was for the plastic surgeon who'd done the last bit of work that smoothed things on his face out a little, kept him from looking like Deadpool.

He just wasn't going to talk about what he'd done to get so crisp.

She didn't look like she wanted to interrogate him. She looked like she wanted to taste him.

Yeah, right. Maybe in some other lifetime. He looked away from those hypnotic eyes and examined his thumb.

"That looks painful," Jen said, turning to the sink and twisting the faucet handle. "Here, let's rinse it off a little."

Her camper was so small, he didn't even have to stand to reach the sink, he just leaned a little to the right. She took his hand in hers and guided his thumb under the cool stream. As she gently rubbed the dirt and gore from around the wound and the rest of his hand, the room began to feel smaller and warmer. Intimate. It smelled good, too. Like cinnamon rolls. He wondered if that was from some sort of candle or if it was her.

Damn. He was sitting here, hand throbbing like it had been run over by a tank, and other parts of him were starting to throb like he hadn't been laid in years. Which he hadn't, actually. Not since before what happened, happened.

Well, that train of thought certainly cooled his mood.

"I think it's clean, but it's still bleeding." Jen turned off the water, reached for a soft, clean dish towel, and carefully blotted his hand dry.

Blood still seeped from beneath the nail, so Tanner pushed the towel away and grabbed a paper napkin from the holder on the counter. "Don't want you to have to bleach your stuff," he said, then added, "for bloodstains. Not because there's anything icky in my blood. I mean, I get tested for HIV and hepatitis and shit anytime I have surgery."

"Oh. Okay." She blinked at him like it hadn't occurred to her to worry about blood-borne pathogens.

Maybe most people didn't think about that when they saw blood. Tanner shook his head. He'd spent way too much time reading the walls of VA waiting rooms over the past couple of years.

"You say that like you're a regular."

"At getting surgery? I was for a while. I had a lot of ground to cover with skin grafts, so it took a few trips under the knife. I think I'm well done now, though." He grinned and waited to see if she got his joke.

"Oh, you're very punny," she said, rolling her eyes.

"I try," he said with mock humility.

She smiled, and then there was another one of those moments where they were looking at each other, and he had the thought that if he wanted to kiss her, she'd let him. Which was absolutely crazy. He was a relative stranger—an acquaintance at most—and she'd brought him into her place because she was nice, and maybe a little naive—not because she was attracted to him. But damn, she was hot in that nightshirt—those long legs extending under the hem… She was curvy and fit and pretty and…out of his league. He blinked and broke the spell before it got weird.

"Let's get you bandaged up so you don't get all germy." She opened the first aid kit and dug around until she came up with a roll of gauze and some sterile dressing stuff.

"Jeez, just find me a big Band-Aid and I'll be fine. Two little ones if you don't have a bigger one."

"That's going to hurt like heck if it bumps something," she argued. "At least let me pad it a little."

He thought about being all manly-man about it and brushing her off but changed his mind, mostly because it would give him an excuse to sit in her cute little camper and breathe in her sweet scent and pretend, if only for a moment, that he had a right to be here.

In just a few minutes she had his hand all wrapped up and secured with tape.

"You look like you know what you're doing," Tanner said, holding up his hand and admiring the tidy job.

She smiled. "I had to learn first aid for self-preservation. I'm kind of clumsy, and my mom faints at the sight of blood, so—" She stopped talking then.

Tanner figured she didn't want to say too much about her life if she was trying to fly under the radar.

Well, that was cool, actually. He wouldn't ask her to show him her secrets if she didn't ask him to show her his.

"You should probably put some ice on that," she said. "Let me grab a freezer bag—"

"I need to get going," he said at the same time, rising to his feet.

"Oh. Okay." She stood there, big eyes wide and…disappointed?

"I've got a couple of miles to go to get back to the ranch, and the guys are probably already wondering what happened to me, so…"

"I'll drive you!" she said. "Let me get my keys." She whirled around, and Tanner admired the way the fabric of her nightshirt clung to her body.

"No," he said. He'd do something stupid like ask her out if he spent any more time with her. "I'll run. It's good for me. It's good for Trixie to run off some steam."

They both looked under the table, where Trixie lay on her side, snoring blissfully.

"I don't think Trixie has any more steam to let off right now," Jen said.

"Come on, Trixie, let's go home!" Tanner called.

Trixie didn't even open an eye, but she did raise her lip and snarl.

"Y'all didn't just growl at me, did you?" He reached carefully under the table and grabbed Trixie's collar, gave a tug, and she still didn't get up.

Jen laughed. "If you want her to go home with you, you might have to carry her. Come on, I'll drive you. I want to see this Big Chance Dog Rescue anyway. I mean…I know where it is, and I know it's too dark for a tour, but you need a ride and I have a vehicle. It's even mostly de-stinkified from Khloe and Kim's ride earlier."

Ah hell. She was irresistible.

"Okay," he said. "But do me a favor?"

"Sure," she said, twirling her key ring around a finger.

"Put on some more clothes?"

She looked down, and it took no seconds for the color to bloom on her face. Then she was past him and slamming the door to the private half of the camper. Her "I'll be right out!" was muffled but clear as day.

Tanner smiled. He forgot about scars and shame and fear, was just a guy getting to know a girl. And for the first time in a long while, he felt *good*.

Chapter 9

"Hey, Sar'nt, I need your John Hancock on some checks." Tanner put the checks and a pen on the ranch house's kitchen table. Adam was ladling scrambled eggs onto a couple of plates while Lizzie poured coffee. Trixie shoved her nose into Adam's lap but he ignored her, and she shuffled back a few steps to sit hopefully nearby. "Sorry to interrupt your breakfast," he added. Everyone tried to give Adam and Lizzie home alone time as much as possible since they lived in the same house as the headquarters for the rescue, but Tanner was in a hurry to get his chores done today.

"Sure, sit down, want some eggs? Grab a plate," Adam said. The cool thing was that Adam and Lizzie never seemed to mind when someone interrupted their meals. *Other* personal time was a different story, but they tended to go upstairs and shut the door for *that*.

"No, thanks, I ate."

"Suit yourself," Adam said.

Trixie whined and was ignored. Giving up on handouts, she trotted down the hall to see if she could stir up trouble with D-Day and Loretta.

"Coffee?" Lizzie asked, handing Tanner a mug before he answered.

"Thanks." He helped himself to cream and sugar, and sat down while Adam and Lizzie got themselves arranged for breakfast.

It had taken a few months to get comfortable around Adam. He was very sergeant-like on the outside—a little gruff, very much an in-charge-and-get-it-done kind of guy. And Tanner, arriving at the Big Chance Dog Rescue with a heavy conscience, knew Adam would see through his bullshit in an instant and call him on it. And then there was the crap with that shyster who stole a butt-ton of cash from the rescue while Tanner was standing right there handing him passwords. Everything had been resolved, however, and no one held Tanner's lapse against him, which only added to the weight on his soul.

But in the process, he'd gotten more comfortable around the boss.

"You're here bright and early," Adam commented as Lizzie said, "What happened to your hand?"

"Uh, yeah…little accident with a hammer," he said, feeling an inexplicable urge to hide his wounded thumb behind his back.

Lizzie eyed Tanner over the edge of her coffee cup.

"How'd you do it? Do you need to see a doctor?" Lizzie asked.

"I'll be fine." Tanner took a sip of his own coffee and didn't meet Lizzie's eyes.

"*Hmph.*" Adam tucked into his eggs.

Lizzie apparently wasn't as hungry because she was still questioning. "Heard you get dropped off last night…"

Since she wasn't likely to let him off the hook, Tanner supposed he might as well try to control the narrative instead of letting her make stuff up.

"Yeah. I went for a run with Trixie, planning to stop by Jen's place and take a look at her setup, like you *volunteered* me to do. Trixie found Jen's goat and her little sheep things wandering in the bushes, so we got them untangled and took them home, and then I fixed the latch on her gate."

"And Jen was there?" Lizzie raised her eyebrows. "Did you find out if it's *her*?"

"It was indeed the woman y'all met yesterday in town," Tanner said, crossing his arms over his chest.

Lizzie narrowed her eyes in a "We have ways of making you talk!" way, but he also knew Lizzie wouldn't spread news that she wasn't 110 percent sure of.

"And for rescuing her livestock, she came after you with a

hammer?" Adam asked, indicating Tanner's bum hand with a chin jerk.

"Naw. I was trying to fix the gate in the dark, and my aim was off. Got the thumbnail, and it bled a bit. She bandaged it up for me and drove me home—not that I needed a ride," Tanner added, seeing Adam's mouth quirk up on one side. "But because Trixie plumb wore herself out and wouldn't get up to come home with me."

Adam shook his head. "She's a stubborn one, isn't she?"

Tanner chuckled. "Definitely smarter and more determined than any horse I've ever worked with."

"Speaking of—"

"Hang on. I hate to miss dog—and horse—business, but I've got to go to work," Lizzie interrupted, rinsing and putting her plate in the sink and going to the coffee maker for a refill. She leaned down to kiss Adam. "See you guys," she said and pushed through the screen door, admitting Jake, who nodded a greeting to Tanner and Adam and went to help himself to coffee.

Adam continued as though there had been no interruption. "Speaking of horses. Have you given any more thought to what I mentioned the other day?"

Jake leaned against the counter sipping coffee, his normal relentless energy stilled for the time being.

Suddenly Tanner wished Lizzie was back in the room, teasing him about Jen. He blew out a breath. "I don't think adding horses to the mix here would be a good idea."

Jake coughed, and Adam glanced at him, then shifted his focus back to Tanner. "That's too bad. I think Jake's been looking forward to shoveling something besides dog crap."

Jake snorted and took another sip of coffee.

Adam asked, "Why don't you think we need horses?"

Because I don't think I can do it? Because horses can smell a fraud a mile away and they know who not to trust? "Don't you think you've got enough here to keep you busy?"

Adam raised an eyebrow. "*I* do."

Ah. So Adam was throwing Tanner a bone to keep him occupied.

"Actually, I've kind of got a…*thing* I wanted to talk to you about that's likely to keep me busy for a while, too."

"A thing?"

"Yeah. This Jen. The woman with the escaping goat."

"And what about this mysterious Jen? What's the deal there?"

"There's no deal. We didn't even—" Tanner shook his head.

Adam's face broke out in a grin. "I was going to ask what kind of help she needs out there and what we've got that will work, but now I need to know what you 'didn't even.'"

Tanner rolled his eyes, feeling like a damned teenager with a crush on the head cheerleader. "There's nothing to tell."

"But you like her, huh?"

"Yeah, sure. She's okay, I guess." *Seriously? She was more than okay. She was…not for him.*

He got himself on track and said, "She's in over her head. I think she bought the place she's living in without seeing it in person, and it's more run-down than she expected. That, and she doesn't have much experience with the livestock she's taken on."

"That could turn out badly," Adam said.

"She's doing her best, considering what she's got to work with." He thought of that fence she had rigged up. Had he seen a spatula in there? "Right now, I'd like to get her fence in better shape, to keep her animals in their space. I thought maybe I could volunteer to help her out, I guess. I'll keep up with my chores here, though."

"Well, if she's willing to learn, you're the guy to teach her the ropes." Adam got to his feet and clapped Tanner on the back. "And I'm not worried you're going to up and disappear on us. You work harder than anyone here—except Jake, of course."

Jake snorted and rolled his eyes.

"You and Jake can look around and see what we've got that'll help. If your Jen really feels the need, she can pay us back in fresh vegetables or something."

"That might take a minute," Tanner said, wondering if she even had space cleared for a garden. He needed to get over there in the light of day and see what was what. "And she's not my Jen."

Jake coughed pointedly.

Adam ignored that point. "No problem. We've got a busload of new recruits coming Monday, but you know how that goes. You need to be here to do the meet and greet, but in the meantime, you can take a few days and help her out if you want."

Tanner didn't know if that was a good idea. Spending a few days playing farmer with Jen might find him hoping to find her in the hayloft—if that old barn still had one.

A cacophony of dogs with an undertone of diesel engine drowned out the rest of his thoughts.

As all three men looked through the window, Adam said, "Huh. Who do you think this is?"

Jake coughed again.

Tanner's spidey senses went on full alert.

Jen swam reluctantly up from a thick sleep where she'd been floating on a raft in a warm pool, with a man in a cowboy hat drifting next to her, telling her how smart and creative she was, which was nice, but didn't he think she was sexy, too? An insistent chime centered somewhere in the vicinity of her right ear tugged her toward dry land and consciousness. She didn't want to wake up. Waking up meant sore muscles and sunburn and bug bites...

It wasn't until she'd groped around under the pillow and found a flat plastic thing and rubbed her finger across the front that she clocked into the fact that her phone had been ringing.

"Hello?" she rasped.

"Hi, baby, are you okay?"

"Mom. Hi. Yeah. I'm…okay." Jen sat up and rubbed the sleep from her eyes, checking the time. *Ten o'clock? Wow. The animals must be—*

Yep. She could hear Angus and the girls putting up a fuss. "Sorry. I overslept."

"I'm checking in to see how you're doing. I haven't heard from you for a few days."

Jen stifled a yawn-sigh. "I'm good. Tired, obviously. I've been really busy. How are you?"

"We're doing okay, but we miss you like crazy."

We. Which included *Brock. What about you, Mom? And why do we care about Brock?* All he missed was Jen's contribution to his revenue stream.

Why couldn't Mom see what a slimeball he was?

"The show's doing okay, as I'm sure you know."

No, she didn't know. She hadn't once checked online to see if there were any new episodes because she couldn't take any more comments about her own "disappearance," but that sounded selfish even to her own sleep-addled, caffeine-deprived brain, so she only said, "That's so great. I…" *Wish you needed me to come back, even though I wouldn't.*

Mom went on, "We've got some new ideas cooking, some really exciting stuff."

"Yeah, what's that?"

"Oh, no. Brock would kill me if I blabbed before the big reveal."

What was that supposed to mean? What on earth was Brock talking her into doing now? Jen's stomach sank. Her mother wasn't allowed to tell her what she was up to?

"But maybe you can come back. Maybe we can get you in on what we're going to do."

"Oh well… I'm pretty busy with my own project, you know?"

"Yeah? What are you up to?"

"I've got some livestock now, and I'm putting in my garden"—or at least she would be soon—"so maybe you could come visit."

"Oh, I'd love that!"

Jen's heart squeezed. She really missed her mom. She knew Joanie would get a kick out of the animals Jen had adopted and would have some good ideas for making clever housing for the bunnies and chickens. She could probably turn the serviceable chicken coop into a multilevel, self-cleaning showpiece.

"I'll have to talk to Brock and see when he thinks that might be doable."

"What's Brock up to?" Jen choked out.

"Oh, he's so busy, I don't even know where he is sometimes. He's been scouting locations all over the state to shoot, and meeting with… Well, that's part of the surprise, but he's working his little butt off, let me tell you."

The last thing Jen wanted to hear was anything about Brock's butt, but she managed to listen to her mom ramble on for a bit.

"That's great, Mom. I look forward to finding out what you've got going on."

"I wish you'd come back and join us again."

"I can't, Mom. You know I have to do this thing here now." *And I can't come back to be part of "us" as long as Brock is part of us.*

"I know you want to prove yourself, and I am proud of you. But…you're all alone at that place. Something terrible could happen. I'm afraid you'll get hurt out there tilting at windmills," Mom continued. "You never know when one of those big blade things is going to break off and crush you, baby."

"Thanks. I…I'll watch out for windmills."

"Okay, sweetheart. I'll let you go. Remember I love you to the moon and back."

"I love you too, Mom."

Chapter 10

"Honey, I'm prouder of you than I ever could have thought," Mama said as she enveloped Tanner in a tight hug.

Tanner didn't say "Aw, geez, Mom, not in front of the guys," mostly because he couldn't breathe, but also because her affection always left him feeling a pang of guilt for not living up to the notion of who she seemed to think he was. He didn't deserve her hugs. Instead, he hugged her back and told her he loved her and he was glad to see her, in spite of the unwelcome surprise she'd brought with her on this unexpected visit.

Tanner shot a glance at Adam who, along with Jake and Marcus, stood watching him from the porch. All seemed uncertain that their surprise had been a good idea.

It had not.

Mama had shown up a couple of hours ago, "just passing through," a few hundred miles out of the way, to deliver Tanner's roping partner and former best friend, Bullet, a delivery that didn't seem to be a big surprise for Adam, Marcus, or Jake.

"I think he looks real happy there, honey," Mama said, watching the palomino gelding give a half-hearted head toss. The horse didn't look happy at all. He looked half-starved and unkempt and depressed.

"I thought he was happy at home with the other horses," Tanner said, one last wish that this could somehow turn out differently than him being in charge of an equine therapy branch of the Big Chance Dog Rescue.

"He wasn't happy at all without you, especially after I sold off the others."

Tanner rubbed his chest, feeling an actual pang at the thought of his best friend alone and miserable as his home was auctioned off. Mama had told Tanner that if he wasn't coming back to run the ranch, she was going to start selling off the land and the herd. In the abstract, it hadn't bothered Tanner at all to know the Beauchamp Ranch would be parceled out to a developer. He wasn't going back there to run things since he couldn't live in a town where everyone knew him. Knew *about* him and wouldn't have welcomed him. If his dad were still alive, he wouldn't have wanted Tanner there, either.

But learning that the time had come, that his road home was washed out, came with a bit of a sting. He'd refused to consider what would happen to Bullet, hoping Mama would sell him to some local rodeo wannabe and never mention him again to Tanner.

Instead, here was his truth, a living, breathing reminder of all Tanner had messed up. He wondered if he could find Bullet a new home. Trixie, the traitor, was standing on her back legs, front paws on the fence, barking encouragement to Bullet.

"After you left, Bullet got mean. He wouldn't let anyone else ride him and bit anyone who tried."

Tanner shook his head and swallowed. Bullet had been the sweetest horse around, before Tanner ruined him.

"I hope you like our little surprise," Mama said. "You were surprised, right?"

"I definitely was." Tanner hadn't had to fake surprise, but he had to work to let her think he was pleased. He didn't know what he was going to say to Adam after Mama got back on the road. *Thanks for not inviting her to stay for happy hour?* He didn't think he could bear tipsy Mama wanting to talk about Daddy.

"Come on and walk me over to the camper," she said of the motor home she'd purchased for her retirement travels. It looked about two feet farther from the grave than that thing Jen was living in. At least this one had tires instead of cinder blocks.

"You sure you're comfortable driving this beast?" Tanner asked when they got across the farmyard.

"What? You think I need a penis to push a gas pedal?"

From behind him, Tanner heard Marcus hoot with laughter. "No, ma'am, I don't. I just want you to be careful."

"I am careful." She put her hands on his face and looked into his eyes. "You look real good now, honey." She stroked his face. "I hope you'll get out there and get me a daughter-in-law."

"Sure, Mama."

"You know Kelsie Lynn's still single, right?"

The sound of her name didn't make him want to throw up from shame and misery anymore, but that ship had sailed a long time ago. "That's not…that's not going to happen. You know that, right?"

Mama sighed. "Surely y'all could let bygones be bygones."

"I'm hoping she's moving on. I don't know about her. But I wouldn't blame her if she didn't, and no." *Please don't ask any more questions.*

"Well then, get out there and find you a girl. That Lizzie and Emma can fix you up, you just ask them."

"I'm just not… Dating's not a priority right now." He thought of Jen and her ramshackle homestead. Rebuilding a woman's fence was *not* dating.

"I don't see why not. What else you got to do at night out here? They's not even cattle to tend." She clucked disapprovingly. "And here you are in the prime of your manhood. I don't know how you're going to make me any grandbabies out here with no one but your own left hand for company."

"Mama!"

Tanner heard someone on the porch snort.

Mama just waved her hand at Tanner. To the peanut gallery, she said, "You all can fix him up with some nice girls, can't you?"

"We'll do our best, ma'am," Adam said.

"Hawkeye! Winchester!" Mama hollered at the dogs she'd adopted during her last visit to the Big Chance Dog Rescue. They were too old to be trained as assistance dogs so they were adopted out. Mama had fallen in love with the old guys ar.d couldn't bear to separate them, so... "Let's go, boys!" The elderly English bulldog—Winchester—and the equally decrepit wire-haired pointer ambled toward the camper.

"I got you, buddy," Tanner said as he bent to boost Winchester with his short legs up the steps, and then repeated the action for Hawkeye whose legs were plenty long but painfully arthritic. Trixie tried to follow, but Tanner tugged her back to his side.

With one more big hug—and Tanner did not get a tear in his eye—Mama was in the Rhinestone Pup Tent, as she'd dubbed her rig, and there was nothing left but the aroma of diesel exhaust.

"Your mama's a force to be reckoned with," Marcus said, coming up next to Tanner and clapping him on the shoulder.

"She is, indeed." Tanner stood watching the dust settle behind the disappearing bus, then turned toward the pasture. What the hell was he going to do now?

"What did she give you there?" Marcus asked, pointing at the canvas tote bag Tanner held.

"Just some books and stuff." The bag held his old chaps, along with other useless memorabilia from his young rodeo days.

"So..." Adam said, coming with Jake to join Marcus, until they were all leaning on the fence, watching Tanner's horse plod a few steps, then stop to touch noses with Trixie. "I...guess I should have found a way to ease you into this horse thing, but your mom was so excited to surprise you..." Adam's voice trailed off.

Tanner understood the implicit apology and shrugged his understanding. "I guess I'd rather take care of him than have him sent to the glue factory, and I want you to know I'll pay for his upkeep."

"Not necessary, especially if you'll let our recruits ride him."

Tanner looked at the skin-and-bones horse and thought about what his mom had said about Bullet getting ornery. "I don't know if that's going to work."

"Up to you," Adam said.

Tanner was grateful to know that Adam meant it.

"Come on, Trixie," he said now. "Let's leave Bullet to himself for a while."

Trixie reluctantly trotted after Tanner into the bunkhouse and his room. Tanner pulled the stuff out of the bag and put it into his bottom drawer, where it would languish until he got up the energy to throw it all out.

As he lifted the stack of programs and certificates from the bottom of the bag, a photo fell out. It was Tanner, so young and fresh he barely recognized himself, sitting on Bullet. He glanced at himself in the mirror and wasn't sure he recognized his current self, either.

Chapter 11

"GOOD MORNING, MR. BIGFOOT," JEN SAID, DROPPING A PIECE of lettuce and an apple core in the stock tank. She figured—hoped—he could dig up enough bugs to satisfy his need for protein. The turtle, who'd tucked his head and limbs inside his shell when she first appeared, stuck out enough of his nose to investigate the fresh food. He took a cautious bite of lettuce, and finding it to his liking, he began munching.

"Oh shoot. I should be recording this." She turned on her camera.

"Well, it looks like Mr. Bigfoot is pretty happy at the moment, so let's go check on the bunnies. They're still staying in the chicken coop, since the chicks don't arrive for a couple more days."

A wooden shutter covered a mesh-screened window in the side of the coop so she could check on the occupants without going all the way inside, so Jen unlatched it and flipped it up, and looked in to see. "Oh look, they're play— Oh, no. That's not playing."

She quickly straightened from the window and relatched the shutter to give them some privacy.

"Um, I'm pretty sure that lady said these rabbits are both females, so maybe they're lesbians, but just to be on the safe side, I guess I need to make a note to research rabbit gestation periods. And if rabbits can be neutered."

Great. More potential mouths to feed. How was she going to take care of everything she had here if she wasn't even sure she'd be able to feed herself? The goal was to be self-sufficient within a year, but she was afraid her meager savings would run out before then.

She planted her camera on its tripod in the ground, then stepped back so she had some scenery (such as it was) behind her. "Today is garden day!" Her imaginary garden was filled with tomato plants, green beans, sweet corn, herbs, and greens, but her right-now garden was about a quarter acre of fenced weeds, surrounded by more weeds.

She looked at it with trepidation. This was going to take forever. Maybe if she could clear a few square feet, she could find enough space to start some beans. It was only May, but a long, hungry winter loomed ahead.

She pictured herself crawling back to her mom and Jerkface. She grabbed her shovel and rake, gloves and water bottle, and trudged toward the garden.

The gate only had one hinge, so when she unlatched it the whole thing hung crooked, and it took every ounce of Jen's strength to move it far enough to slip inside. It was a sturdy enclosure, though. That fence was about eight feet high. Probably high enough to keep out all but the most determined deer.

If only the goat pen was so sturdy. When she'd dropped Tanner off at the Big Chance Dog Rescue last night, he'd muttered something about coming back to help her reinforce it, but she shouldn't count on him. She was, after all, doing this *herself*.

Although she found herself thinking about him a lot. Not just about how damned sexy he was in those running shorts he wore—or the cowboy boots and jeans she'd seen him in in town—but she wondered about his life. She assumed the burn scars were received in battle, and that was what brought him to the Big Chance Dog Rescue, but he hadn't volunteered anything about his military service. That was okay; she wasn't going to volunteer anything about her past, either.

"Not your business," she reminded herself. "You absolutely, positively don't have time for a guy." In her experience, guys—especially new guys—took up way too much mental energy and literal time. "You're going to have enough trouble getting this homestead off the ground without the distraction."

She planted her camera again and checked the angles before turning it on. After stomping around a bit, she found she'd flattened enough grass to reach an area where the plants looked different. She bent down and thumped the edge of a plank that lay on its long edge. "Oh, this is good," she said. "The previous gardener here made enclosed beds. I can trim the grass and clean up the beds without worrying that the grass is going to overtake the growing space."

She wiped away a drop of sweat trickling along her brow and glanced at the sky. The Texas sun had already heated things up, and it wasn't yet noon. Good thing she'd brought her industrial-sized water bottle.

Jen thought about her mom's call as she worked. Brock was a class A jerk. Jen wasn't jealous. She was *worried*, and feeling guilty, which made her angry because she wasn't supposed to be responsible for her mother's broken man-picker.

She took a deep breath. Brock wasn't her future stepfather, any more than any of those losers her mom had allowed to move into their home before she got herself together. And Joanie wasn't dating Brock, so it was less likely she'd start depending on him too much, right?

And even if Joanie slipped, Jen wasn't her mother. She didn't need a man to make her feel complete, to make her feel worthy, or to help her make it on her doggone homestead.

After about an hour of serious weed pulling, she'd amassed quite a pile of thistle, dandelion, chickweed, and grasses, and a whopping three square feet of cleared dirt. Her hair was soaked with sweat, and her T-shirt wasn't much drier. Rising to her feet to stretch, she heard her knees crack. Her back ached. She opened her water bottle and tilted it to her mouth. Nothing. Time for a refill.

Maybe she should switch tasks for a while. There was an old-school reel-type lawn mower in the shed, and she went to retrieve it.

The door creaked and groaned as she fought to move it. The hinges would need to be replaced, but not today. She squeezed inside, squinting into the dusty gloom.

God, it was hot here. She knew this part of Texas wasn't any hotter than Austin, but she didn't spend hours and hours outside sweating there. She went to the air-conditioned gym to work out, and when she worked in the yard she'd shared with her mom, she was done before she got good and sweaty.

Well, this homesteading thing was *supposed* to be challenging. She was up for it. She dug into the pile of cast-off farm implements.

Ten minutes later, she revised "challenging" to "hell on earth." There was a lawn mower, but she hadn't registered that it was semi-buried under an old bed frame, pieces of something that looked like it belonged on a space shuttle, and about six miles of old nylon rope twisting everything together.

She finally dragged the mower out of the pile of junk and found that one wheel was wobbly. This would have been fixable, but her screwdriver fell apart on her. How the heck did that even happen? The metal part just popped out of the resin handle. So she found some pliers, held the shank with the pliers, and managed to get the wheel sort of tightened.

Then she dragged the mower to the garden. Where the grass was so long and the blades so dull that the reel was wrapped tightly and fricking stuck in the grass before it went two feet.

Not for the first time, Jen wondered if she might have made her point about being independent and successful some other way—like getting a PhD in astrophysics or single-handedly brokering peace in the Middle East. And what was her point, anyway? Oh yeah. Something about proving that she could be a back-to-basics girl all on her own.

Maybe she should have tried to do this on a tropical island, where she could eat coconuts and fish and enjoy cool breezes from her palm-frond hut.

A gnat dive-bombed her, and the humidity doubled down.

She'd put on a long-sleeved T-shirt as a form of sun protection, but now it was sticking to her skin, and her jeans felt like a double layer of thermal fleece, holding in all the heat and humidity in Chance County. She should go inside and change clothes.

The distance from the garden to her camper seemed to have doubled in the time that she'd been working. Tripled, even. If she passed out from heat exhaustion, no one would find her unless they noticed the vultures circling her carcass. On the other hand, there was no one to judge her if she decided to strip out of her soggy, stinky clothes right then and there and stride stark naked across her yard.

She peeled off her shirt and tossed it in the air. Where it snagged on the top of the world's highest fence post. Damp red cotton drooped in the sun like a dead flag. She toed off her boots and wriggled out of her jeans. The hot, dry air made her suddenly bare, damp skin prickle with goose bumps. *Wow.*

That felt amazing, actually. She wiggled a little. She took the elastic from the end of her braid and ran her fingers through her hair, knowing it would be a tangled mess in two minutes and not caring a bit. Her bra was wet. And cutting into her shoulders. Might as well lose that, too, right?

She felt kind of ridiculous, but she unclipped her bra, slipped it off, and laughed as she shot it like a giant rubber band that landed a whopping three feet away.

Angus and the girls bleated, and she looked to see them watching her. What did animals think of goofy humans, she wondered. Probably if the humans weren't delivering food they didn't much care, but they were making a bit of noise.

There was another sound, too. An engine. And tires on gravel. *Oh, no.*

She couldn't see the vehicle—it had stopped out of sight, blocked by the barn—so she had a few seconds to try to get her clothes back on. But her shirt was out of reach at the top of a damned pole, and those jeans—already too tight, and wet to boot—were going to be a bitch to put back on.

She was going to have to climb the fence for the shirt and hope it was long enough to cover her butt while she fought her way back into the jeans. Slipping her feet back into her boots, she grabbed the fence and started to climb.

That was when she heard the barking and Trixie darted into view.

Before Jen realized what was happening, the dog had her bra in her mouth and was dragging it through the dirt as she ripped at it with her sharp little teeth.

"Hey! Stop it! That's my best bra, you mutt!"

Jen tried to step back down, but her foot slipped, and suddenly she found herself stranded in midair, arms and one leg wrapped around the fence post, the other wedged into a space in the wire fence.

Chapter 12

TANNER HEARD THE SWEARING BEFORE HE CAUGHT SIGHT OF the source, hanging in midair from a tall fence post, all red hair and white skin. Was she *naked*?

Holy crap. Except for a pair of boots and some seriously tiny bikini underwear, she *was* naked.

Meanwhile, Trixie pranced around beneath her, shaking her head and whapping what looked like a red—

"If you know what's good for you, you'll get my bra from that dog before she kills it," Jen growled from her perch.

"*That's* what you need me to do?" Tanner asked, dropping to one knee and reaching out to Trixie, who ran over and flipped her head around so one bra cup landed in his hand. Apparently, this was one of those front-close deals, because Trixie had the other cup in her teeth, a bunch of straps dangling or stretched between them. He started to pull, but then realized that he had fallen right into Trixie's trap, because she immediately scrambled backward— excited for a round of tug-of-war. "Come on, Trixie," he coaxed, reaching for her collar.

The dog snarled and hopped away, always just out of Tanner's reach.

"Maybe I should let her go for the moment and help you down?" Tanner called.

"I spent seventy-five dollars on that bra and I want it kept intact."

Tanner glanced up at Jen, who had on an I-really-mean-it face, which was kind of impressive considering her position. He gulped and looked down at the bit of lace and stuff in his hand, did some mental budgeting, and let it go. "I'll buy you a new one," he said, moving closer to Jen.

"Fine," she said through gritted teeth.

Tanner was torn between needing to rescue her while somehow keeping his eyes averted and wanting to stand back and appreciate the view. And over all of that was the conviction that he had no business here, that this woman was so far out of his league he wasn't even worthy of carrying her bat and glove.

Keeping his eyes as chaste as possible, Tanner tried to figure out how to help her down. She had one leg stuck in the wire fence, which had to hurt. Her hands and the other leg were wrapped around the post to keep her weight off the fence leg.

"So, um…"

"Yeah, I know," she said. "I'm not strong enough to hold my weight up if I let go of the post with my leg."

Tanner cleared his throat. "I could, uh, boost you up long enough to get your fence leg out."

"Okay, that could work," she agreed.

He got into position behind her and gazed up at her backside. It was a really nice backside. A scrap of nylon barely covered her bottom. A couple of dimples on her low back peeped above the waistband of her panties. He suddenly realized he loved butt dimples.

Focus, Beauchamp. You're not here to cop a feel or stare at her underwear, which probably covers more than her swimsuit. He needed to get his hands around the tops of the backs of her thighs and push up, while hoping that all the blood rushing to his groin didn't make him pass out—

"I know what you're thinking," she said.

"I doubt it." He reached up and cupped his rough hands around those muscular thighs and their silky-smooth skin. He started to push up, hoping his shoulder wouldn't give out on him. This was so damned awkward. He took a moment to give thanks that the guys back at the ranch couldn't see him right now.

"You're thinking 'How can a woman who spends seventy-five

bucks on a bra wear drawers she clearly bought on clearance at Walmart?' Right?"

Tanner laughed.

Jen laughed.

And somehow, he didn't drop her, she got her leg untangled, and he eased her to the ground, where they both stood grinning at each other.

"You're awesome," she said, putting up a fist for a bump, which put a bounce in her perfectly not-quite-a-handful-but-definitely-a-mouthful-sized breasts.

And then they both realized he was standing there staring.

"Sorry." He turned away as fast as his bum leg would let him and gathered up a handful of bra bits.

"It's okay. You can turn around," Jen said.

In case her version of *okay* meant her bare breasts would still be front and center, he glanced over his shoulder at her before committing to the turn.

It was safe-*ish*.

"What do you think?" she asked when he faced her again.

She was posed, leaning against the fence post, crazy hair framing her face and flowing over her shoulder like she was some kind of high-fashion model. One who wore Walmart panties and jeans around her chest, legs tied between her breasts like some bizarre high-fashion bikini top.

"Perfectly adequate," he said.

He'd said those words: *perfectly adequate*, Jen thought as she scrounged in a drawer for a fresh bra. He had to be saying that on purpose, as in he'd seen the video of her meltdown.

So why hadn't he said anything about it sooner? Probably because he was going to take advantage of her ridiculous fantasy that she could move out here to Nowhere in Particular and restart her life in relative anonymity. He was probably planning to out her in a blaze of embarrassing tweets.

She froze with her head and arms halfway through a tank top. What if he'd recorded everything that had just happened? Her fingers were numb as she tried to tug the top into place. If Tanner had taken video of her hanging from that pole in her underwear, the world would think she got off on having her boobs flapping around in the breeze and had a fetish for pole dancing with splintery wooden poles.

What a jerk. Here she'd been thinking he was such a nice guy, and how she'd like to get to know him better. Had even been wishing she were in a position to get to know him *much* better. But not if he was going to make secret sex tapes to…to do what with, exactly? Ruin her reputation? She'd managed to do that pretty well herself, but still. It was *her* reputation. She was the only one allowed to make a fool of herself, damn it.

She yanked up a pair of shorts, fastened them, and stomped back outside, where Tanner was… What *was* he doing?

She'd expected to find him tapping on his phone, gloating about how he'd managed to scoop the tabloids on his literal exposé of Jen and her whereabouts. Instead, he was near the goat pen, unloading stuff from the back end of his truck.

"What are you doing?" she asked as she shoved her feet back into the boots Tanner had thought to deliver to the front stoop of the camper.

He didn't pause, but said, "I said I'd come fix your goat pen, and here I am."

She walked toward him. "But…" *Aren't you here to make a fool of me?* "I didn't think you really meant it."

Now he did pause to look at her. He tilted his head, considering her words. "I meant it."

"Most people don't." Now that she was closer, she scanned him from head to toe. There was nowhere she could see that he could be concealing a camera. She glanced into the truck. It was old, and a bare-bones model—no dash cam or tailgate cam.

He abandoned the roll of fencing material he'd been moving and leaned back against the truck, crossing his arms over his chest. Trixie, snoozing in the shade from the cab, raised her head a millimeter, then laid it back down.

His eyes were soft when he said, "You need to hang out with a better class of people, if you're so used to empty promises."

With that, all the wind went out of the sails of her angry boat. She swallowed down the tears that threatened to spill just because this guy was being nice to her. Was he a better class of people? He sure seemed like it.

Ridiculous.

You don't have the time for this, she reminded herself for the ninetieth time. Maybe she should make that her mantra.

Apparently realizing she wasn't going to say anything, he gave a little nod and said, "I'd have been here sooner, but I had an unexpected visitor."

"Oh yeah? Who?"

He started to shake his head as if to say it was nobody, but then he said, "My mother."

"Omigod! Your *mom's* visiting? What are you doing *here*? You should be home hanging out with her!"

"She left again. She was just 'dropping by' on her way to Corpus Christi to bring me my horse."

"Wait. She showed up out of the blue to bring you a *horse*? You didn't know it was coming?"

"Yeah, she did. And no, I didn't." He shrugged, as though it didn't make much sense to him, either. "Adam—that's the guy who owns the ranch here—was in on it. She wanted to surprise me, and he went along."

"So, I take it you were surprised?"

"You have no idea."

"Tell me."

He looked like he was going to protest, but then he leaned on the rake he held and said, "I used to rodeo a little." He said *rodeo* like it was a verb. "I thought I might get back to it when I got out of the army, but after I got home—" He shook his head.

"Does it hurt to ride? From your injuries?"

He closed his fist over his chest, as though to say *hell yeah it hurts, my heart hurts*, but instead said, "A little. The scars pull, my hip bothers me sometimes. I'm just not that into it anymore."

From the faraway look in Tanner's eye, Jen suspected there was a hunk of internal pain that he wasn't going to tell her about, and if he wasn't into it anymore, there was something in him that had pushed him away.

"Your poor horse was just languishing away at your mom's place and she brought him to visit you, huh?"

"Pretty much. Adam's got some batshit-crazy idea about me starting a therapy horse project, but I'm not sure I'm the man for that job. Besides, ol' Bullet's in pretty bad shape right now—he's really skinny—so he may not be the right horse, either."

"Huh," Jen said. Tanner was so patient with Trixie, and even had a way with stubborn Angus. He probably would be good at something like therapy horses if he were so inclined.

But Jen knew what it was like to be bullied into working on something she didn't want to do, so she said, "And poor Bullet's alone over there with all those dogs?"

"He's a little cranky, so I think he appreciated being left alone. He's likely takin' himself a nice long horsey nap."

She laughed. "Well, for Bullet's sake, I'm glad you had somewhere else to go."

His eyes crinkled when he smiled. Their eyes met, and a shiver of heat, not unpleasant, ran through Jen's bloodstream.

Tanner cleared his throat. "About this fence. I have a couple of ideas, if you want to hear them."

She tried to protest, to tell him that no, she didn't want to hear his ideas because she was supposed to be doing this on her own, but after her morning, she thought maybe she should let in a little outside information. After all, she accepted all kinds of advice she found on the internet from complete strangers. Besides, he'd actually asked her if she wanted to hear what he had to say, instead of launching into a mansplanation of why everything she was doing was wrong. "Sure. What are you thinking?"

"That garden over there's got some serious fencing in place. I don't think even Angus could get out of there."

She looked at the garden, where she'd imagined tidy beds of tomatoes, peppers, and herbs, then at Angus and the girls in their ramshackle pen. "I guess you're right, but if I move them over there, I'll have to build a whole new shelter for them and start over on a place to garden—this spot's too shady."

"Agreed."

Wait, what? He agreed with her argument?

He took of his ball cap and resettled it on his head. "But your garden's a mess. You're going to kill yourself before you get all those weeds cleared out. What if we move Angus and the sheep over there during the day, let them eat the mess? Then you can bring 'em back here and shut them up in the shed at night. By the time the garden's clear of weeds, you'll have this area all snug and safe."

That was kind of brilliant, actually. "I like it," she said.

It was a good idea. The reality of convincing Angus to go where she wanted him to, however, was a little less straightforward. As soon as she unlatched the gate and reached for his collar, he shoved past her and darted toward the lane.

"Doggone it, Angus, get back here!" she yelled, trotting after him, which only made him move faster.

Tanner, who'd assumed (apparently wrongly) that she could handle moving her goat and sheep on her own, had been unloading fence posts. He dropped his load and jogged toward the lane at an angle to try to catch Angus before he made it to the road, but Angus was faster.

Not faster than Trixie, however. The little dog had been chewing on a toy, watching the action from the bed of the truck, but when people started running, she decided it was time to get involved.

Yapping happily, she took off after Angus and cut him off before he got away, nipping at his heels and turning him, then herding him back to his pen, circling him to keep him cornered against the fence.

Jen caught up, grabbed Angus's collar, and leaned down to give Trixie a major ear rubbing. "That was awesome, Trixie!"

Tanner had come back, too, and leaned against the fence. "I'll be damned. Maybe ol' Trixie is good for something besides stirring up trouble."

"I think you might be my new best friend!" Jen told the dog, getting a big swipe of tongue across her face in response.

———————————

After they got the animals secured in the garden, Tanner started to ask her how she wanted the new fencing laid out, but Jen interrupted him.

"I really appreciate all this," she said hesitantly, "but I have to ask... How much will I owe you when we're done? My budget's pretty tight..."

Tanner shook his head. "No worries. This is all surplus." At her dubiously raised eyebrows, he said, "No, really. See, Emma Collins... You met her in town the other day."

Jen nodded.

"Her late husband's parents gave her their hardware store when they retired, which we turned into the Big Chance Training

Center. That was the old Feed and Seed, and there was a lot of stuff left over when they had their going-out-of-business sale. We moved anything we thought we might need out to the ranch when we cleaned out the building, and this is part of that stuff."

Her eyebrows were gathered above her very cute wrinkled nose, where freckles had begun to appear. "But if it's stuff you'll need on the ranch—"

Tanner waved her concern off. "We've got more than enough fencing supplies to last a lifetime. Adam said to tell you that you can repay us in fresh vegetables when your garden gets going."

Jen rolled her eyes. "Y'all might be waiting a while."

Tanner shrugged. "We've got time." Especially Tanner. He had his whole life stretching ahead of him, looking long and lonely. Meeting Jen, coming here to help her, was a respite from what had become a pretty lonely existence. He had Jake, Marcus, and Adam, as well as Lizzie and Emma, but he wasn't likely to ever have an easy relationship, especially not with a woman as nice and whole-some as Jen.

"And that's another thing," she said, oblivious to his thoughts. "Don't you have to work? Surely you shouldn't be wasting time over here."

He'd really prefer being here, especially since his horse had shown up, bringing with him memories that were better left, if not buried, at least lying low. "Things are slow at the moment. I have some chores I share with another guy, Jake, but to be honest, he'd rather do everything himself. He hates to sit still. I also do the books, but I'm all caught up right now."

To keep himself from sounding like he was completely useless, he added, "I'll be busy as hell in a few days, though. We've got a squad of recruits coming in, and they need more wrangling than a hundred heifers in a thunderstorm."

"Is that so?" She smiled at his words, so he laid the cowboy on a little thicker.

"Yes, ma'am. I'll be busier than a squirrel on the first day of nut-hunting season."

She snorted. "Working harder than a rowboat going up Niagara Falls?"

He laughed. "Now you get it."

"What do you do with these recruits?" she asked. "Besides teach them how to handle their service animals."

"I don't actually do much of the dog stuff," he admitted. "When the recruits come, they meet a bunch of the dogs and take turns with them, practicing basic commands and teaching them a few tricks. That's mostly so Adam and Emma can get a feel for what dog might be best for which veteran's needs. Jake and I are there to reinforce the basics and keep an eye out to make sure no one is mistreating the dogs or sneaking them food.

"And we're there to listen. Hang out. Part of the appeal of our program is that we're also vets, so we've been through some similar experiences, and we get the crap they're trying to deal with as civilians. That's pretty hard to find out in the real world. We're not there to be therapists or counselors, just friends." It was okay as long as he only had to listen, not share.

"And this horse therapy thing. That's supposed to be part of the listening and relating stuff?"

"I guess. I haven't researched it because I don't want to do it. I think there'd be a bunch of training for me if it was going to be a formal thing."

"Why don't you want to do it?"

Tanner tried to laugh it off. "Oh, honey, there's a whole passel of reasons I don't want to get involved in that sort of thing."

She held up a hand and said, "I'm sorry. I shouldn't pry. Not my business."

"No, it's…it's okay." If she'd have pushed it, kept asking, he'd have pushed back and not answered, but there was something about Jen, about her goodness and kindness and openheartedness that made him want to pour it all out there. He couldn't do that, couldn't open that box, so he gave her a little—the dust on the top, but it was something.

He rubbed the space between his eyebrows and said, "When I was rodeoing, I didn't ride bulls or broncs. I'm too big for that. The little guys tend to do better there, but I was pretty good at calf roping. I learned to rope because I had visions of grandeur, working with my dad on the ranch, bringing home the bacon…er, steak." His dad. Big, strong, and in control of the world. He *didn't* smile at the memory. "But when Dad saw how good I was, he pushed me to get into junior rodeo. He had his own vision, which had me going to college on a rodeo scholarship."

"Wow, you must have been really good," Jen said.

Good and selfish, self-centered, self-absorbed. "Dad was pretty militant about my schedule, school, practice. He'd been a marine sergeant and you know what they say—once a marine, always a marine. I…rebelled." To put it mildly. To put it honestly would be more than he could bear to see in Jen's eyes. She'd asked why he didn't want to do the horse thing, though, so he had to tell her. Maybe then, when she knew at least part of his backstory, that understanding look in her eye would turn to judgment, and he'd be able to get over his stupid crush before he made a fool of himself.

"Anyway, I decided I wasn't going to college, and I didn't care about winning. I started doing stupid shit, like skipping practice, getting mouthy with the officials, generally making a nuisance of myself. Somehow, though, I kept winning." Because deep down, he loved it. Loved riding Bullet, roping, winning.

Jen had gone still, listening to him talk, and he grew self-conscious. The scar on his cheek, which he rarely noticed, began to pull uncomfortably. But he was also aware of Jen. Of her big eyes, her scent, the curl that had escaped from her ponytail.

His throat tightened, but with a deep breath, he got through the rest of it. "Anyway, I got drunk before the championship and almost missed my turn. Then when I went, my reflexes were off, and I gave Bullet the wrong cues. He was so well trained, he listened to me instead of his own instincts and went right when he should have gone left. Then when I tried to correct, he lost his footing, fell… It was bad."

"Were you hurt?" Jen asked.

"Me? I had a couple of broken ribs. Bullet, though—he was messed up. Without getting too technical, he had a really bad sprain. Almost had to be put down." Probably should have been. It might have been kinder than to leave him alone to become a sad, beaten-down nag, alone in the pasture at the ranch. But once again, Tanner had only been thinking about himself, about what he wanted, and he had wanted to keep his horse.

"My dad agreed to let me keep him, but I had to do the rehab. Hours every day working with Bullet to get him back in shape. But I was still acting like a damned little kid, so I half-assed it and Bullet didn't recover fast enough and my rodeo scholarship chances were shot. I couldn't have worked as well with another horse, even if we'd been able to afford one. My dad was pissed, I said I didn't want to go to college anyway, he said I'd never amount to anything if I didn't go to college. I said, 'Screw you, I already enlisted in the army,' which pissed him right off, being a Marine…"

Tanner stopped then. He didn't need to share the corollaries to that story—about how he'd had a girlfriend but had flirted and made out with every rodeo princess he met when he competed, and what came of that, what he'd learned about his dad during one of those competitions, about what happened with his dad after he'd come back from his deployment, charred and damaged. The fact that he'd hurt his horse and then not cared for him ought to be enough to take that look out of Jen's eyes.

Instead, she stepped into him, slipped her arms around his waist, and *hugged* him. "I'm so sorry that happened," she murmured into his shirt. Her touch, the comfort she offered, was so unexpected, so surprising, that tight feeling came back to his throat, his chest.

He awkwardly patted her on the back.

She stepped back and looked into his eyes. "I can understand why you might be hesitant to get involved with horses again. That's a heavy weight to carry around."

He blinked. That wasn't exactly the response he'd expected. He cleared his throat. "At any rate, I'm going to have to start working with Bullet again as soon as he's got some meat back on his bones. Need to at least make sure he's safe to have around humans and dogs. So yeah. You'd better take advantage of me while you've got me here."

She raised an eyebrow, and he realized what he'd said. His whole damned face and neck were burning, not just his scars.

But she grinned and said, "I'll just have to do that," and tugged on a pair of leather gloves, which were surprisingly sexy considering they were made for stretching barbed wire. "Now. What should I do with you?"

Chapter 13

"AHWEEEE!" *SPLASH!*

A warning siren—complete with doggy breath—sounded right next to Tanner's head, jolting him from sleep and rewarding him with a face full of slobbery kisses.

"Thanks a lot." He reached over and turned off his alarm.

Tanner wiped his face and sat up as Trixie did a doggy version of the Cupid Shuffle around—and on—his bare feet. "Ouch!" He looked around for his boots and thought fondly of the nights when he just wore them to bed.

It wasn't the combat-boot nights, but the cowboy-boot nights—after a long day at the rodeo, camping out with his teammates, a saddle for a pillow—now those were some great nights. As a matter of fact, he'd been dreaming about one of those rodeo weekends, celebrating a good score, full of hot dogs and snack-bar popcorn, exaggerating the near-misses as well as the wins. Those were good nights, even with the mosquitoes and sunburn, when he was young and strong, and it was fun to be scared to death.

He froze, realizing he didn't remember the last time he'd thought about his rodeo days fondly. As a matter of fact, he didn't realize he even had those memories until just now. All he'd ever brought up before—on the rare occasions that box cracked open—were the bad times. The times his dad told him he was ashamed of him. The times he'd embarrassed his mom or hurt his girlfriend. Maybe that's what talking to Jen about that stuff had done for him. Made space for some good stuff.

Wasn't it supposed to be the other way around? Didn't people usually keep the bad shit *under* the good stuff?

Trixie paused in her breakfast dance to bark at Tanner and get him going.

"Shh. I'm moving." He carefully reached his bad arm out to grab his jeans. He might have overdone it at Jen's yesterday, needing to prove—to himself, anyway—that he could still work hard. It wasn't as bad as some of those earlier days, when the scar tissue covering his shoulder felt so tight, he wanted to cut it loose with a knife. Today he only felt like crying a little as he pulled up his Levis and shoved his feet into his boots—he'd come back and get socks and a shirt before going out to work. But now he had to get Trixie fed before she woke every other living creature on the ranch.

As Trixie was wolfing down her breakfast, Tanner heard a whinny coming from the other side of the bunkhouse. "I hear ya, Bullet," he muttered, feeling a wave of nostalgia for the mornings he was wakened by the sound of his horse whinnying from the paddock, demanding his morning rations and a day filled with attention from Tanner.

The sky was gray, the air thick and heavy. A few drops of rain plopped on Tanner as he refilled Bullet's water tub. He didn't care much for rain even without thunder and lightning, but he tried to shrug it off. It would go away eventually. After a scoop of grain and a quick check to make sure the horse was secure in his new stall, Tanner convinced Trixie to follow him back inside so he could get his own breakfast, which he was looking forward— "Damn it, Jake! Did you eat the last of the Cap'n Crunch?"

"Sorry." The voice came from directly behind him.

Tanner would have jumped out of his skin if it wasn't so tightly bound to his damaged body. Instead, he only whacked his knee on the doorframe when he turned to see Jake standing there, pajamas rumpled, and blinking sleep from his eyes. The only thing detracting from Jake's toddler-on-steroids look was the stubble on his chin and the scar on the side of his head.

His irritation gone, Tanner asked, "Are those *penguins* on your jammies, dude? Did you steal those from a Hallmark Christmas movie?"

Jake looked down and shrugged, unfazed by Tanner's teasing. "My grandma sent them to me. Besides, the purple pig ones are in the laundry."

The outside door to the kitchen opened, admitting Marcus, his support dog Patton, and the sound of a couple dozen dogs clamoring for their breakfast. "Heads-up. Adam called and he's going to be here with the recruits ahead of schedule."

Tanner cursed. Jake's eyebrows gathered, and Tanner knew his friend was thinking about the change in his schedule. His recovery after the head injury that had rearranged his wiring was nearly miraculous, but sometimes the little things tripped him up.

"Come on, I'll help with the dogs," Tanner said, giving up on breakfast.

"It's my week," Jake pointed out. "You're on KP duty for humans."

"Yep, but today's menu called for cold cereal, and we're out of Cap'n Crunch," Tanner said. "Might as well help you."

Forty-five minutes later, watching storm clouds gather, Tanner wondered what had made him volunteer to get dragged around a pasture by a recently rescued Newfoundland, while trying to avoid land mines of the excremental variety. Half of the dogs here were so new they didn't know how to behave on a leash, and Tanner's ability to fake patience was a bowl of Cap'n Crunch short this morning.

A roll of thunder preceded a few drops of rain, then a few more. "Hurry up, pooch," he told the dog whose leash he held. "Get your business done before you freak out about the weather."

Sore muscles and all, Tanner found himself wanting to dig a few more fence postholes today. He'd had a good time with Jen yesterday, talking about nothing—and then talking about some things, working together to make sure her little homestead was getting closer to usable. Too bad that wasn't his reality.

His reality was standing in an increasingly chilly rain, waiting for a dog to take a dump.

Well, yeah, there were a lot of things that sucked more than what he was doing right now. There was war. There was getting your life blown up and your skin barbecued. There was surviving that shit and realizing you'd have been better off dead.

Tanner tipped his head back and let the rain wash away his self-pity. It would come back, it always did, but there was something about being here on this ranch that kept him from putting a gun in his mouth. Recently, he'd realized he actually wanted to live, if only to steal a few minutes of fantasy about a girl with long, lean limbs and a streak of dirt across her cheek.

The dog he was with finally did her thing and tugged Tanner toward the open door of the barn/kennel, turning her head to give him an anxious look when he didn't rush to follow her. *Ridiculous human, acting a fool in the rain.* When they got under the roof, she gave a great shake and splattered Tanner as though to emphasize her disgust. Trixie, who'd been lounging in the dry barn showing off to the dogs who hadn't earned off-leash privileges, barked at her.

"They're here!" Jake jerked his head toward the driveway, where a short school bus chugged into the farmyard. "Go get dressed."

Tanner jogged across the open space to the bunkhouse. Fortunately, his recruit-greeting uniform was clean and hanging on the back of his door. He left his soggy stuff in a pile on the bedroom floor to deal with later and struggled into clean jeans and a Big Chance Dog Rescue T-shirt.

Within seconds, he was in the wide-open space that served as front yard, parking lot, and parade grounds, but was still later than Marcus, who held up a clipboard and a handful of canvas tote bags while juggling an umbrella. "You the checker or the gifter today?"

"Gimme those bags," Tanner said, taking them from his friend, who gave a grateful nod and let his free hand rest on the brace harnessed to Patton's strong golden-retriever back. Marcus didn't need the dog much, but when it rained, or when it was especially cold, Tanner knew he ached, and today was one of those days.

"Where's Jake hiding?" Marcus asked.

"Finishing up with the dogs," Tanner said.

Jake preferred not to meet all the new people at once, as the noise and confusion stressed him out (for some reason the noise and confusion in the kennels soothed him), so he'd been exempted from their little swearing-in ceremony.

The bus stopped a few feet away, the occupants inside gathering their belongings after their long ride from Dallas.

Lizzie and Emma came out of the ranch house carrying golf umbrellas even though the rain had slowed to a drizzle. Lizzie stood by the door of the bus, greeting Adam as he opened the bus door.

Tanner wondered what it would be like to see Jen coming through the front door, waiting to greet him like some sort of returning hero. It was a good thing he'd told her he'd be busy for a few days with these recruits, because if he kept going to her place as he had been, he was likely to hope for that sort of greeting and get his heart broken.

"Okay, let's do this quickly so we can keep you guys dryish and get you settled in," Adam said, as he followed D-Day down the steps.

The six new recruits tramped off the bus and got lined up, while Tanner sorted through the bags he held, making sure the names on the tags were in alphabetical order. In addition to a lot of paperwork and dog training gear, each bag held a T-shirt with a recruit's name on it, which they'd be expected to wear for the first day until everyone knew one another's names.

Adam began to speak. "Okay, recruits, you've made it to the Big Chance Dog Ranch, home of the Big Chance Dog Rescue. You already know that you're all veterans, and we thank you for your service. We've been where you are now and understand the challenges that come with the transition to civilian life, especially for those of us with physical and mental scars. A service dog isn't going to cure you. It won't make everything the way it was before. Taking care of these animals is a lot of work. These dogs are not pets, and the training never stops. But if you're willing to put in the work, and understand this isn't a magic pill, we hope your service animal will help you find a new normal that works for you."

For some of them—like Tanner—that new normal might be surviving in a holding pattern between regret and shame, but hopefully most of them could find some peace and happiness.

Tanner was still sorting through the bags—the Hernandez shirt was in the Chen bag, but the Chen shirt wasn't in the Hernandez bag.

Adam continued, "The Big Chance Dog Rescue was formed a couple of years ago because I found myself out here on my grand-dad's land, trying to decide between hanging myself or becoming a hoarder-slash-hermit or a homeless alcoholic."

There were a few uncomfortable chuckles from the recruits.

"Yeah, I can joke about it now, but at the time…I didn't know what to do with myself. After I left the army, I didn't feel like a real person anymore." He paused and put a hand on D-Day, who leaned against Adam's leg. "But then a woman I'd known in high school decided I should help her train this ridiculous dog she'd found, and before I knew it, I was so busy working with D-Day here that I forgot how miserable I was. Friends I'd served with showed up, along with a few more dogs, and we realized we were all going to make it. It seemed selfish to keep it to ourselves. There are many other service dog organizations, and we don't claim to have anything special, but we do have a mission. We're grateful we can pass it along to you."

Okay, there was the Chen shirt, in the Rico bag.

As Adam began introducing the staff to everyone, Tanner was

trying not to get frustrated, because the Rico shirt wasn't in any of the other bags. *There it was.* Right in the bottom of the Rico bag.

"And this guy over here with his head in a goody bag is Corporal Tanner Beauchamp."

Tanner straightened and started to salute, but it was half-assed because Otis, the one-eyed barn cat, chose that moment to bolt across the wet ground in the middle of everyone. The other dogs ignored Otis, but Trixie considered it her personal mission to eradicate cats and tried to give chase.

"No." Tanner held the leash firmly and tugged Trixie back into position. The dog gave him a reproachful glance but settled back on her hindquarters as the recruits began to line up to formally check in, which meant Tanner was finding the bag for Air Force Captain Tim Chen and handing it to him.

"Thanks," Chen said, taking the bag and moving off to let Hernandez take his place.

"Rico," the recruit after Hernandez said as Tanner double-checked the bag. He hadn't been paying attention to faces as the vets listened to Adam give his spiel, and the name "Rico" hadn't chimed any alarms in Tanner's mind. It wasn't an unusual name, after all. And to be honest, the face that stared at Tanner now wasn't one hundred percent familiar. It was harder, harsher, and lined. But then Ben Rico grinned and said, "Hey, man!" and threw his arms around Tanner's shoulders in a familiar bear hug.

Oh, hell no. He wondered if Jen needed any emergency help that might take up, oh, the next six weeks or so.

Chapter 14

Jen sat beneath her camper's awning, Ginger the newly named rabbit on her lap. She'd spent most of the afternoon watching rainwater gather from the four corners of her property to puddle in the middle of her yard. At this point, she knew she wouldn't be able to get the bunnies back to the rabbit coop without scuba gear and wondered if she should feed the goats their supper now, before she was stranded from the garden, too. Fortunately, their new temporary digs were on high ground, and they seemed plenty satisfied with their diet of weeds.

She'd brought the rabbits over to be groomed before the rain started and had amassed a fairly respectable paper bag full of fur. She'd watched spinning videos and knew that this fiber was spinnable, but her internet crapped out before she'd learned how to store it until she had enough. Was it something that had to be washed before she put it in a plastic tub? Was a plastic tub good or bad? Not that she expected him to know, but she would have liked to bounce her ideas off Tanner. But she already knew he wasn't coming today.

And here, from her wet, gray perspective, Jen could see that this homestead idea had been way beyond her capabilities. Not only did she know way less than she'd thought about caring for livestock and growing food, but she'd apparently missed the chapter on what to do if your yard was a flash *lake* zone.

She put Ginger in the kiddie pool where she and Fred immediately started *dancing*, which was what her mother had told her eight-year-old self when she'd seen the dogs across the street getting busy. And bunny *dancing* was a whole different ball game than dog nookie. The term *going at it like rabbits* was indeed appropriate.

Instead of taking advantage of the crummy weather and giving herself a day off to go shopping in the nearest town big enough to have at least a Walmart, or to have lunch somewhere besides her kitchenette, Jen was sitting here all glum and lonely, wasting a perfectly good Saturday afternoon.

Well, if nothing else, she could call her mom and check in.

Brock answered. "Hello, Jennifer," he said. He tried to turn his nasally whine into a television announcer baritone, but it didn't work.

"Brock?" Jen checked her display to make sure she hadn't pushed his contact by mistake, but no, it was her mom's phone.

"The one and only, babe."

A million possibilities ran through Jen's mind at once, colliding into a suggestion she didn't want to consider, so she didn't ask any questions. "Can I talk to my mom, please?"

"Sorry, babe. She's...busy right now."

Busy? What did that mean, exactly, with that weird hesitation? Before Jen could frame the question, Brock went on.

"She'll be okay, though. You know, just a little rough patch."

Jen's stomach knotted. "A rough patch? Is she—"

"She's fine. I'm taking good care of her. But you know, she's been really out of sorts since you cut out on her."

Cut out on her? She'd thought of her departure as more of a bird leaving its nest. It wasn't like she'd broken up with her mom. Was it? Did her mom feel like she'd felt every time one of those loser guys she couldn't stop falling in love with left her for greener pastures?

Jen had been so sure those days were over. That her mom knew better now.

Jen had flashbacks to the last guy who'd dumped Joanie. Not to him exactly, but to his aftermath. As much as Jen had celebrated his departure, Joanie had wallowed in misery for weeks. Months. It had taken a lost job, an eviction notice, and a visit from Grandma

Lucy to get her mother dressed and out the door to her doctor for some new meds and back on her feet.

"Listen," Brock said. "Maybe you should come on home. Don't you have all of that silly homestead business out of your system by now?"

The self-pity and doubt that had been plaguing her for the past several hours was gone in a flash. "'Silly homestead business'?" she said.

"Oh now, you know what I mean. I respect your right to stretch your wings a little, but you also owe a lot to your mom, don't you?"

Yes. Yes, she did. She owed her mom a daughter who could do what she set out to do, who could accomplish things. Especially when that mom was doing well and not getting mixed up with an asshole.

"Have her call me" was all Jen said to Brock before hanging up.

She thought for a moment about getting in her car and driving home to make sure Joanie was okay and that Brock's boots were not under her mom's bed, but there was a lake in the middle of her yard, cutting her off from her car.

Note to self: Park car closer to the road when foul weather is forecast.

Well, she could call her mom tomorrow and have a nice, long talk.

Meanwhile, she'd sit here and watch Fred and Ginger *dance*. How had her life gotten so work-centric that she'd lost contact with friends she could call when she was lonely? Friends who would tell her that her mom was going to be fine, that Joanie was a grown woman who'd had enough therapy over the years to tell Jerkface to hit the road when she got sick of him. Friends who'd do normal things with her like come over and bring a gallon of margaritas and make her feel like a normal person.

Lizzie and Emma probably did that for each other. They seemed like they might even do it for Jen if they knew her better, but Jen hadn't even exchanged phone numbers with them.

She wondered what Tanner was doing. He'd said they were getting new recruits—new veterans who were getting dogs—today. They might be sitting around the bunkhouse having some meaningful sharing time, or maybe they were working out, one big, happy, sweaty muscle party. Although they were probably just drinking beer and telling lies.

Being normal.

In reality, Tanner was doing everything in his power to avoid Ben Rico and his sunny disposition. "Hey, buddy! Hey, how's it hanging? It's good to see you, man! I can't believe I got chosen for this program, and then to see you here? That's just fucking icing!"

Tanner had made an excuse about seeing if the meat he'd put out for dinner was defrosted yet and retreated to the bunkhouse's kitchen.

Jake came in, shaking drizzle from his hair. "Rain's not stopping," he said.

Tanner just grunted and pulled the enormous pan of pot roast fixings from the fridge.

"Is that guy your friend?"

Was. "We served together." He put the pan on the stove while he opened the oven door, then slid the roast home.

"He said you were a champion roper. I didn't know you were a rodeo star."

Tanner turned to glare at Jake. "Aren't you supposed to be the quiet one?" he asked.

Jake grinned. "Only when it suits me."

Tanner rolled his eyes and loaded a few glasses into the dishwasher.

"So...?" Jake was still there.

For crying out loud. Tanner gave up and turned to face Jake. "So what?"

"He said you would have taken the junior title if you hadn't had some bizarre accident, and if you'd come back and started competing again as a pro, you'd be ranked."

"I doubt it," Tanner said, refusing to give that thought space in his mind. He'd shut that shit down the minute he'd woken up in the hospital.

Jake shrugged. "You probably still could. It's all muscle memory, right?"

"No." No fucking way.

"You've got your horse here, you could try."

"Not gonna happen. Don't you have dog shit to shovel?"

Jake, all sincerity and good intentions, blinked and took a step back as though he'd been struck.

"Shit, I'm sorry." Tanner ran a hand over his face. "I'm a little on edge."

Jake's forehead creased with concern, and he said, "Maybe you should go visit your lady friend for a while."

Tanner almost agreed. He could escape his past and spend a few hours in Jen's world, where he wasn't a loser egomaniac who didn't deserve to be called a hero, a champion, or a decent human being.

Right on cue, as though summoned from the gods to add an exclamation point to Tanner's damnation, Rico pulled open the screen door to the kitchen and stepped inside.

"I'm going to go shovel some shit," Jake said and left.

What the hell? *Now* the man was going to leave him alone?

Tanner didn't say anything to Rico, but began scrubbing non-existent crud from the stainless-steel sink. He watched from the corner of his eye as Rico wandered around the kitchen, looking at the photos and cute little sayings Lizzie had put on the walls. His prosthetic leg made an awkward thump every time he took a step, a sound that grated Tanner's nerve endings and took up a chant inside his head: *You suck You suck You suck.*

Finally, Rico cleared his throat and said, "Adam told me he's trying to talk you into starting up some equine therapy here along with the dog training."

Of course he did. "I don't think that's a good idea," Tanner said.

"I'd love to be your first client, student, whatever you want to call me."

Maybe my first victim? What was Rico's angle here? At least he wasn't spouting recriminations and demanding explanations. *Yet.*

"Bullet's not up for riders now," Tanner hedged. "He's been pastured at my mom's place for a long time."

Rico shrugged and smiled. "I'm willing to let you take him for the first ride, make sure he's still saddle broke."

Tanner was so surprised, he almost laughed. That was something Rico had always said, whether they were going on patrol or eating at a new roadside stand. *I'm willing to let you go first...*

"I—"

"Listen, I get it," Rico said. "You might be right. I might bust my ass the first time the horse takes off and I can't feel my foot in the stirrup. Hell, I might not even be able to get the hell up there." He lifted his prosthetic leg and gave it a rap. "But I'm game to try. I miss riding, don't you? Just getting up there and taking off? That rush of feeling all of that power under you, knowing that horse is only tolerating your presence?"

Tanner did miss it. But when he'd ridden Bullet, before he fucked everything up, he and the horse were one animal. And he didn't want to risk that now. Bullet remembered Tanner and knew Tanner wasn't worth sharing his power with.

He was saved from responding further when Lizzie and Emma entered the kitchen, talking and laughing about something one of the dogs had done.

"Hey, guys!" Emma said.

"Hey, Tanner," Lizzie added after nodding at Rico. "Tomorrow's the welcome cookout."

"I know." They always had a barbecue, complete with beer and horseshoes, the first night after a recruit class arrived. A few locals usually showed up, like Joe Chance, the mayor, Lizzie's parents, and Adam's grandfather.

"Will you make sure to invite your Jen? I feel bad for her out there all alone on that homestead. I think she'd like to spend a few minutes with someone besides you, don't you think?"

His Jen? "I, ah, can ask." He gauged Lizzie's expression to see if she was asking because she was still trying to figure out if Jen was the notorious internet flasher or if she was just being nice, but ultimately decided to give Lizzie the benefit of the doubt. Tanner only had the brainpower to be suspicious of one person's motives at a time, and the winner of that award today was Ben Rico. Why was he so determined to renew their friendship, and what did he want from Tanner?

Chapter 15

"No, ma'am," the man behind the counter said. "I'm positive. Strangest thing, too. I was gettin' my coffee fix over at the Big America"—he held up his beer-barrel-sized insulated mug—"and was tellin' Wayne and the boys that I couldn't dawdle and chat since it's baby-chick season and we had a couple of orders coming in. Somebody asked if they was all gonna be for Jim Stein out on Route 15, and I said 'well, no, there's some for that new gal out there on Happy Beef Way. And there was this fella in there, also gettin' coffee, said he knew you and was coming to see you and he'd just bring them chickens out to you.'"

"Really?" Jen was stymied. She only knew one guy in this part of the state, and she didn't know why he'd go all the way out to the Big America to buy coffee. "Was his name Tanner?"

"No, ma'am. I know them boys out there on the dog farm, and this fella was from somewhere else. Drove a bright-green Prius." He shook his head as though he couldn't understand why any self-respecting man would drive a Prius.

"He didn't give you his name?"

"No, ma'am. Maybe I shouldn'ta given him your birds, but he said he was going your way."

The man looked sincere, so Jen tried not to be upset, but what the hell? It was weird enough to get a box of live chickens through the mail that you'd think you would make sure the person they were going to was the person who got them, although maybe that was just based on where Jen was from, not here in farm country. Who the heck could have taken off with her chickens? The man had said it was a bright-green Prius, but she hadn't seen one on her drive into town. Something like that would have caught her attention, she thought. She forced a smile. "Okay, thank you. I'll get home and see who brought my chickens to me."

A million ideas crossed her mind on her drive back to her place. Had the internet gossips gone to all the trouble of tracking her down? Surely she was old news by now. Unless someone with a drone had been stalking her and had gotten pictures of her with her shirt off again, this time hanging from a fence post looking like some sort of redneck stripper.

Just in time to distract her from paranoid fantasies, her phone rang. The drive home seemed like a perfect time for a showdown about Jerkface Brock. She put the call on speaker, and the car in drive.

"Hi, Mom!"

"Hiiii, Jennifer."

Was it her imagination, or did Mom sound a little hesitant in her greeting? Jen figured she might as well dive in, no matter how many rubber bands were dancing around her insides. "How are things? I tried to call you yesterday, but Brock answered your phone. Did he tell you I called?"

"Um, yeah, he did."

"Sooo...that was kinda weird for me. That Brock answered your phone and you weren't shooting a segment or anything."

There was a moment of silence while the fields flashed past, and Jen turned onto Wild Wager Road.

"Honey, I need to tell you something."

Damn it. Jen's eyes filled before her mom even told her the thing. She let the tears fall, because she needed to see where she was going, but that didn't work, so she pulled to the side of the road.

"Brock and I have become romantically involved."

Jen didn't speak because she knew that anything she said would come out as a whine. Or a scream.

"I know you don't like him all that much, but I think if you gave him a chance, you'd see that he's a really caring man. He's been taking good care of me since you left—"

"Why do you need someone to take care of you?" Jen cut in. "You told me you were okay. You gave me your blessing and encouraged me to fly from the nest!" Yep. Whiny. The only thing worse than having to hear herself cry-talk would be if— "Is he there now?"

"No, honey, he hasn't moved in yet."

"Yet?" Jen had only been gone a couple of weeks. "How long have you been involved with him?"

"Well, you know we've known him for months, and—"

"You've been screwing him for months? How did I miss this?"

"No. Listen to me, Jennifer." There was a pleading note to Mom's voice that Jen didn't like to hear. It sounded too much like the old mom. The mom who knew that this new guy was the one. So much better than the last guy. Until he went out for a gallon of milk and never came back, leaving Jen to pick up the pieces of her mother. Again.

"I'm listening."

"We didn't get together until the day after you left. We had a meeting to talk about how to reframe the show, and I was just… It just hit me that you were gone. And I started to cry, and Brock comforted me, and then—"

"Okay! Okay, I don't need details." Jen was doing her own pleading now. "So Brock took advantage of your weak moment, and you…responded."

"It's not like that," Joanie protested. "It's not like we jumped into bed right then and there."

"I'm glad you waited until you got home, I guess."

"Now that's just bitchy, Jennifer," Joanie snapped.

"You're right." Jen sighed. The irrationality train had left the station, but Jen tried to dampen all of the free fuel. "I apologize. I just—*Brock?* You had to break your winning streak with *Brock?*"

"He's so sweet. He really is. And working so hard. He's out day and night making sure the show's running smoothly. And even better, he takes care of me when I'm feeling down."

"How down are you feeling?" Jen asked, alarmed.

Joanie chuckled. "I'm perfectly fine. I'm still taking my antidepressants. I just get a little sad sometimes. I think it might be perimenopause. You know I've been having those crazy heavy periods, and the doctor said my body's having one last hurrah before it shuts down. And doggone it, I'm not letting go of these hormones without a fight. And if I found a younger guy who wants to spend time with me, and he makes me feel special, then by golly I'm going to do him until the cows come home."

"Eww. Can you…will you talk to your therapist about him and make sure you're doing what's best for you?"

"I already have, and she reminded me that I'm an adult and entitled to date whoever I want."

Jen sighed. "Okay. I get what you're saying. I just don't trust him."

"Can you trust me?" Mom asked. "Trust that I am okay?"

"I guess I have to."

"I love you, sweetie," Mom said.

"I love you too." Jen stifled the urge to argue a little more. To beg a lot more. She very carefully hit the end button and put the phone in the cup holder.

And then she banged her fist, hard, into the steering wheel.

Bullet nickered at Tanner when he approached the paddock, the sound a flash of a familiar, homelike feeling. But this wasn't home and having Bullet here was all wrong. The big problem with that, however, was that Bullet didn't have anywhere else to go.

Neither did Tanner, for that matter.

Bullet could have been a great partner for a young rider just starting to learn roping, if Tanner hadn't been such an idiot. Now Mom said Bullet wouldn't let anyone else near him, but Tanner hoped that with a little time and attention, the horse would come around. He just wasn't sure he was the right man for the job. Bullet might not let him in. Tanner ignored the uncomfortable pang in his chest when he thought about letting someone else take the horse.

"Sorry, buddy. I thought you'd be okay after I left."

Bullet tossed his head and stepped back when Tanner let himself through the gate. At least he was reacting, which was more than he'd seemed to do when he'd first arrived. Trixie barked in protest when Tanner told her she had to stay outside. "You'll just get into trouble.

"I brought you a present," Tanner told the horse, pulling a peppermint from his pocket and holding it out on the flat of his palm. Bullet sniffed the air suspiciously and came a couple of steps closer. Tanner waited patiently, and finally Bullet stretched his neck and carefully lipped up the candy, but stepped away quickly before Tanner could reach up to stroke his neck.

All he planned to do today was to get a halter on the horse and lead him around a little to get reacquainted, but it seemed as though that might not be on the agenda just yet.

"I've got a whole pocketful of candy for you, buddy. All you've got to do is hang out with me." He fed Bullet another peppermint, and this time the horse stayed a little closer.

It took four more candies before Tanner was able to reach out to stroke his horse's nose, another one before he could run a hand along his side.

"He sure is a pretty horse."

Tanner jerked in surprise when Rico spoke, a move that sent Bullet backing away. "Damn it, you scared him off."

Rico shrugged. "He'll come back. If you're half as good a horseman as you claim to be, you'll be up and riding him in no time."

"Was."

"Was what?" Rico leaned on the top rail of the fence.

"Was a hell of a horseman. Not anymore." Getting Bullet to come as close to him as he had was only because he'd been bribed. Horses knew when a person was no good, and Bullet was no fool.

"Aren't you supposed to be learning how to sit and stay?" Tanner asked Rico.

"I'm taking a break to bother you."

Rico was still as annoying as he had been when they'd served together. The man didn't know how to shut up. "Okay, you bothered me, you should go back now."

"Nah. Not for ten more minutes."

"That's fine. I'm done here anyway," Tanner said, opening the gate to let himself out. "Come on, Trixie!"

Trixie didn't come on. As a matter of fact, he didn't see her. She normally would have wandered over to the barn to stir up trouble in the kennels, but everything was quiet over in that direction.

"Trixie!"

Tanner scanned the barnyard, calling to no avail. Rico hadn't seen her, he said.

"Well, hell." Tanner scratched his head. "She's been doing really well at staying with me, but I guess she got her feelings hurt when I left her out—"

A horn blared from the direction of the road. And kept blaring.

He didn't hear any tires screeching to a stop, but Tanner took off running anyway. If that dog had been killed, Tanner'd never forgive himself.

But the horn was still honking by the time Tanner made it to the end of the lane, at which point it stopped abruptly.

There, on the edge of the road, sat a blue SUV with the hood up and a very fine backside—one that Tanner was coming to recognize—bent over the engine.

"Jen?"

Jen straightened and banged her head on the hood. "Ow!" She turned with a scowl, rubbing her head with one hand, a handful of wires in the other. "I think I broke something."

Tanner took the wires from her and bent to see where she'd been tinkering. "Yeah, I don't think those were supposed to come out like that."

She put her hands on her hips and blew out a breath. "Well, I never liked that horn, anyway."

"It's fixable," he told her. "Did you see Trixie, by any chance?"

"No. Did you see my chickens?"

"Your chickens?"

"Yeah, my chickens." She said it with such force that Tanner was tempted to take a step back. Her cheeks blooming with anger, she said, "I went to pick them up at the post office, and the guy said someone who knows me picked them up and was bringing them to my place. You're the only guy I know in town."

Tanner shook his head. "Sorry, wasn't me."

"Damn it." She stomped her foot and threw her hands into the air. "What the hell?"

"As my granny would say, you seem a mite vexed."

She narrowed her eyes and pursed her lips, looking for all the world like she was about to light into him and tan his smart-aleck hide, but then she stopped, bowed her head for a second, and looked back up at him, a reluctant smile crossing her sweet face. "Your granny would be right, but I don't mean to take it out on you."

He shrugged. "You can holler at me all you want if it makes you feel better."

She tilted her head and looked at him like he was some kind of rare specimen, her expression soft.

"You. Are. An amazing man, Tanner Beauchamp."

He shook his head, not sure what had given her that idea, but liking the way she smiled at him.

Then she took a deep breath and seemed to come back to reality. "I'd love to stay and chat, but I've got to go see if my birds are sitting on my front porch. If I see Trixie, I'll let you know."

She started toward the car door, but then stopped and turned back. "Would it be forward of me to ask to exchange phone numbers? That would make it easier for me to reach you if I do see your dog. And, you know, if you see my chickens. Or want to ask me out for a beer or something."

Tanner rattled off his digits, too thunderstruck to say anything else.

She typed the number into her phone and then said, "There. I sent you a text so you'll have my number, too."

"Okay." He just stood there like a dumbass, watching her.

"Okay. Well, I guess I'll see you." She stood on her tiptoes and kissed him before trotting back to her car.

She got buckled in and turned the key. Nothing happened. No sound at all came from under the hood. A few curse words came from inside, though.

Chapter 16

JEN SPENT THE RIDE BACK TO HER PLACE—IN THE PASSENGER seat of Tanner's truck—in a half-mortified, half-elated state of mind. Granted, she hadn't been thinking much at all when she laid that smackeroo on Tanner's lips, but if she had to explain herself, she'd say her plan was to surprise him and drive away, leaving him to stew over her suggestion that he ask her out.

Instead of roaring to life, however, her car hadn't even peeped when she'd turned the key, no matter how many times she tried. She'd looked up to see Tanner standing next to her window, hand to his mouth. She'd had a brief impression that maybe he was so blown away by her kiss that he was trying to hold on to the feeling, but recognized that he was really just covering a laugh at her predicament.

He was perfectly straight-faced and gentlemanly—because of course he was. He wouldn't let an embarrassing little kiss stop him from being Captain America—when he said, "I think you pulled out the wrong set of wires."

And now they both rode silently in the beat-up ranch truck, Tanner scanning the roadside for Trixie, Jen looking for Trixie, too, but also smelling that amazing Tanner smell while feeling like an idiot for throwing herself at him.

Fortunately it was a short trip, because she was on the brink of apologizing and asking him to forget that anything untoward had happened, and she knew she'd crossed a line and if he wanted to pursue sexual harassment charges against her, she'd understand completely and never use that phone number he'd given her except under the direst circumstance.

She tried to think of what to say as they bumped along her

muddy lane, but when her camper came into sight, Tanner said, "What's that?"

He barely had the truck in park before Jen was on the ground running toward a crushed cardboard box next to her lawn chair. As she got closer, she saw what looked like blood smeared on the outside. "Oh, no, they're all dead!"

———————————

Tanner's blood boiled at the thought someone might have let Jen's birds get hurt or worse. "Let me see," he said, gently moving her aside so he could peer inside the destruction. There were no chicks in the box at all, neither alive nor dead. *Damn.* Whatever had gotten in here had killed and eaten every single bird.

"What could have done this?" Jen asked, her voice small.

"I don't know. Most predators prefer to hunt after dark, but I guess if there's a free lunch in the open—" He winced as he realized calling her chickens *free lunch* was a little insensitive.

"Dang it." Jen plopped down on her top step, hands hanging limply between her knees, staring at the ground. "Poor things." After a moment she looked up at the sky and said, "I'm so sorry I wasn't there to get you guys. I hope you're in a really nice coop in heaven."

Now probably wasn't the time to tell Jen that she could order another box of birds and have them by next week, so Tanner just eased himself into the nearby lawn chair, prepared to sit with her until she felt better.

He needed to make sure Trixie was okay, but knew she had probably circled around from wherever she'd gone and was lolling in the shade with D-Day and Loretta.

He quickly realized he was wrong about Trixie when a bark sounded from the barn.

"Is that Trixie?" Jen asked, rising and heading that way.

"Better let me go see," Tanner said, trying to get in front of her, because even if it hadn't yet occurred to Jen, he was afraid that—

"Trixie, what—" Jen crouched next to the dog, who stood in the open doorway, and examined the bloody fur around Trixie's jaw.

"Oh hell, Jen, I'm sorry," Tanner said. "She got away from me while I was working with Bullet. She's never gone after anything live before. If I knew she could do something like this—"

Jen turned and put a hand on his arm. "She's a dog. She didn't do anything wrong."

No, but Tanner had. If he'd just been paying more attention to what he should have been doing instead of fucking around with the damned horse… "Come on, Trixie," he said, leaning down to grab the dog's collar.

But Trixie wasn't coming. She pulled against him and growled. He barked a sharp "No!" and pulled her collar again, but still the dog fought going with him. She shook her head and danced a few steps into the dark barn when he lost his grip.

"Is she hurt?" Jen asked.

"I don't know. She's never acted this way before."

They contemplated the dog in silence for a moment, and that's when they heard the soft peeping sound coming from a dark corner of the barn. Trixie darted inside.

"Is that—?"

"Be careful!" Tanner grabbed Jen's shoulder to stop her from following the dog in case she went into attack mode, but they both froze when they caught sight of Trixie carefully herding a handful of chicks into a group, then lying down next to them. She whined up at the humans.

"She's taking care of them!" Jen said, wonder in her voice. She leaned down, Tanner's hand still on her shoulder, and counted, "One, two three…all six are here, safe and sound. What a good girl you are, Trixie! Isn't she a good girl?"

When Jen straightened and turned toward him, Tanner realized he'd put his arm around her, and she was now pressed against him, those big brown eyes staring up into his. His voice was raspy when he answered, "Yeah. She is."

She glanced from his eyes to his…lips. She was looking at his lips. Which made him look at hers, softly parted, her tongue slipping out to wet the bottom one, and of course he hadn't stopped thinking about what she'd done on the side of Wild Wager Road, how she'd kissed him so quickly but so powerfully, though maybe that was just because he was so caught up in her, everything she did was impressed into his memory, and why was he thinking about a barely there kiss when there was the potential for—

"I'm so sorry," Jen said, pulling out of his arms and waving a hand around in the air as though to erase what had been just about to happen. "I didn't mean to get so fresh there, ha-ha." She turned away before he could speak, before he could even think, and started scooping up chicks. "Here. Can you hold these guys while I get the other two?" She dumped four chicks into his hands. "We need to get these babies into their brooder. The book says they have to stay at a very particular temperature, and they need water as soon as they arrive, and heaven knows how long they've been in this nasty barn, and who left a box of baby chicks in the hot sun in front of my camper anyway?"

Tanner blinked and followed Jen the mother hen from the barn to her camper, where he spent the next hour building a brooder from a cardboard box, a heat lamp, and a small plastic swimming pool.

———

It wasn't until afternoon that Jen remembered she'd wanted to record the chick unboxing event. As a matter of fact, she hadn't recorded much of anything she'd been doing lately, mostly because Tanner was around a lot. She'd get her camera out and do a little post-work recording, but her aim had been to show herself actually doing the work. It was possible Tanner would let her record them both working, but she wasn't a hundred percent sure he really knew that she was an internet niche celebrity and didn't want to make things weird between them—like they weren't already weird, with her constantly getting in his personal space and acting like a sex-starved desperado.

After they got the chicks settled in their brooder/swimming pool, Tanner and Trixie left with a promise to get Jen's car fixed and returned to her soon.

Jen had protested, of course, and told him that she'd call a tow truck, even though towing was an added expense she'd rather avoid. She was actually planning to look at YouTube videos geared toward people who accidentally destroyed the wiring in their cars, and then jog over there in the dark to fix it. It was entirely possible that Tanner knew what she was plotting, though, because he told her that his roommate, Jake, loved to work on cars and would be offended if Jen took it to a shop to be repaired.

Jen couldn't quite understand how she could offend a man she'd never met, but she didn't want to risk it. She felt like she needed all the good energy she could collect at the moment. It had been a crazy day, between the chicknapping, the stuff with her mom, and kissing Tanner, and it wasn't even suppertime.

It was five o'clock somewhere, though, so she dropped her gardening tools off in the barn and headed toward the camper to wash up and pour herself a big glass of cheap pink wine and think about the kiss that had happened and the one that hadn't.

She was totally embarrassed, but figured she could explain it away as a friendly little peck for a friend who'd shown up at just the right moment. Surely she'd kiss a girlfriend for being her friend indeed, right? Okay, not on the mouth. Probably not even on the cheek. But that thing in the barn where Tanner had his arm around her, and she looked up at him and felt his lean, strong body hot against her chest, her thighs, and wanted him to kiss her so much she thought she'd actually willed him into doing it…until the dog had leaned against her leg and brought her back to sanity. Good ol' Trixie, saving the day.

Saving the chicks.

She'd barely gotten a jelly glass out of the cabinet—because jelly glasses seemed much more appropriate for cheap wine than cheap plastic wineglasses—when a thought had her reaching for her phone.

She brought up her contact list and found Tanner's number.

Whose blood was on Trixie's fur? Do you think she bit whoever brought the chicks from the post office?

Why would Trixie bite someone who was just dropping a package on Jen's doorstep? She seemed very protective of the chicks. At the time of the drop-off, she wouldn't have even met the chicks. Unless she was hanging out and saw something?

Jen had barely hit Send before her phone chimed with an incoming text.

Except instead of a response to her questions, it seemed that Tanner had been pondering something else altogether.

About going out for that beer. Does it count if I invite you to the ranch for a barbecue?

Jen hadn't even caught her breath before another text came in, answering her question.

I wondered that too. I'll pick you up in an hour.

Holy crap. She had a date. With a guy. With a hot guy who she'd been fantasizing about since she'd met him. In the middle of all this crazy stuff, one thing seemed like it might be working out right.

Chapter 17

"You sure she's your date?" Marcus asked Tanner as they watched Jen, head bent together with Emma and Lizzie, talking about something *else* they all had in common. The three women had been inseparable since Tanner had arrived with Jen an hour ago.

After greeting Jen and introducing her to the guys, it had taken Lizzie exactly no minutes to come straight out and ask, "Are you by any chance Jennifer Greene from *Homemade with Joanie and Jennifer*?"

Jen had laughed, given Tanner a side-eyed glance, and said, "Yeah, I guess my plan to remain incognito is a miserable failure, isn't it?"

"Oh, we're not going to blab," Emma assured her. "I can't imagine what it's been like to have your, uh, *life* broadcast around the world for everyone with a social media account to comment on."

"Yeah, it was a little rough there for a while, but things seem to have died down. Or maybe it's just that my internet connection is a little patchy out here."

Everyone had laughed, and then Lizzie and Emma swept Jen along with them into the house where they remained until the men had the food ready, reemerging with quart mason jars filled with something red and laughter-inducing.

To be honest, Tanner's feelings had been a little hurt that Jen had abandoned him. All the way from the ranch to pick her up, he'd questioned what he thought was going to happen with a girl like her. At that moment, from across the yard, she looked over at him, her eyes shining and cheeks pink. She smiled, then bit her bottom lip and looked away.

"Oh yeah, she knows she's here with you," Marcus said, slapping Tanner on the shoulder as he rose to leave the table.

Tanner surreptitiously adjusted his position on the hard picnic bench, before being strangled by his Wranglers.

Trixie, off her leash for the first time since her big escape that morning, lolled beneath the picnic table, hoping for scraps.

After he'd picked up Jen, they talked all the way back to the ranch about everything and nothing, about the chicks, and who Trixie might have bitten, and laughed about Kim and Khloe, who, since their temporary move into the garden, had taken to chasing Angus around. It didn't matter then who Jen was in her real life. She was a woman who for whatever reason had decided she liked Tanner, and he felt pretty good about that.

At least until Rico came over, carrying what had to have been his fifth or sixth beer and holding the leash of a young dog named Ferris. He sat and got the dog settled before speaking. "Your girlfriend's pretty hot," he said, not exactly slurring, but his consonants a little softer than usual. "Did you ever imagine, after all that shit over there, that you'd be here, livin' the good life, looking forward to gettin' some of that later?"

"Jesus Christ, Rico, have some respect, would you?" Tanner fought the urge to lash out physically. "You want to lose your other leg?"

"Whoa, man," Rico said, hands up in a conciliatory gesture. "Sorry. I forget I'm back in the land of polite humanity sometimes."

Tanner didn't answer, just took a slug of his nearly empty beer and thought about getting a new one. He didn't, though. He wasn't afraid he'd turn into a fool, but every time he let his guard down and relaxed, shit came back and bit him in the ass. Most guys drank to appease the gods of PTSD. Tanner's version thrived on alcohol, waited for him to fall into a buzzed stupor and led him to sleepwalk and God only knew what else. He just knew he woke up in strange places—the basement, the front yard, the middle of the road—ready for battle and terrified he'd made a decision that was going to get everyone he loved killed.

At least he hadn't had any waking flashbacks since he'd moved here to the ranch.

Just then Jen laughed and stood, turning toward him. He watched her come his way. She wasn't dressed up—just had on regular jeans and a tank top under an open-front plaid shirt and sparkly flip-flops glinting in the setting sun, but to him, she looked better than any fashion model could. She looked approachable, and welcoming, and *real*.

"Wow, I haven't really talked to you since we got here," Jen said, sitting on the picnic table bench and leaning back against the table edge, opposite of the way Tanner sat.

She turned a little sideways, her knee brushing the side of Tanner's thigh, so she could see Rico. "Ben Rico, right?"

"Yes, ma'am." Rico gave a small salute.

"And you were in the army like Tanner and the other guys?" She indicated Marcus, Adam, and Jake.

"I was in the army *with* Tanner," he corrected.

"Really?" She shot Tanner a look. "I didn't know you had a friend here. I mean, you know, a friend other than the ones who already live here."

"Rico's not—" Tanner almost said *Rico's not my friend*, but knew that would open a can of questions he wasn't sure he wanted to answer, so he only said, "Rico's been working with Emma and Adam pretty much full-time since he got here, learning the ropes with the dogs."

"No kidding," she said, which Tanner was pretty sure translated to *I can't wait to get you alone so I can ask you why you're not hanging out with your buddy*.

"I'm not so busy I can't take a minute to learn how to ride a horse again, though," Rico said.

Tanner wondered if the man might not be less inebriated than he let on.

"I love to ride," Jen said. "Or at least I used to. I haven't been on a horse since I was…twelve or so. Back when I lived and breathed horses. I even tried to make a saddle for our cat."

Tanner smiled, imagining a preteen Jen collecting her cat and convincing it to sit still so she could get its tack on.

"I think Tanner should get us in the saddle. Adam wants him to start a horse therapy program. Don't you think he'd be good at that? He's supposed to be some hotshot cowboy, right?" Rico was pushing awfully hard, and Tanner was working harder to sit there and stay cool.

"I think Tanner should make sure his horse is healthy, then do whatever he wants," Jen said.

What Tanner wanted to do right that minute was to grab this woman and kiss her. It was such a little thing, taking his side like that, but in this world where his every decision seemed to be fucked up, it felt like…vindication or something. And then after he kissed her, he wanted to take her somewhere private and do a lot more than kiss…

As though she read his mind, Jen asked, "So do you want to show me around the place before it gets too dark to see?"

"Sure," he agreed, a little too quickly. *Down, boy. She's a nice girl and you're reading too much into this.* They rose, and putting a hand at the small of her back, he said, "Let's start with the kennels. Come on, Trixie, let's show Jen—"

Trixie was gone again.

"Do you really think she'd go all the way back to my place again?" Jen asked as they drove slowly along the increasingly dark road, peering into the shadows, occasionally calling for Trixie.

"I didn't think she'd go all the way there the first time," Tanner said, his tone clipped.

"I'm sorry."

Tanner sighed and scraped a hand through his hair. "Not your fault."

"Well, I know that, but that was a sympathy *sorry you had to leave your party.*"

He barked a laugh. "Nothing at all to be sorry about there. I was about to start inventing excuses to leave."

"Oh." Had he not wanted to take her there in the first place? Or... "I didn't mean to be a neglectful date and bail on you the minute we got there. It was just that Emma and Lizzie were so friendly, and I got kind of swept up..."

He laughed. "They can be a little overwhelming. No, it was nice to see you having a good time. You looked like, um, like you belong there."

Jen looked over at him, but he was watching the road. Or deliberately not looking at her? That statement had seemed to carry a little more weight than about *her* belonging there, but it felt good anyway. There were so few times in her life when she'd felt like she belonged somewhere.

"How long have you been at the ranch?" she asked.

"About a year."

"Has it been a good year?"

His head snapped around, and he narrowed his eyes as he considered her question. "It's been interesting," he finally said.

He didn't elaborate, and she wasn't sure if she should push or not, so she settled on "Okay."

But then eventually he spoke again. "After I got hurt, I was in and out of the hospital for a long time. Took a lot of pain pills. I don't know if I got addicted, but I was definitely messed up, and it took me a while to get my head clear. Scared my mom. What I didn't realize at the time was that her finances were pretty tight, and she could have used my help to pick up some of the workload, but I, ah, didn't do much but sit on the couch and play video games.

Eventually she read about this place, about what Adam, Marcus, and Jake were starting up, and decided she'd found a solution."

"So she packed you up and brought you here."

Tanner chuckled. "Yeah. Except they weren't open for business yet, and they weren't exactly expecting me. It was a little—a lot—embarrassing." He shook his head. "But the funniest thing. We were getting back in the car, and Marcus just... He asked if I knew how to use a computer, and I said yes, because, duh, doesn't everyone? And all of a sudden, I had a job as the bookkeeper, in charge of all the money."

"Wow, that's...that's a lot of trust to put in someone they just met," she said, then tried to backpedal. "I mean—not that you're not trustworthy, it's just—"

"No, you're right. It was stupid of them to just give me the keys to the castle, so to speak."

"I don't know if it's stupid..."

He shook his head, then did that thing where he ran his hand through his hair. Then, apparently coming to some sort of decision, he said, "I'd only been here for about a month when I let some con man see our account information, which he used to steal all of the ranch's money."

"Oh shit," she said, imagining how terrible Tanner must have felt.

"'Oh shit' is right. Screwed us up something fierce."

"But you couldn't have known..."

"He showed up in a big SUV with tinted windows. His name was Butch, and he wore dark sunglasses inside the house."

She laughed.

"But you know what?" He went on, his voice softer now. "The guys never—not one time—blamed me for the screwup. They never bring it up, and they didn't let me out of bookkeeping."

"See? They didn't think it was your fault, either."

He shrugged. "Anyway, they eventually caught the guy and got the money back, thank God."

"And here you are, still resident bookkeeping cowboy without cows. But hey, at least you have a horse again."

He blew out a breath. "Yep. I do have a horse."

"How's he doing?"

Tanner shrugged. "Not bad, I guess. He seems to be eating more, and he's letting me touch him more. Worked on getting some of the knots out of his tail today."

"That's awesome." She smiled and patted him on the thigh, which felt natural to do, but also weird and kind of inappropriate, and also hopeful, like they'd crossed some desert of intimacy. Except she had the feeling they were only on an oasis, that there was still a good distance to cross.

To the woman who hadn't let herself get close to anyone in far too long, it felt good, and scary, and exciting. She looked at Tanner, at the face that was simultaneously strong and handsome and ravaged, and thought maybe this homesteading adventure was going to turn out better than she could have anticipated.

Tanner turned on his blinker to signal the turn into her drive. "Well, here we are. Let's hope Trixie's here and that she hasn't had any more run-ins with— Oh shit."

There was Trixie, all right. Running back and forth at the end of the lane, barking at Jen's tiny herd, keeping them from wandering down the road.

Chapter 18

"THEY WERE SNUG AS BUGS WHEN I LEFT. I SWEAR IT," JEN complained as Tanner helped her urge the goat back into his side of the shed and secured the sheep. "You were here when I checked them!"

"I was. You did."

"And it seems like Trixie somehow knew they were getting in trouble and showed up to save them from themselves."

"She does seem to like it better here than at the ranch," Tanner agreed, an idea forming in the back of his brain.

"I just can't figure out how they're getting out. It's like they've grown opposable thumbs. Monkey hooves."

Tanner grinned. Jen had a knack for making the most annoying jobs fun. But she did have a problem here, and he'd be damned if he could figure it out. "I guess you could try a padlock," he suggested. "Seems kind of crazy, but even if they are somehow using super-goat-tongue power to get that latch undone, I doubt they'd be able to get in your camper and take a key off of your table."

"Oh, please, I'm already a little freaked out here," she said, giving the shed latch a final tug before leaning back against the fence rail and looking up at the sky where a few stars were peeking from between clouds that had rolled in over the past few minutes.

She didn't look freaked out. She looked peaceful, her profile in moonlight so perfect. Her throat, long and slender, made him want to nuzzle in and taste her skin there…

Wait. They were talking about something. He searched his memory. *Oh yeah.* "Maybe you should use a keyed lock for the gate. It would give you peace of mind."

"Yeah, you're right. I'll pick one up the next time I'm in town."

"Speaking of which," Tanner said, "Jake said to tell you he'll have your car fixed in the morning. We'll bring it to you first thing."

"I really appreciate this," she told him. "I tried to tell Jake, too, but he was pretty scarce."

"Yeah, he doesn't talk much under the best circumstances, and big crowds kind of overwhelm him. It wasn't personal."

They were quiet then, each lost in thought. A low rumble of thunder sounded in the distance, and for once it sounded romantic instead of reminding him of rocket-propelled grenades.

If he were a different man, Tanner might have turned then and taken her in his arms, kissing her senseless.

Instead, he said, "I have something for you," and pulled a DVD out of the big pocket in his cargo shorts.

"What is it?"

"I found a copy of *Gremlins*. You know, about the cute little things that turn into monsters if you feed them after midnight?"

She took the DVD and looked at the cover. "Oh yeah! That's... that's sweet," she said, then cringed and stepped back. "Sorry."

"Sorry?"

"For saying you did something sweet. That's like...insulting the man code or something, isn't it?"

He laughed. "I guess it's okay," he said, rolling his eyes at his own corniness. "Just don't, you know, broadcast it on your show."

There was another beat of silence, and he heard her shift, a shoe scuffing against grass. She cleared her throat. "I guess I should have been more open about who I am—or was. Hiding in plain sight didn't work very well, did it?"

Tanner shrugged. "You're entitled to your privacy. I hadn't heard about any of that business until Emma and Lizzie talked about it, but it seems like you got a pretty crummy deal, losing your show like that."

"Oh, I didn't lose my show," she said. "I left it. I'd been itchy to try something new anyway, and the big, uh, *reveal* seemed like a perfect time to try my wings. My mom says she's okay about all of it, but I still feel a little guilty about bailing on her so abruptly."

"But isn't she still going strong? I mean, the shows still gets good ratings, right?" He felt her looking at him and added, "I'll admit I was curious."

"The show's good. You're right. Maybe I just miss her. We've always been really close."

"You can always go back," he said, then immediately regretted it, hoping she didn't take that as a suggestion.

"I can. It's been suggested. But not the way things—" She broke off as her phone rang. She took the call, said "Hello," and Tanner heard an indistinct male voice coming through the receiver.

"I'm fine," she said. "Is my mom okay?… Why are you calling?… No, everything's fine here. What makes you think it wouldn't be? No, everything here is *fine*… What are you talking about? I spoke to her this morning… I'll call her again… Why not?… Goodbye, Brock." She hit end and put the phone back in her pocket and put both hands in her hair, pulling at it as she growled in frustration.

"Everything okay?" Tanner asked, though it was obvious that it wasn't.

"That was *Brock*," she said, as though that should make everything clear, but at his blank look, she said, "He's the *Joanie and Jennifer* show manager/producer/asshole."

"Is he the guy who—"

"Who insulted my perfectly adequate breasts? That's the one."

"Say no more. I'll kick his ass," Tanner said, only half kidding.

"He's apparently moving in with my mom. Can you believe that?"

"And this relationship is a new development?"

"And not a good one, not at all. She was doing so well." She paced a few steps, then came back. "My mom used to have these episodes of depression between relationships with major losers. But apparently 'used to' isn't over anymore."

"That sucks."

"One of my first memories is of my mom sobbing because some guy she thought would love her forever and fix all of our problems wound up being a no-good loser who couldn't—or wouldn't—hold down a job, and who stole our grocery money and left us in debt."

"Geez" was all Tanner could say.

"Except maybe it wasn't my first memory, because maybe it was my third or fourth or ninth—they all kind of run together. I don't even remember my dad. I was raised more by the families I watched on TV than any real parent."

"What changed?"

She tilted her head at him.

"You said she was doing well, at least until recently. I assume something must have changed that made her break the cycle," he clarified.

"Yeah. I got arrested for shoplifting poster board."

"Poster board."

"Yeah." She laughed in a definitely unamused way. "I had an assignment for my seventh-grade history class. I was supposed to make a family tree, and I had this great plan where I'd substitute people on TV for my real family, which consisted of me, my mom, and sometimes my grandmother, who had her own issues with alcohol and gambling. Anyway, Mom's last boyfriend—Chuck— had left a few days earlier and hadn't come back, and I couldn't get her out of bed. Which was fine. I was used to fending for myself, but this time I got to the little drugstore on the corner and realized I didn't have any money. Mom had lost her job for being absent so much, and I was afraid to ask her for anything. So I had the brilliant idea to act like I was going to use the restroom, prop the back door open, then circle around and sneak in the back to steal the poster board.

"I didn't think about closed-circuit cameras and observant

shopkeepers. I think they would have let me go except they knew things were messed up at home. God knows they'd filled enough prescriptions for my mom over the years. So I was caught, they called the police, and Children's Services told my mom to straighten up or they were going to put me in foster care."

"You must have been terrified," Tanner said.

"We both were. Mom didn't have a job or any prospects of a new one. I think I outcried her that time, which really freaked her out." Jen laughed, for real this time. "I said I'd help her find a job and we could sell stuff we made and make a TV show about it. I was all about living the TV life, right? And crazily enough, that's what we did. We spent her last five dollars on chocolate ice cream, and we sat at the kitchen table with a notebook and markers and started making lists of things we knew how to do, and we started doing them. We made doll clothes out of thrift store stuff, and dishcloths out of recycled yarn, and started selling them all at a flea market. Meanwhile, Mom started seeing a doctor that the social worker set her up with, and she got better, and we turned all of those dishcloths and doll dresses into *Homemade with Joanie and Jennifer*."

"Wow. That's truly amazing," Tanner told Jen, sincerely. "What an amazing kid you were. Are."

"But then!" She thrust out her arms, the DVD case in one hand, waving around like a weapon. "I called my mom last night and *Brock* answered, and he was even smarmier than usual, insinuating that my mom was falling apart without me and has been crazy with worry over me, even though every time I talk to her I tell her everything's okay, and she sounds fine. If she's falling apart, it's because that asswipe is screwing with her mind."

The DVD case made a whistling noise as it flew past Tanner's right ear.

"And *then* he was asking all these questions about how things are out here, insinuating that I can't hack it out here because nothing's going well, and telling me I should come home where it's *safe* and where he can *help* me. He's such an asshat."

Tanner couldn't help it; he started to laugh.

"What? Why is this funny?" She stood there in the dark, hands on her hips, DVD finally still.

"First, let me hold on to that movie before you kill me," he said, taking the case from her. "Second, you called ol' Brock an asshole, asswipe, and asshat. That's a lot of asses."

She ground out, "Well, he's all of those and more!" But then she seemed to relax and let out a little laugh. "I'm not going to let any ass-butt jerkface ruin my night, though. Apparently it's eighties movie night at Casa del Jen. Would you and Trixie like to join me for a screening of *Gremlins*?"

Jen awakened to a blank TV screen and an anxious Trixie pacing and whining softly.

"No. Not that way! Get out! Get out!" Tanner's shouts were nearly drowned out by the raging storm. The thunder that had been a low rumble an hour ago had progressed into a series of fierce explosions, which must have triggered the nightmare that had Tanner in its grip. He thrashed, fighting the afghan they'd snuggled under to watch the movie. As soon as his arms were free, he grabbed Jen by the arm, yanked her over his body and rolled with her, taking them both to the floor in a tangle of limbs and bedding.

She didn't fight, understanding instinctively that whatever was happening in the recesses of his mind, Tanner was trying to protect her. Instead, she said, "It's okay, Tanner. I'm okay. We're okay," as lightning flashed and the rain beat on the metal of her camper's roof.

"No! No, you dumbass, we're—" He broke off, blinking, staring down at Jen as if he'd never seen her before.

"It's okay," she repeated, hoping—

"Fuck." He let her go and scrambled away, as far as the tiny floor of the trailer would allow. "*Fuck!*" He slammed a fist into his thigh. Hard. Once, then again.

"Tanner, no!" Jen tried to reach him, but he was on his feet.

"Get away from me!" In two steps he was at the door, then the door was banging behind his disappearing form.

"Damn it, Tanner, come back here!" Jen shouted into the night. She ran barefoot into the storm, searching for him in the darkness.

There he was. Next to the barn, slamming his fist into the rotting wood again and again.

"Stop it," Jen said, reaching him, trying to grab his arm, but he shook her loose and turned away, breath heaving in and out, hands fisted in his hair. Rain mixed with blood and ran darkly down his arms, streaking his white T-shirt gray in the nearly nonexistent light.

He stood that way for a long time. Jen didn't move, either—uncertain how to help him, not even knowing if she should try. At least he wasn't hurting himself now.

A soft whine drew her attention down. Trixie had followed them outside, her body appearing to shrink as her fluffy coat became soaked. "It's okay," Jen said for what seemed like the hundredth time, lifting the little dog into her arms and stroking her head.

"Go back inside," Tanner said, turning to look at her.

"You too," Jen said, unmoving.

He looked away, nostrils flaring as he prepared to protest, then blew out a breath and nodded.

Good. He seemed to have figured out that her stubborn streak ran as deep as her determination.

Jen led the way into the camper, holding Trixie under one arm to keep her from jumping onto the couch and doing the wet dog shake over everything, stopping in the doorway of the bathroom.

Reaching into the cabinet with her free hand, she tugged at a pile of towels, which tumbled to the floor. She cursed and tried to pick them up without losing Trixie.

"Here." Tanner stood inches away, holding his arms out for the dog.

He gently took Trixie as Jen picked up the towels. She put two on the edge of the sink and spread one to cover the dog in Tanner's arms. Together they worked to get the drippiest of the rain out of Trixie's fur before she wriggled away to hide under the table, but that was okay. When she wound her little body up to let go with a good shake, she barely misted her own little cave.

Jen handed one of the remaining towels to Tanner and picked up the other for herself. The tiny space was suddenly even smaller than normal with Tanner so close, watching her, waiting for... what? As though he knew she was feeling awkward, he looked away and backed up until he stood next to the door.

"I—I've got some sweats you can put on," she stammered, and stepped into the main room. She grabbed dry clothes and thrust a pair of sweatpants at him. "Here. I'll be right back."

Jen's skin pebbled in the air-conditioned chill as she ripped off her soggy clothes and toweled off. She wrapped her wet hair in the towel and wrestled her way into a dry T-shirt and jeans.

She opened the bathroom door a crack. "Can I come out now?"

"Yeah."

She stepped out and found Tanner was not only dressed but had mopped up the floor and had his wet stuff in a pile. "Here. I'll add that to my stuff in the shower."

She heard him rummaging in her kitchen.

"You have tea bags in here somewhere?"

"Behind the pots and clean socks," she said.

Her sweats rode low on his hips, and she could see the patches on his torso where skin had been harvested to repair his burns. It was like a map of his pain, only she didn't know how to navigate that map.

The fun, easygoing guy making wry comments about the movie was gone, replaced by a distant stranger.

He pulled his head out of the cabinet and looked at her with raised eyebrows. "Pots and socks?"

"It's where they fit. You gotta use every inch in these things."

She combed the tangles out of her hair while he heated water in the microwave and rearranged the skillets and pans until he found a box of green tea bags. Neither spoke until the microwave dinged and he'd put a steaming mug on the table in front of her. His tension was back, that intensity that both drew her forward and worried her at the same time.

He moved to the other side of the table, crossed and uncrossed his arms. "I'm sorry—"

"No." She cut him off. "Don't be sorry."

"I don't know what else to be," he said. At that moment he looked so bleak—his eyes were so dark and deep, and he seemed so lost—that she wanted to touch him, to take him in her arms, but suspected that if she touched him, he'd disappear in a puff of smoke.

Chapter 19

THE STORM HAD LET UP AND WAS NOW ONLY A DRIZZLE. A cool, rain-scented breeze flowed through the camper's open windows, but Tanner was suffocating. "I, uh, I should go," he said, looking outside. "It's not pouring anymore."

Jen held up her phone, which displayed a red flashing WARNING notice. "This is just a little break. There's more coming."

"I'll be fine," he said.

"Don't make me chase after you again," she said, both eyebrows raised in a not-very-threatening threat. "I'm out of large sweatpants, and you'll have to sit around here naked until everything is dry. For that matter, I'm completely out of any clean dry clothes. We might both have to sit around here naked."

He felt a smile crack through his misery. "Is that supposed to keep me from going back out in the rain?"

She smiled back, little crinkles at the corners of her eyes. God, how could she be so cool with him right now? She should be shoving him out the door and locking it behind him.

"I'm sorry if I hurt you, you know, earlier. Are you okay?"

"Yep. I'm pretty sturdy," she said. "You were trying to protect me from something, not beat me up. Was that a flashback?" she asked curiously, but not in the way his friends back home had asked about things, not like they were rubberneckers passing a wreck on the highway, but like she actually cared.

Which was somehow worse. Worse because if she cared, she would wind up disappointed.

"It was just a nightmare. A…bad nightmare. I'll be okay." Which was what he'd told his mother over and over again until she'd packed him in the car and delivered him to the ranch. Where would the guys send him off to if he couldn't keep it together here? A rubber room at the VA?

"I really do need to go," he said, his skin suddenly too tight, and not just where he had scars. He shivered. When had it gotten so cold in here? "Come on, Trixie."

The dog didn't come out from beneath the table. When Tanner looked underneath, he found her cowering behind Jen's legs.

"She's shaking," Jen said. "She doesn't like the storm, either."

As he reached beneath the table, he realized Jen wasn't including herself in the *either*; she'd recognized that he was struggling. His hand wasn't steady, and he missed the dog's collar, lost his balance, and fell back, barely missing the refrigerator with his head.

He tried to laugh and shrug it off, but Jen didn't laugh along. Instead, she was on her knees, straddling one of his legs. She'd grabbed the shaky hand and was peering at him closely. "You're white as a sheet."

"I'm fine," he insisted, trying to pull his hand away. "I'm not some old grandma."

Now she laughed, still holding his hand between hers, where it was warm and soft. "I don't think of you as anything near an old grandma." Her cheeks were pink, but her gaze was steady as she regarded him.

It was suddenly much warmer here on the floor than it had been a minute ago, and his shiver wasn't so much from cold fear as it was from desire.

Her eyes moved over his face, and for once he didn't freeze, though he worried about what she'd see. His instinct to turn away, make a joke, and deflect her interest wasn't gone exactly, but it was hiding.

He returned her gaze, hoped she didn't look down, because if she did, she'd see—aaand there went her eyes.

"I was beginning to wonder," she said, her voice husky and low.

His voice cracked. "Wonder?"

"If you like me back the way I like you." Now she was smiling at him, a wry twist to her pink lips. "I'm about out of signals to send."

"Signals?"

She sighed dramatically. "I think I've done everything but twerk in your direction."

He cleared his throat, but was still raspy when he said, "So you're saying you're into me."

"I'm saying that if you're into me, I'd like very much if you took some action, because if I make another move on you, it will seem very much like desperation."

He raised an eyebrow. "I dunno. I'd like to see you twerk."

She snorted, and he laughed, pulling her down so she was half lying on him, supporting herself on one elbow next to his shoulder, her legs intertwined with his. He turned them so they were mostly on their sides, though there wasn't much room to maneuver.

He cupped her cheek and brushed his rough, scarred thumb across her bottom lip as softly as he could. He felt the whisper of her breath over his skin, the tip of her tongue as she touched it to him, reaching nerve endings deep in his soul.

How had he gotten here, on the floor of a run-down camper, with this beautiful, vibrant woman pressing her lithe, amazing body against his? He didn't know, and for once he didn't question it, just said, "I'm going to kiss you now."

He was taking his damned sweet time with it.

Jen was about to implode, waiting for him to close that final centimeter gap between them. She'd done her share and made it clear she wanted him; it was up to him to make it happen.

She must have sighed, or wriggled, or done something else to telegraph her impatience because he whispered, so close now that she *felt* the words as he said, "Kissing you now."

And then he was. Kissing her. His lips met hers, which had become so hypersensitive she felt everything like a long, firm stroke to her core. She arched into him, no longer caring who was kissing whom, just knowing she was on fire.

His tongue ran over her lips, and she opened her mouth to him, tasting him back. Teeth scraped over sensitive skin, nipping, soothing, making the rest of the world disappear.

He had one arm behind her head, the other hand cradling her face, and she'd never felt so safe, so protected, so *wanted* before. She touched him, the arm that wasn't trapped beneath her running over his torso, feeling soft skin and rough scars, hard muscle. His breath stuttered when she stroked his stomach, traced his hip bone.

Her body ached for him, her breasts dying for the pressure of his hand, which he moved from her face to her hip, where it stayed for way too long.

And still they kissed.

He stroked his hand up her side, taking her T-shirt with it, until her breasts were free, and then he finally touched her, squeezed, stroked, and *yes*, tasted.

Her hands were in his hair then, and her legs shifted restlessly, needing to soothe the ache in her core, until she found his erection between them, and somehow, incredibly, he pressed through layers of fabric, just barely against the apex of her thighs, right there, almost, not quite, but definitely there.

Someone was chanting "Oh my God, oh my God," and it must have been her, because his mouth was busy sucking her nipples, first this one, then that one, a little harder, a little softer, tension in her entire body mounting tighter and tighter, and she was bumping against his erection again and again, and—

She spent eternity frozen, every muscle in her body contracted as she came apart, wave after wave of pleasure swamping her senses so that she wasn't aware of anything but Tanner, soothing her body with his hands, stroking her through the aftershocks of her orgasm, holding her tightly as she began to relax, keeping her safe in his arms.

And yet she still quivered with need.

She ran restless hands over Tanner's back, to his—her—sweatpants, around to the front, covering him with her hand, cupping him, stroking through the soft fabric, but that wasn't enough. She needed him *in* her.

He groaned when she slipped her hand over the waistband, slid her thumb over the slippery head of his cock, stroked him.

"I need… I want… Can we…" she stammered.

He grabbed her hand, holding it between their bodies, breathing heavily. "I'm not exactly prepared—"

"Under the kitchen sink," she said, jerking her head to indicate the cabinet behind her.

"Of course." He chuckled. "That's where I keep mine, too."

"And because you never know when you're going to want to have sex on the floor of your camper."

He grinned. "You're amazing. Just fucking incredible."

Then there was more of that incredible kissing while they pressed themselves as far against the opposite wall as they could while he opened the cabinet far enough to reach inside, and—

"In the flowerpot. Can you feel it?"

"No…"

She was going to have to get up, even though her legs felt like rubber because her muscles had abandoned ship.

"Wait. Got it." He shut the door and loosened his hold on her, presenting a strip of condoms.

———————

This was happening. This was actually going to happen. There was a strip of condoms in his hand, and Jen was squirming next to him, trying to get her pants off, trying to get his pants off, and he was going to have to get this condom on and get inside her and not come the second he did, not because he'd never had sex before, not even because it had been a really fucking long time since he'd last had sex, but because this woman was more than he ever could have imagined, more than he ever deserved, and he was so hard, but his brain wouldn't stop—

"Do you need help?" Jen asked, panting slightly.

"No." He might have sounded too sharp, but if she touched him, now that he could feel her bare thighs pressed against his, the scent of her arousal making him both weaker than he could imagine and ready to climb castle walls and fight dragons, it would all be over. "I've got this," he said, kissing those incredible lips once more, trying not to get distracted but finding it hard to stop. Other parts of him were hard, too, so he reluctantly drew his lips away from hers to focus on what he was doing, and he got the damned thing on, almost coming because she was watching him do it, and while she watched, her own hand slid down...

He closed his eyes and groaned. "There is so much I want to do right now. I want to touch you, and taste you, and watch you touch me, but—"

"If you don't get inside me in the next ten seconds, I'm going to literally die right here on this floor, and now you only have four seconds."

It took him two to have her on her back, his knees between hers, poised over paradise. "Are you ready?" he asked, sliding his fingers between her folds, making sure she was good and wet, because—

She growled. "You're late."

He lowered himself slowly as she squirmed, making a slight mewling sound as he guided himself toward her entrance.

"Please," she panted. "Please."

"You gotta stop wiggling," he panted back.

"Oh." She reached between them then, her hand hot on him as she made sure he was—*in.*

He didn't think he'd ever felt so incredible in his life. He probably had, though. Probably the last time he'd been... No, he wasn't going to think about that now. But damn, the sighs and whimpers she was making, her creamy skin, that crazy red hair, knowing she'd already come in his arms once, ready to make it happen again...

"Would you stop thinking and start moving?"

So he did. He rocked into her, again and again until he thought he'd die, as the heat gathered at the base of his spine, deep inside of him, growing tighter until he was sure he couldn't hold out any longer. But he did. Somehow, he managed to hold on, just a little longer, until once again, gripping his shoulders with steel and crying out, she came.

Her body tight, tighter, pulsing around him, he followed her over the edge, falling farther and harder than he'd ever gone before, into oblivion.

Chapter 20

SOMETHING COLD AND WET STARTLED JEN FROM THE BEST night's sleep she'd had in—

Oh wow. There was a furry little dog—a matted, tangled mess of a furry dog, panting her doggy breath right into Jen's face, adding her cold, wet nose as needed. There was a big, warm pallet of Tanner behind her, arm slung over her waist, light snores buzzing in her ear.

"Hey, Trixie," Jen murmured, edging from beneath Tanner's arm, trying not to disturb him. She suspected he didn't sleep much, so every extra minute was golden.

She tiptoed to the bathroom, though she knew each step jolted the entire camper. After she took care of business, she brushed her teeth and looked at herself in the mirror. Not too bad, she decided. No big raccoon eyes, since the little makeup she'd put on for the barbecue at the ranch had mostly been washed off in the rain between the movie and the… Whoa. The best sex of her life. Which was probably why her lips were so red and puffy this morning.

And why she was still naked. And why she was going to sneak back into bed with Tanner and find out if morning-after sex might be half as amazing as night-before sex.

She opened the door as softly as she could, but found that Trixie, having failed at getting Jen to immediately scrounge up breakfast, was on her pillow, licking Tanner's face as he waved a half-asleep hand in the air.

Okay, well, morning-after sex might have to be after-Trixie's-fed-and-pottied sex. "Come here, Trixie," she said, grabbing the first thing she could find in the way of pants—the ones she'd given Tanner to wear for all of half an hour last night—and her T-shirt.

She checked on the chicks, who peeped softly in their pretty new cardboard box. She'd have to move them to the swimming pool incubator soon enough. For now, they were fine, though.

She glanced at Tanner, but he appeared to have fallen back to sleep. She opened the camper door and tiptoed out behind Trixie, who immediately bolted for the goat pen, where Angus and the girls bleated their desire for freedom—and breakfast.

Angus, Kim, and Khloe were happily munching breakfast, and she'd just opened the container of rabbit chow when the camper door opened. Tanner came out, wearing his jeans, carrying the still-damp shirt.

His naked chest was incredible in the morning light. He rocked a farmer's tan like no one ever had.

But he was dressed. In his wet jeans. Jen's stomach dropped as cold heat rushed through her body.

"Hey, uh, I need to get going," he said, fiddling with the truck keys, finding them way more interesting than Jen's face, apparently.

"Oh. Okay." Why hadn't it occurred to her that he might be all *Wham! Bam! Thank you, ma'am*?

Because he hadn't been a jerk before now.

It was on the tip of her tongue to ask if he wanted breakfast, or at least coffee, but every morning-after she'd ever witnessed with her mom, every time the next perfect guy left... It all came back to her, and she was not going to be that girl. Or rather she wasn't going to *act* like that girl, no matter how she felt.

She straightened her shoulders and mustered her best smile and said, "Thanks for, um, the movie and... Anyway, thanks."

"Sure." He looked at her, a slight crook to his mouth which gave her a moment's hope. But then he focused on Trixie, who was busy running circles around the goat and sheep. "Come on, Trixie," he called.

Trixie ignored him.

"Shit," he muttered, and strode off toward the goat pen. "Damn it, Trixie, come here!" he said, not quite angrily but definitely without his usual patience and humor.

Jen's heart was feeling like it had little spiderweb cracks, and all she wanted to do was curl up with a pint of Ben & Jerry's to spackle it, but she managed to say, "You know, she can stay here if you're in a hurry. I'll get her corralled and you can collect her when you bring my car back."

Did her attempt to sound upbeat come off as needy? Was there too much *I hope you're coming back to hang out with me and not be weird*?

Tanner turned to her then and said, "You know, I was thinking. Maybe you should adopt Trixie. She seems to like it better here where she's got some livestock to protect."

Jen blinked. "But isn't she your dog?"

He shrugged. "Not really. I've been working with her since she came to the ranch, but she's too interested in shepherding everyone to be a service animal, so I know she'll be adopted out."

"I don't know what to say." She wanted to say *How can you let that sweet little pup go?* And also she wanted to say *Yes, yes, yes!*

"Think about it. She can stay here for the time being." He stood there for a long moment as though he were trying to make a decision. Then in one swift motion, he came close, pecked her lips with his, and walked back to his truck like his boots were on fire.

"Okay, well... Have a nice day!" she called after him, as he opened the door and got in his truck.

He didn't look her way as he lifted a hand on the way down the driveway.

If he could have, Tanner would have timed his arrival at the ranch to coincide with everyone else's let's-go-to-town-and-walk-the-dogs time, but the universe knew better than to let him have that kind of luck. No, instead of finding the ranch deserted, it was filled to the brim with wide awake and painfully observant soldiers, sailors, airmen, and marines.

"Woo-hoo, Beauchamp doin' the walk of shame!" fought with "Does she have a sister?" and "I hope you used protection!" as he stalked across the dining room floor of the bunkhouse to his quarters next to the kitchen. He helped design this place. Why hadn't he insisted on private entrances?

He managed to flash a devil-may-care smile as he entered his bedroom, but lost it the second the door was closed.

He flopped onto his bed, but jumped up immediately, remembering that his pants were still damp. Cursing, he struggled out of the pants and shirt, tossing everything in the corner. He'd get it into the washer before it got moldy. Or he wouldn't. Dragging some clean stuff out of a drawer, he started to get dressed for a day of getting crap from everyone. It would have been one thing if he'd come home with a smile in his heart after a nice morning roll in the hay. He could put up with teasing for that, but instead, he was all about screwing up an amazing time with an incredible woman.

He was such a loser!

He felt bad for the way he'd acted around Jen, like what they'd done, like *she* didn't matter to him in the slightest. But that wasn't true; he was just nervous when he'd first awakened, and like a chickenshit, he'd feigned sleep until she was outside and he had a chance to gather his wits. Which of course had given him time to get freaked out about whether or not she had regrets, so he'd been nervous when he'd gone outside, wanting to give her space, to let her know he wasn't planning to move in and become one of her mom's user-loser boyfriends.

But when he'd blurted out that he was leaving, she hadn't seemed to care one way or the other. For a moment something flashed across her face, but he couldn't tell if it was pain or relief, and the fact that he didn't know was yet another example of why he had no reason getting cozy with Jen.

She deserved a man who could gauge her feelings better. Some kind of knight in shining armor, rather than a loser who left a path of destruction everywhere he went.

But in the end, she'd smiled and told him to have a nice day.

Have a nice day?

What did he expect? For her to drop to her knees and beg him not to leave? No, even if that's what she wanted, she wouldn't do that, especially not after his awkward-as-hell goodbye kiss. That was a kiss-your-fourth-grade-girlfriend kiss.

At least he had another chance to make things right today when he and Jake took Jen's car back to her.

Dressed, he shoved his feet into dry boots and prepared to catch more grief. He opened his bedroom door and came face-to-face with Adam, the one man on the ranch who had not been in that dining room when he'd come in.

Was he here now to dole out some extra-special boss-type abuse?

"Good. You're dressed. Take a walk with me."

Or maybe he was there to give him his walking papers.

Tanner knew better than to fill any silence with bullshit, so he didn't ask any questions or offer any unasked-for answers, just nodded and followed Adam back down the hall, through the nearly empty dining room, and out into the muggy sunshine.

"Nothing like a good thunderstorm to make sure the humidity doesn't fall below a hundred and ten percent," Adam said.

"The mosquitoes will be mighty happy for a few days," Tanner agreed. They walked without speaking for a few minutes, following the fence line past the kennels, past the agility yard, and stopping next to the field Bullet was calling home these days.

The horse in question snorted and trotted around the small field, slowing to a walk before stopping a few yards from Tanner and Adam. He eyed them mistrustfully, but Tanner thought he recognized a hint of mischief in his old friend.

"He looks a lot better than he did when he got here," Adam said.

"Yeah, we're going to have to start cutting back on the grain before he gets *too* fat."

"Too fat for, say, a saddle?" Adam asked.

Tanner let out a sigh and hung his head for a moment, although he knew the minute they started walking this way that this was going to be the topic of conversation. "Yeah. Too fat for a saddle." He held up a hand to forestall anything Adam might say next and added, "I still don't think he's the right horse for this kind of a gig, and I'm *sure* I'm not the right guy."

Adam took off his ball cap, ran a hand through his hair, put the hat back on, and squinted at the sun. "I disagree. I think you're the perfect man for the job. I don't know about the horse, but if he can't earn his keep, he might have to go."

"I'm paying for him," Tanner said. "You don't have to worry about his *keep*." He knew that sounded sarcastic, but damn it, he wasn't in the mood for this argument right now. Surprisingly enough, he didn't have to be.

"Where's Trixie?" Adam asked now.

"She's...she stayed at Jen's place. I was about to come talk to you about her."

"Jen or Trixie? 'Cause if it's Jen I might have to refer you to Lizzie and Emma."

"Ha. No, Trixie. I suggested Jen might want to adopt her. I should have talked to you first, but she's already flunked out of service-dog training, and she keeps taking off and going over there anyway. It seems like a good placement."

Adam nodded. "She takes after you."

Tanner bristled. "I thought you said we weren't talking about Jen."

Adam slapped him on the shoulder. "Take it easy. Just kidding. She seems nice, and for whatever reason, she likes you."

"She is. Nice." He left out the information that she might not like him so much anymore. "And she and Trixie get along well. She's got that goat and a couple of sheep, which seem to be entertaining enough to keep Trixie busy."

"Staying all alone out there most of the time"—Adam shot Tanner a side-eyed smirk—"it'd be good for her to have a dog. And even though Lizzie's ten miles away at the moment, just in case she's listening, I have to add that I'd make that suggestion to anyone living alone in a rural area. Always a good idea to have an extra set of eyes and ears around the place."

"I agree. A few weird things have happened out there, and I'll sleep better knowing Trixie's guarding her six."

"On the nights when *you* don't have her back." Adam held up a hand. "Sorry! You left yourself wide open for that one."

Tanner shook his head and laughed.

"What kind of stuff has happened?" Adam asked.

"I've fixed that fence and gate several times now, but the animals keep escaping."

"Maybe she's got an especially clever raccoon in the neighborhood?"

Tanner tilted his head, considering. "Could be. But she also had a thing with the chicks she ordered through the mail. Someone claiming to be a friend of hers picked them up at the post office, but she doesn't know anyone in town but us." He went on to explain about the blood and the way Trixie guarded the chicks like they were her pups.

"She have a crazy ex-boyfriend?" Adam asked.

"Not that she's mentioned."

"Look out for her, and we'll keep our eyes and ears peeled, too. Let me know if you need help with anything," Adam said, meaning he was willing to gather his friends and help with an ass-kicking if necessary.

It was good to have friends, even if you didn't always understand why they put up with you.

Chapter 21

JEN WAS NOT GOING TO SIT AROUND AND WAIT FOR TANNER TO come back with her car. He could just drop it off and leave the keys under the mat as far as she was concerned. She had things to do, errands to run, and she was going to go do them.

Or at least she would if she had a car.

Damn. She sat on the step of the camper and sighed.

How had a morning that had started off with so many good feelings shifted so quickly to *Boy, you really misread that situation, didn't you?*

Had she? She went back over the previous twenty-four hours. Was it just yesterday morning she'd missed her chicks' arrival, broken her car, kissed Tanner, found her chicks, and wrangled herself an invitation to a barbecue? Well, to be fair, she hadn't really wrangled the invite. She might have suggested to Tanner that she'd like him to ask her out, but he'd been the one to text her. And then later, he'd given her a present. That was surely an official declaration of interest. Or at least friendship. Then he'd fallen asleep on her couch and had that terrible nightmare, after which there had been awkwardness, followed by the most amazing sex of her life.

But maybe that had only been one-sided. Yeah, he'd participated, and he'd actually taken the lead, but geez… She'd all but thrown herself at him, and he was a guy, after all. A young, healthy male presented with a willing female.

No. She wasn't going to go down the road of reducing a man to a hormone-driven, brainless sex machine, incapable of restraining himself. If she did that, there'd be no hope for a relationship with him, although there might be a chance for more incredible, mind-blowing sex…

Wait.

A relationship? Was that what this was?

Well, yeah. Any interaction between human beings could qualify as a relationship.

But not a *relationship*. That was a little more special.

And that wasn't what she was here for. She was here to live out her vision, which she couldn't do back in Austin because relationships—her relationship with her mom, and her mom's *relationship* with Brock—screwed everything up.

Her head hurt, and she wasn't going to figure anything out about Tanner, how she felt about him, how he felt about her, or the meaning of life right now. What she could do was get her head back in the game and get on with her plans to have an amazing homestead that she could share with the world via the magic of the internet. She sat for a few minutes longer, soaking up the sun, slapping at mosquitoes, and appreciating the sights, sounds, and scents of what she'd accomplished so far.

She heard bees buzzing, birds chirping, and Angus butting his head into the shed wall.

She smelled flowers blooming, grass growing, and Angus pooping.

Okay, well, it wasn't all supposed to be roses and butterflies, was it?

Having grown bored with the goat and sheep, Trixie trotted over and pushed her head between Jen's knees and nudged her hands until Jen petted her. Ruffled her ears. Scratched above the base of her tail. In return, Trixie rose on her hind legs and planted her front paws on Jen's shoulder, plastering her face with wet kisses.

"Aw, thanks, Trixie. I was feeling kind of low there for a minute."

The dog sat on her haunches, gazing expectantly at Jen.

What was she supposed to— "Food. You want food. What, that half of my breakfast burrito didn't cut it for you? I don't have any dog food. What should I give you?" She stood, opening the camper door. "Come on, let's go see. Then, when we have a car, we can go to Pet World in Cherokee and stock up on—" Jen stopped. "I guess I made my decision, didn't I? Guess what, Trixie?"

The dog pranced a few steps and then sat, vibrating with expectation. Probably more for breakfast than what Jen was about to say, but that was okay. Trixie was a dog, not a human man, and *she* was allowed to be motivated by her body's needs.

"If it's okay with the people at the ranch, I'm going to adopt you and make you a formal family member. If that's okay with you."

Apparently it was, because Trixie didn't say otherwise, especially as Jen opened the door to the tiny refrigerator and started pulling out eggs and cheese and ham.

Jen's share of their omelet had worn off completely by the time she, Angus, Kim, and Khloe declared the garden devoid of weeds. Her stomach growled, and she finished off the last of the water in her jug.

"I think it might be time for lunch," she told the camera and her animals. "Unfortunately, I still don't have anything to eat that I grew here myself, though I did spot some blackberries growing along the southern fence line. Next time I go to the grocery store, I might have to pick up some ice cream. Ooh, you know what, Trixie? I think I have the stuff to make some ice cream in the fridge right now. What do you say? I bet we can make some doggy ice cream, too!"

She got the livestock back in the goat pen, made sure there was enough water for the bunnies and Mr. Bigfoot, and headed to the camper to get started on lunch—and dessert.

Just as she reached the door, Trixie began to bark and dance excitedly, darting toward the lane. Jen's car appeared, followed by a truck, sun glinting off the windshields. The truck was different from the one Tanner usually drove. Her heart sank, assuming Tanner was blowing her off, sending his friends to drop off her car so he wouldn't have to see her.

In spite of her genuine appreciation for the free car repair, she had to work to muster a smile when her car door opened. It took her a moment to realize that it *was* Tanner driving. The driver of the truck didn't get out, and between the tinted windows and the bright sun she had no idea who it was, but he'd said Jake would be helping him so she waved and called, "Thank you!"

It was the guy Tanner called Rico who rolled the window down, however. "How you doin'?" he said, waggling his eyebrows.

Waggling his eyebrows. Seriously?

And right on cue, Jen felt the heat of a blush cover her face.

Sheesh.

Though to be fair, she'd been out in the sun without a hat, so maybe no one would notice.

And why did she care?

Because Tanner was walking over to her, holding out her keys as though he barely knew her, like he was the neighborhood car-fixer guy about to say "Here you go, Ms. Greene. Let us know if you have any problems…"

Trixie, God bless her, lent a helping hand by leaping with joy at the great Tanner's return, practically bouncing off him in her insistence that he stop right now and make a big deal over her.

"Well hey, little lady. How's it going? Are you having fun?" He grappled with the dog, rolling her over to her back, giving her tummy a thorough scratching as she squirmed and fake-growled, wagging her tail so hard Jen thought she might take flight.

"Wow, she's really glad to see you," Jen said.

Tanner looked up at her, grinning. "She was never this glad to see me when she lived with me. I think being here suits her."

A sudden wave of no-good-reason emotion hit Jen, filling her eyes and sinuses, making her blink hard.

Tanner peered at her and his smile slipped into concern, then discomfort, and he looked like he was about to say something when the truck's horn blared so loudly that all three—Jen, Tanner, and Trixie—jumped.

"Come on, Romeo, we're on a B-double E-double R-U-N. Beer run!"

Whatever Tanner might or might not have been about to say was lost due to the interference of the man in the truck. Tanner rolled his eyes and hollered, "Are you fifteen, or what?"

"Then I'd be too young to buy beer."

Tanner flipped him off and rose to his full height. He handed Jen her keys and said, "Here you go."

"Thanks."

"Did you decide…about Trixie?" he asked.

She had; she wanted the dog, but the way Trixie had greeted Tanner, Jen wasn't sure. "I think she wants to be with you," she said.

"That's okay. You don't have to take her," Tanner said, shrugging. "She's a sweetheart. Someone will adopt her."

"No, I–I do want her. I'd love to keep her, but what about you? Don't *you* want her?"

"I think she's happier here," he hedged. "She's a little too much of an attention hog at the ranch, and we've got several who could be good service dogs if we can get them trained."

That was about as unanswery as an answer could get, but Jen decided she wasn't responsible for making sure Tanner was in a satisfying dog-human relationship. She wanted Trixie, so she'd adopt her. "What do I need to do to make it official?" Jen asked. "I'm sure there's a fee, and some paperwork, right?"

"Don't worry about the fee. We accept donations from people who come to our adoption events, but you're, you know, friends and family, so I'll get you in touch with Emma to transfer micro-chip info and vaccination records."

Friends and family, huh? That feeling started to crawl through her heart again. That simultaneous wedge of longing and sorrow that lodged in her gut and made her eyes try to leak.

"Come on, man!" Rico called, honking the horn again.

"So…I'll talk to you later, okay?"

"Sure. Thanks again."

Tanner trotted back to the truck, cursing at Rico the whole way.

"Well, Trixie," Jen said as he drove away, "I guess it's just you and me. One little happy family."

"Beer run? Really?" Tanner said to Rico when he was back in the truck, glancing in the side-view mirror to see Jen, but he only caught the shutting of the camper door as she and Trixie entered her trailer.

"Well, we're running to the store and we're getting beer, right?" Rico asked, shrugging good-naturedly. "Come on, man," he said, giving Tanner's arm a playful punch. "If you really like this girl, a little teasing's not going to put you off, is it?"

Tanner didn't think anything could put him off when it came to Jen, but damn, everything had changed last night.

Hadn't it?

They'd gone from friendly to intimate in the blink of an eye, and then to awkward even faster. Although maybe that was a long, slow blink. She was so open and welcoming, he felt like he'd known her his whole life.

He knew he'd made a mess of things, but hopefully he could make it up to her later. He just had to figure out how.

Unfortunately, drawing the short straw and going into town to do the grocery shopping with Rico wasn't helping him come up with good ideas.

"Whatever happened to that girl you always talked about when we were deployed?" Rico asked, incapable of leaving a quiet stretch alone. Even though everything in Tanner's world was different, some things hadn't changed. "What was her name? Amber?"

Tanner answered, "It didn't work out."

Rico snorted. "I figured that much. What was it? She screw your best friend? The whole football team?"

"It just…didn't work out."

"But there's got to be a reason. Were you worthless in the sack? Or was it her? Did she just lie there with her eyes closed?"

"What the fuck is it with you? People break the fuck up for all kinds of reasons, for fuck's sake."

"Well, that may be true, but it must have had something to do with sex because that was a lot of fucks you gave just then." Rico laughed.

Tanner was not going to punch him. He wasn't. He wanted to, but he wasn't going to do it.

"Sorry, man, I'm just yanking your chain," Rico said. "My girlfriend dumped me, too. She was willing to put up with me and my peg leg, but I was such an asshole about everything, she gave up and started seeing my brother."

Tanner looked at Rico and saw the hurt underneath the razzing, and recognized the defense mechanism. Push them away before they can push you, right?

"I guess I did the same thing," he said. "Amber and I dated in high school, and she was more into me than I was into her. I was going out and doing all that rodeo crap and meeting other girls… But then I enlisted, and I discovered that I desperately wanted her to be there when I came home—not because she was the right girl. I was just scared, I guess, and needed that anchor. But then I came home all busted up and toasty to boot, and she figured out we really didn't have anything in common…"

Rico nodded, the skin around his eyes tight. "Bethany, she had this life that was all sorority shit and wedding showers and *career planning*, and it was just all so…like something from a movie set, ya know?"

"Yeah. It all seemed fake, all magazine-perfect and Pinterest, and the real stuff was dirty and tasted like sand and sounded like explosions and smelled like—"

Rico held up a hand and laughed. "Yeah. We don't need to remember the smells."

"Anyway," Tanner said, "I was in a lot of pain with all the skin grafts and shit, and she was so damned perky. I just told her I didn't want to see her anymore. And I didn't. It wasn't like I was being all noble and shit. I just couldn't relate to her."

"So you relate to this Jen better, with the YouTube channel and the homemade jelly?"

Tanner laughed. "Maybe I'm just seeing life from a better place now."

"That's cool, man. I hope it works out."

And Tanner realized that he hoped it did, too. Like maybe… maybe he could let a little hope in and see where it took him. As far as trying to convince Jen he wasn't a total dick? He supposed he could make some kind of grand gesture and *call* her.

They'd reached Big Chance and had just turned into the Shop 'n Save when Tanner's phone rang.

"Hey, man," Marcus said. "There's something wrong with your horse. I think you better come look at him."

Chapter 22

TANNER HAD SAID HE'D TALK TO HER LATER, HADN'T HE? JEN was sure of it. He hadn't said when, and she hadn't been about to ask him because that would have been so totally Joanie, but he had said he needed to get her in touch with Emma.

So she waited for his call.

Not, like, sitting in the camper watching the phone, waiting for it to ring, but she had been carrying it with her, only occasionally stopping her work to make sure she had reception and that her battery was charged. Heck, she'd even left it in the car (okay, on the charger, but still…) when she and Trixie went to the pet store and the garden center that afternoon.

Which made it absolutely nuts that she jumped so high when the damned thing did actually ring.

She waited two rings, picked it up, looked at the screen, and in her best I'm-not-a-basket-case voice said, "Hi, Mom."

"Hi, baby. How are you doing?"

"I'm…good." She wished really hard that she could tell her mom about Tanner and about his non-call and ask her advice, but since she didn't want to open any extra paths to share about Jerkface Brock the asshole-wipe-hat, she kept all of that to herself. Instead, she told her mom about the garden: "I planted a bunch of stuff this afternoon: tomatoes, peppers, zucchini, cucumbers…" And the chickens: "They're so cute. I named them Huey, Dewey, Louie, Mo, Shemp, and Curly."

"But aren't they all girls?"

"We're not into all of that gender-specific stuff here."

"Oh, okay," Mom said. "What are you doing right now?"

"Right now, I'm waiting for my homemade ice cream to freeze.

Trixie and I found some blackberries today and we're going to mix those in with it."

"Trixie? Who's Trixie?"

"Oh. Um, Trixie's my dog."

"You got a dog?" Her mom's squeal was loud enough that the dog in question stood up and started to bark. "Send me pictures. Oh my God, I have a grandpuppy!"

Wow. For someone who'd never even let Jen have a gerbil, her mom was awfully excited.

"I am developing the cutest dog and cat outfits you've ever seen. How much does she weigh? I'll reserve Trixie the first set. Maybe she can be a special guest. Which reminds me. Will you be a special guest?"

"Um, I'm kind of working on my own YouTube show, remember? It might be a while before I can get it together to be a guest on *Homemade*," Jen said. *And remember that I hate your asshole-wipe-hat boyfriend more than liver and onions so there's not a chance in hell I'm going to make a guest appearance anywhere near him!*

"Oh, no, not that. I didn't tell you? I can't believe I haven't told you the news. Oh. But that's why I called you, isn't it?"

"What? What's up, Mom?"

"Brock got us an hour special on the Shopping Extravaganza Network! Can you believe it?"

"Wow, that's…amazing." It really was. The fact that Brock, the world's least useful manager, had scored a spot on a shopping channel was also kind of impressive. But… "What are you going to be selling?"

"Oh, you know, candles, wreaths, goat's milk soap, that sort of thing."

"Wow," Jen said. "And you've been…you've been making that much stuff that you'll be able to fill that many orders?"

Her mom laughed. "Oh, honey, don't be silly. I'm not making anything myself. I don't think even you and I together could make that much stuff. Brock found a supplier in South America who's going to put our brand on their product. Isn't that incredible?"

"But that's—" *Not what our brand is about. At least it wasn't when it was our brand.* "That's great," Jen said, hoping her mom's enthusiasm was enough to cover for Jen's lack thereof.

"And I want to ask you to be my first special guest. I say my first because I'm sure that after our first episode, they'll ask me back to do more. Especially if you come on there with me."

Oh, no. Jen would seriously rather go back through the whole boob-flashing episode again than be on a shopping show where she'd be selling faked homemade goods. Even if the people buying the stuff probably knew it wasn't homemade, there was no way she could do that. "I don't think that's a good idea," Jen said. "I–I've got a lot going on right now, and I don't think I can get away…"

"Nonsense. You can ask a neighbor to watch your chickens while you come for a visit."

"I really can't, Mom."

"After all I've done for you?"

The words were like ice—dry ice and liquid nitrogen—along Jen's spine. How many times had Jen heard her mother ask some guy that question as he was walking out the door? How many times had Jen feared the aftermath, because those words could not stop someone from leaving?

Not even Jen.

"Mom. Listen to me." Jen took a deep breath. "I love you. I want only the best for you. And I want that for me too. When I left *Homemade with Joanie and Jennifer*, you said you understood that I needed to do things my way, and that I had to do that on my own, right?"

After a heavy sigh, her mom said, "Yes. But…but you've spent a few weeks out there now, working your butt off. And seeing how hard it is. Don't you have this homesteading thing out of your system?"

"No, Mom. I don't. It's hard. It's *really* hard, and I don't know if I can make it work or keep up with everything forever, but I'm going to keep trying until I'm absolutely sure I can't—or don't want to—do it."

A shuddering breath, and then in a small voice, Mom said, "Baby, I love you more than anything. If that's what you need, then I know you can do it."

"Thank you."

"I just wish you'd come home for one day."

"I'll check my calendar," Jen said, praying she'd have to make an unchangeable doctor appointment for a completely curable major disease on that day. Or that there'd be a flood that only blocked roads to Austin. Or that she'd even grow a backbone.

"What did the vet say?" Rico propped a sneaker-clad prosthetic foot on a bucket next to the stall door where Tanner leaned, staring at his horse. Bullet stood, head down and legs stretched out so far it looked like he was trying to touch his belly to the ground. And hell, maybe he was.

"He's got colic," Tanner said.

"Like babies get? Doesn't that mean they cry all the time?"

Tanner rubbed the bridge of his nose. He didn't really know what it meant in babies, but in horses it could mean anything from an exploded section of dead intestine—which was a death sentence—to an unpassed fart. "He had too much of a change in his food, and his belly isn't happy."

"But he'll be okay, right?" Rico asked, looking from the drugged, uncomfortable horse back to Tanner, who probably didn't look much happier.

"I hope so," Tanner said. Dr. Chance, the local veterinarian, had come and gone, leaving Tanner with strict instructions to make the horse walk fifteen minutes out of every hour, try to get him to drink, and not feed him anything until the vet came back to check him again in the morning. And if he lay down and refused to get back up, call right away.

This was all his fault. He should have known better than to turn Bullet loose on all that grass and local hay. But he'd been so glad to see the old horse eating, he hadn't stopped to think about how new vegetation could upset the flora and fauna in his gut, causing his intestines to bloat and possibly twist. It probably wasn't such a big deal for most animals, but Bullet always had been a persnickety cuss, only eating hay from home when they traveled for rodeos.

The good news was they could hear things gurgling around in the big horse's belly. The bad news was he hadn't taken a dump in hours.

"We just need to make sure he keeps moving so things get jostled around in there some," Tanner told Rico.

"Anything I can do to help?"

"Just send some coffee after a while," Tanner said. "I'll be okay. I just need to keep an eye on him."

Probably he could go inside and come back out to check every few minutes, but he wanted to be completely sure he'd done everything he could for Bullet.

After a phone call to his mother, she confirmed that the horse hadn't been eating as much at home because she'd sold off the pasture Bullet liked, and he didn't like the grass on the other side of the barn as much, and then their hay supplier had changed his plantings, and the old cuss went on a hunger strike.

Which he made up for the minute he got to Chance County and made himself sick.

"You want anything to eat?" Rico asked before he headed inside to make coffee.

"No, I'm good, thanks." Tanner waved Rico on, really glad the guy was around, which was crazy as hell because Rico, who had been a thorn in Tanner's side since the day they'd met on the plane to the Middle East, had switched from sarcastic obnoxiousness to sincere support.

"I'm Rico, like Puerto, except I'm Italian," the man with the dark wavy hair and the Brooklyn accent had said, then proceeded to spend God knew how many hours telling everyone his entire life story—and that of his ancestors as well, all the way back to Caesar, it felt like.

He was also a master of bloviation. If you told a story, Rico had one twice as good and twice as long. Tanner wasn't impressed. He knew the man wasn't a bad guy. Hell, he called his mother more than Tanner called his own mom. The guy just grated on his nerves.

Rico's never-ending chatter was part of the reason Tanner had insisted on the shortcut the day of the explosion. Shame and regret, never far from his consciousness, sent a fresh wave to swamp him. Rico might still get on his nerves, but he'd always been Johnny on the spot in battle, and he had Tanner's back today. And he hadn't once thrown Tanner's mistake—the big, unforgivable fuckup of all time—up in Tanner's face.

Their talk in the truck seemed to have helped them both, that mutual acknowledgment of the way things had changed and the trouble they had getting back to normal, which had more to do with the things they'd seen and done rather than the injuries they'd sustained. Rico also hadn't made any more inappropriate comments about Jen since then, which was cool.

Jen. Tanner needed to call her, but guys kept coming out every few minutes to check on him, to check on Bullet, and he didn't want to get interrupted. Not that he thought they'd get in the middle of any big, long phone sex conversation, but more likely in case she needed to cuss him out for being such a chickenshit this morning.

He tried texting, but gave up after erasing the fifth pathetic attempt.

He'd find a minute to call her in the morning.

Chapter 23

"A week, Trixie. It's been an entire week since the big nookie event, and he hasn't called me once."

Jen decided the little whine Trixie let out was sympathy, not a reminder that Jen could have easily called Tanner instead of waiting for him to call her like some sexist princess. She didn't want to seem pushy. She wanted *him* to seem pushy.

Jen kept chatting to Trixie, who was a great travel companion as long as they didn't go any farther than one town over. Otherwise, she got a little carsick.

"We'll be home in a couple of minutes, and you can run around and see your friends. They'll be glad to see us, especially since I got more of everyone's favorite foods."

One of the best parts of having a canine companion to talk to was that Trixie didn't care if Jen hopped back and forth between topics without warning. She just seemed to love to hear her talk. "But back to Tanner. His horse is totally better by now," Jen said. When Jen finally called Emma to formalize Trixie's adoption, Emma had mentioned that Tanner's horse had colic, and he'd been in the barn with Bullet almost constantly, and Jen forgave him for not calling. But then when Emma and Lizzie came to visit last night, bringing dinner and mojitos, they told Jen that the horse was all better. She didn't ask anything else about Tanner because she didn't want to seem desperate. Living and working together as they all did, they surely knew there had been, as it now qualified, a one-night stand.

"We don't need a man, do we, Trixie? We don't even want one, right?"

Trixie didn't answer, just hung her head through the open

window, sniffing the air as they drove past the Big Chance Dog Rescue. Jen was way more dignified and only slowed down a little to peer through the thicket along the road, trying to catch sight of a man and his horse.

She turned into her own driveway and pulled up close to the barn so she could unload her supplies. She turned off the engine and listened for a minute, watching Trixie scent the air. Jen didn't know why, but she always felt a little better if she knew Trixie was comfortable getting out of her car when they came back from an errand. The mysterious thing with the chicks still creeped her out, she supposed.

Trixie gave a bark, her doggy seal of approval, and Jen opened the door. Before she got out, however, Trixie did some more serious sniffing, but then apparently deciding everything was fine, bounced over Jen's lap and trotted over to check on Angus and the girls. Her next stop was the lane, where she stood sniffing for another long minute. She did that at least twice a day. Jen thought Trixie was looking for Tanner.

Who hadn't called, even once, to check on the dog!

For crying out loud. It was one thing to ignore the hookup, but his dog? What a jerk. She was well rid of him.

After she got the various animal chows unloaded and put away, she checked on the rabbits. Ginger was much fatter than she had been when she'd first arrived. Jen made a mental note to google rabbit maternity wards.

She stopped to pet Angus, Kim, and Khloe and check that the gate was secure. There hadn't been an escape since Trixie moved in, but she was a little paranoid.

She planned to work in the garden for a bit, but needed to stop and check the chicks first.

They'd outgrown their cardboard box and moved into the plastic swimming pool, and would be ready to move outside before she knew it.

When she opened the camper door, she heard them cheeping frantically, emphatically enough that Trixie ran straight to the pool and peered over the side, whining nervously.

"What's the matter, guys?" Jen looked in and saw what had them all so upset. Their food dish was completely empty. "You guys ate all that food? I filled it all the way up before I left." She had, hadn't she? Maybe not.

She made sure there was plenty of feed to last them another hour or so at least and changed into gardening clothes. A liberal coating of sunscreen, a healthy blast of insect repellent, and a great big water bottle, and she was ready to go.

"Come on, Trixie. It's garden time." She turned on her camera, stopped to do another quick chick update, and went outside.

They stopped to give Mr. Bigfoot some salad left over from the night before, and Trixie circled the old stock tank, sniffing and growling. "What's wrong?" Trixie ignored her and took off, running around the whole yard, smelling everything in sight, peeing on most of it, which was par for the course. Jen shrugged and went about taking care of her reptile.

"Come on, Mr. Bigfoot, we brought lunch!" She put the food down on his food rock and looked around. She'd done a pretty good job of fixing up the old stock tank, if she did say so herself. The bottom was mostly rusted away, and a tiny oak tree had sprouted through one of the holes, and there were piles of strategically placed rocks here and there providing shelter and sunbathing spots. She'd partially buried a sloping paint tray that, filled with water, provided a tiny swimming pool/drinking fountain.

But today, the turtle wasn't in any of his usual places. He wasn't on the big triangular rock; he wasn't under the half-rotted log. He was missing.

Jen looked in every shadow, every crevasse, patted the ground all around to look for holes in case he'd dug an escape tunnel. He was gone. Which meant someone—or something—had helped him out. A frisson of fear ran down her spine, and she looked around. She didn't feel like someone was watching her—Trixie would be on to that—but she was almost positive someone had been there.

But who would take her turtle?

It was probably a raccoon. Or maybe an eagle or something had swooped down from the sky and snatched poor Mr. Bigfoot from his habitat. Wherever he'd gone, hopefully he'd tucked up inside his house and stayed there until it was safe to come out. At which point he'd trot into the woods or a nice field and find other turtles to hang out with, living a nice, long life.

That was what she chose to believe, anyway.

She didn't have a ton to do out there today, just some weeding and watering and debugging. She'd discovered the most horrifying giant green caterpillar on one of her tomato plants yesterday. Checking online, she'd learned it was a tomato hornworm and was a voracious destroyer of tomato plants. A bottle of diluted lemon juice infused with cayenne pepper and garlic in hand, she was going to protect her tomato plants to her dying—

They were already dead.

Everything in her garden was dead.

But her plants hadn't been eaten. Instead everything was all wilted and brown. Her tomato plants, her pepper plants, her cute little bean sprouts—all dead.

"Damn it!" she shouted, then added a few dozen other expletives. And repeated them for good measure.

It did not revive her plants.

Suddenly, she remembered her camera was on. This wasn't what she'd hope to record, but it was what was really happening, so she said, "I'm not having the best day ever. Things seem to be going wrong at a faster rate than I thought they would. I mean… everyone expects a little drama now and then, but I didn't think my turtle would disappear and my garden would die on the same day. Oh. My boyfriend ditched me, too." What the hell, she could edit it later. "I mean, he wasn't technically my boyfriend, as in 'Do you want to go steady?' but I kind of thought we were headed in that direction. I must have been really terrible in the sack, because he took off the morning after and hasn't been back."

She turned off the camera and picked up her water bottle. Maybe today was a good day to crack open that gallon jug of white zinfandel she'd been hoarding. Do a little day drinking, wallow in self-pity, get up tomorrow and try again.

When she got back to the camper, however, she opted for ice cream. Starting fresh tomorrow with a hangover might not be as much fun as it sounded right now. And besides, she was a the-tough-get-going kind of person who needed a few minutes to regroup.

She plopped into her lawn chair and took a bite. It was pretty good, if she did say so herself. She had a little bowl with Trixie's doggy ice cream, and she put it down next to her. "Trixie, come here! Ice cream!"

Trixie didn't come.

"Come here, girl! Come get your ice cream!"

Oh no. She should have never taken her eyes off the dog, but she'd been too busy feeling sorry for herself to watch Trixie. Her own ice cream forgotten, she got up and started looking and calling. She went back to the garden, but the dog hadn't gotten trapped behind that fence. She was starting to get scared now. What if Trixie got lost and a wild boar—or hell, a damned chupacabra—ate her?

She came out of the barn in time to see Angus stroll past the chicken coop, glance inside, then continue toward the lane. The goat-pen gate was hanging open, Kim and Khloe still inside bleating and anxiously pacing.

"Damn it, Angus!" She sprinted after the goat. Fortunately, he was self-assured enough to believe that he didn't need to speed up to elude her. He was right. Just before she reached him, a tree root jumped out of the yard and grabbed the toe of her boot, sending her sprawling. Angus stopped and looked at Jen, gave a lusty *baaaah* and kept on his way.

Jen got to her feet. Brushed off her knees, swiped at the sweat and dust in her eyes, and stalked after her goat. She was *not* going to cry. This venture of hers was supposed to be hard. It was going to get harder. A stupid goat who wouldn't stay in his stupid pen was *not* going to get her down.

"Angus, get back here!" she yelled.

Angus ignored her.

"I mean it!"

He kept walking. Jen chased him, catching him just before he turned from her lane into the road.

"Come on, you jerk," she said, tugging the goat's collar to aim him back at his pen.

Angus didn't want to turn around.

The more she pulled, the more he didn't move.

Kim and Khloe cried behind her. "Come on, Angus. I'm sorry I called you a jerk and cussed at you. Can't you hear the girls? They miss you."

Or were they cheering him on?

She was going to have to stand here hanging onto two hundred pounds of goat until he decided to go her way or she went his way, wherever that led, or one of them died out here in the two thousand percent humidity and two-hundred-degree heat. How was she going to get through this next year if her stupid livestock wouldn't even cooperate?

And her doggone dog was gone.

Her chest prickled from the heat and her legs itched from mosquito bites. Her throat tightened, and her vision blurred.

She gave in and started to cry in earnest.

That was how Tanner found her a couple of minutes later—with her arms around the neck of her goat, sobbing into his stinky locks, at the entrance to her worthless homestead.

There was just enough room to pull his truck into the lane, and Tanner turned carefully to avoid hitting Jen and the goat.

Jen, who'd been hugging Angus a moment before, must have registered the sound of his truck because she raised her head. She barely glanced his way before turning away and… Oh hell, was she wiping at her eyes? Was she crying? *Oh, no, no, no.* Tanner didn't do tears. That shit could be contagious, and it made you do things you didn't want to do. Like propose to your high school girlfriend before you left for boot camp, or agree to let your mother take you to the middle of Texas and dump you at a sleepaway camp for lost veterans.

He'd been feeling awkward enough for coming out here after not calling for so long. He'd expected a cold shoulder maybe, but not tears.

He took a deep breath and got out of the truck, shutting the door behind him. Trixie, the little stinker, stuck her head out of the open window and panted happily.

Jen turned toward him with a smile that was a little too cheerful.

"Hey, good morning," he said, crooking a thumb over his shoulder. "I had a visitor show up a few minutes ago." *Don't ask her how she is. Do not ask.*

"Hi," Jen said. "Angus and I were just out for a little walk."

Even with bloodshot eyes and blotchy cheeks, she was so damned pretty it made Tanner's stomach flip—although that could also be a side effect of not letting her obvious distress get to him, which he was ignoring pretty well, he thought.

Until she gave a tiny sniffle.

Well, hell.

He couldn't help it. He pulled her into his arms, where she

leaned her head against his chest and sobbed for all of about five seconds, then lifted her head and said, "Nope. We don't do this. We don't stand around crying."

He kept one arm around her and tilted her face up to his, checking her eyes, wondering if she'd lost her shit. In spite of the tears, she didn't look like Gollum. "Who's we?" he asked.

She laughed wetly and stepped out of his embrace. "Just repeating a pep talk my grandma used to give me."

In spite of his earlier misgivings, Tanner hadn't minded holding her, so he said, "It's okay if you need to cry."

"Nope. Won't do any good. Won't fix my gate, won't bring back my garden, won't get my mom to ditch that jerk Brock." She drew a shaky breath but let it out and seemed much better for the moment. "But Angus—"

"Already back in the pen."

Jen turned to see what Tanner had noticed over the top of her head—Trixie had herded Angus right back into the pen and sat at the gate, guarding the exit.

"What the heck?" She marched over and glared at the goat, then turned her attention to the dog. "I'm very glad to see you back, Miss Trixie, but I'm afraid you've earned yourself a leash, since you can't seem to decide where you live."

Trixie stood on her hind legs and put her front paws on Jen's waist, and Jen hugged her, giving her head a good long pet.

Tanner was no dog whisperer, but when Trixie had shown up at the ranch, run right to him, and started barking and running in circles, it had seemed an awful lot like she had a plan and was now apologizing for scaring her mom.

For his part, Tanner went to shut the gate of the goat pen but found that the fence half of the latch was missing, bolts and all. He found the whole latch hanging from the gate. It looked as though the bolts had broken out of the post, which could happen if the wood was rotted, but this was a brand-new fence post.

Jen was now next to Tanner, looking at what he was seeing.

"Did you come out here and…drill the bolt holes bigger?" he asked.

Her expression said that was as ridiculous to her as it was to him. She crossed her arms over her chest, hugging herself as if she were cold, and said, "Some more weird things happened."

Tanner tensed. "What kind of things?"

"Mr. Bigfoot's missing. I went to feed him, and he's gone. I checked everywhere in his stock tank, but he's not there. I mean… maybe some wild animal came along and carried him off? Also, my garden's dead. *Everything.* It's like it had a drought, but I've been watering it regularly, and everything died at one time. Maybe I have a fungus or something? So okay, that stuff could be coincidental, but then the chicks ate a whole day's worth of food in, like, two hours, and now that I think of it, that's the scariest of all."

Tanner scratched his nose. "The chicks eating all their food too fast is scary?"

Jen sighed and said, "Yeah. I filled their feeder to the top this morning before Trixie and I went to Cherokee to run some errands, and we checked on them when we got back. They were freaking out, and their feeder was totally empty. That much food should have lasted all day."

He nodded. "Seems like someone dumped out the food maybe?"

"Yeah. I mean…it's possible I forgot to fill it this morning, but I could swear I topped it off before we left."

"Are you still keeping them inside your camper?" he asked now.

"Uh-huh." She nodded slowly.

It was bad if someone was coming onto her property to mess with her animals, steal her turtle, or kill her garden. That kind of thing could get you shot, no questions asked. But someone going into Jen's living space? Completely, absolutely unacceptable.

Chapter 24

Jen watched Tanner stalk away, yanking his phone from the side pocket of his cargo shorts. She figured he was calling his friends at the ranch, but when he came back, he said, "The sheriff's dealing with a drunk-driving accident, but he or one of his deputies will come by later."

"The sheriff?"

"Don't you think this should be reported?"

"Well, yeah, I guess I do. It's just been all these little things, though, things that can be explained away. I didn't figure the police would take it seriously." They wouldn't in Austin, anyway, where it seemed like it didn't count unless you had video of your stalker climbing in your bedroom window.

"When someone has been in your camper without your permission? That's serious. I don't know that the police can do much besides drive by now and then, but at least they'll keep a lookout. And I'm going to start sleeping here."

Jen saw red. Complete, utter red. "Ex*cuse* me? You think you can just participate in the Big Bonk, disappear for a week without a word, and then show back up here and think your white-knight routine is going to get you back into the palace? The hell you say!"

Tanner ducked his head, but Jen could still see the smile he tried to hide, and it fed the hell out of her anger.

"Oh. You think this is funny? I may be willing to do more than *kiss* on the first date, but I'm not *easy*."

"Oh, no, Miss Jen, you are *not* easy," he said. " Things got crazy at the ranch, and I didn't get a chance…couldn't find a…" His voice trailed off as though he realized there was no good excuse for not telling her what was going on.

Jen crossed her arms and cocked her hip, all tough girl on the outside, heart thumping, stomach churning on the inside, and waited to hear what he said next.

"My horse got sick, and at first I was waiting to find out how he was going to do before I called you, but then I was up with him for about thirty-six hours straight and crashed hard once he was out of the woods."

Jen imagined Tanner pacing the barn with worry over his horse, knowing he probably felt terribly guilty, but still… He didn't have time to shoot her a text?

"How's Bullet?"

"He's doing okay. Ornery as hell 'cause I won't let him out to graze more than a few minutes at a time, trying to ease him into being used to new grass and such, but he's healthy, and he's actin' more like the horse I used to know."

"That's great."

"Yeah." Tanner shook his head, then looked her straight in the eye. "I'm sorry. I screwed up from the minute I woke up that morning after…what did you call it? The Big Bonk." His mouth tilted up in a half smile. "I confess that I was a little out of my element and didn't quite know what you'd expect of me."

"Staying for coffee would have been good," she said.

He nodded. "And I shoulda called later, but I didn't know what to say, and I kept finding excuses, and then it had been so long, I felt like an ass. I feel like an ass. I am—"

Jen shook her head. "I can't believe that after everything I saw my mom go through, I'm still naive enough to think—"

"Stop," Tanner said. "It's not naive to expect to be treated with respect, and you deserve better than some washed-up cowboy who's too chicken to call a woman because his *feelings* are too intense."

Jen blinked. He was admitting to having *feelings* for her. That was…

182   TERI ANNE STANLEY

"And listen. I'm not planning to come riding my stallion back to your, uh, palace, but I am going to find out what's going on here. The thought of someone messing with you while I was off being a teenager makes my stomach hurt. I'll sleep in the barn to keep an eye on things."

He really meant it, and the thought that he was willing to sleep in that nasty barn so Jen would feel safe warmed her to her toes.

"And I won't be wearing my white armor. More like dingy camo."

"Oh." She pondered that a moment, then said, "You can wear your white armor if you like."

He shook his head and said, "It doesn't fit me. Never has."

"So about how you're not planning to, uh, ride your stallion into the palace... Is that because you don't want to? I mean, it's not like the Big Bonk was supposed to be the most significant sex of our lives or anything. I mean, even if it wasn't that great for you—"

"Stop that," Tanner demanded, pointing a finger at her, eyes hot. "I'm not sure what you qualify as great bonking or mediocre bonking or whatever, but that was the best sex of my life, and if—" He broke off then, eyes wide, as though he'd said something he shouldn't have.

Whatever he didn't mean to give away had an electric effect on Jen. She'd gone from wallowing in despair to anger in a short time, so why not shift right into overcome by lust? She looked up at his mouth, licking her lips. "The best sex of your life, huh?"

He swallowed, and she didn't think she'd ever seen a sexier Adam's apple. She moved closer to him, the heat from his body adding to the heat from hers, and instead of that making her want to melt, she wanted to make it even hotter.

Draping her arms around his shoulders, she brought her body against his, feeling all of his hard places—some very hard—nestle into her softer spots. "Do you want to come inside?" she asked.

His voice was raspy when he answered, "Yes, I believe I do."

And they forgot about dead gardens, sick horses, and escaping turtles for a very long time. At least until the sheriff showed up.

Chapter 25

JEN UNPINNED HER SHEETS FROM THE LINE AND SORT OF folded them, or maybe wadded them up with style. There was another storm brewing, and she didn't want to go to bed on wet sheets—or no sheets, which was a distinct possibility the way she and Tanner had been burning them up for the past couple of weeks.

They'd developed a routine: Tanner got up and went to the ranch first thing in the morning and did his thing there—taking care of book work and looking after Bullet, working with the veterans in whatever way he was needed, helping Jake with repairs.

Meanwhile, Jen worked around the homestead—doing the million and one things that had to be done to ensure there would be food and shelter in the coming weeks. The chickens were growing like weeds and had moved into their coop. The rabbits had moved into an impressive—if she did say so herself—bunny condo, made of a couple of plastic fifty-five-gallon drums, a bunch of scrap lumber, and a few yards of wire mesh.

She'd also taken Fred to have his little bunny balls removed—she'd figured out which one was the male based on who wasn't growing to twice their original size—and made an appointment to have the any-day-now babies neutered as soon as they were old enough.

She'd replanted some of her garden in buckets and barrels filled with new, store-bought potting soil. It turned out the sheriff's deputy who'd come in response to Tanner's call was a gardener who thought her soil might be contaminated, so she'd sent a couple of samples to the county extension service for testing. He also said he'd make sure someone drove by a couple of times

CHARMING TEXAS COWBOY 185

per shift and they'd keep an eye out for a green Prius like the post-master had described during the chicknapping. Fortunately, Dr. Chance didn't think that the animals had been harmed by grazing in that garden, though he did warn Jen to be on the lookout for signs of illness. Meanwhile, Jen watered her bucket garden and kept an eye out for Mr. Bigfoot.

Then sometime before the sun went down, Tanner came back to the homestead. They'd talk about their day and watch a little TV or read. And then they'd make love. Sometimes it was fast and furious, sometimes it was slow and sweet, sometimes it was just... regular, which was also very, very good. Waking up in Tanner's arms was the best way to wake up, ever, Jen decided.

There had been no more unexplainable incidents, thank-fully. Angus didn't escape, Trixie didn't run off, and the plant life flourished.

But today...today, something was off. Or maybe everything was off.

Jen knew that part of her discontent was her mom's premiere on the shopping show next week. She'd once again asked Jen to appear with her, and again Jen had refused. It hadn't helped that Brock had gotten on the phone at one point and dared her. "What's the matter, Jennifer, are you scared?" And then insulted her. "I know you're finding out that homesteading isn't as fun and easy as you expected it to be, aren't you?"

Jen was a mess of confusion—wanting to support her mom, but needing to see her homestead through. No, a trip to Austin for a few days wouldn't mean the end of her dreams, but the thought of showing up there and having to deal with Brock...nope. Nopey, nope-ity, nope.

But her current disquiet was about more than feeling guilty that she was going to let her mom down. Tanner had been rest-less, too, and not his usual self that morning when he'd left for the ranch.

As a matter of fact, he'd been edgy last night, too. Maybe Jen had hurt his feelings by not paying enough attention to him or something. Instead of snuggling on the couch to watch TV, she'd sat alone at the kitchen table to put together some trailers for her show. She finally felt like she had enough footage for a couple of episodes, and she knew making a trailer for each planned episode was a sure way to know if she had a cohesive story. She had her website ready to launch and planned a few tweets to let her followers know something was coming. She planned a soft launch, not being able to go whole hog and lay out big money for advertising. She'd have to build her audience organically, though hopefully quickly enough to earn a little money before winter, or what passed for winter in Texas.

"Hey, what are you doing over there?" Tanner had asked, once he got her attention and she took off her headphones.

She explained what she was doing, and he nodded, then said he'd leave her alone and went out to make the rounds, check that everything was battened down and secure for the night, that there weren't any random vandalizers hiding in the bushes. He was gone longer than usual. So long that Jen had crawled into bed to wait for him.

She must have fallen asleep, because she woke up when he slid in next to her, but he didn't move to take her in his arms as he usually did. So she turned to him and kissed him. What followed was the sweetest, most tender sex they'd ever had, and they'd drifted off to sleep shortly thereafter.

Sometime in the middle of the night, Tanner woke her with his thrashing and cursing. It was his first nightmare since he'd been staying with her, and as she thought about it now, she was worried.

Something was wrong. She'd asked him this morning before he left for work, but he just said, "What? Nothing's wrong," but he hadn't kissed her goodbye. He just left.

Laundry gathered, storm brewing, Jen checked on the

livestock one more time and went inside to post her show teasers on YouTube.

———————————

Tanner gathered his purchases and got out of the truck. He looked up at the sky. There was definitely a storm brewing, but he thought it was far enough away that if he hurried, he could get his work done before he got wet.

He waved at the camper, where he could see Trixie at the window, barking in joy at his arrival. Jen was oblivious. She had her headphones on, eyes fixed intently on the screen of her laptop as she worked away at her project.

Her project. He knew that, in addition to getting her own show off the ground, she felt guilty about leaving the show she'd had with her mom and was troubled about her mom and this Brock jerk, who sounded like one more asshole there to take advantage of a good woman.

He'd been thinking about all of that recently, wishing there were some way he could lighten her load. He'd even had a nightmare about Jen—that he was running around trying to keep insurgents from hurting her, but every time he shot at one, he left a big hole in the wall for more to sneak through. When he'd left her this morning, bleary-eyed from lack of sleep, he'd noticed she had her own dark circles—caused by him and his damned nightmares.

The last thing he wanted was to add to her problems. He shouldn't have come back here with Trixie last week. Yeah, Jen would probably—would definitely—still have hurt feelings, and that would be his fault, and the past week had been great—a glimpse of what could be, if only…if only he weren't so damaged. Bringing his crap to a relationship was just irresponsible and selfish.

Well, he couldn't undo the past week, but he could make sure she was safe from here on out. He got to work and had just finished up, taking care of his trash and putting his tools back in the truck, when the first raindrop fell.

He dashed toward the camper, just as Jen opened the door and said, "Hey! You're here... Why didn't you come in?"

He stepped inside and shut the door behind himself. "I'm in now. I wanted to get some stuff done before the storm hit."

"What did you do?" she asked, looking out through the window.

"Something I should have done a while ago. Unlock your phone and give it to me for a minute."

She looked at him funny, but did as he asked.

He found the app he needed and downloaded it, entered the numbers he'd written on his hand, and pressed a few more buttons... "Here. Watch this." He pushed the first button, and a light over the barn came on. He pushed it again and it went out.

"What is this? Remote control lights?" she asked.

"Remote control all kinds of things," he told her. "It's a security system for the whole farm. There are two cameras—one from the barn, looking toward the camper"—he showed her how to access the screen that did, indeed, show the camper—"and one from the camper toward the animals. Everything has motion sensors, which you can override to work remotely, turn on and off whenever you want. You can check on things from anywhere, and it will let you know if something happens."

"Wow. That's...that's a lot. How much did you spend? Let me pay you back."

"No. Not necessary. I've got the money, and...I'll feel better if I know you're safe while you're here alone."

She looked at him funny. "What's going on?"

"Nothing," he lied, worried that he'd given too much away, but he wasn't quite ready. He was a selfish bastard, but he wanted just a little more time.

His cell phone rang, saving him from those searching, probing eyes.

"Hello? Hey, Lizzie," he said into the phone.

"Hey, Tanner. Sorry to bother you while you're with your Jen."

"She's not my— What's up?" he asked.

"I just wanted to make sure you invited *your Jen* to the adoption ceremony. Tell her to bring Trixie. Even though she's already officially Trixie's human, we'll add them to the program."

Crap. He'd forgotten all about that. "Yeah, okay, I guess."

"You guess?" Lizzie laughed. "Maybe I should have called your Jen myself instead of putting you in charge."

"She's not—" *She* was looking at him right now, wondering what the hell was going on. "Yeah, okay. I'll take care of it." He said goodbye and hung up.

"What was that about?" Jen asked when he had his phone back in his pocket.

"Lizzie was reminding me to invite you to our dog/handler graduation and adoption ceremony Sunday after this one. It's kind of a big deal, I guess."

"Kind of?" Jen laughed. "It's kind of the whole point of things, isn't it?"

"Yeah, it is. But anyway, she wants to include you and Trixie."

"Oh. Wow. That's…that's nice." She bent down to Trixie, who was under the table, and said, "We'll even get our hair done and a pedicure. At least Trixie will." She straightened. "Now what was all that 'she's not' stuff?"

"Huh?"

"You kept saying 'she's not…'"

Oh. "It's stupid," he said, shaking his head.

"What? Come on, tell me," she insisted.

Well, hell. He shouldn't tell her, but instead, he opened his mouth. "They—Lizzie and Emma—keep teasing me and referring to you as *my* Jen, which is ironic because they're the die-hard feminists who remind everyone who needs reminding that women are not objects to be owned, so…" He let his voice trail off with a shrug.

Jen had those big brown eyes fixed on him.

"See? I told you it was stupid. As if—"

"I'd like to be your Jen," she said, cheeks pink. "I kinda thought we were getting there. Had gotten there. Except—"

He shook his head and looked down. "You're right. It's not a good idea." He realized he was rubbing the scars on his jaw and shoved his hand into his pocket.

"Wait, what?"

He took a deep breath. He was being a damned coward. He was cowardly and selfish for thinking he could come here one more time, have one more beer on Jen's mini patio, spend one more night in her arms, knowing it had to end. "You're going back to your life. Which is awesome. I'm so glad you're getting to do what you love and share it with the world. But I don't have a place in that."

"Why—why not?"

Trixie had come out from beneath the table and had begun to pace nervously between them. Tanner wanted to scoop her furry little body up and hold on to her, but he needed to get through this and get out.

"Listen, Jen," he said, "I'm a mess. My life up to now, up until you came into it, my life has been pointless, when I wasn't destroying other people's lives. I've screwed up almost everything I've ever tried to do, and I hurt people. Good people who don't deserve it."

"What are you talking about? Bullet? Your parents, because you think you disappointed them?"

His laugh was as bitter as the bile he felt in his veins. "You have no idea."

"Then tell me. Don't I deserve to know?"

"No. It's really better that you don't. Call me shallow, but I'd rather you just think I'm an ass than give you the facts to prove it."

Her eyes were filling with tears, and her cheeks were getting blotchy, and he hated himself more than he'd ever thought he could. He wished more than life that he could be the man she needed him to be. He *loved* her, damn it.

Which was why he had to go.

"Listen, Jen... Being with you has been pretty awesome, you know? You...you're a great person, and your life is just going to get better and better because you deserve it. But I've got some baggage and...I just think it's better if we end things here on a high note."

"This is a high note?" she asked. "You standing in my kitchen breaking my heart is a high note?"

"Well, it was up until right now," he said, hating his own guts ten times more than she possibly could.

"I don't understand," she said.

"I don't want to hurt you."

"Well, you are. Hurting me," she said. "But I'm not going to beg. I'm not going to lie around and feel sorry for myself and think my life can't go on without you. Just so you know."

"I know," he said, feeling lower than dirt. He was hurting himself, too. But in the long run, he knew she'd be better off. "I'd better go."

Chapter 26

"Come on, Trixie. He's not coming back. Let's go have some ice cream, okay?" She coaxed the dog back from the lane, and they went inside to get their second batch of the day. It was good the blackberries were about exhausted because Jen's pants were getting a little tight.

She felt like she'd eaten her weight in junk food the past week, trying to stuff her feelings about Tanner. She still didn't understand what she'd done to drive him away. She'd been back over it again and again, but nothing came up. Yeah, he gave her all that *we come from different places and I'm not worthy* bullshit, but she wasn't buying it.

She'd even gone so far as to invite Lizzie and Emma over for a chick movie night, trying to keep herself from going crazy until she saw Tanner again. She'd see him at the adoption ceremony, right? Surely he wouldn't avoid her? She just had to see him again. Look in his eyes and have him tell her one more time that he didn't want to be with her. Lizzie and Emma had come over, full of plans for the coming ceremony which sounded more like a big party to Jen, who tried to muster some enthusiasm. Then before she got to ask if they'd rather watch *Steel Magnolias* or *Beaches*, she burst into tears and started talking about Tanner.

The women were sympathetic but unhelpful. "He doesn't share much with anyone," Lizzie said. "He's all-in most of the time and participates in everything, but there's a point where he kind of shuts off. But that's not really unusual. Sometimes our veterans have a wall inside them they can't let down. A lot of times the dogs help with that, but not always."

And so Jen had spent a week feeling lost and confused and not at all interested in her homestead that was now producing a few small cherry tomatoes and would have at least three green beans ready to pick tomorrow. Which would be good because it would keep her busy for at least a minute or two while she *didn't* go to the big graduation ceremony at the ranch tomorrow.

The one bright spot in the week had been the arrival of six baby bunnies. They were still tiny pink squirmy things. Fortunately Ginger was a patient, trusting mother, because Jen couldn't stop herself from checking on them three or four times a day, and Trixie was very interested in the new smells in the bunny zone.

She and Trixie finished their ice cream, and Jen picked up her phone. She needed to call her mom because today was her big day.

"Hey, Mom, I just wanted to wish you good luck on your show today," Jen said.

"Oh, Jennifer, I appreciate this so much. I'm so nervous!"

"You're going to be fine. You're great at this stuff."

"But there will be live people calling in on the phone! I'm going to have to talk to them!"

Jen laughed. If there was one thing her mom was a pro at, it was talking to strangers. "Really? You're worried about *that*?"

Her mom laughed, too. "You're right. I'm just… Everything's so up in the air right now. I'm not sure this show's the right thing to do."

Jen was surprised. Her mom had seemed so certain and steady the last couple of times they'd spoken. "What changed?" she asked.

"I think maybe I did," Mom answered. "I need to tell you—and you have to promise not to say 'I told you so,' but I broke things off with Brock."

Jen was stunned. "What… How…"

"I don't trust him," Mom said matter-of-factly. "He'd take off at all hours and be gone forever and refuse to tell me where he went. All he'd say was that he was working to make my life better, but I'll tell you, my life was not better when I had to spend every minute worrying about what he was doing and who he was with. I'm not that girl anymore. So I told him I don't want to see him anymore."

Go, Mom. "Wow. What did he say?"

"He gave me some malarkey about how he was the best thing that ever happened to me, and that he'd show me how great he was and then I'd beg him to come back."

"Oh geez, Mom, that's...that's kinda scary."

"I know, and I promise that the next time I get swept off my feet, it won't be just for the sex. Although I don't even know if the sex was that great."

Jen felt her face screw up and was glad she wasn't FaceTiming with her mom. "You don't have to share—"

"I mean"—her mom went on as thought Jen hadn't spoken—"he did oral sex like he was eating watermelon, and no girl wants to feel like her lady parts are watermelon, do we?"

"I—"

"Oh well, I'm just glad to be done with him. And now I need to get off of here. I'm going to be late for my hair appointment, and then I have to meet the makeup lady. Are you going to watch the show?"

"I'm going to try," Jen said. She'd been so depressed that she hadn't even checked yet to see if she could get the channel here. Emma had invited her to her place in town to watch, because she had every channel ever invented to satisfy Marcus's sports and documentary habits. Emma wouldn't be there, though, because she'd be working with the veterans and their dogs at the ranch, doing some last-minute testing.

She wished her mother good luck, promised to call her later to hear all the behind-the-scenes stuff, then hung up.

She woke up her laptop, hoping to find she could access the show through her computer. It was bad enough she didn't have anyone to watch the show with; she'd hate to have to put on a bra and deodorant to go to someone else's house. The internet was slow, so she closed her fancy new security app since it was the middle of the day.

And then her laptop gave her the blue circle of death. She restarted things and waited for a reboot.

Trixie, who had been lounging under the table, came out and sniffed at the door.

"Do you need to go potty?" Jen asked, rising.

As she got closer to the door, Trixie started to growl and *bite* the doorknob. "Trixie! What's wrong with you? I'm coming, I'm coming!"

As soon as she opened the door, Trixie darted through the space before Jen could stop her. She heard a yelp of pain and saw the dog's body fly through the air.

"What the hell?" She went barreling outside without stopping to think that whoever had just kicked her dog was waiting for her.

"Hi, Jennifer," Brock said, looking for all the world like he'd just stepped out of a magazine ad for used cars. "I need a favor."

Tanner cursed himself for being a fool as he carried the saddle from the barn to the paddock. He'd finally admitted to Adam that he thought Bullet was ready to ride, and now he'd found himself about to saddle the old boy up to try to ride him.

"Hey, you want some help?" Rico asked. Eisenhower, the German shepherd he'd been paired up with, sat quietly at Rico's side, alert and waiting for a command. The dog's job now, until he was retired, was to help Rico do things that his prosthetic leg made difficult. Though Rico was fully mobile, he fatigued easily and was never completely pain-free. Eisenhower would fetch things from the refrigerator or find the remote or a phone. Another job was to keep Rico from being knocked off-balance in public spaces. He was a big, ferocious-looking guard dog who wouldn't hurt a fly but who would keep strangers at a distance.

The really cool thing Eisenhower could do, however, was to remind Rico to take his meds. Three times a day, no matter where they were, a bell on the dog's collar would ring, and Eisenhower would nudge Rico until he got out his packet of medicine, opened it, and gave Eisenhower the treat at the bottom of the container.

When Tanner learned that this was one of Eisenhower's most important jobs, he was stunned. He had no idea that the attack that had taken Rico's leg had also knocked his brain around enough that he sometimes had seizures. Fortunately, the medicine he took was both relatively mild and effective, so he was able to live his life fairly normally—although whatever *normal* meant was up in the air.

Right now, Tanner wanted to tell Rico that he did need his help. He wanted to ask the man to give him a leg up and to hold Bullet's reins while Tanner cinched the saddle. Unfortunately, Bullet wasn't too fond of any dog larger than about forty pounds. Trixie was his limit, which was unfortunate because there were a hell of a lot of big dogs at his new home. That was something Tanner would have plenty of time to work on, now that he was back in his tiny bunkhouse room, feeling miserable. It was crazy how much he missed Jen.

"Thanks, but I think I need you to have both hands free to call 911 here in a few minutes."

Rico laughed, but Tanner was only half kidding.

He walked up to the horse, soothing Bullet with his voice, telling him it was all going to be fine, they were just going for a little ride like old times. But the whole time his heart was racing and his chest felt tight. He was sweating like he'd run a marathon in the Amazon jungle. And he'd promised Adam he'd get on Bullet today and ride him. It wasn't a do-or-die thing—he knew Adam would give him more time if he really needed it—but the fact was, it wasn't Bullet who was the problem. It was Tanner.

The last time he'd ridden this horse, which had been shortly after being released from the hospital, he'd been thrown and injured badly enough that he had to go back to the hospital for several weeks. He shouldn't have been riding in the first place—he was still healing from a round of skin grafts—but when he'd gotten home, after the crap he'd seen and done, he just wanted to do something that had once given him pleasure.

But within five minutes of getting back in the saddle, a snake had spooked Bullet, who reared up and dumped Tanner. It messed up man and horse.

Both had needed Tanner to get right back in the saddle, but with his new skin torn and bleeding, he physically couldn't do it. Mentally, he really couldn't.

A month later, when he'd healed and been given the go-ahead, he'd taken the horse out of his stall, saddled him up, and stood there sweating and breathing so fast he blacked out. He came to as he hit the ground and scared the horse half to death. It was a miracle old Bullet hadn't trampled him.

And now, a couple of years after the last time he'd tried to ride, he was going to force himself to get on the horse. He knew he was a chickenshit coward. *Knew* it. Had proof in the ruined lives he'd left in his wake, but he had to do this today. Not so Adam would let him keep Bullet here at the ranch, but so he knew he had a shot at someday, somehow, becoming a better man.

Lord knew he wasn't there yet. He'd spent the past week tossing and turning, trying to sleep, only to dream of fires and screams and explosions. He knew the resurgence of nightmares was because he'd screwed up and gotten involved with Jen. He'd gone and fallen in love with her when he knew he couldn't be with her long-term. He'd hurt her, because she thought he'd broken her heart, but she'd be fine. She just needed to look around the world and realize that there were a million better fish in the sea. She'd forget Tanner the minute she met someone new.

Now Tanner believed that if he could ride Bullet again, if he could overcome his fear, shove it down and away, he'd be able to find a new purpose. One that wasn't about doing the books or anything Jake couldn't do alone, but about being a contributing member of the team. He didn't know when he'd changed his mind about what Adam wanted him to do. It had been gradual, an insidious little germ that had gotten in his brain and multiplied in spite of his best efforts to stop wanting things. And he did want to ride. Didn't he?

"So are you gonna do this or what?" Rico asked from the other side of the paddock fence.

Bullet swung his head around, looking at Tanner with one enormous liquid black eye. Tanner knew this wasn't going to go well, but he was going to try anyway. He flipped the stirrup down and gathered the reins, hoping that his shaking wasn't visible to anyone but himself. He grabbed the saddle horn and lifted his foot.

Bullet snorted and sidled away, rearing when Tanner tried to calm him.

For a few minutes, Tanner spoke softly but firmly to the horse, hoping he sounded more confident to Bullet than he did to himself. He once again lifted his foot and this time got it in the stirrup and began to pull himself up before Bullet snorted and bucked, tossing Tanner onto the hard ground.

"You okay, man?" Rico called. "You sure this is a good idea?"

Tanner shook his head. "I thought he was ready, but I guess we'd better wait and try again another day." Another day like the fifth of Octemer.

"Tanner! Oh my God, Tanner!" He turned to see Lizzie running across the yard, a limp and bloody Trixie in her arms.

Chapter 27

"BROCK, THIS ISN'T THE WAY TO IMPRESS MY MOM," JEN SAID, trying to keep the pleading note from her voice, also trying not to think about the fact that she was in a car with a psychopath—sociopath—whatever, badguyopath. And every true-crime story she'd ever read or listened to said you should never get in the car with a kidnapper. But here she was. Hands cuffed and feet tied, buckled into the passenger seat of the green Prius.

"When did you get this car?" she asked. "It's an interesting choice."

"Maybe it's best if you shut up now," Brock said in a pleasant tone Jen had never heard, which was extra creepy. He went on, all singsongy, "I put up with you because your mother loves you, and I was glad to see you go because then your mother loved me, but she seems to think she needs a break because she says I drove you away, so I'm bringing your stupid ass back so she can see I'm on her side."

Maybe this wouldn't be so bad if she just sucked it up and rode to Austin with him, got to her mom, and then called the police, but Brock reeked of whiskey, and he had a bottle under the front seat that he'd opened and swigged from before starting the car.

She had to find a way to either convince him to stop or... something. Dying in a head-on collision with a semitractor trailer wasn't on her agenda for the day.

He started to turn left out of her lane instead of right, and she said, "Go the other way. You need to go right."

"How do I know you're telling me to go the right direction?" he asked. "Why should I believe you?"

"Because if I can't get you to let me go, I want to make sure we get to Austin." Or at least somewhere closer to Big Chance. Where there would be people who might be able to help her. But this might also be putting her mom in danger. He had a gun and was off his rocker, and she didn't want to take him straight into the city where there were so many other people who could get hurt. She was so confused. She wasn't one of those people who got all laser focused and strong when their adrenaline surged. She was more the huddle-in-place-and-pray type.

If only there were some way to signal for help.

Her phone rang. *Well, that would sure be a way.* But the gun in Brock's hand suggested otherwise. "You answer that and you're dead," he told her. She didn't really think he'd kill her—showing up on her mom's doorstep with a dead Jen hopefully wasn't part of his plan—but she also didn't want to tempt him to take out her knees or anything theatrical and terrible. She sat still and felt the vibration of potential help calling—even if it was a telemarketer—and listened to the ringtone until it stopped. But then it started again.

"Damn it, can you turn that thing off?" he asked.

"I–I think so," Jen said, squirming to reach into her pocket with her bound hands. The call went to voicemail—the caller *hadn't* been an auto-warranty specialist—and she unlocked the phone, turned down the volume, and hit Redial—

"Now give it to me," Brock said, snatching the phone from her and tossing it onto the dashboard without looking at the display.

"Turn left right up here," she directed, although if she was really going to send him through Big Chance, she'd have kept them going straight. This was Forest Hill River Road, which ran parallel to Wild Wager Road and led to some sparsely wooded rises that were part of the Chance River watershed. Not a location with a lot of people who might come to Jen's rescue, but also not many people who could get hurt if he got crazy and started swerving or shooting.

And just maybe, if she could get away, she might be able to make it to the ranch for help. Of course, Brock would follow her, and then she'd be dragging a lunatic with a gun into the middle of a bunch of people and dogs.

Her best hope right now was to sit tight and hope Tanner picked up the call she'd just placed and listened.

"Don't you think this is a pretty road? It's Forest Hill River Road. Pretty fitting, don't you think?" Jen asked as loudly as she could without being too obvious that she was projecting to the phone on the dashboard.

"Wha?" Brock jerked the wheel. He was definitely drunk. Great.

"We're on Forest Hill River Road," she said, holding on to the Oh Jesus bar with both hands (since they were cuffed together—otherwise she'd have braced one on the dash) as they rounded a curve going way too fast. The hills seemed higher now that she was going up and down them. Right here, one side of the road went uphill, the other side went down, and Jen was on the downhill side.

"If you say so."

An armadillo chose that moment to waddle into their path. Jen gasped as Brock slammed on the brakes and whipped the steering wheel around, sending the car careening over the side of the road and down the hill.

The sound of the little car crashing through bushes and grass was drowned out by Brock's cursing—until they slid off the edge of an embankment. It seemed like hours as the car bounced, tilted, and landed upright, wedged into a crevasse of boulders and brush and God only knew what else.

For the longest moment, there was only the sound of breathing and the *tink-tink* of the engine cooling. But then the *tink-tink* was joined by a *drip-drip*. And a smell.

"Brock, we're leaking gas," she said. "We need to move away from this car."

"Don't you move," he ordered, still holding onto the gun.

"Okay. But do you smell the gas?"

"Shut up. Let me think."

Jen politely didn't snort in derision. Instead, she carefully slid her tied feet along the foot well, locating her phone which had bounced off the dashboard.

"Don't move," Brock told Jen again, then got out of the car to assess the damage.

While he had his back turned, she managed to reach the phone on the floor, but she barely had time to tuck it under the edge of her shirt before he turned back to her.

"One of the fucking wheels came off. We have to walk out of here. Get out of the car."

"You have to untie me," Jen said. "I can't get out. Hurry, before we blow up!" She didn't know if that was true—she thought she'd read an article about how cars rarely blow up after crashing—but she didn't want to take any chances. Besides, if Brock was in a hurry, he might make a mistake.

"Flip your legs up here," he ordered, holding the gun on her while he reached below the seat to retrieve his nearly full bottle of bourbon, then into the back seat for a backpack.

She squirmed, fighting gravity and the tiny interior to get her feet over the center console and into the driver's seat.

And then Brock had a dilemma. He had to put the gun down to untie her feet. Or...

"We're going to uncuff you long enough to get your feet free. When you're out of the car, the cuffs go back on."

Well, that wasn't going to help much, but at least it gave her a chance to put her phone in a pocket while she squirmed out of the car. She glanced about frantically for a way to escape, but his bullet would make it faster than her feet could take her anywhere. They stumbled a few steps away before he stopped to make her put the cuffs back on, and a few feet farther before he used the ropes that had tied her feet to fashion a harness with the knot on her back. He wrapped the other end around his wrist, so she was bound to him by a leash. As long as he held the other end, there was no way she could get loose.

He took a long slug of whiskey, slid the bottle into his pack, and looked around. Back the way they'd come, toward the road, would involve scaling a ridge covered with sticker bushes and boulders. "We need to find a car. If we go back up to the road, we could pretend you're hurt and when someone stops, hijack them."

"I don't think that's such a good idea," Jen said, the idea of involving innocent people in this crazy escapade making her stomach churn. Some poor rancher just driving along the road, stopping to help someone and getting his truck stolen—or worse, his life? Not happening. "What if we head that way, toward the east—" She pointed the other direction, through the woods, which she was pretty sure would eventually bring them closer to town. "There are farms and ranches that way. There should be cars."

The Big Chance Dog Rescue was that way, too, and while the thought of taking this unhinged creep anywhere near the dogs and people she'd come to care about made her ill, she also knew that if anyone was going to be able to help her, it would be Tanner and his friends. And there was the slightest chance he was listening to her on the open cell-phone line in her pocket.

"Okay. She's got him moving east into the woods off of Forest Hill River Road," Tanner said, pointing to the map Lizzie had pulled up on her phone. "Headed this way."

Everyone looked toward the vast expanse of wooded land that bordered the ranch. Some of that was part of the VanHook Historical and Recreation Park, but most of it was several square miles of private land used for hunting. Fortunately, nothing was in season at the moment, and it was the middle of the day, so they weren't likely to be mistaken for big game.

But they had other problems.

"Depending on where they went off the road, it's about two and a half, three miles as the crow flies," Lizzie said.

"It's not a straight shot, though. It's hilly, and there's a lot of dense brush in there," added Adam. "Lots of places to get lost."

"And snakes." That was Jake.

"It's hot as hell out there," Marcus said. "I wonder if they have water."

"I always carry water when I go kidnapping," Rico said, then, "Sorry, *shit*. I'm sorry," when everyone turned to stare at him.

Adam's phone rang.

Tanner's brain raced. It would likely be an hour, maybe two before Brock and Jen got through the woods, and anything could happen between now and then. How many lifetimes ago had they found poor Trixie? Then the phone calls to Jen that had gone to voicemail until she'd called him back. He'd answered her call, then realized she was in trouble—terrible trouble that he could have prevented. That interminable minute between screeching tires and silence, and her voice again. *Alive*. She was okay.

At least for the moment.

The blood on Trixie's fur was from a small cut on her head which wasn't deep or long, so they'd cleaned her up and gotten her a long drink of water. She seemed back to normal except that she hadn't strayed more than a couple of feet from Tanner since she'd come back. Emma had checked her out and said she seemed fine, just exhausted from her long trip in the heat of the day.

Adam put his phone away. "The sheriff's dealing with a domestic incident that turned into a murder-suicide on the other side of the county. He's calling in a SWAT team from the next county, but it's going to take them a while to get here."

"They could be here by then," Lizzie said.

"And we'll be ready." Adam gave Tanner a reassuring nod.

Tanner tried not to panic. This was worse than any mission he'd been on while deployed. He had training for that. He knew how to shut off his own reactions, channel the adrenaline into step-by-step actions and just do the job. This, though… What were you supposed to do when the woman you loved had been taken *hostage*? He couldn't detach from Jen and the fear he heard in her voice, the terror he felt at the thought she might get killed. And then to think that he was pacing around here chewing his damned fingernails while she suffered… That wasn't going to happen. He had to get in there and find her.

The phone he had glued to his ear came to life again.

"Shhh!" Tanner hit the speaker button and everyone gathered around to listen.

Jen said, "*It sure is hot out here.*"

There was a muffled response.

"*I don't suppose you have anything to drink besides whiskey in that pack, do you?*"

The unintelligible response was short and sharp.

"*Okay, but I really could use a drink. Do you think that's a creek up ahead, between those two tall rocks? I wonder if it will be safe to drink.*"

"She's telling us where she is!" Emma whispered. "Good girl, Jen!"

A few seconds later, Jen said, "*Be careful!*"

This was followed by a lot of yelling and confusion—pained cries from Brock and a protesting "*Hey! Ow, crap!*" from Jen.

Tanner's blood pressure rose a hundred points. Not being able to see what was happening made all of this so much worse because his imagination was painting a terrible picture.

He wanted to yell into the phone, to ask what was going on, but a moment later Jen told him.

"*Oh my God, Brock, are you okay? Your ankle… Is it broken?*"

Brock must have been much closer to Jen now than he'd been while they were walking because his response was loud and clear. "*It's just sprained. I'll be okay in a minute.*"

Jen said, "*Okay, but it's really swelling up fast. If you give me the handcuff key, I can make a splint—*"

"*You're not touching me. Shut up and let me think.*"

There was the sound of glass clinking, presumably the liquor bottle hitting the ground.

"*What time is it?*" Brock asked. "*I dropped my phone over there. Get it for me. And don't think you're going to get away with anything. I've still got this gun.*"

"*And you still have me tied up.*"

"*You can reach it,*" he said.

There was some shuffling and Jen said, "*Here.*"

"*I can't see it. The sun's too bright. Damned trees everywhere but right here. What time is it?*"

"*Four o'clock. Why?*"

"*Because Joanie's show is going to be on in an hour. And if I can't be there to show her how much I love her, we're going to call her instead.*"

There was a beat of silence, then Jen said, "*I really think we should get help for that ankle. Can't you call her from the emergency room?*"

"*I think you can shut. The fuck. Up. And sit. The fuck. Down.*"

There was a cry then, Jen's voice crying in pain.

Tanner couldn't take it anymore. "That's it. I'm going in."

"I understand your feelings," Marcus said, holding up a hand when Tanner would have pushed past him toward the barn. "But we can't just go running in there with guns blazing."

"*We* aren't. *I* am." Tanner had been unsure about almost everything he'd tried to do his whole life, and he wasn't sure he could rescue Jen. What he was sure of, however, was that if he didn't go in there and try, he'd never forgive himself.

"You don't even know where they are!"

"They're in a clearing near a creek with a couple of big rocks. They told us that." Rico held up his phone. "There's only one spot like that, according to Google Earth."

"Can you draw me a map while I go saddle Bullet?" Tanner asked.

"Yeah, but you can just take my phone. I know you have to keep your line open to listen to Jen."

"Thanks. What's your password, in case your phone goes to sleep?"

"Easy to remember. 80085."

"That's…"

"Boobs, right?" Rico grinned. But then he got serious. "You're going to ride the horse? Is that a good idea? You said you weren't sure he's ready," Rico said.

Tanner shook his head. "*I* wasn't ready. I am now."

Chapter 28

LYING IN THE DIRT—OR RATHER, ROCKS, WEEDS, AND DIRT—Jen took inventory of her body parts. Her right knee was going to have a hell of a bruise, as was her left elbow. These were the parts that had taken the brunt of it when Brock had yanked the rope that tied her to him. She had to give the jerk credit; he'd tied the rope in such a fashion that she couldn't reach the knot with her cuffed hands. And in spite of his inebriation and the ankle injury, he was still strong enough to both hold that gun on her and pull the rope hard enough to topple her over.

She gingerly pushed herself up and carefully maneuvered into a sitting position.

Brock watched her from the corner of his eye while he took a long pull on his liquor bottle and tried to shift to a more comfortable position.

Jen didn't think he'd be successful. His normally skinny white calf was swollen above the cuff of his sock and had already turned an angry red. She wasn't anything close to a doctor, but that much red so soon after an injury had to mean something in that leg was bleeding more than it should.

"Help me take off my shoe," Brock ordered now.

"I don't think that's a good idea, Brock. If something in there's broken, your shoe's probably kind of holding it all together."

"Well, it fucking hurts, so take it off, okay?"

"Okay, okay." She scooted down to his foot and carefully untied and loosened the laces.

Brock moved to lift his foot and toe the shoe off with his other foot, but screamed in pain. "It hurts. Oh damn, it really hurts."

"Brock, we need to get help. Let me call for help."

"No way. Just let me sit here for a few minutes."

She wasn't sure Brock was in danger of dying from a broken leg in the next few minutes, but if he didn't let her get help, they'd both die of dehydration and heat exhaustion soon enough.

There was a phone in her pocket, though. Was it still on? Was Tanner even listening? In the few seconds between retrieving the phone and getting it into her pocket, she thought it looked like there was a call in progress, but she wasn't sure. And it could have cut out by now. She needed to get it out and check, sneak a call in to 911. *Something*.

"It's time for Joanie's show. I can't fucking believe she wouldn't let me come with her. But when I call her, when she sees how I was willing to go to such lengths to bring your sorry ass to her, to make her happy, she'll come get us." He had to put the gun down to use both hands, one to shade the sun's glare from the screen and one to push buttons and hold it.

Jen was tempted to try to kick the gun away, but he was still sober enough to put it on his far side, so she'd have to stand up to get to it, and he'd be able to grab the gun and shoot her before she disarmed him.

It's okay, she told herself. *You can wait him out. Tanner will find you.*

But what if he didn't? What if he'd sent her call to voicemail? He already told her he didn't want to be with her, so he might have been willing to cut ties to the point of ignoring her calls.

Don't let that crap drag you down, Jen reminded herself. *You might never meet a guy who cares about you the way you want to be cared about, but you're not your mother. You do not need him to save you, literally or figuratively.*

Brock cursed and slammed his phone down on his thigh, which jarred his ankle, making him curse even louder. "Bitch won't take my calls. Sending them straight to voicemail. After everything I've done for her." He uncapped his booze and took another big drink.

Oh great. She and Brock were in the same *But why won't you answer my calls?* brain space.

Well, Jen was nothing if not a great rationalizer, so she said, "She probably can't answer while she's getting ready to go on the air. Maybe you can get the show on your phone."

Brock blinked at Jen, then looked at his phone. Then he tossed it to her and picked up his gun. "Do it for me. No funny business."

Okay, so he'd reached the point of being too drunk to browse the internet, though he still had the use of his gun hand. She could work with that. If they could reach her, Jen's mom would hear how messed up Brock was and find a way to send help.

Jen managed to find the show, the overly cheery voice of Misty Marvin herself saying, "In just a few minutes, we've got a very special program planned, so get those phones charged and make sure your credit cards are handy because you're about to have ringside seats to a brand-new exclusive product line from the creator of *Homemade with Joanie*—Joanie Greene!"

Jen was surprised at the pang of sorrow she felt hearing *Homemade* announced without her name in the title. She really, really missed her mom right now.

"Gimme that," Brock said, then "How the hell am I supposed to watch this and call her at the same time?"

Jen mentally rolled her eyes. "Maybe we can wait until they say it's time to call, then we can switch to the phone app."

Brock closed one eye and squinted at her suspiciously, holding the muzzle of his gun to Jen's temple. "If you screw this up, I'm going to screw *you* up."

Jen had no doubt that he meant exactly what he said.

Tanner dismounted from Bullet when he was about a hundred yards from the clearing Jen had described so he could proceed on foot. This wasn't a good time to charge in like, well, the cavalry because he'd likely get everyone shot.

"Thanks, buddy," he murmured to Bullet, who blew out a big horsey breath and took the brim of Tanner's hat between his teeth, tossing it on the ground. In spite of how worried he was about Jen, he had to stop and hug the horse's neck, just for a second. One of Bullet's favorite games from *before* was to take Tanner's hat and toss it aside. "Be good. I'll be back as soon as I can."

It wasn't steep terrain but it was rocky, and there was a lot of brush that would snap and crackle with each misplaced footstep, so it was slow going. He'd put the phone in his pocket, hoping the battery wouldn't die on him. He hadn't been able to hear much over Bullet's hoof steps, and now there was some sort of interference coming in because he could hear faint music like from a commercial or something. Damn this outer-nowhere cell phone reception.

He carried a rifle, a semiautomatic pistol, and enough ammo for a month-long siege. Nothing like getting outfitted for a mission by a crew of Army Rangers and a handful of war fighters from other branches, all champing at the bit to get involved. Adam had taken charge, however, and decided he and Rico would come in on foot behind Tanner and provide backup, while everyone else would stay at the ranch in case they'd gotten the location wrong and needed to redeploy.

He reached the creek Jen described and worked his way up the opposite embankment until he heard... *What was that?* It was the same broadcast he was getting over his phone. It wasn't interference; they were watching TV through a phone. He clicked off his own phone in time to hear a painfully perky woman introducing "a very special guest with a very special brand of makerism."

"*New here to our Shopping Extravaganza Network audience is Ms. Joanie Greene!*"

"*Hi, everyone,*" a woman, presumably Jen's mother, said. "*Thanks so much for having me.*"

Hoping Brock's attention was on the screen and not his surroundings, Tanner hazarded a glance over the edge of the rise and saw that Jen and Brock were about fifty yards away. She appeared to be okay, and he didn't give a shit how Brock was except as it applied to how easily Tanner could get Jen away from him. Considering there was a gun in the hand not occupied with the phone, it wasn't likely to be a walk in the park.

"Dial," Brock said, and held the gun up as he passed the phone to Jen.

Jen thought for a split second about texting her mom instead of calling, but Brock was wound so tightly, watching her every move, that she didn't want to take a chance. If they called and got Joanie on the line, she'd know something was wrong because she'd know Jen would never, ever go anywhere willingly with Brock, especially after Joanie told her she'd ditched him.

It took her a couple of tries because she was so scared, her brain wouldn't hold the phone number beyond 1–800. Finally, she wrote the digits in the dirt and managed to get them dialed. She put the phone on speaker, but the line was busy. She tried again. Again, same result.

"Hurry up!" Brock ordered.

"I'm trying but it's not going through."

The third time was the charm. Except the call went through to a prerecorded message. "Our system will not accept calls from this number. If you feel you have been blocked in error, please visit the customer-service web page at—"

"Are you kidding me?" Brock was incredulous, and while Jen was disappointed, too, she had to give her mom kudos for thinking ahead. It would really suck to get a phone call from your skeevy ex while you were on live TV. "Put it back on the show," Brock ordered, taking another slug from his bottle.

The only thing Jen could think to do was to wait for Brock to drink until he passed out, and then somehow get out of this harness. At least she knew there was no way he could follow her. That leg was seriously messed up. She was afraid he might have screwed up his circulation because the red staining his leg earlier was beginning to darken. What happened if you lost the blood supply to your leg? The affected parts would die from lack of oxygen, and then you'd probably go into septic shock or gangrene or whatever and die a horribly agonizing death. Jen didn't want that to happen to Brock. Even though he was an evil pig, she didn't wish suffering and death on him. How long would it take? Would they both die of thirst and sunburn first? And what if Tanner was the one to find her bloated, decomposing body? Would he blame himself? Could she freak herself out any more completely?

She shook her head and focused on her mom's show.

Jen was between Tanner and Brock. Tanner was a good shot, but not that good. Besides, lethal force was a last resort. Not so much because Tanner didn't want to kill the monster who held his woman in jeopardy but because he didn't want Jen to have to live for one second with Brock's brains splattered on her body, or that image in her head. It was obvious Brock was focused more on watching Joanie at the moment than shooting anyone. Of course, Tanner wasn't a hostage negotiation specialist, so what did he know? He'd driven the damned vehicle when his squad went on patrol.

The one thing he did know was that the woman he loved was in danger, and he was going to save her if it was the last thing he did.

They were next to one of the big rocks Jen had mentioned in her description of the place, so there was no way to come up behind the guy and get the gun away from him. Unless…

Tanner sized up the second big rock, a few feet away. If he could get up on the rock, he might just be able to jump down on Brock. A six-two, two-hundred-pound pissed-off soldier landing in his lap would definitely distract the asshole long enough for Jen to get away. But the way things were situated, he'd crush Jen on his way to crush Brock.

He thought about it for a couple more seconds, then carefully picked his way around to the other side of Brock's makeshift hideout.

Once he was in place, he pulled his phone from his pocket and checked. Grateful for the small miracles, he found that not only did he have reception, but he had some battery left. He tapped around on Google for a minute, spent another minute downloading an app for the shopping network, entered all of his personal information, including his PayPal account, and finally got to make a call.

He didn't think he'd get through, but surprisingly, his call was answered on the second ring.

"Hello, you're on Shopping Extravaganza!" he heard from the chipper call-center person. "I see you're a brand-new member! I bet you'd like to order one of Joanie's homemade soy candles, wouldn't you?"

"Actually," he said, keeping his voice low, "I'm a friend of Joanie's daughter, Jen—Jennifer—and I need to give her a very important message about Jen."

"What is your name, sir?"

"Tanner Beauchamp." He spelled his last name for her.

"And what is your message?"

"I—I'd like to deliver it directly to Ms. Greene. It's an important message from Jennifer."

"Hold on one moment, sir!"

Instead of elevator music, he heard the show while he was on hold. While he waited, the perky cohost said, "What do you know, Joanie! It seems we have a message from a very special person today."

"Is it Jen?" Joanie guessed, her voice sounding so hopeful that Tanner felt guilty.

"No," Ms. Perky said. "This might be even better. It's Jen's friend Tanner!"

There was silence while Jen gasped.

"Would you like to speak to her *friend*? Is he her *boy*friend?" the perky lady cooed.

Joanie was no fool, however, and she sounded suspicious when she said, "Jen didn't have a boyfriend the last time I spoke to her. What's the message?"

"Go ahead, caller!" Ms. Perky said.

Oh crap. He was on live.

"Uh, hi, Ms. Greene. My name's Tanner Beauchamp, and I'm a friend of Jen—Jennifer's."

Chapter 29

Jen wanted to cry and laugh at the same time. This whole ridiculous mess was getting nuttier by the moment. Now *Tanner* was chatting with Jen's mother on a shopping channel show.

"Who the fuck is that?" Brock threw his liquor bottle. It didn't break, but spilled some.

"Shh. Listen," Jen admonished him.

Joanie said, "*I don't know you. How do you know Jennifer?*"

Tanner, sweet Tanner, replied, "*I, ah...I live a few miles down the road and I've been helping her out on her homestead.*"

"*Oh! Are you one of those veterans from that dog place?*"

"*Yes, ma'am.*"

"*Wonderful! Jennifer told me about your place and what you're doing for other veterans. I thank you for your service both now and while you served our country.*"

"*Yes, ma'am,*" Tanner said.

"*You know, Jennifer told me all about her sweet little Trixie. I have to thank you for helping her out. I worry about her out there all alone.*"

There was a slight pause, and Jen could imagine Tanner wanting to tell her mom that she was right to worry. That Brock had shown up and taken her hostage.

Instead, he said, "*She's a fine woman, Ms. Greene, and she's doing an amazing job out there, putting together a homestead anyone would be proud to live on.*"

Jen's heart clenched. Did he really think that?

"Aww, dats so sweet," Brock mocked. "What's he trying to do? Get in your mom's pants too? He got a mother-daughter fantasy?"

"Shut up, Brock," Jen snapped. She'd really had just about as much as she could take of him, gun and all.

Meanwhile, the shopping network host was having a terrible time regaining control of her show.

"*Well, isn't that just lovely?*" the woman said. "*You'll have to get Jennifer to come to our show and tell us all about her exploits, won't you?*"

Tanner and Joanie ignored her.

"*What moved you to call today?*" Joanie asked.

"*Well, Ms. Greene, I have a problem, and I need your help.*"

"*Oh my goodness, look at those phone lines lighting up!*" the host said. "*We've got a lot of people waiting to talk to you about these lovely candles you've brought today.*"

"*How can I help you, Tanner?*" Joanie asked.

"*I'm having a little trouble finding Jen today. See, Trixie wandered into the ranch this afternoon, and when I tried to take her home, Jen wasn't there.*"

Trixie was okay. Jen hadn't allowed herself to think about the dog, fearing the worst, but if Trixie really did show up at the ranch, that must mean she was fine. And Tanner knew Jen was missing. He'd have seen her car sitting next to the barn, and even if he didn't know where she was, he knew she wasn't where she should be.

"*What's your point, young man?*" asked an exasperated host. "*We're going to have to move on here.*"

"*I need you to give Jen a message,*" Tanner said.

"*Oh, that's so sweet!*" Joanie exclaimed. "*You are her boyfriend, aren't you?*"

"*I… Not exactly.*"

Jen's heart sank, although why it did was anyone's guess. Yeah, she'd wanted him to be her boyfriend, even though she didn't have time for a boyfriend, certainly didn't *need* one.

"*But you care for her, right?*"

"*I'm…*"

Jen held her breath, waiting for him to finish with "Just a friend."

Tanner's voice was a little froggy and she had to strain to hear him say: "*I'm in love with her.*"

Jen's heart beat so loudly, she almost missed the rest of it.

"She's like a cool stream flowing next to a couple of big ugly rocks."
He was in love with her? What...?

She ran the rest of his words through her head. *He knew where she was. Holy macaroni.* He knew. He was going to save her.

"Well, that's certainly an interesting analogy," the host said. *"But for the last time, what's your message?"*

"Tell her I said: Duck!"

Jen didn't exactly duck, she kind of leaned away and looked around, but as she did, Brock cursed and yanked on the rope harness, pulling her over onto her side, knocking the breath from her body. Something hit Jen's shoulder, and Brock wasn't just cursing, he was screaming bloody murder because the thing that hit her shoulder was an elbow or a knee belonging to a very angry man who'd also landed on Brock. Jen got to her feet and pulled the rope wrapped around Brock's flailing arm, tugging to free herself and keeping him from using both hands to fight back as Tanner grappled with him. The rope loosened, and she scrambled out of the way, nudging the gun out of grabbing distance. Brock thrashed and howled as Tanner fought to subdue him, finally flipping him over and sitting on the backs of his legs while he wrenched Brock's arms behind him and secured them with zip ties he pulled from somewhere.

As soon as Brock was secure, whimpering facedown into the dust, Tanner rose and picked up the gun. He pulled and pushed some things until a bullet popped out of the top and the thingy that held all of the other bullets was in his other hand, then he put it all in his jean pocket.

Finally, he looked at Jen.

"Hi," she said, while he ran a hand through his hair and brushed some of the dust from his jeans.

"Hey," he said back. "Are you okay?"

She nodded, but said, "Probably not. I mean, I think I'm okay right now, but I'm pretty sure I'm going to have a meltdown later."

"Adrenaline. That's normal. Make sure you drink lots of water and eat something so you don't go into shock."

"What about me? What about my shock?" Brock spat out.

"We'll let the sheriff deal with you," Tanner said.

Brock began muttering about lawsuits and civil rights, but neither Jen nor Tanner paid him any attention.

"*And we'll be back in just a few moments while we tell you about what's coming up next!*" came from Brock's phone, which was still streaming.

"My mom's got to be freaking out," Jen said as her own phone buzzed in her pocket. She dug it out and put it to her ear. Tanner walked a few feet away and pulled out his own phone and pushed some buttons. "Hi, Mom?"

"What on earth is going on there?" her mom asked. "Are you okay? What happened?"

"Oh geez. So much. But I'm okay."

"Tell me."

"Brock was holding me hostage out in the middle of the woods, and Tanner came from nowhere to jump down on Brock and now he's tied up and I guess the police are coming."

"Oh my God," Joanie moaned. "He *hurt* you? Did Brock hurt you?"

"I'm okay," Jen said again, because what else could she say? "Don't you have a show to do?"

"I think that ship just sailed," her mom said.

"Oh, no. I'm so sorry. I mean, it's not my fault, but it's because of me—"

"Stop," Joanie said.

Jen stopped.

"I don't want to do this stupid show anyway. You're right. The crap Brock ordered is just that. Crap."

"Oh. Well, that's okay then," Jen said. "I mean, it's not okay, because… Oh, Mom, I was so scared!" She started blubbering and hiccupping and sobbing and making no sense at all, and her mom was trying so hard to help her calm down to tell the story but it wasn't helping—

Tanner took the phone from her hand and led her to a boulder, where he urged her to sit as he said, "Hi, Ms. Greene? It's Tanner again." He explained what had happened, and what was going to happen next, and assured Joanie that Jen would be fine, that she was safe.

As he talked, answered questions, and made assurances, Jen gathered herself and took a few deep breaths. She accepted a bottle of water that Tanner had brought with him and drank about three-quarters of it in one gulp.

"Sure, Ms. Greene. Yeah, I think she can talk now." Tanner handed Jen the phone. He said he had to see about…something, but Jen didn't catch it all because her mom was talking a mile a minute.

"I'm so sorry this happened to you! Oh, that jerk. I just want to kick his stupid self all the way to hell."

"I think he's suffering pretty well as it is," Jen said, glancing over at Brock who seemed to be in some sort of a trance, staring at nothing as tears ran from the corners of his eyes to pool in the dirt below his head.

"Are you sure you're okay?" her mom asked about sixteen times, then finally said, "Okay. I guess I have to deal with the people here. You have a good guy there, though. You hang on to him."

"Yeah. Okay," Jen said, watching Tanner walk back up the hill he'd apparently gone down, Bullet pacing patiently behind him. "I'll call you when I get home."

"I love you, punkin," Joanie said.

"Love you too."

Jen put her phone in her pocket and wondered at Tanner walking with his horse like he did that all the time. "Is that how you got here? On Bullet?"

"Yeah," he said, rubbing the bridge of Bullet's nose. "Seemed we needed a little motivation to get back together."

"Is that right?" She smiled, because it also seemed like this little escapade might have brought her and Tanner back together, too.

Chapter 30

Tanner called Adam and asked him to let everyone know that Jen was okay and that Brock was secured. Adam messaged a few minutes later that the sheriff was on his way. Then while Tanner was going to retrieve Bullet, he got a call from Lizzie.

"Omigod, Tanner. You're not going to believe this. You're viral."

"What? Why?"

"Because everyone who was interested in Jen's perfectly adequate breasts has been wondering what happened to her, some of these people were watching Joanie on the shopping show, and when you called in, they recorded it all. Someone posted it on Facebook, and there are already memes of you. I didn't know you were a high-school rodeo star."

"Why would anyone care about me?" he asked.

"Because you're like a real-life romantic hero. You put yourself out there on live TV to rescue your lady love."

Oh, no. He didn't deserve to be considered a hero. Especially not Jen's hero. And he should have never said he loved Jen, because even though it was true, it would be harder to walk away from her.

He said goodbye to Lizzie and led Bullet into the clearing.

Jen looked up and smiled at him like he'd hung the moon, and it made his stomach clench because while he'd do almost anything to see that smile from her as often as he could, he was even more sure now that was impossible.

"Hey," he said as she approached him and Bullet, who lowered his head and allowed her to stroke his neck. Actually hung his head over her shoulder like he was hugging her.

Jen beamed. "I think he likes me. Good thing, huh?"

How could he not like you? Tanner wanted to ask. Instead, he said, "The sheriff will be here in a couple of minutes. I'm going to get out of here as soon as he shows up."

"Why?"

"I need to get Bullet back to the ranch before the sun sets." Which was true—*ish*. He'd packed some serious flashlight power when he'd headed out, enough to assure his horse safe footing all the way back to the ranch. But he needed to go for himself even more. Soon. He'd commented on Jen's adrenaline rush, but hadn't let on that his own was messing him up. His emotions had just started the decline from kicking-ass elation to...something else. If he stayed here any longer, he'd be a weeping mess.

Jen narrowed her eyes at him. "Is that the only reason? Your horse?"

He tried to look innocent, he really did, but he'd never been innocent a day in his life, and she wasn't buying what he was trying to sell.

"You know the sheriff's going to want to take a statement, right?" she asked.

"Tell him I'll call him in the morning." He didn't know what else to say. His throat was tight, and his eyes were beginning to sting. "I'm, um, glad you're okay."

"You're glad I'm okay? What does that mean? I'm glad we're both okay, but what's next?"

"I told you, the sheriff will be here..."

"What about us?"

He pushed out a breath. "There is no 'us.'"

"What happened to 'I'm in love with her'?" she asked, stepping back from Bullet and putting her hands on her hips, eyes shooting fire. She'd never been so damned beautiful, the sun's last rays glinting off of her hair, her skin, her *her*. "And that other thing. The thing about the cool stream and rocks? That was almost poetic!"

"That was me letting you know I was in the vicinity."

She didn't say anything, just glared.

He cleared his throat. "Listen. Twitter's apparently already… twittering about you. *People* and *Us Weekly* are going to be right behind *BuzzFeed* and *Huffington Post* trying to get to you, and you don't want me anywhere in your vicinity when that happens."

"Tell me why not?" She actually stamped her foot.

"Because, as shitty as this situation was, as terrible as it could have turned out, it's turning into your big break. Your brand or aesthetic or whatever is going to be off the charts."

She tilted her head and said, "Did you just use the word 'aesthetic'?"

He flapped a hand at the air. "I read something about that when I looked you up when you first got here."

"So what's that got to do with you running away right now?"

"Because I'm bad news. Bad shit follows me wherever I go, and I'll do something to ruin you, or your career, or someone you love—"

"I don't understand," Jen said, more softly now, taking a step toward him, reaching to put a hand on his arm, but if she touched him now… He backed up out of her reach and tried to ignore the hurt that crossed her face.

"I have killed people."

"You were in a *war*."

"Where I killed most of my squad."

"How?" She crossed her arms and tapped her foot, like she was waiting for him to lie.

He didn't. "On that last patrol, there were five of us in my vehicle. I was driving. We were on our way back to the base, and there was a lot of traffic in the street we were supposed to be going down. We had a specific route to take, which had other patrols here and there to provide security for teams that were in transit. But I was in a hurry to get back because I was tired, I had to take a leak, and I wanted to see an LSU Tigers game that I had money on. I took a shortcut. Rico kept saying, 'You're going to get us killed, man. You need to go back to the route,' but I ignored him. Because I wanted to watch a *basketball* game."

Jen wasn't tapping her foot now. She was as still as the rocks casting long shadows over the ground.

"I didn't go back to the scheduled route, and we got a grenade tossed right through the driver's side window. Landed in the lap of the man next to me—Lieutenant Steve Mulcahy. He was thirty, had just gotten news that his wife was expecting twins. There was almost nothing left of him to send home to her. Private Bobby Washington's head was crushed when we crashed into a house. Rico lost a leg. You know what happened to me, but that's what I deserve because it's always been about me and about what I want."

"You couldn't have known—"

"Bullshit. I knew it was dangerous. They told me not to go that way, but I went anyway."

Jen didn't say anything, but Tanner could see her formulating another argument about why it wasn't his fault or why he shouldn't blame himself.

"You want more?" he asked. "I killed my father. I'm the reason my mom's a widow and had to sell the ranch."

"What?"

"There's a little more to the story about all of that rodeo business." Tanner's neck was so tight he was afraid his head might pop off, but he had to get through this. "My junior year, the year I did win at the finals, I caught my father screwing the mother of one of my teammates. Everyone would go to these big rodeos and camp out, but usually only one parent for each kid would go because someone had to stay home and mind the farm, right? Well, my dad was such a big rodeo fan, my mom was always the one who stayed home. Turned out he was also a fan of Mrs. Chess. That was part of why I started acting like an idiot.

"But anyway, I kept the secret for many years, until I came home from blowing up my future in the army. I'd been such an ass to my fiancée that she dumped me, and I guess I was smarting from that because when my father came to visit me and said he'd do everything he could to help me get back on my feet and get back on Bullet so I could return to the rodeo, I said, 'Why, so you and Mrs. Chess can go at it again?' My mom was standing in the doorway to my room. I just didn't see her.

"My mother left him that night. The next day, my father took a shotgun out of the back of his truck, shoved the muzzle in his mouth, and pulled the trigger."

"Oh, Tanner." Jen's face was drawn, terrible in realization, making her look ten years older. He'd made that happen, too.

"There's more, about how he left her with almost nothing except a miserable excuse for a son, why she had to sell that ranch and buy a damned motor home to live in, but I think that's about enough, don't you?" He didn't wait to see the condemnation in her eyes, just mounted his horse. "I hear sirens, and those lights over there? That's Adam and Rico coming. I've got to go."

Tanner turned Bullet toward home. Well, toward the ranch, anyway. He wasn't sure if he had a home because now he was pretty sure the toxins that made up Tanner Beauchamp would soon poison everyone.

"Wait. Tanner." Jen stepped in front of Bullet and put a hand on the horse's neck, looking up at Tanner, imploring him, tempting him to dismount and take her in his arms. "I'm so sorry for all you went through, but you're not bad. You're good. Look at how much you've helped me!"

Tanner swallowed and with every bit of determination he could muster nudged Bullet so that her hand dropped off, and then ground out the worst thing he could think of to say. "Give it up, Jen. You don't want me. You just want someone to save you."

He clucked to his horse and started off without looking back, but he sure heard her next words. "Well, I sure as hell don't want you to be my white knight."

Chapter 31

Tanner had been right about the media storm. By the time Jen finished with the sheriff, got home, showered, and poured a glass of wine, every social media platform had something up. Jen and Tanner were both memes. There were pictures of her taken from that horrible perfectly adequate video, and someone had put together a TikTok rap remix of Tanner's quote about Jen being like a cool stream. And then, of course, she became a perfectly adequate stream.

The one that broke her heart the most, however, was footage—and how in the hell anyone could have found Big Chance and gotten a drone up that high that fast—of a shot of Tanner on Bullet, plodding into the sunset. It looked for all the world like Tanner was shaking. As in sobbing. The caption read: "Wholesome Homemade Princess Rejects Rodeo Bad Boy."

His words echoed through her brain: *You just want someone to save you.* Was he right? Was she the needy, pathetic person she'd sworn she'd never become?

Trixie's bark announced the arrival of Jen's mom. Trixie's bark, Angus's bleat, and the motion-sensor light and camera in the yard. Even though Brock and his stupid pranks were no longer a threat, Jen was still glad Tanner had installed the stuff.

Joanie blew through the front door of Jen's camper carrying snacks and drinks and a casserole. "The sheriff's cruiser is right behind me. Do you want me to tell him to go away?"

"No," Jen said, dragging herself to her feet. "I'll see what he wants." Surely she'd already told him everything. What else was there?

"Howdy, Ms. Greene," the deputy said. "Sorry to bother you

again tonight, but we found something in Brock's trunk and wanted to know if you recognize it." He opened the back door of his SUV and pulled out a five-gallon bucket.

Jen was terrified to look. Knowing Brock, it might be a severed head.

As the deputy approached, however, Jen heard scratching along the plastic walls. She looked in. "Mr. Bigfoot! You're back!"

She grabbed the turtle from the bucket and carried him over to check him out in better light near the camper. He waved his arms and legs in the air and opened his mouth as though saying "Feed me."

She thanked the deputy, tucked Mr. Bigfoot under one arm, and stepped inside the camper to grab some fresh grapes. "I'm not sure how to tell if you're dehydrated or anything, but if you don't eat these grapes, I'm taking you to see Doc Chance first thing tomorrow." She put Mr. Bigfoot in his tank and tossed in the grapes.

She walked back to the camper and invited her mom inside. She picked up her wine. "Here. I've got another glass for you."

"Put that wine down until you've had your supper," Joanie ordered. "And tell me *everything* about Tanner."

Jen tried to eat, but the tuna casserole—her favorite—tasted like sawdust. She did manage to choke down a 3 Musketeers bar, however.

As for telling her mom *everything* about Tanner, she only told her mom *almost* everything. She told her about how nice Tanner had been about being tackled on a dark and deserted road, about how he'd fixed her fence, installed her security system, and invited her to meet his friends.

"So why isn't he here now?" Joanie asked.

"He says he can't be with me because he's not some sort of perfect superhero guy. He's got stuff in his past that he seems to think makes him unsuitable. The war really messed him up, but it's not just that."

"Do you know what the stuff is?"

"Yeah."

"Is it bad?"

Jen thought about it. "It's bad. It's ugly. But it's not a deal breaker for me, and I think Tanner's put way too much of the responsibility for the things that happened on his own shoulders, if that makes any sense."

Joanie nodded. "Sure. He's got baggage. His is heavier than most. But he clearly cares for you. If you want him, go get him. Make him see that you want him."

"But that's not…that's not all. I think I've been too needy. I don't know if chasing after him is the right thing to do," Jen confessed. "It's so tempting to think he could not only be Mr. Right, but that he'd be the one to rescue me from myself, or whatever. I'm not going to—" She cut herself off and shook her head, but Joanie understood where she was going.

"You're not going to be me."

"I didn't mean—"

"Stop," Joanie said, putting her hand on Jen's knee and waiting until Jen met her eyes. "You are not me. You learned my lessons long before I did, but I've learned them. That's why—before I knew he was a crazy kidnapping stalker—I broke up with Brock. Because he was doing all of those things that I wanted guys to do for me back when I did that stuff."

Jen managed to follow that logic and nodded.

"Does he ever 'should' you?" Joanie asked.

"Huh?"

"Does he 'should' you? You know. Like, 'Hey, hon, you should clean the bathroom more often.' Or 'You shouldn't let the dog sit on your lap.' You know what I mean?"

Jen did. And he didn't. "He seems to be okay with who I am and what I want to do. He didn't even laugh when he saw I used kitchen utensils to make the fence taller."

"Well, maybe he should have laughed about that," Joanie said.

"True."

"Listen, I obviously don't have a template you should follow when it comes to relationships, but if you've found a guy who cares about you, and who you love right back, who makes you happy and most importantly lets you be you—then that might be a guy worth keeping around."

Jen thought about it, then nodded. "I'm not exactly sure how to make that happen."

Joanie hugged Jen and said, "I'm not sure, either, but I bet an opportunity will present itself if you just watch for it."

Chapter 32

"Okay, Bullet. Let me see that hoof one more time." Bullet reluctantly let Tanner lift his foot and take the pick to it. Tanner had cleaned the horse's hooves when they'd gotten back last night, but he'd ridden him again this morning and didn't want a stray pebble to ruin their renewed relationship. If only the rest of his life was so easily managed.

Had he done the right thing pushing Jen away? Yes. Definitely. He had to remember that he was saving himself a lifetime of heart-ache because eventually she'd realize she'd made a mistake by let-ting him into her life, and it would hurt even more later.

Although it hurt a hell of a lot now.

He was grateful to his friends at the ranch for not bringing up any of the crap that was going around the internet about Jen. Tanner had seen some of it. He wanted to make sure Jen was safe, that the trolls weren't ganging up on her too much. Though what he'd do if they were, he wasn't sure. He did know he'd sit at the end of her lane every night until forever to protect her if he needed to, and troll all the trolls while he was at it. He didn't really care what they said about him; he just didn't want anything to hurt Jen.

He didn't know if anyone knew exactly how ugly he'd been to Jen yesterday, but everyone had been tiptoeing around him. He knew Lizzie had spoken to Jen last night because she'd told Adam and Adam had told him. "I figure since you're not over there your-self, you should know that Jen's okay. Her mother drove out here for a few days."

Tanner was relieved to know this because he already felt lower than the junk he was digging out of Bullet's hooves, and he'd have worried about her being scared out there on her homestead.

He ran a comb through Bullet's mane again, though he should probably stop before the old guy regressed from attention overload. But damn. Tanner couldn't sit still. Jen had been invited to the graduation ceremony scheduled for tomorrow, and he suspected Lizzie and Emma had told her about tonight's pregraduation bonfire. He had no idea if she was going to show up, and what he'd do, what he should do, if she came. Pretend like they were casual acquaintances? Ignore her completely? Beg her to forget every negative thing she knew about him and ask her to take him back?

Bullet jerked his head, more than done with being fussed over.

"Hey, Beauchamp." Rico hiked across the yard, his prosthetic leg making his gait awkward but not slowing him down in the least. Eisenhower, off leash for the moment, trotted ahead of him. "Eisie, stop!" Rico warned, before the dog got too close to Tanner and Bullet, who was still not too sure about the big dogs. "So. Now that you're back in the saddle, so to speak, you gonna let me ride your horse?"

Tanner sighed. "Rico, it's just not a good idea. I don't think I could keep you safe."

"Jesus Christ, man. I'm not made of fucking glass. Hell, I've got fewer body parts than I started with—less of me to break. I trust you."

Tanner, who'd been on a razor's edge all day, snapped. "Why the hell would you trust me to keep you safe? I didn't do it in Afghanistan, why would I do it here?"

Rico blinked in confusion. "What are you talking about?"

Now it was Tanner's turn to be befuddled. "Because I got half of us killed, and you and I are...are..."

"Gimps?" Rico suggested, eyebrow cocked.

"You're not a gimp," Tanner said.

"No. I'm not. And neither are you, man. I look at it this way. War changes everyone on the inside. You and me, we got the outward signs. It's those guys with no visible panty lines"—he crooked his thumb over his shoulder to indicate Marcus and Adam—"they're the ones with deep, dark damage."

Tanner shook his head. "That's not relevant. I'm not...I'm not a good person."

"You're what?" Rico asked. "Are any of us good? What does that even mean? We all made decisions over there that were bad. They just weren't as bad as the alternatives."

"I was shit to begin with, but how can you even stand to be near me? I drove you down the wrong road on purpose and got you blown up."

"What are you talking about? You didn't get us blown up on purpose, and you definitely made the better choice that day!"

"Where were you when that grenade went off? Two men died!"

"Man, don't you remember? Didn't they tell you?"

Tanner didn't want to remember. His heart started beating so hard he could barely think over the noise in his head. He said, "Tell me what? I took a short cut, and you were bitching at me, and then—and then it happened."

"That's all you know?"

Tanner must have looked completely clueless, standing there with his mouth hanging open.

Rico blew out a breath. "Damn, man. We were sitting on that road, stuck behind a bunch of vehicles. They were stopped because an IED had gone off and blown a hole in the road. We got word to turn around and go back the way we'd come, to circle around the outskirts of town to get back to base. But you were like, 'Screw it, I know this way will get us there,' and that's what you did. The other vehicles we were behind that day? The ones behind us? They all got gunned down right after we turned. Every single man and woman. If we'd stayed on course, you and I would be dead, too."

Tanner was literally staggered by that information. "I don't remember that. I just remember arguing with you, and then waking up in the hospital. They told me about the grenade, but I guess...I don't know if they told me the rest of it."

"Do you remember me coming to visit you?"

"What?"

Rico laughed. "I didn't think so. They had you on so much shit because of those burns, I don't know how you knew your name. Unfortunately, I was conscious for almost every damned thing." Rico slapped him on the shoulder. "Listen, man, I promised to help gather wood for the bonfire, but remember...I'm ready to ride whenever you want to get me up there, cool?"

Tanner nodded. As he led Bullet back to the barn, he began to wonder if everything he'd ever known, ever thought about his life was real. And as he'd hoped, wished, wanted since the day he'd met Jen Greene, maybe he wasn't to blame for so many bad things.

It could be he didn't need some unattainable redemption. Maybe it was as simple as having the hard conversations.

He pulled his phone out of his pocket and dialed. "Hey, Mama? You got a few minutes to talk?"

An hour and a few manly tears later, he entered the dining room, where Adam, Marcus, Jake, and the soon-to-be graduates were sitting down to lunch. "Hey," he said.

"Hey, man," Rico said, moving his plate to make room for Tanner at the table. "You been makin' things right with your girl?"

"Not exactly," Tanner said. "It's going to take more than a phone call, I'm afraid."

"Unfortunately, we don't have crow on the menu tonight," Jake said, ladling a big glob of taco casserole on a plate and handing it to Tanner.

Chapter 33

"I don't know, Mom," Jen said as she tugged at the neckline of the dress she'd squeezed into. She was going to have to lay off the homemade ice cream, that was for sure. On the other hand, her boobs looked more than adequate. "What if he's not even there? What if he just turns and walks away? Or worse, asks Adam and Marcus to escort me off the premises?"

"Then you'll just have to try again tomorrow. Your girlfriends will help if you ask, I'm sure."

And they would, Jen realized. She had made actual friends here in Big Chance once she'd eased up on the whole *I don't need anyone*. Still. "I don't know. This seems kind of contrived."

"What, not authentic?" Joanie asked, raising an eyebrow.

"Well, yeah, kind of."

"Listen, kiddo. There's nothing more real than a woman putting her heart out there, hoping the right guy picks it up."

Jen blew out a big breath. "Well, I'll cross that bridge if I have to. Maybe I'll get to the party and he'll be waiting for me at the front gate with a dozen long-stemmed roses and a ring box."

"A ring box?"

"Yeah, that might be pushing it," Jen said, rolling her eyes at herself.

She took one last glance at the mirror. "I guess that's about as good as it's going to get." She had on a little makeup, a lot of bug spray, and she was ready. "Are you sure you don't want to come with me?" she asked her mom.

"No, I really don't," Joanie said. "I'll meet everyone another time. I'm going to take a walk and admire your neighbor's Happy Beef."

Jen snorted. "Mom, that sounds wrong on so many levels."

"Well, you never know." Joanie winked. "Now where's Trixie? We want to get her dress on."

Jen shrugged, knowing that as soon as Joanie strapped the little polka-dotted dress to Trixie, the dog would go find something incredibly nasty to roll in, if she hadn't already. "I let her out to go potty a few minutes ago."

Joanie went out, calling, "Come here, Trixie girl!"

Jen slipped on her sandals and picked up her keys. She was on her way out when Joanie reappeared in the doorway. "Um, Jennifer? Did you latch the gate for the goat pen?"

"Oh, for crying out loud. Is Trixie gone too?"

"I can't find her."

"Kim and Khloe?"

"I don't see anyone but Fred, Ginger, and the Rockettes."

"Okay, Mom. I'll go find them. Will you check on the chickens and Mr. Bigfoot?"

"Got it," Joanie said. "Call me when you find them."

Jen had just turned onto Wild Wager Road from Happy Beef Way when she caught a glimpse of white disappearing into the brambles on the side of the road, followed by Trixie, yapping on the heels of Kim. Or Khloe.

"Oh no you don't!" Jen yelled, as she slammed the car into park and jumped out onto the road. "You get back here!"

It occurred to her as she followed the animals into what seemed to be an endless maze of—what was this stuff? These thorns had thorns and they were grabbing at her clothes—and she probably should have changed from these cute little strappy sandals into her barn boots. And brought the cell phone from the center console.

Jen managed to catch up with Khloe, Kim, and Angus in a small clearing in the middle of all the brambles, Trixie keeping them in a tight cluster. It was getting dark.

"Okay, you guys, you're going to come with me, and we're getting out—" She turned in a circle. Which way had she come in? She wasn't that far from the road, but she had no idea which way that was.

She was not going to hyperventilate. She wasn't going to cry. Well, maybe she was going to cry a little. She was really looking forward to going to the ranch tonight to see her friends, even if Tanner wasn't one of them anymore.

A branch cracked nearby.

Trixie growled.

Angus and the girls gathered together in a tight bunch, ready to defend against whatever predator might be watching them.

Jen remembered the chupacabra she'd gotten so hysterical about the night she'd met Tanner, and was scared all over again.

She searched the ground for a decent-sized rock or a broken branch to use as a weapon. There—next to the tree. Her heart was pounding so hard, she barely heard the rattling before she felt the sting.

"This is stupid," Tanner said, moving to dismount from Bullet's back.

"You stay up there," Emma warned him. "It's not stupid, it's so romantic I'm already crying."

"She needs to know you really mean it when you tell her how you feel," Lizzie added.

Bullet snorted, though it was unclear whether that was in agreement with the women or with Tanner.

Tanner wasn't at all sure he should be trying to get Jen to forgive him for being such a total jerk to her; it wasn't like he suddenly found himself king of the world. But he'd promised his mother he'd ask her to give him another chance.

He was still reeling from their earlier conversation. Mama said that Tanner hadn't given her any news the day she heard him accusing his father of adultery. She'd known for years about his dad's infidelity; she'd just never had the energy to do anything about it until she heard the pain in Tanner's voice as he accused him. She said she felt terrible for letting her boy think it was ever okay to treat a woman like she didn't matter, so she decided right then and there to send his dad packing.

What neither of them had known, and Tanner hadn't known until a couple of hours ago, was that his father not only had a woman problem but also had a gambling issue, and there were some men who were very unhappy with him. Something about many thousands of dollars in questionable loans from a shady bank. Tanner's mom actually owned the ranch, and when she kicked him out, he lost his collateral and took the low road out.

Mama hadn't lost everything, because there had been a little life insurance without a suicide clause, but it had been close.

She'd worked through her feelings around the whole situation a long time ago and only felt terrible that Tanner had believed he was somehow responsible.

Then she lit into him for keeping that sweet little Miss Jenny Homemade a secret from her.

"Well, Mama," he'd said, "I knew it wasn't going to work out, and I never expected everything to blow up like it did."

"What are you going to do to get her back?"

Tanner had explained, "I don't think that's going to happen. I hurt her pretty bad."

"You're going to go ask that girl to give you another chance because she should get to decide what's good for her, not you."

"How much longer do we have to wait out here before we know she's not coming and I can go lick my wounds?" he asked now. They'd already been here at the end of the ranch's driveway for half an hour, and it was hot as hell.

"She's coming," Lizzie promised. "I talked to her a couple of hours ago."

"She might have changed her mind. She should have. If I were her, I'd never go anywhere I might run into me."

"Seriously?" Emma glared at him. "You got all dressed up, took a ton of crap from the guys, and you're going to let a little thing like a long wait send you running?"

"Yes," he said, and would have crossed his arms if he could have. Something in the middle of his back itched.

"No," Lizzie and Emma said in unison. "You're going to have to go get her."

"That's not going to happen," Tanner said. "I'll give it ten more—"

He was cut off because he saw something coming around the bend of Wild Wager Road. It was Trixie, barking her head off.

This wasn't normal look-at-how-cute-I-am Trixie stuff. She reached the driveway and pranced and hopped around Bullet's feet, then stood on her hind legs and frantically pawed at Tanner's boot, then took off a few steps back the way she'd come, then returned to bark at Tanner again.

Senses on full alert, he said, "Something's wrong. I'll go with Trixie."

"Do you want us to come? Or to get the guys?"

"I'll go see what's going on and call you if I need help." He shifted in his seat and gave Bullet the signal. "Okay, guys, let's go."

He followed Trixie for about a mile, to the area where he'd first come across Angus stuck in the brush. Jen's vehicle was pulled to the side of the road, but there was no sign of woman or goat.

Trixie ran to a spot in the brush and panted, whining and looking at Tanner expectantly.

He dismounted and looped Bullet's reins through the rear door handle of Jen's car. The horse would probably take the whole door with him if he decided to get loose, but hopefully he'd stay put. He stepped toward the bushes, actually glad he'd forgotten to take off his stupid outfit. He took a deep breath and said, "Okay, girl, don't get too far ahead of me."

What was a harmless layer of bushes next to the road seemed to thicken into actual gloomy woods after about five feet. The branches glanced off most of his body, but the occasional thorn caught him in the elbow, or the knee, though his hands took the worst of the damage as he tried to protect his eyes. It was so dark he could barely see his own hand in front of his face, so he was startled when he suddenly found himself crashing into a clearing. He was even more surprised when he felt something hard whack him across the chest, followed by an "Oh shit!"

Chapter 34

"OH MY GOD," JEN GASPED AS TANNER BENT FROM THE WAIST and tried to catch his breath. "Are you okay? I'm so sorry. I was so scared, and I thought there was another snake, a bigger one coming, although that's silly. Even if it was Everglades-sized, it wouldn't make that much noise, right? I know I'm babbling, but—" She paused as she took in his appearance. He was wearing something. "Is that an Imperial Stormtrooper costume? With spray paint on it?"

Tanner held up a finger to indicate he needed a moment.

Jen fell silent, watching Tanner, amazed that he'd shown up to rescue her—yet again. Trixie, who'd run off right after Jen met the rattlesnake, must have gone to fetch him. Lassie had nothing on this dog, and Jen mentally reminded herself to get some extra treats for Trixie.

She waited for him to collect his breath, feeling her arm begin to throb as the adrenaline wore off. She did her best to hold it straight down at her side and ignore the pain for the time being. What was with that outfit? Was he in the middle of some kind of role-playing game with the rest of the guys at the ranch? Was he supposed to be Han going to fetch Leia, or was he an actual minion of Darth?

Tanner's wheezing finally slowed, and he turned his head to look up at her. "It *was* a stormtrooper costume. We repurposed it. I'm a knight in tarnished armor."

"You are?"

He shrugged. "Actually, I'm not a knight at all, and any armor I have is in my own head." He straightened and took in the scene. The full moon lent some illumination. "Are you okay? What happened? And what's wrong with your arm?"

"Wait a minute. Explain the knight thing. Are you guys LARPing back at the ranch?"

"Are we *what*?"

"LARPing. You know, live-action role-playing. Like at Renaissance fairs."

His expression was both incredulous and adorable, and Jen wanted to kiss him so much right then that her lips were practically numb.

"Okay, so no to the LARPing." She used her good arm to wipe sweat from her brow. Was it getting hotter instead of cooler? Weird. "Well, whatever. I guess it's good for walking through sticker bushes."

He looked her up and down. "That's an interesting choice for farmwork," Tanner said of her snug dress and strappy sandals.

"Yeah, probably next time I'll go for jeans and flannel." She winced. Damn, this arm was starting to bug her. Her fingers were getting hard to move.

"Jen, what happened to your arm?" Tanner asked again. "Why are you holding it down like that?"

"I got bitten by a little rattlesnake. I'll be okay."

Tanner took a full second to be incredulous that she was so casual about being bitten by a damned rattler. Then his training kicked in and he said, "Sit down on that log and don't move."

She sat, and he pulled his phone from his pocket and saw that it was blowing up with missed calls from Lizzie, Marcus, and Rico. He really needed to remember to take his phone off "do not disturb" when he wasn't sleeping.

He ignored the missed calls and hit 911, told the operator what was going on, and she said, "Aren't you the same fella that called me yesterday about that nutjob kidnapper?"

"Yes, ma'am, but we're in a different location this time. We're in the woods off of Wild Wager Road. I'm going to carry Jen to the road. Her car and my horse are there. Tell the paramedics, they won't be able to miss us."

She spoke to someone in the room, and then came back to Tanner and said, "Okay, honey, they're on their way, but listen. Maybe y'all ought to plan your dates somewhere a little less rustic next time. Take her to the Dairy Queen for a sundae."

"Yes, ma'am," Tanner said and hung up, hoping Jen would be able to go out for ice cream soon, even if it wasn't with him. He knew bites were rarely immediately deadly, but she was going to have issues if she didn't get antivenom soon.

He hit the callback button and waited for Marcus to answer.

"Yeah? What's going on?" Marcus greeted him.

Tanner explained, then said, "EMTs are on the way, but we've got a horse and a bunch of livestock out here. Can you guys come help? You might need floodlights and a machete."

He hung up and turned back to Jen.

"Okay, Jen, here's what we're going to do. I'm going to carry you out of here, and you're going to stay as still and quiet as possible. How long ago did the bite happen?" He stripped off the top part of his costume and used his pocketknife to disassemble and refashion it into protection for Jen.

"Fifteen minutes?" she guessed. "It can't be that bad, it didn't hurt that much. It hurts a little now, though," she said as Tanner pulled the arm protectors over Jen's legs.

"I'm going to get you to help. You're going to be just fine, but we've got to go back through the thorn bushes to get to the road. I'm going to lift you up, and you're going to hold that chest protector over as much of the top part of you as you can with your good arm."

"I can walk, you know," Jen said, though her words were a little slurry. "My faith—*face*—feels a little numb."

"You need to not move any more than you have to. I'm going to carry you," Tanner said, and lifted her into his arms.

"What about Angus and the girls?"

"My friends will take care of them. I'm taking care of you."

"I need you to call my mom," Jen said.

Tanner shouldn't have felt a pang of disappointment at her words. Of course she wanted her mother to take care of her. She didn't need Tanner hovering around her, other than to carry her to safety. Wasn't that what she'd been telling him all along? It wasn't like he'd been fantasizing about riding to the hospital with her and having time at her bedside to state his case and win her back. That would be sick. But even so, this evening wasn't exactly going to plan.

After a few yards of thrashing through the brush, the skin of Tanner's arms felt like it had been shredded, but at least Jen was fairly well protected, and his legs were okay. "Not too far now," he told her.

"You know, I'm glad you came to rescue me," she said. "There are some things I want to talk to you about. I was coming to the party, but I got sidetracked by my animals."

"Shh…" Tanner said. She should be quiet to save her energy, and he wasn't quite ready to hear her tell him to get lost, because surely that's what she wanted to talk to him about.

Jen, however, wasn't interested in shh-ing. "Let me just say this before I lose my nerve. For the past ten years, I've been chasing success by doing things myself, by trying to be authentic and real, and to show the rest of the world how to do the same. I moved out here to Big Chance because I wasn't happy trying to do things someone else's way and wanted to prove I didn't need anyone in order to be who I wanted to be."

Jen looked up at Tanner. "But then my goat escaped. And I met a chupacabra, and I learned that I can't figure out everything I need to know all by myself. Not even with Google. I need people.

And I don't care if my homestead show is a flop or a big hit. I don't need internet fame, a hashtag, or my own homemade homestead empire to be a success. I saw Big Chance as a starting point for bigger and better things, but what I found was everything I need. New friends who are becoming good friends. Belief that with their help, I might just make it."

Here it came, Tanner thought, as he took the last few steps before leaving the briars and stepping onto the roadway. The big *but*. As in *I have friends, but I don't need a man*. His heart was breaking, and he wanted to tell her to stop, it was okay, he didn't want to hear it. Like maybe it wouldn't hurt so much if it wasn't spoken out loud.

Tanner heard sirens in the distance as he crashed out of the woods, but Jen was still talking. He tried to tune her out because he needed to keep his shit together and make sure he called her mother as she'd asked and talked to the EMTs.

"*But* the most important thing I learned is that friends are awesome, and sheep and goats and chickens and turtles are cool, but if you're not there to experience it with me, I'm going to be very sad."

Tanner carefully deposited Jen on the hood of her SUV and took the chest plate from her. The bitten hand was swelling, he thought, but the EMTs would be here in a minute. When he would have stepped away, she grabbed a fistful of his shirt with her uninjured hand and pulled him in close, back into her orbit, where he couldn't ignore her. "Did you hear me?" she asked.

He gave up and let the words she'd just said echo around in his brain. *If you're not there to experience it with me, I'm going to be very sad.* He looked at her face in the moonlight, even more beautiful than the first time he'd met her because he knew her now and loved her. Loved her enough to leave her, but—

He shook his head. *If you're not there to experience it with me, I'm going to be very sad.*

"I heard what you said, but I don't know what you mean."

The scream of the ambulance was loud now, the lights flashing as the truck arrived, stopping in the middle of the road a few feet away.

Jen yelled, "I love you, you big goof. I want you to be in my life." She tugged him closer, and he lowered his head so he could hear her say, more softly now, "I don't need you to save me, but I need you to love me and balance my crazy ideas with your good sense, to watch eighties movies with, and to make love all night long for as long as you want me."

Timing was everything, Jen thought, as Tanner disappeared in the swirl of people that was suddenly milling around in the middle of Wild Wager Road. A sheriff's deputy pulled up—the same one who brought Mr. Bigfoot home the night before, she thought—and there was a paramedic girl and a guy, who asked Jen a million questions about the snake, which she couldn't answer because she hadn't actually seen it. Her arm *really* hurt.

Her mom showed up. "Oh, Jennifer, are you okay? What were you thinking, going into those woods in the dark!"

"It wasn't that dark at the time," Jen tried to explain, but then a pickup truck full of men and dogs arrived, carrying chainsaws and Weedwackers and giant clippers, for some reason, and her mom went to talk to them, and Tanner was all the way over there, too, and the paramedics were entering a bunch of stuff on an iPad, and one of them was on the phone, and then all of a sudden they were helping her onto a stretcher and loading her into the back of their truck.

"Wait," Jen pleaded as they secured her in place and set up an IV. "I need to talk to Tanner." Even though he wasn't going to come to the back end of the truck and respond to what she'd said to him because it might be uncomfortable and awkward, she at least wanted to let him know...something. She was feeling a little light-headed.

And suddenly, there he was. Climbing into the back of the truck and sitting next to her while the female paramedic—her name tag said "Julie"—while Julie got out a bunch of gauze and started to wrap it around Tanner's arms.

"Oh my God, are you hurt? Did you do that carrying me out of the sticker-bush forest?"

"No sticker-bush forest is too thorny if you need a lift," Tanner said, smiling at her. And Jen's heart gave a little flip that she didn't think was due to snake venom coursing through her bloodstream.

"Angus!" Jen tried to sit up. "And Trixie! Angus and the girls are—"

"They're fine," Tanner said, putting a gauze-covered hand over her good hand. "The guys are going to cut through the brush to get them free, and then they'll make sure they all get back to your place. Your mom and Lizzie are going back to your place to pick up some of your stuff and meet us at the hospital. Rico's going to look after Bullet, Jake will drive your car home, and Marcus and Emma will stay at the homestead tonight to make sure everything's secure. Adam's going to look after everyone else."

"Wow," Jen said. "Your friends are awesome."

Tanner shrugged. "I like to think of them as *our* friends."

And there was that crazy heart flip again. But he hadn't said anything about what she'd said before the ambulance showed up. On the other hand, he was gazing at her with so much heat, she thought she might burst into flame. Although that might also be fever from the snakebite.

"So, what's with all the graffitied Star Wars garb?" Julie the EMT asked, indicating Tanner's legs, which still bore the semi-spray-painted plastic pieces.

Tanner blushed, but he kept his eyes on Jen's as he said, "I needed to make a big apology to Jen, here, for being so far up my own back end that I couldn't see straight. I had this not-very-eloquent speech prepared about not being a hero, but that I could scare up some secondhand tarnished armor if she ever decides she needs me."

Jen sighed.

"I don't understand most of that, but it looks like your armor came in handy tonight, huh?" Julie said, then leaned into the cab of the truck to speak to the driver.

"So what happens now?" Jen asked, heart in her throat.

"Well, the doctors will check you out and pump you full of medicine, and in a few days, after you're recovering, they'll send you home."

"And then…?"

"Well, you'll have chickens to feed and a garden to weed. When are you going to launch your show?"

Really? They were going to talk about her show? After that moving speech about tarnished armor? She shook her head. "I don't know. I may do a few episodes of *Homemade with Jennifer and Joanie* from the homestead, if Mom's okay with that. I'm definitely going to introduce Angus to the world. I think I found my calling as a goatherd."

Tanner laughed out loud as he leaned down and planted a gentle kiss on her lips. "Please. No more goats until we've built you a fortress with no exits, okay?"

"We? Does that mean…you want to be my guy?"

"That means I love you more than I can say." He rubbed the bridge of his nose. "So…it seems I might have been overreacting a little about how much of a slime bucket I am."

No, duh. "Is that so?"

"Listen," he said. "Some new information has come to light, and I'm confused about a lot of things that I thought I knew before, but I do know this. I love you, and I'm going to do everything in my power to make you happy for as long as you want me around."

"I think," Jen said, "that sounds perfectly adequate."

Epilogue

"COME ON, BUDDY. LET'S GO." RICO FLICKED THE REINS AND kicked Bullet's flank, but Bullet didn't move from his spot in the middle of the ring. Rico tried it again. "What the hell, man?" he called to Tanner, who leaned against the fence, along with Adam and Lizzie, Marcus and Emma, Jake, and Jen. "I waited six long months to come all the way back here, expecting your horse to give me a ride, and he's just standing here ignoring me."

"Hey, you're the one who insisted you were ready," Tanner yelled back. "Show us what you've got."

"Damn it, Beauchamp, what'd you do? Drug him or something?" Bullet didn't seem so much drugged as bored. If he were a cow, he'd be chewing his cud like a boss.

Tanner laughed. "No, man, I swear I didn't do anything to him. Just fed him and saddled him up."

"You suck at being a riding instructor," Rico groused. "Come on, Bullet! Let's go for a ride."

"I'm not a riding instructor. I'm a horsemanship facilitator," Tanner said, trying not to roll his eyes at his new job title. He had a lot of work to do before he—or anyone else—could call himself qualified in horse therapy, but in the meantime, the Big Chance Rescue was going to acquire a couple more horses which Tanner and Jake would train and make available for riding when veterans came to work with their dogs.

The ranch had now graduated three sets of veterans with service dogs, for a total of fifteen teams. They'd also started hosting camps for existing teams to return to the ranch and brush up on training skills, deal with any problems that were cropping up, and reconnect with one another in a low-stress environment.

"Seriously. What do I gotta do to get this horse to move?"

"It's not what you've got to do," Jen finally said. "It's what Trixie's got to do. Come on, girl, get in there."

Trixie, who'd been impatiently waiting for the signal, bolted into the ring and ran a couple of circles around Bullet, who'd perked up at her arrival. After a minute, Trixie settled down and stood in front of Bullet, facing away from him.

"Walk, Trixie," Jen said.

Trixie began to walk in a counterclockwise path around the ring, and Bullet fell right in behind her.

"Are you effing kidding me?" Rico dropped the reins and lifted both hands in surrender. "The dog can make the horse walk?"

"Hang on," Jen said. "Trixie, trot."

"Whoa, shit!" Rico lurched in the saddle and grabbed for the reins as Bullet picked up his pace to match the dog's. "I've only got one and a half legs to hold on with here!"

Jen didn't want to torture the man, so she said, "Trixie, walk," and both dog and horse slowed again.

"That's a pretty fancy trick," Rico conceded, once Tanner had gone into the ring and helped his friend down. "How'd you teach them that?"

"I didn't," Tanner said. "It just happened. I was working with Bullet one day, and Jen and Trixie were hanging out, and all of a sudden Trixie was in the ring with us. Just kind of evolved from there."

"Well, maybe your next horse will follow people orders, huh?"

"That's the plan."

"I gotta say, it looks like you're pulling it together here." Rico nodded to indicate the new barn that was going up behind the riding ring.

It turned out that having an internet celebrity for a girlfriend had a few perks.

Jen had posted some videos after her snakebite incident.

Fortunately, she had no long-term issues, though it had taken a couple of months before she said she felt normal again. That was fine. Tanner had been more than happy to wait on her hand and foot. But after she'd posted the vlog-style videos about the bite, and what she was harvesting from the garden, and how fast the baby bunnies were growing, her viewership began to grow exponentially. It seemed that everything she'd been through over the past year, from exposing her perfectly adequate breasts to being kidnapped by Brock, had given her a boost when she officially launched *On the Homestead with Jen and the Gang*.

Tanner didn't mind being grouped with Angus, Khloe, Kim, Fred and Ginger, and Mr. Bigfoot—well, not much, anyway. But when Jen introduced her friends at the Big Chance Dog Rescue and horse farm, she attracted a whole new level of viewership. Now she had a segment each episode where Adam or Emma gave dog-training tips, and where Tanner reluctantly talked about horses. Unbeknownst to anyone in Big Chance, one of Jen's viewers set up a GoFundMe and collected over a hundred thousand dollars, which they donated to the ranch for improvements.

Hence the new barn. The ranch was also making a decent chunk of change selling Big Chance Dog Rescue merch: T-shirts, mugs, and hats with their logo paw print were almost as popular as the doggy shirts that read I SUPPORT SERVICE ANIMALS FOR VETERANS.

The ranch was doing great. Tanner had turned the bookkeeping over to someone with an accounting degree and was full-time horse trainer and homesteader. He'd officially moved in with Jen the month before.

The homestead…well, it was a work in progress. After Jen invested a serious amount of sweat equity, the garden had finally started to produce. Jen and her mother were doing their best to make zucchini into the new kale and seemed to develop a new zuke recipe every week. Good thing, too, because they were harvesting enough squash to feed all of Big Chance and half of Austin.

Angus didn't escape very often anymore, though he still managed to figure out a way out of his pen once in a while. Trixie had gotten pretty good at bringing him back without incident.

The rabbits were all happily growing lots of fur and *not* reproducing.

And Tanner and Jen? They were about as happy as two exhausted farmers could be.

"Hey, Tanner?" Jen said as she dug her car keys out of her pocket. "I'm going to run over to Fredericksburg. I'll be back before dinner."

"Sure, babe. What's in Fredericksburg?"

"Um…a thing I saw on Craigslist this morning."

Tanner groaned. "What kind of thing?"

"You know…like a llama."

Tanner heard Rico laugh.

Before she walked away, she draped her arms around Tanner's neck and pressed her body against his, which never failed to defuse whatever argument he might make. She kissed him, long and sweet. "I think I'll name him Rupert."

Big
Chance
Cowboy

Prologue

Afghanistan, nine months ago

"Hey, Collins, are we clear?"

Marcus Talbott's voice crackled into Adam's earpiece, barely suppressed tension thickening the soldier's Kentucky drawl.

Tank snuffled next to Adam, tugging at his lead. "Hold back," Adam murmured into his mic. The dog hadn't alerted to explosives but continued to weave his head back and forth, every now and then pausing when he caught a hint of something that troubled his world-class nose. He didn't stop for long in any one spot however.

Adam forced himself to breathe in and out for a count of five and tried to let Tank take his time. Adrenaline and exhaustion fought for dominance in his blood, and it was only long hours of training and experience that kept Adam from urging Tank to give the all clear so the team they were assigned to could do their thing. Everyone was tired and ready to end this. Four other highly trained soldiers crouched close by, weapons ready to blast their target the moment Yasim Mansour showed his evil, drug-dealing, bomb-building self.

It would have been safer to make sure the run-down shack was clear of innocents, then blow the bastard up from a distance, but that wasn't an option. Mansour had important information about the next link in the chain of terror.

"If he's in there, he'll be in the back bedroom," First Lieutenant Jake Williams whispered through the airwaves. The kid was still wet behind his West Pointy ears but smart as hell. He knew everything there was to know about their insurgent of the moment, so Mansour would be exactly where Jake said he'd be.

It was up to Adam and Tank to make sure the path to the bad guy wasn't booby-trapped. And Tank, the chillest IED-detecting dog Adam had worked with, wasn't ready to stop searching. Tank raised his head, ears pricked, then sniffed at a shadow. He looked back at Adam as if to ask if he should keep going. Adam nodded, mentally promising Tank half of his own dinner tonight for working overtime on this mission.

"Come on, Sar'nt," Talbott urged.

Adam held up a hand that he hoped the team could see through the dim, dusty twilight, asking for patience. He and Tank had been assigned to this unit for a couple of months now, and the team knew how he worked with his dog, had accepted the pair as one of their own. Some of the younger guys treated Adam like a respected elder, but others, especially Talbott, added Adam to their own special brotherhood, which was probably why the lunkhead was screwing with him now.

"I've got a date with some pictures of your sister," Talbott continued. "So, you know..."

Adam sent another hand signal, one used for offering opinions to bad drivers and other assholes around the world. Tank was tired, damn it. So was he, and in no mood for Talbott's normally tension-defusing banter. Talbott chuckled in Adam's earpiece, about to continue, but then Jake spoke. "There's a light on in the back bedroom now. I can see two people. We need to get moving before they vaporize through a vent." These guys had more escape routes than a meerkat colony. "Can you give us an all clear?"

Adam considered the dog. Tank stared back at him, patient and trusting. He'd done his job, and it was time for Adam to do his part and make the final call.

Once again, Adam raised his hand, this time with the go signal. He clicked his mic and murmured, "Stay on the right." He summoned Tank to his side and waited for the team to silently enter the house and gather behind him. Adam and Tank would take point until they reached the end of the hallway, then Talbott would sweep around and kick in the door.

The door.

Why was there a door? Most of the rooms in these houses had curtains, if anything. It niggled at Adam, but everything made his hair stand on end these days, even someone knocking on the side of the damned latrine. There was a door because the bedroom wasn't really a bedroom. It was a command center for one of the biggest scumbags in the Middle East.

Talbott, no longer joking, jaw set, moved silently toward Adam and Tank. He was followed by Emilio Garcia, Max Zimmerman, and finally Jake, the young lieutenant.

The operation began like clockwork. The soldiers moved past each other in near-perfect silence, the only noise the sound of their own adrenaline-amplified heartbeats.

And then it all went to hell.

———————————

Later—days later—when the brass debriefed him, Adam said Tank suddenly started to freak out, barking and fighting the leash, and tried to run to the front of the line of soldiers. The dog knocked Talbott against a shelf on the wall. If that was what triggered the bomb or if it was the men in the room beyond, no one would ever know. The ensuing explosion blew every damned one of them into the street, and not a single man could remember exactly what happened.

Not Adam or Max Zimmerman, who each had a mild concussion and a few bumps and bruises. Not Marcus Talbott, with a cracked pelvis, knee, vertebra—if it was bone, Talbott's was broken. Not Jake Williams, who was in an induced coma following surgery to relieve pressure in his brain. And not Emilio Garcia, because he was on life support in Germany.

Why hadn't the dog alerted to the danger? Tank wasn't talking. He was lying under four feet of desert sand, his collar hanging from a post.

Chapter 1

Present day, just past the middle of nowhere, Texas

HOUSTON WAS THREE HOURS AND A COUPLE OF BROKEN DREAMS behind her when Lizzie Vanhook crossed the Chance County line, right about the same time the Check Tire Pressure light in her dashboard blinked on.

Crap. She'd been in the homestretch. There was something symbolic about an uninterrupted beeline home, to the place she planned to find her center of gravity. Maybe start doing yoga. Eat all organic. Drink herbal tea and learn to play the pan flute.

"Get over yourself," she said to the boxes and suitcases in the back end of the SUV. She'd do that getting over herself thing just as soon as she checked this tire at the truck stop.

Flipping the turn signal, she pulled into Big America Fuel and stopped near the sign for *Free Air*. She stepped out onto the cracked gray asphalt and bent to search for the pressure gauge her dad always insisted she keep in the pocket of the door but came up empty.

It's here somewhere. Lizzie would admit to giving a major eye roll for each Dad-and-the-art-of-vehicle-maintenance lesson her father had put her through, but she was secretly grateful. She was surprised Dad hadn't sent her text updates about the traffic report in Houston before she left this morning. There wasn't much going on in Big Chance, so he watched Lizzie's news on the internet and always called to warn her of congestion on the way to work. Her throat tightened when she acknowledged the reason he hadn't sent her a text today was because he was at the clinic in Fredericksburg getting his treatment. He and Mom might claim this prostate cancer was "just a little inconvenience," but Lizzie was glad she'd be home to confirm he was as fabulous as he claimed to be.

She abandoned the driver's side and went to the passenger door, hesitating when she noticed the dog leaning against the nearby air pump. The *big* dog. It was missing some significant patches of hair, and the rest was black and matted. Its *big*, shiny teeth were bared in what she hoped was a friendly smile. Its football-player-forearm-sized tail thumped the ground, raising a cloud of sunbaked, Central Texas dust. Lizzie sneezed. The dog stopped wagging and raised an ear in her direction.

"Good boy," she told it, hoping that was the right thing to say. It was one thing to misunderstand the intentions of a tiny fuzzball of a dog and need a few stitches. Ignoring a warning from something this size could be lethal. It had to weigh at least a hundred pounds.

She kept the beast in her peripheral vision while she bent to search for the tire gauge. *Ah ha!*

"Y'all need some help?"

"No!" Lizzie straightened and turned, the pressure gauge clenched in her raised fist.

"Whoa there!" A sun-bronzed elderly man, about half Lizzie's size, held his hands in front of him in a gesture of peace.

"I'm sorry," she said, relaxing slightly. "The dog—" She gestured, but the thing was gone.

"Didn't mean to scare you, darlin'," the old man said, tilting his *Big America* ball cap back. "We're a little slow today, so I thought I'd check on you." He indicated the vacant parking lot.

"It's fine," she said. She should remember she was back on her own turf, where it was way more likely that a stranger at a gas station really *did* want to help you out rather than distract you and rob you blind. "It's been a long drive, and I'm a little overcaffeinated."

"No problem. You local?"

"Yes," Lizzie said. Even though she'd been gone for years, it was about to be true again.

The attendant squinted at the tool she carried. "You got a leaky tire?"

"I don't know." She stooped to unscrew the cap of the first valve. "The little light went on while I was driving." *Nope.* That one wasn't low. She put the cap back on and continued her way around the car while her new friend followed, chatting about Big Chance. He wondered about the likelihood the Chance County High School quarterback would get a scholarship offer. Lizzie had no idea; she hadn't been keeping up. He speculated on the probability that the Feed and Seed might close, now that there was a new Home Depot over in Fredericksburg. She expected she'd hear about it from her mom and dad if the local place was closing and wondered if her friend Emma still worked there.

It had been ages since Lizzie had spoken to Emma, and a wave of guilt washed over her. After swearing to always be BFFs, Lizzie left for Texas A&M and only looked back on Christmas and Easter. She'd gone to Austin for Emma and Todd's last-minute before-he-deployed wedding but hadn't been able to come home for Todd's funeral.

Finally, the last valve was checked, and she screwed the cap back on. She reached through the open window and dropped the tire gauge on the passenger seat while she said "Everybody's full. Must be a false alarm." She wrinkled her nose as she caught a whiff of the interior of her car. *Sheesh.* The service station probably sold air fresheners; maybe she should invest in one. Compared to the breezy, wide open spaces of home, her car smelled like an inside-out dead deer. She wanted to get home, though, so she decided to deal with it later.

"Well, everything's got enough air," she told the attendant. "I don't know why the light went on."

"Those sensors are a waste of time, if you ask me. You don't have nitrogen in there, like those fancy places put in, do you?" he asked, then launched into a diatribe about modern technology.

One of the things she'd not missed about Chance County was the tendency of the residents to ramble as long as possible when given the opportunity. "Well, thanks again," she told the man. "I've got to run."

It wasn't until she was backing out onto the main road that she realized the awful smell inside her vehicle wasn't just long-drive funk. There was something—something big and black and furry—sitting in the middle of her back seat, panting and grinning in her rearview mirror.

"Ack!" She hit the brakes, then jammed her SUV into forward and pulled into the parking lot again. She opened the door to jump out, barely remembering to put the SUV into park before it dragged her under. She finally whipped open the back door and glared at the scruffy passenger. "Out. You. Out."

She looked around frantically for the old man who'd been chatting her up, but he was nowhere to be seen.

The dog panted and tilted its head at her.

"Out. I mean it."

It wasn't wearing a collar, not that she'd reach in to grab him anyway, in case he mistook her hand for a Milk-Bone.

"Come on, puppy. Seriously. Get out."

The dog sighed and lay down, taking up every inch of her back seat.

She was afraid to leave the thing alone in her car, so she pulled her phone from her pocket and stood next to the back end. She Googled the number for the Big America station and waited for the call to connect.

"Y'ello," said the gravelly voice she'd been chatting with a moment ago.

"Sir, this is Lizzie Vanhook. From the air pump just now."

"Sure, darlin'. What can I do you for?"

"I'm right outside."

"I see ya."

She looked up, and sure enough, he was waving to her through the glass.

"There's a big dog in the back of my car."

"Oh, yeah," the man said. "He showed up here a week or so ago. Kind of invaded, so we've been calling him D-Day. Real sweet little guy."

She eyed the sweet *little* guy. *Uh-huh.* "Could you come help me get him out of my car?"

Laughter. "I don't think you can get that boy to do anything he don't want to do."

"But he's in my car."

A sigh. "Well, I've been threatening to call the animal control officer for a few days now, but I kept hoping his family would come looking for him."

"Don't you think the shelter would be the first place they'd go?"

With a snort, the man said, "There's only room for a coupla dogs over there. Don't even take cats. They'd probably have to fast-track that one to the gas chamber, seein' as how he's so big and would eat a month's worth of food at one meal. Besides, he's ugly as sin, with all them bald spots."

Right on cue, D-Day sat up and stuck his nose through the open window, giving Lizzie's arm a nudge and turning liquid coal eyes up to gaze at her. Reluctantly, she stroked his surprisingly silky head. And then she gave his ears a scratch. *So soft.*

D-Day licked Lizzie's hand. What the heck was she going to do with this guy? Mom and Dad weren't too crazy about dogs. Lizzie loved dogs, but Dean, her loser ex, had been unwilling to get a dog of their own. As a matter of fact, one of their biggest fights was the weekend she'd volunteered to babysit a friend's perfectly mannered labradoodle. Then, when Lizzie called her mom for support, she'd gotten an "I don't blame him. Dogs are a pain in the neck."

"I can't take this dog with me." Lizzie sounded defeated even to her own ears, which contradicted her plans for an optimistic return to Big Chance and a fresh start.

The attendant said, "I'll give the shelter a call. Shame, though. I think he's still a pup."

Those big black eyes stared up at her. D-Day needed a fresh start, too.

Lizzie decided that Mom would tolerate a canine house guest if Lizzie promised he was moving on. "Never mind," she said. "Thanks anyway."

Who did she still know in town who might take a dog? The Collins family came to mind right off the bat. Adam Collins specifically. *Oh no.* She wasn't going to start thinking about him, now that she was moving home. Not. At. All. And really, she wouldn't be running into him. It had been years since he'd joined the army, and his main goal in life, other than becoming a military policeman so he could work with dogs, had been to get—and stay—as far from Big Chance as possible.

She got back in the car, rolled down all the windows, and turned the fan to full blast.

"Listen," she told the dog, who leaned over the seat and licked her ear. "I'll bring you with me. But we're stopping to get you a bath at the car wash on the way through town right before we go to the vet. Then I'll find you a new home as soon as possible."

The dog barked.

"No. No dogs for Lizzie. I mean it."

"Beer, bologna, and white bread. That's all you're gettin'?" The middle-aged grocery clerk—her name tag said *Juanita*—glared at Adam as though he'd personally offended her. "How's a big boy like you gonna survive on that?"

Adam fought the urge to wipe away the cold sweat that had

broken out along his hairline in spite of the frigid air-conditioning inside the Big Chance Shop 'n Save. He'd about reached his out-in-public time limit. *Don't snap her head off. Just smile politely.* She was simply being friendly, in that judge-everything way people had in Big Chance. "Well, ma'am," he found himself explaining, "it's just me, and..."

"Hmmph." She crossed her ample arms instead of scanning his food items.

Come on, he silently begged. *You don't really want to see me go into full frontal meltdown, do you?* He looked around for a self-checkout, but the store apparently hadn't been upgraded since he'd left for the army, and it was old then.

The clerk—Juanita—peered at him now, eyes squinched up to inspect him. "You're that Collins boy, aren't you?"

I used to be. "Yes, ma'am," he said.

"I heard you was back. Holed up out there like some kinda hermit on your granddad's ranch. You know he used to come in here and talk about you like you was the second coming of Patton."

He was momentarily stunned that Granddad had spoken of him at all, much less with pride. For Granddad, the greatest praise he'd ever offered Adam was "Well, you didn't fuck that up too much, I guess." Maybe it was just as well that his grandfather had lost most of his grip on reality these days, because he wouldn't even be able to say that much about him anymore.

Adam told Juanita, "Thank you. That's nice to hear."

She shook her head. "So sorry for how he's gotten to be. He was a good man in his day."

Granddad was something, all right. "Yes, ma'am. Thank you."

"Your sister's doing a good job with him, though."

"Yes, she is." Unfortunately for her. The war Emma had fought at home, while Adam was deployed, was as bad as anything he'd suffered overseas, and she wasn't free yet. If only he'd known how bad things were here, he could have...what? Gotten out sooner?

Not reenlisted—twice? He didn't know if he could do things differently, because until that last mission, finding IEDs with his dog had been the one thing he was good at.

Now here he was, sweating through his clothes in the grocery store, wanting nothing more than to get back to hiding out in the place he'd avoided for the last twelve years, at least until he could move on again.

Juanita still hadn't scanned his loaf of bread or his lunch meat. Or—*please, God*—the beer. The country music playing on the intercom seemed to get louder, even through the buzzing noise, which Adam knew didn't exist anywhere but in his head. The sound, always present at a low hum when he was in town, intensified. He inhaled on a count of ten and exhaled.

"Sooo…." He waved at the supplies, hoping to get checked out and into his truck before his vision narrowed any further.

"You still in the army?"

"No, ma'am."

"You were in a long time."

"Yes, ma'am." Hell, he'd planned to stay in the military until they pried his dog's leash from his cold, dead hand, but that wasn't how it had worked out.

She nodded. "You need some meat. Homer!" she barked over her shoulder at the elderly man standing a few feet away.

Adam flinched at the volume. Nothing compared to an IED or gunfire but jarring in its own way.

"Yep?" Homer moved a step closer, tilting his head in Juanita's direction.

"Go get some a' them pork chops, and bring me a couple big Idaho bakers. Oh, and a bag of that salad mix!"

Homer nodded and shuffled off.

"Ma'am, I don't need—"

"Yes, you do. You can't keep that fine body strong on nitrates and Wonder Bread."

Adam snorted. He wasn't having any trouble staying in shape out on the ranch. There was enough work to be done that he could sweat from morning until night for a year and not finish all the hammering and scraping and scrubbing.

"Am I right?" She raised her eyebrows. "You need to keep up your strength."

Homer thunked Juanita's order down on the counter.

She pushed the twelve-pack toward Homer and said, "Take this beer back to the cooler and bring me a gallon of that sweet tea."

"Really, I—" Adam reached for his beer, but the old man was already staggering away under its weight.

Juanita shook her finger at him. "No ifs, ands, or buts. You get some good food in you." She stopped then, her eyes wide and sympathetic. "Unless…you don't have anyone to cook it for you, do you?"

He assumed she meant a woman. But instead of mustering some righteous feminist indignation on behalf of his sister and all the women he'd ever met, he just felt tired. It was good that he lived alone—no one besides himself to make miserable. "I do know how to cook, Miss Juanita. I don't do it much, though."

Juanita snorted. "That's ridiculous. What do you eat for breakfast? You're not buying any oatmeal or even Pop-Tarts." She held up a hand. "Don't tell me you eat at that cesspool diner at the truck stop out on 15."

"No, ma'am." He'd tried it once, in the middle of the night, figuring that would be a safe time, fewer people. Something about the vacant, litter-strewn parking lot reminded him a little too much of his time in the desert, though, so he hadn't been back.

"Well, that's good, anyway," Juanita said. "But you better not be going to that superstore over in Fredericksburg, either. They got radiation in their eggs, you know."

"Really?" Adam didn't mind a little radioactivity. It was a failure to find the right balance of desperation and antianxiety meds that had him stuck buying food in Big Chance instead of going farther away, where no one knew his name or cared what he bought to eat.

Juanita smiled and slapped the counter. "You know what? You gotta get offa that property. Bein' alone ain't healthy. You come on to town some Saturday night. There's movies in the high school gym, bingo at the Catholic church, and there's gonna be a big shindig on the Fourth of July in the square. There'll be a band and dancing and food trucks and everything. There's all kinds of unmarried women there, just dying for a big strong man to take care of. Some of them girls are divorced, but don't let that stop you from givin' 'em a chance. They probably know how to cook, too."

"I've got a lot of work to do out there at the ranch. It keeps me pretty busy." And away from town with its memories. Although, if he did wander through the town square one night, he wouldn't run into anyone he'd thought about over the long nights in the desert. Last he'd heard, *anyone* was seriously dating some land developer mogul-type and living the big life in Houston.

Homer returned with the jug of tea, plunking it on the counter next to the paper-wrapped bundle from the butcher and several plastic containers, one containing something green that he leaned to look at—beans?—and one full of coleslaw.

Juanita nodded. "That's better."

"Can I keep my bologna and bread?" Adam asked. Maybe he could get out of here with his bachelorhood intact if he hurried.

"Fine. But you better not come back in here and buy more of that crap."

The chances he'd be back soon were getting slimmer by the minute, and a grab-and-go convenience store diet was looking better.

He gathered his bags and stepped into the already oppressive early summer afternoon. His white pickup truck sat alone in the parking lot, and only a few cars passed by. Big Chance was still more or less alive—there was someone down near the vet's office—but most people had the sense to stay in their air-conditioning today. A plastic grocery bag blew from between two buildings and did the twenty-first century tumbleweed thing down Main Street toward him. He put out his foot and caught it on the toe of his boot. He bent over and pulled the plastic free, wadding it up and shoving it in his pocket while keeping an eye on the street. A quiet neighborhood wasn't any less likely to wield danger than a busy market place, but it was easier to avoid distractions.

Except for the activity two blocks away, where a woman struggled with what was probably a dog but looked more like an elephant calf. It wasn't stupid, whatever it was, and it barked in protest. *Smelled one veterinarian's office, smelled them all*, it seemed to be saying, and no one ever saw the vet just for the treats and pats on the head. Adam suppressed a pang of longing—dogs had been a big part of his life for as long as he could remember, but the smarter, more experienced part of him was glad he didn't have the responsibility and problems anymore. The woman shook her head at the dog, a move that seemed familiar. He couldn't see her face, but when she tripped over the dog, who had stopped to sit in the middle of the sidewalk, there was something about the way she tossed her hair as she laughed that took him back.

Back to memories of the night before he went to boot camp, when he'd kissed a girl in the dark summer night. Kissed her and touched her and *wanted* her like he'd never known was possible. He'd never had any doubts about joining the military, wasn't afraid of basic training, knew how to handle himself, but that night, holding Lizzie Vanhook in the moonlight, he'd felt a trickle of regret and longing for what he was leaving behind.

A car door slammed nearby, jerking him back to his own space. With a hot prickle of anxiety, Adam shook his head and turned toward his truck. Time to make tracks back to the ranch and get back to work. He'd promised his sister he'd stop and visit Granddad this afternoon, but he'd been in the presence of humanity for long enough.

He glanced back down the street, but the woman with the dog was gone. Just as well. Lizzie would never have settled for the likes of him, and now he was even less respectable than when he'd been the kid with dog crap on his cowboy boots, who thought this little redneck town was the worst place in the world. He'd had no idea how much worse the outside world could get. As of now, Big Chance was just one more reminder that the kid he'd been hadn't turned into the man he'd expected.

Chapter 2

"Elizabeth Marie! If this thing isn't out of my house in the next two minutes, I'm going to drag it into the front yard and lasso it to the next car that drives past!"

Uh-oh. Mom sounded a little…shrill. *D-Day, what did you eat now?* It might be time to get him out of the house for a while, take him for a ride. Lizzie wanted to look at some of the properties her dad's real estate agency was listing. Since he didn't seem to have the energy to think about work right now, she wanted to step up and help.

She grabbed her car keys, purse, and the leash. "Come here, D-Day!" She headed toward the dining room, hoping the dog had learned his name since the last time she'd tried it, forty-five minutes ago. "Come on, buddy!"

"Elizabeth…" Mom's voice was lower now, almost calm, which was possibly even worse.

"Coming!" She broke into a jog and skidded around the corner to find the source of the chaos. "Come on, D-Day. Let's go for a ride!"

But D-Day wasn't interested in a ride. He wanted in on Mom's Big Chance Hometown Independence Day planning party, which consisted of seven other local ladies, a pitcher of margaritas, and enough diet-busting food to fill the Astrodome. This last part was clearly what D-Day was most interested in, because he stood perfectly still, his enormous face resting on the edge of the dining room table.

Meanwhile, her mom's friends began to gather around Lizzie.

"Oh, Lizzie, it's so lovely to see you back in Big Chance," one woman said. "I'm so sorry things didn't work out for you in

Houston," she added in a stage whisper. "But don't worry. You'll find someone else."

Lizzie smiled as politely as she could, desperate to escape the inquisition. She clipped the leash to D-Day's collar and tugged, but he didn't move.

"It's so nice that you're willing to help out at the agency until you're able to settle down," another woman said.

Until you find a husband to support you, she knew the woman meant. She didn't need to *settle down* for that. "I'm just glad I could be here to help out." Lizzie gritted her teeth. "Come on, D-Day."

He didn't budge. Worse, he'd locked eyes with Ms. Lucy Chance, supreme goddess of the universe herself. The older woman sat frozen, a half-bitten miniature quiche hanging from her creased, orange lips.

Seriously? Could he choose a less appropriate target? Ms. Lucy held most of Big Chance, Texas, in the palm of her hand. She had more dirt on the residents than anyone else in the county. She was also the president of the Third Savings Bank of Big Chance (no one knew if there had ever been a first or second), and Third Savings was the only bank in Big Chance. Ms. Lucy knew who charged porn sites to their credit cards and who bought seventy-five boxes of Thin Mints last year from the local Girl Scouts. As far as Lizzie knew, Ms. Lucy didn't use her power for evil, but the threat was always there, and no one wanted to tip her over the edge.

"What the tarnation *is* that?" the old lady whispered, not looking away from the dog.

"D-Day." The dog ignored Lizzie and licked his chops, sending a string of drool flying over the crystal dish of trail mix.

"Good Lord," Mom swore, swept the bowl out of sight, and grabbed the lemon squares before they got contaminated.

D-Day seemed to grin at Ms. Lucy. The dog, who might be a Great Dane/buffalo mix, weighed more than Lizzie did, and *she* was no delicate flower. If she got into a tug of war with him, she'd lose. "Come on, buddy." She had to get him out of here before something awful happened.

But then Ms. Lucy asked, "Can I pet him?"

"Uh...sure." Lizzie nudged D-Day with her hip, and he obligingly stepped over to the older woman, who reached out to stroke his giant head.

As a side effect, his back end started wiggling with delight. Hoping to avoid a tail-induced accident, Lizzie said, "D-Day, sit." At which point he rose onto his hind legs and planted his front paws on either side of Ms. Lucy's Jackie Kennedy pink skirt.

"D-Day, no!" She pulled back on the leash as hard as she could without strangling him, but he didn't move. "D-Day, down!"

Nothing.

"Come on, D-Day. Let's go, big guy. Seriously." *Crap.* She'd promised herself she'd never beg a man for anything. Did begging a male dog count? "I'm so sorry, Ms. Lucy. I'll save you." Somehow. And then maybe her mother would forgive her for ruining her party, and Lizzie would magically lose thirty pounds *and* win the lottery.

Coiling the rope around her fist, she reached for D-Day's collar, intending to lever his giant body off the woman's lap and wedge herself between them. But before she could get into position, she heard something.

A giggle?

Holy crap.

Ms. Lucy was *laughing* while D-Day licked her. And not just her face. He lapped at her from collarbone to hairline, and Ms. Lucy had her hands in the patchy fur around his neck, hugging him.

Lizzie tried again. "Let's go, D-Day."

"Noooo!" Ms. Lucy begged. "He loves me! He's just a big old wubba dubba boy, isn't he?" she asked, kissing D-Day back. Fortunately, she didn't seem to be using as much tongue as the dog.

While Ms. Lucy made googly eyes at D-Day, Mom took Lizzie's arm and hissed, "You've got to get rid of this dog."

"I'm sorry, Mom. I'm trying to get him to behave. I really am."

"I see that, but it's not working, and he's simply too much for you to handle."

She opened her mouth to argue, but the fact was, Mom was right. But who was going to want to adopt a dog with the body of a *T. rex* and the mindset of a Jack Russell terrier? "I'll figure something out."

"Elizabeth."

What now?

Mom was looking pointedly at D-Day's underside.

"Yeah. Okay." Lizzie prepared to put her weight into moving the dog this time, because she'd seen what Mom was staring at. D-Day was clearly at least as enamored of Ms. Lucy as she was of him, because he was humping the dickens out of her right leg. "Let's go, dog. I really mean it this time."

With a long, lingering look in Ms. Lucy's direction, D-Day followed Lizzie to her car.

"What do you say, D-Day? Want to go meet a friend of mine?" Lizzie asked when he'd jumped into the back seat.

Mom had said Emma Collins-Stern still worked at the Feed and Seed down on Main Street, and Emma's family had trained police dogs when they were younger. Even though they hadn't seen each other in person for a decade, Lizzie hoped Emma would help her out. Maybe even let D-Day stay at the ranch for a while.

Lizzie drove down her parents' street and turned onto Main, passing the old Dairy Queen, which, along with the Feed and Seed, Todd's parents had owned, back when he was Adam's best friend and not Emma's husband.

And there she went, thinking about Adam again. Her secret fantasy knight in dusty cowboy boots. At least that's how she'd thought of him until she'd thrown herself at him and chased him away. She shuddered, slamming a lid on that embarrassing memory and focusing on the now. Seeing Emma would be fine. Adam was probably still in the army, and if not, he'd have moved as far from Big Chance as possible.

He always swore the last place he'd spend his life was the ranch where he and Emma had grown up after their parents died.

Going to visit Emma would be easy-peasy. No worries.

Lizzie didn't see Emma when she finally wrangled D-Day into the Big Chance Feed and Seed. This may have been because she'd only spoken to her friend a few times on Facebook over the past ten years or so, and Emma didn't post pictures of herself. Heck, her profile picture was her first day of kindergarten.

Also, D-Day, yanking Lizzie six ways to Sunday, had her a little distracted.

She went into the store looking for the quiet, bookish girl with the long black hair, heavy eyeliner, and thick glasses she remembered.

A young woman with a blond buzz cut, countless piercings, and electric blue eyes glanced up from a ledger on the paint counter.

"Is Emma Collins here?" Lizzie asked the punk pixie.

"Maybe."

D-Day chose that moment to spy something at the end of the aisle he needed to investigate at warp speed.

"Damn it, D-Day!" Lizzie yanked the dog's leash, but he didn't stop, dragging her halfway through the store, until the clerk stepped around the counter and said, "Down," in a calm, authoritative voice.

D-Day immediately dropped to his haunches.

"I'm so sorry," Lizzie said. "I'm trying, but I can't control him to save either of our lives."

"I can see that," the other woman said, laughing. She straightened and met Lizzie's eyes. "You're going to have to get a handle on that."

"That's kind of why I'm here." A tingle of recognition swept over her, and Lizzie looked more closely at the girl—woman. "No way. Emma? It's you! It's me. Lizzie."

"I see that, too." Emma grinned and reached over the dog for a clumsy hug. "I'd know you anywhere."

"Really?" Lizzie was surprised. "Sometimes people don't." As Dean had pointed out every chance he got, the years hadn't been kind. Nor had Doritos and M&M's, her comfort foods of choice. Of course, he'd met her after she'd starved herself half to death and was running 10Ks every weekend. The snack foods came back into her life after they'd been dating a while.

"Are you kidding?" Emma laughed. "You're prettier than you were back then, if that's even possible."

Whatever. Lizzie didn't want to get into a reality smackdown in the farm supply store, so she let the over-the-top compliment pass. "So how are you? What are you…up to?" She didn't add, *you know, since your high school sweetheart drove off a bridge?* Or better yet, *How's your jerk-face stud muffin of a brother? The one with the giant chip on his shoulder? And by the way—will you help me train my dog?* Not a good way to resume a friendship.

Emma's smile chased away the flash of darkness that flitted through her eyes, and she spread her arms wide to indicate her surroundings. "Living the dream of single, successful girls everywhere."

"That's, um, that's great." Lizzie glanced around the nearly empty store and wondered how the place managed to stay open. Especially with shrines to a dead soldier hanging from every available bit of wall space. The shelves might be nearly bare, but the walls were covered with photos of the late Todd Stern, mostly either in his football uniform or his army uniform.

"Yeah," Emma said. "I'm really grateful to the Sterns for this job. After they had to sell the Dairy Queen, I wasn't sure if they'd keep me on here."

After an awkward pause, Lizzie said, "I'm really sorry about Todd. I'd have come back for the memorial service, but I was out of town when I heard."

"Thank you. And you sent flowers. That was nice. It's been hard, but I've been keeping busy. It really is okay." And the way Emma said it let Lizzie know that while she would probably never be over Todd's death, she was getting by and didn't want to talk about it right now. "What's going on with you? Last time I saw a Facebook update, you and Dean were just getting back from a Caribbean cruise."

"Oh." Lizzie's shoulders slumped. "Yeah. That was pretty much the last time I had anything positive to say on social media. Dean…moved on to 'other opportunities.'" *Found a thinner, prettier girlfriend.* "And I've moved home." *Given up, tucked my tail, and skedaddled.*

"Is that a good thing?"

Lizzie gave a quarter of a second's thought to how much Dean had hurt her and another quarter to how much more peaceful she'd felt after deciding to come back to Big Chance and said, "Yeah. It is. There's nothing for me in Houston, and my dad needs help here. It seemed like a good time for a fresh start." And maybe she'd be better at life here than she'd been there.

Emma's musical laugh contrasted with her hard-ass look. "There's *nothing* fresh in Big Chance." She sobered slightly. "I heard about your dad. Prostate cancer? That sucks."

"Yeah, thanks. His prognosis is good, but"—*he seems to have lost his will to live*—"he's got a long road ahead of him."

Emma started to speak, stopped, then said, "I was going to offer some sort of 'Gee, this might be a good time for him to retire while you sashay to the helm of the family business' optimism, but the market here doesn't exactly support a lavish lifestyle."

Lizzie shrugged. "I don't care about lavish. The Lifestyles of the Rich and Feckless demographic I worked with in Houston wasn't exactly where I fit anyway." *To put it mildly.* She needed to change the subject, so she asked, "How's your grandpa? Does he still have the ranch?"

A shadow crossed Emma's features, and Lizzie regretted the question. Before she could apologize, Emma said, "No. Granddad and I are living in the little house in back of the store." She pointed toward the rear exit. "He's got dementia, and the ranch got to be... not safe. So we're here in town, and Adam's staying out there."

Adam.

Lizzie had been carefully not thinking about him for at least ten minutes, and she'd never thought he'd be living in Big Chance again. What was he like now? Her teenage dreamboat, becoming a studly soldier turned—what? "Is he, uh, still in the army?"

Emma blew out a frustrated breath. "No, he got out a few months ago. He's been living alone on the ranch, hiding from the universe, I think."

"That's too bad." Though maybe he'd taken off his camouflage and put his Wranglers back on. She suppressed the shiver that ran through her at the thought of seeing him in either. Or nothing.

The conversation lulled, and D-Day saw a new opportunity to escape. Lizzie dropped her purse to grab his leash with both hands while her belongings scattered across the floor.

"Here," Emma said. "Let me take him while you gather your stuff."

"Can you take him until, I don't know, until he's a good dog? I could use some help."

Emma looked like she was going to laugh off Lizzie's request, then realized she was serious.

"I wish I could. But Granddad takes up all of my spare time. We haven't had dogs since, well, since before Todd died."

"I'm sorry."

"Yeah. Me too," Emma said, squatting down to rub D-Day's ears. "Sometimes I miss working with them. It's so…straightforward, I guess. In the moment. You can't worry about other stuff when you're focusing on a dog and he's focusing on you."

Lizzie didn't know what to say, not sure if Emma was referring to the tragedy of watching the man who'd raised her disappear before her eyes or if she was talking about Todd, or both. And of course, Emma also worried about Adam. She'd mentioned he'd retreated into himself out at the ranch. He'd been to war, and that must have messed him up plenty. Lizzie thought of the earnest country boy he'd been in high school and wondered if he'd lost his optimism.

She tried to push Adam's memory away. That was a long time ago. She might remember the way she'd made a fool of herself over him, but he'd no doubt forgotten her existence. Instead, she said, "Do you have any suggestions about what I should do with D-Day? Mom's already threatened to sell him to a glue factory if I don't keep him in his crate all the time."

Emma raised an eyebrow.

"Well, she'll call animal control, anyway."

"Oh, you can't do that!" Emma looked at her like she was about to drop her grandmother off at Walmart and not come back. "I mean, I'm all for crate training a dog, but not if he's never going to get out and have a life."

"I know. And I'm determined to make sure he has a life. I really didn't want to keep him, but I can't find a shelter within a hundred miles that has room and won't promise not to kill him."

"How long have you had him?"

"I found him a few days ago. Or rather, he found me. I stopped to check my tires, and he climbed in the car and wouldn't get out. The clerk said he'd been hanging around for a couple of weeks. He's not a bad guy," Lizzie told her. Honestly, the ugly beast had started to grow on her. "But I'm staying at my parents' house right now, and they aren't fans of big dogs." *To say the least.* "Aaaand he eats everything in sight. Like furniture. And car parts."

"You do need help," Emma told her.

"Yes. I do." It had been foolish to take on the responsibility for a dog when she'd soon be so busy helping her parents, but what was she supposed to do? Leave him on the side of the road to starve or get hit by a semi?

The doors of the store slid open as someone walked by and triggered the mechanism. A white pickup truck passed, and Emma narrowed her eyes in its direction. "I have an idea."

"Yeah?"

"Yeah." She looked at her watch. "I get off work in ten minutes. Our neighbor Mrs. King stays with Granddad while I'm at work, and she's usually willing to stay a little longer. Do you have the next hour or so free?"

Lizzie was afraid to hope and afraid that Emma's idea was going to make her—and a certain army veteran—very uncomfortable.

Chapter 3

ADAM DID *NOT* SHRIEK LIKE A LITTLE KID WHEN THE TRICKLE of lukewarm water flowing over his head and shoulders turned arctic. He uttered a few high-pitched yet completely manly curses and rinsed off as much soap as he could before his balls completely retreated inside his body. He reminded himself to be glad that Emma and Granddad were living in town in relative comfort while he tried to add sweat equity to a worthless, run-down ranch and appreciated the solitude.

So when he turned off the water and stepped out of the chipped, claw-footed tub, he was surprised to hear a feminine voice from somewhere outside.

"Sit," he heard his sister say, followed by a bark in response.

Oh hell no.

He should have known she'd show up here, since he hadn't stopped at the farm store while he was in town, but bringing a dog here to torment him was just twisted. He looked around for a pair of clean gym shorts with no luck. *Eh.* It was only his sister. Pants were overrated anyway.

Wrapping a towel around his hips, he padded down the steps, dripping water on the warped pine floors the entire way. They'd get refinished eventually, just as soon as he fixed the roof on this old house, painted it, cleaned up the yard…

He was about to open the front door when he heard another female voice outside. Emma wasn't alone.

Ditching the towel, he found a pair of sweatpants in the pile of clean laundry on the couch and shoved his legs in but gave up trying to tighten the knotted drawstring. They hung low around his hips, but since nothing crucial was exposed, they'd have to do.

This wasn't a good time for company. He glanced around the inside of the house at peeling paint and grime-encrusted windows. The view outside wasn't much better, though. Invisible from the road, the dilapidated house faced north toward an ancient barn filled with deserted kennels. The neutral territory between was a quarter of an acre of lawn, er, *weeds*. Rounding out the areas that needed to be cleaned up were a horse shed and paddock that had never, at least not in Adam's time, held a horse.

A loud *bang* was followed by two softer knocks. "Adam! Are you here?"

"Yeah." He was going to let Emma have it for not calling before she visited. He threw open the door and stepped onto the porch. "Dammit, Emma, I thought I told you—"

Emma's presence was a dim shadow in his peripheral vision as Adam stared into the familiar liquid-brown eyes of his dirtiest midnight fantasies.

Lizzie Vanhook. It *had* been her on the street the other day.

He should say something, like *hello*, but a black blur bolting into view caught his attention. Before he could react and get the women to cover or even warn them, he was slammed sideways and tackled to the porch floor.

Deeply familiar impulses prepared him to neutralize the threat.

"D-Day, no!" Lizzie yelled, and her husky voice cut through Adam's narrowed focus. *Dog.* It was a dog. Straddling Adam's legs and playing tug-of-war with the drawstring of his sweats. Another, older instinct arose from Adam's addled brain, and he gave the command before he even realized he'd opened his mouth.

"*Down.*"

The dog dropped to its belly, right on top of Adam.

"Omigod, I'm so sorry." Lizzie knelt next to Adam, tugging ineffectually at the dog's collar. "Come on, D-Day. Get up. Come on."

Her hair was shorter and streakier than he remembered. She

was definitely more grown up, in a very good way. She was a prettier, curvier version of the girl he'd tried to leave behind, and every bit as tempting. But she smelled as sweet as she had the last time he'd seen her.

She noticed his examination, and her expression shuttered.

Turning to Emma, she said, "I don't know if this is such a good idea."

So she was still pissed about the way he'd run off from her the night before he left town.

If only she knew how much more painful that had been for him. Surely, she—what was she doing here anyway?

"Li—" He cleared his throat, masking his uncertainty by shoving the dog off and getting to his feet. "Lizzie."

If she was surprised at his chilly reception, she didn't show it as she rose and moved back a step. "Hi, Adam." Her voice was a little lower, richer, than it used to be. She gave him a quick up and down look, masking her expression, but he felt the judgment anyway. "How are you?"

Lizzie was here. With his sister. And a dog. Which remained in the down position but managed to army crawl right against Adam's leg. He fought the urge to shove the thing away.

Lizzie had retreated to the edge of the porch, arms crossed over her middle, looking like she'd rather be anywhere but where she was. At least she'd gained some self-preservation since he'd last seen her.

"What are you doing here?" He finally pulled his brain together enough to ask. "What's going on?"

"We need your help," Emma said, seemingly oblivious to the fact that he and Lizzie were both uncomfortable.

"What? No." He shook his head but had to ask, "What kind of help?"

"We need you to be a foster parent," Emma told him. "You're out here alone all the time, and it's not good for you. You need company."

He deliberately didn't look at the dog, but a chill ran up his spine anyway. "I don't need company," Adam protested. "It's really good for me to be alone out here."

"No. It's not. You need a companion, and we happen to have one for you."

Nope. No way. He stared at the beast grinning up at him, enormous pink tongue dangling. Adam looked away.

The dog sat up and shoved its head into Adam's crotch. *Pet me.*

Adam stepped back. The dog got to its feet and followed.

"What *is* that thing?"

"That's D-Day," Lizzie said, a note of defensiveness in her tone.

"But what is it?"

"Well, the vet thinks one of his parents was a Rottweiler," Lizzie said.

"And the other was, what, a mastodon?" The dog responded to that remark with an enthusiastic bark and another crotch nudge. Adam shoved its head away.

"D-Day, come here," Lizzie pleaded with the dog, tugging ineffectually at its lead.

For crying out loud. She was beautiful but clueless when it came to dogs.

Before he could stop himself, he took the leash and reminded the dog to sit. It sat. Adam and the dog both worked on instinct—he to lead, the dog to obey the alpha—but he'd sworn off this job. To distract himself from his own contradictory behavior, he asked Lizzie, "What's wrong with its hair? Why is it half bald?" The thing had huge bare spots.

"The vet thinks he had mange, and someone tried to treat it with a home remedy that killed the parasite but also killed the hair."

Adam's gut roiled at the thought of some of the things he'd heard of people doing to their pets, through ignorance, cruelty, or neglect. Nothing like the dogs he'd worked with in the army. Those damned things were treated better than most Thoroughbred race-horses. At least until their handlers got them killed.

The dog nudged his leg, big black eyes rolled up in supplication.

"Down," he commanded, and the dog flopped to the porch floor, staring at him with a vague semblance of adoration.

"See? He does all that stuff for everyone but me," Lizzie huffed, hands on hips. "This is why we need your help."

And yeah, he noticed when she stomped her foot and produced a nice jiggle.

From the corner of his eye, he caught his sister's smirk. He glared at her.

"Here's the deal," Emma said. "Lizzie can't keep him at her parents' house because he's a little more dog than they can handle."

Lizzie shrugged. "We don't have a fence, and he's still mostly puppy. He needs somewhere he can get some exercise. I can't keep him."

"Take it to a shelter," Adam told her.

"Not an option," Lizzie said, shaking her head.

"He'd be killed before we got out of the parking lot," Emma added. "Neither the county nor the city has the funding to run a no-kill shelter."

A memory came to him then, of Lizzie marching through the halls of Big Chance County High School, carrying a clipboard to collect signatures for some cause or other. "Why don't you work your student council magic and get a new one built?"

She lowered her chin and scowled at him from under her eyebrows. "Even if I had that kind of pull, it's not going to solve my problem today."

"I can't help you." He wouldn't back down, either.

"I'm going to find him a new home. I'll post something online tonight, but could he possibly stay with you for a while?" Lizzie asked. "I'll come out and take care of him as much as I can, and maybe..." She bit her lip. "Maybe you could teach him some basic obedience? That would sure make it easier to find someone to adopt him."

"I don't think so," Adam told her, trying hard to ignore the fact that the woman whose memory had warmed many cold desert nights was standing inches away, more enticing than she had been in his exceptionally vivid dreams, and volunteering to visit him— well, visit his property—on a regular basis.

She sighed—a tad too dramatically—and said, "If you won't keep him, I'm going to *have* to take him to the shelter. My mother threatened to poison him if he chewed up anything else in the house. And then when he tried to get romantic with Ms. Lucy's leg in the middle of Mom's Fourth of July party planning meeting, the camel's back broke."

Adam caught himself before he actually smiled. He remembered Lizzie's mother with her perfectly arranged blond hair and always tidy PTA president appearance, giving him a polite but cold smile when he picked up his sister at their house. And Lucy Chance. That sourpuss had been old as dirt when he'd left town. How could she possibly still be alive?

"I'll pay for his kibble and clean up after him," she assured him. "Whatever you want."

He raised an eyebrow, and her lips parted—to offer what?— but she closed her mouth, much to his disappointment. Not that he'd take her up on anything—hadn't Emma said she was engaged or something?—but the recluse gig was boring sometimes. He could use some new fantasy material.

Both women tilted their heads, and he could practically hear the "Pretty please with sugar on top?" that Emma had always tried to use on him as a kid. And then, Lizzie and those open, trusting eyes transported him back to the swing in her side yard all those years ago, looking down at the girl who was way too good for him, begging him to spend the last few hours before he left town with her. But this time, she was asking him to take care of her dog, and he was the last soul on earth she should want to get care from.

Damn it. Emma knew why he didn't want a dog, and she was being manipulative. Well, he wouldn't be yanked around like that.

"I'm really involved with getting this place back in shape," he pointed out. Knowing he should have stopped with *no*, he went on, "There's no way I can give a dog the attention it needs and do all this work." He gestured at the disaster around them.

Sensing weakness, Emma came in for the kill. "Lizzie already said she'd come out to feed and walk him. She just needs somewhere to keep him until he's got a new home."

"I'd really appreciate it," Lizzie said with her refined twang. "I felt so sorry for the poor guy, starvin' to death there on the side of the highway, and—" She cut herself off. "Anyway, I really would appreciate it. I'll make sure he's no bother. If it gets too bad, I'll… I'll call animal control myself."

Lizzie's eyes echoed her experience with disappointments, and he hated that at least one of them was his own fault, but like that long-ago summer night, he knew he had her best interests at heart. He had no business working with dogs, and seeing her here every day, knowing he couldn't take another taste of those long-ago kisses, would be torture.

If he'd ever had the upper hand in this situation, he'd lost it when he'd given that dog its first command, but he wouldn't surrender easily.

"I can't train it."

But once again, Emma had an answer. "What if Lizzie trains him, and you just tell her how? That shouldn't take you away from your incredible *Rehab Addict* activities." She glanced around the property with a critical eye for his lack of progress.

"I can do that," Lizzie said, a little too quickly. "I'm working for my dad, but I've got a really flexible schedule."

He exhaled and looked around at the ranch. His sanctuary.

Could he deal with Lizzie and her peppy energy out here all the time?

He'd hurt her feelings back when they were younger. Turning away from her had been the right thing to do at the time.

But that was then. Now she just wanted him to teach her to train her dog.

"I bet Granddad would come out here and teach her," Emma threatened.

He shot her a glare. Granddad *would* come here and criticize and find fault before wandering into the bushes, looking for the refrigerator. There was a reason Adam suffered through visits in town, a reason that included keeping Granddad the hell away from the ranch.

Emma's mouth tipped up in a smile. She had him.

Fine. "Nothing fancy. You learn 'sit,' 'stay,' 'come,' and 'don't eat shit you're not supposed to.'"

"Oh, thank you," Lizzie breathed, and he felt a little rush of... something. Something light and unfamiliar.

"Seven tomorrow morning. I spent ten years getting out of bed before dawn to take care of dogs. *I'm* not doing that again."

"I'll be here at six thirty."

"You can feed the dog and get it out of the kennel when you get here." He pointed at the barn where Granddad had built a series of indoor-outdoor enclosures. "Put the food on the porch for now. I'll find something raccoon-proof before I go to bed."

"Okay."

The stupid dog rested its head on his foot.

Damn it. *No.* He wasn't going to like the damned thing. He was only keeping it from the pound.

As he stood on the porch, holding the leash and watching his sister and the girl he couldn't forget drive away, he tried not to notice that he hadn't had anything close to a panic attack the whole time he'd been talking to Lizzie. As a matter of fact, the anxiety that had tried to take him down when he first saw the dog had left before it got a toehold.

"That was…interesting." It was all Lizzie could think of to say when she and Emma were in the car and on the road back to civilization.

"I thought it went pretty well," Emma told her.

"You did?" Lizzie thought Adam seemed about as happy to see her as he'd be to see the IRS.

"Considering what a grump he can be, he was practically like that teapot lady from *Beauty and the Beast*."

The round little teapot lady was hardly who Lizzie thought of in reference to Adam. It was hard to believe, but Adam—who had been cowboy sexy in high school with his rare but wicked smiles and hooded gaze—had become a mash-up of the Incredible Hulk, Captain America, and the *Men's Fitness* Cover Guy of the Year.

He'd traded that slouchy cowboy thing he'd had going on for military straight, badass, and simmering danger. His short, dark-brown hair made her fingers itch with the need to touch. But he'd nailed Lizzie with a narrow blue-eyed stare that confused her because it held both hunger and rejection.

Well, she'd been there, done that, and was home in Big Chance for a new start, not a rerun. She was no longer a simpering teenager with a huge crush on her best friend's older brother; she was a professional woman with ambitions and self-respect. She'd spend time around him working with the dog, but she didn't have to let him twist her in knots.

"Seriously," Emma continued, "he's in better shape than a lot of guys who deployed." She hesitated, a faraway sadness making a brief appearance before she refocused on the road. Lizzie suspected she was thinking of her late husband. "War messes people up." Emma waved her hand as though to brush the statement away.

"That really sucks." Lizzie didn't know what else to say. She'd read enough to know that PTSD, if that was Adam's issue, affected everyone differently. "Is he getting help?"

Emma gave a short laugh. "If he was, he wouldn't tell me about it. He won't admit there's anything wrong, even though he can't be in town for longer than ten minutes without sweating through his clothes. He almost never leaves the ranch. And did you see the bags under his eyes? I don't think he sleeps, either." There went that dismissive hand wave again. "I'm probably just hypersensitive."

"Because of Todd?"

Emma nodded. "He shouldn't have enlisted at all, but his daddy and granddad both served in the army, and he idolized Adam. Then I...I told him I thought he should do it. It wasn't a good thing. He came back all kinds of messed up, but I didn't realize how bad it was until it was too late. I should have stopped him."

"It's not your fault."

Emma shook her head and ran a finger under a very shiny eye to keep her mascara from running but then jerked that hand back to the steering wheel. "Oh shit!" An old white pickup shot out of a gravel cross street and swung right in front of their car. With a squeal of brakes, Emma yanked the wheel and honked the horn. The truck sped away, leaving them stopped in the middle of the road in a cloud of dust.

Panting, Emma gripped the steering wheel, staring after the disappearing vehicle. "You okay?"

"I think so." Lizzie's heartbeat said otherwise.

Emma took a deep breath as she released the brakes and cautiously accelerated.

"I guess I forgot how everyone drives out in the country."

Emma harrumphed. "They're not usually crazy like that, not coming out of Mill Creek Road. It's too torn up and full of potholes."

"Is that old farm that Mitch Babcock's family owned still out here? Back in the day, no one lived there, but it had a creek and a couple of big fields. I mean…of course the land is still there, unless it got sucked into another dimension."

"Well, I'm pretty sure the land didn't get hoovered up by aliens. The property still runs up against the back of our ranch. But something happened to the Babcocks a year or so after we graduated. Someone put a No Trespassing sign at the farm, and the next day, the Babcocks' house in town went up for sale."

"No kidding." Lizzie hadn't heard any of this from her parents. "Do you know why?"

Emma shrugged. "Someone said Mitch's dad got caught embezzling money and they had to sell all their stuff before they left town."

"Huh." Lizzie looked back over her shoulder, where the turnoff disappeared into the dust. "Remember how, in high school, kids went out there to…do things?"

"Things?" Emma shot Lizzie a sideways glance.

"Well, I never did," she said primly. She would have. Especially if she'd been able to convince a certain Adam Collins to take her out there with him, but she'd never gotten an opportunity. He wasn't exactly friends with Mitch, though, so he probably wouldn't have taken her if he'd wanted to.

Emma laughed. "Todd and I may have gone a couple of times, but I don't think anyone goes out there now. At least not like we did in high school."

"What, kids don't sneak out to party anymore?"

"Ha. I don't think they sneak, and I don't think they go out. They just do stupid stuff at home."

"Lazy bums."

"Right?" Emma grinned.

"When I was little, my dad used to drive by there and tell me all about how my great-something or other grandfather discovered gold in that creek. I don't think anyone lived there even then.

Obviously, *someone's* still going out there. I wonder who owns it now?" An idea began to take shape in Lizzie's mind, and she reached for her bag. Earlier this morning, her father had given her a few folders from the real estate office of properties he wanted her to look into. She'd only glanced at them before shoving them in her bag—she'd been distracted by a certain large dog. But now, she remembered seeing something about a property out here. She flipped through the top folder until she landed on a sticky note that said *Make sell sheet for 9873 Wild Wager Road.* "Oh." Now she recognized the address.

"What's wrong?"

9873 Wild Wager was where she and Emma had just seen Adam. Why wouldn't Emma have mentioned a plan to sell the ranch? Would Adam sell it without talking to his sister about it? *Could* he? "Uh, nothing," she finally said, flipping through some more pages. "Just something I forgot to ask Dad about earlier."

Lizzie changed the subject then, asking about the Chance cousins, because she'd heard that Joe Chance, who had been their class president, was now the mayor.

While Emma filled her in on years of gossip, Lizzie closed the folder. She'd find out who was officially listing the property and why Emma didn't seem to know anything about it.

Chapter 4

"I'M SO GLAD YOU LISTENED TO REASON AND GOT RID OF THAT horrible dog," Mom said as she dumped artificial sweetener into her coffee. "You're going to be so much happier without that responsibility. Now you can focus on living up to your potential."

"No pressure," Lizzie muttered.

"What?" Mom asked.

"Nothing. I'm just glad to be home," she said more loudly and hugged her mom.

"I'm glad you're here, too."

They did seem to appreciate her help, and that made Lizzie feel good. She looked forward to making them both proud of her. Nothing to distract her except the small matter of a large dog who'd cried as she'd driven away from him yesterday and the cranky cowboy holding his leash.

"Is Dad up yet?" she asked. "I wanted to go over some of these notes with him."

"Here I am." Dad shuffled into the kitchen in his ancient terry cloth robe, the one Lizzie had bought him at least fifteen Christmases ago. It seemed bigger than it used to.

He leaned over Lizzie's shoulder to peer at the open folder, then turned to pour himself a cup of coffee. "That's the old Collins place. What about it?"

"Put that down." Mom opened the refrigerator, took out a bottle of water, and placed it in front of Dad, taking his coffee. "You know you can't drink coffee on treatment days. It'll make you sicker than a flea after getting dipped."

"I'll get sick anyway," he groused, then asked Lizzie, "Why are you looking at that?"

"I'm going out there this morning, and I wanted to know who called you about listing it."

"Why do you have to go there?" he asked.

"Adam Collins is keeping D-Day for now."

Mom harrumphed but didn't comment.

"Since I'll see Adam, I thought I'd find out what price he hopes to get." And why it was being sold, not that it was any of her business.

"Too bad that stream from the Mill Creek farm doesn't run through the Collins place," Dad commented. "That would make it a lot more valuable."

"For cattle?" Lizzie asked. "I know there are about fifty acres, but I'm not sure much of that's good for grazing, if you're thinking someone might want to lease it."

"Exactly," Dad said. "The creek is unreliable anyway, which is why my great-grandfather gave up his gold claim upstream and moved to town, back in the day."

"That, and there wasn't any gold," Mom added.

Lizzie thought again of the discussion she'd had yesterday with Emma, when that truck had come out of Mill Creek Road. Was the creek still running there, even occasionally? Was it still a place kids might like to swim and catch tadpoles? She shoved the idea flickering in the back of her mind deeper for the moment. There was an inaugural dog training session to get through first.

"I guess I should take a look around so I can make suggestions about what work needs to be done out on the Collins place before it's listed." Dad didn't sound too enthusiastic, but Lizzie took hope from the fact that he was at least still acknowledging he had a business to run.

"I'll take lots of pictures," Lizzie assured him.

He opened his mouth to protest, but Mom shoved a piece of toast in with a wink at Lizzie.

"I tell you what, Dad. I'll take notes and photos of everything I think you should see and even stuff I think you don't, and then if you feel better, you can go out with me later in the week."

"We'll see." He shrugged. "Depends on how much life this treatment sucks out of me."

As fear bloomed in her chest, she forced herself to hold her smile. "Great. It's almost a date." She figured that was as close to a commitment as she'd get right now. She slung her bag over her shoulder, the weight of her camera and notebook banging against her hip. Grabbing her coffee and car keys, she moved toward the back door. "I'll talk to you later."

"Will you be here for dinner?" Mom asked before she completely escaped. "We won't be back from the clinic in time for lunch, but I'm making liver and onions tonight."

"Oh. Gee. I'll have to let you know. I might have a...thing. An appointment." She didn't look back to see Mom giving her the "I know you're lying" face and instead made a beeline for her SUV.

"That's okay. I'll save you a plate if you can't get here," Mom called through the slamming screen door. "Be careful!"

Lizzie unlocked the driver's side door and got in. Her old cowboy boots looked unfamiliar as she pressed the brake and started her car. Unfamiliar but very right with her favorite jeans. Not that it mattered. She didn't have to impress anyone today.

Anyone but Adam Collins, her evil brain pointed out. Would he like her just as well in jeans, or would he prefer her in the fancier stuff she'd worn when she lived in Houston?

No, he wouldn't like her in anything, she told herself. That didn't mean he'd like her in nothing—it meant he wouldn't be interested. Which was exactly what she wanted.

Lizzie was glad, too. She was. She really was.

———

Adam was staring at the cracks in his bedroom ceiling when Lizzie's tires crunched over the gravel driveway. He wasn't ready for this. Not for getting out of bed or for dealing with that dog, which had cried for an hour last night after he'd tried to leave it in the barn. He'd finally given up and brought the thing inside to sleep in a crate, but only because the caterwauling was about to give Adam a panic attack—not because he gave a damn about the dog's feelings, alone out there with no other animals for company.

He ignored the sound of toenails rattling the metal bottom of the crate as he stumbled to the bathroom.

The four minutes of sleep he'd managed to get had been populated by explosions and body parts—both human and canine—flying into his face. He could have taken a pill. The VA docs had given him a pharmacy's worth of choices, but none helped, and some made the nightmares worse. He brushed his teeth, then shoved his head under the faucet to rinse the sweat from his hair. Finally, he grabbed his best threadbare towel and rubbed his head, opened the bathroom door, stepped into the hallway, and crashed right into a warm, soft body.

Adam jumped back to avoid bulldozing Lizzie and the dog as surprise, which felt too much like fear, shifted into the default emotion, anger, which escaped through his mouth. "*Damn* it! What are you doing?" His voice was huge in the tight space. D-Day leapt and barked at the end of the leash.

"I'm sorry," Lizzie squeaked, eyes wide as she flattened herself against the wall.

Regret flooded through him, although he told himself that he should feel glad about scaring her. Then maybe she'd stay away.

He took a long breath, trying to slow his beating heart, and stepped back into the open bathroom doorway. "What are you doing?" His voice was still sharp.

Something pressed against his leg. Apparently, the dog didn't have Lizzie's sense, because it nudged him with its big nose and grinned. The dog rolled to its back, exposing its belly in hopes of a good scratch. *Dumb ass.* It should have every hair on its body raised in an attempt to look bigger and badder to threaten the asshole who had just yelled at its mistress.

He gritted his teeth. He didn't want any dog right now, much less one that didn't know how to act like a soldier. He reminded himself that he was in a totally different situation—he was home. Not some half-burned-out village teeming with insurgents waiting to blow him up. And this dog was going to be trained to be a loving pet, not a single-minded warrior.

"Are you okay?" Lizzie had moved closer, laying her hand on his arm. The contact wasn't unpleasant, and he didn't flinch, as he did when most people got within touching distance. As a matter of fact, her soft skin against his felt nice, almost cooling his overheated insides. Of course, now that he'd noticed, he stiffened.

She stepped back as though she'd been burned. Flash frozen, more likely. "I shouldn't have barged in," she said, "but I couldn't find D-Day in the barn. I was afraid he'd escaped, but then I heard him bark inside. When you didn't answer, I figured it would be okay to come in and get him for breakfast and potty."

Speaking of which, the dog had given up on that belly rub and gotten to its feet. It pranced around, looking a little anxious.

"I had the water on. I didn't hear anything." Obviously. "Take him outside. I'll be there in a minute. After I'm dressed."

He knew he was being an ass, and he was also suddenly, uncomfortably aware that he was standing in the hallway outside his bedroom in nothing but his boxers. And Lizzie had noticed, too.

Great. Both times he'd seen her so far, he'd made a half-naked fool of himself.

He cleared his throat. "Just so you know, I don't always run around mostly undressed." Not that he needed to justify himself. *She* was the intruder here.

Her lips tilted up. "That's good to know. So next time I come over, you'll be lounging about in your fuzzy footy bunny pajamas?"

His mouth almost won the fight and cracked a smile, but he managed to only grunt.

"We'll wait for you outside," she said.

"Good." He gave her a nod and stepped toward the bedroom but did make a last-second turn to watch her walk down the hall.

Acknowledgments

Hey, y'all, we did it!

Writing this third "dog guy" book has been a *process*, to say the least. Between a couple of job changes, home changes, and other life things my focus has wandered a time or two. And then there was this pandemic thing…but as arduous as the writing was, I love this story. I knew as soon as I met Tanner in Lucky Chance Cowboy that he'd have to find a special woman, and I hope you'll agree that Jen is pretty special.

I have so many people to thank for going through this with me!

My agent Nicole Resciniti helped me develop and publish this series, but more than that, she's been here through all of my drama and tears, offering support and guidance. You are a rock star. I love you and the entire Seymour Agency family to the moon and back.

My Sourcebooks team has been amazing. Deb Werksman, I can't tell you how much your patience and flexibility have helped me get my head back in the game every time it tried to escape. And Christa Désir, thanks a million for your incredible story surgery, and huge thanks in general to everyone who read and commented on this manuscript and worked to get this puppy out into the world!

To my Ngwenya Lab colleagues, thanks for listening to me ramble about things that have (almost) nothing to do with neurosurgery. I love working with you all.

Writing is a solitary pursuit, so knowing that I have readers who enjoy my books and are waiting for the next one is really motivating, and to those of you who've written asking about my next book—here you go! I want to send a special shout-out to @Alys.inbookswonderland on Instagram, who sent me an especially uplifting message on a particularly dark day.

Thanks to my mom who gives me a pep talk every Thursday night, and to my in-laws who don't blink at my nutty ideas.

I have a family who have gotten used to my tendency to space out on them while stories are brewing, and my three favorite kids are always willing to try to drag me back to the present, and still love me even when I kick and scream about it. Seriously. You guys are my favorite kids.

And as always, all the thanks to Tom, my real life hero. I love you more than anything.

About the Author

When Teri Anne Stanley isn't working as a professional science geek, she's usually writing, though sometimes you'll find her trying to convince her rescue dogs that "sit" doesn't mean on the couch. She's definitely *not* cooking or cleaning.

In her endless spare time, she's an amateur genealogist and a compulsive crafter. Along with a variety of offspring and dogs, she and Mr. Stanley enjoy boating and relaxing at their estate, located in the thriving metropolis of Sugartit, between Beaverlick and Rabbit Hash, Kentucky.

Visit her at teriannestanley.com.

COWBOY CRAZY

**Sparks fly in this enemies-to-lovers cowboy romance
from bestselling author Joanne Kennedy.**

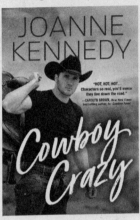

Sarah Landon left the Western way of life the day her father died. Now,
she works PR at Carrigan Oil, where, like Sarah, her boss Eric believes the
new West of oil and energy will inevitably replace the old West of cowboys and cattle. But his brother, Lane Carrigan, is the burr in Eric's behind
and will do anything in his power to save the old cowboy way of living.
It's Sarah's job to smooth things over with Lane, but how can she do that
when the handsome cowboy makes a mess wherever he goes?

"Full of heart and passion."

—Jodi Thomas, *New York Times* bestselling
author, for *Cowboy Fever*

For more info about Sourcebooks's books and authors, visit:

sourcebooks.com

HOW TO COWBOY

Broken trust, damaged hearts, and injured horses get a second chance in this emotional romance from Jennie Marts.

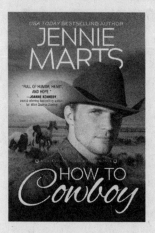

After one injury too many, Cade Callahan gave up the rodeo for a simpler life working at his cousin's horse rescue ranch. Suddenly, his life turns upside down when tragedy places his estranged daughter Allie in his custody. Cade tries everything he can to help Allie heal, including hiring Nora Fisher as her at-home physical therapist. The next few weeks of rehabilitation will be challenging for everyone, but as Cade and Nora lean on each other, they just might heal their broken hearts and find a way to love again.

"Full of humor, heart, and hope."

—Joanne Kennedy, award-winning, bestselling author, for *Wish Upon a Cowboy*

For more info about Sourcebooks's books and authors, visit:

sourcebooks.com

COUNTRY MUSIC COWBOY

**Opposites attract in the latest Kings of Country
romance by *USA Today* bestseller Sasha Summers**

Travis King needs to rein in his bad boy ways or his record label is going to drop him, and an awards show performance singing with one of the industry's rising stars is the perfect start to rebranding his image. It wouldn't be so bad if Loretta Gram wasn't cold as ice. No matter how hard he turns on the charm, she won't give him a break. It looks like this cowboy has finally met his match…

**"Sasha Summers writes romance that will
keep you reading into the night."**

—Jodi Thomas, *New York Times* bestselling author

For more info about Sourcebooks's books and authors, visit:

sourcebooks.com

HOPE ON THE RANGE

Welcome to the Turn Around Ranch: charming contemporary cowboy romance from *USA Today* bestselling author Cindi Madsen

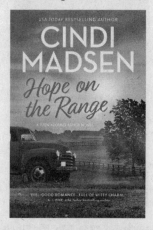

Brady Dawson has been in love with Tanya Greer for as long as he can remember. But running the Turn Around Ranch with his family doesn't leave much downtime for relationships. Now that Tanya is contemplating a move to the city, it looks like he might never get his chance... Faced with the realization that he might lose Tanya forever, he'll have to cowboy up and prove to Tanya that the Turn Around Ranch is the perfect place to call home.

"Feel-good romance...full of witty charm."

—A. J. Pine, *USA Today* bestselling author

For more info about Sourcebooks's books and authors, visit:

sourcebooks.com

COWBOY HEAT WAVE

**Love is catching fire in Kim Redford's
Smokin' Hot Cowboys series**

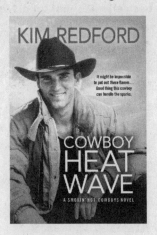

When Audrey Oakes witnesses a mustang herd theft, she looks to hunky
cowboy firefighter Cole Murphy for help. Cole is out to protect the last of
his mustang herd, and he isn't sure that Audrey is an innocent bystander.
But he does know two things—that Audrey is hiding why she's really in
Wildcat Bluff County. And, that there's a red-hot connection between
them...

**"Scorching attraction flavored with just
a hint of sweet innocence."**

—*Publishers Weekly* Starred Review for
A Cowboy Firefighter for Christmas

For more info about Sourcebooks's books and authors, visit:

sourcebooks.com